P9-CET-020

MOLTEN DESIRE

He stared down at her.

She had attempted to tie her hair on top of her head, but the riband had slipped and masses of coppery curls fanned out over the coverlet, framing her profile with burnished gold. Sooty lashes swept her bruised cheeks on which trails from her tears stood out white against the grime. De Larra stepped back, fighting the sudden twinge of pity which threatened to destroy his common sense. She looked so young, so vulnerable.

Suddenly Shona awakened.

With a start, she reached for the bolster, but his hands imprisoned hers. She struggled frantically to free them so she could scratch his face, but his grip was like a band of steel.

Her head was jerked back as he pulled on the ends of her hair, forcing her to look at him. His eyes were staring, probing, demanding. His gaze kindled a molten flame deep within her, and her eyes widened at the unfamiliar sensation.

"What do you want from me?" she hissed.

His eyes glinted with raw desire. "Just this, my little beauty."

He pulled her into his arms and his mouth claimed hers fiercely. . . .

PROUD CAPTIVE
DIANNE PRICE

ZEBRA BOOKS
KENSINGTON PUBLISHING CORP.

ZEBRA BOOKS

are published by

Kensington Publishing Corp.
475 Park Avenue South
New York, NY 10016

First printing: November 1986

Printed in the United States of America

For my father,
Benjamin Henry Hathaway.
His love still sustains me.

Chapter 1

Shona Cameron strode impatiently down Cross Street toward the blacksmith shop, muttering oaths under her breath. She carried a heavy iron pot with a broken bail in one hand, her sodden kerchief in the other. She batted the cloth angrily at the swarms of no-see-ums undulating in serpentine clouds before her face, knowing that even if she lived to be a hundred, she would never become accustomed to the hordes of stinging insects and the hot, sticky climate of Carolina, so unlike her native Scotland.

Her rough, hand-woven, toadflax gown chafed her legs, and she tried mightily to ignore the discomfort. After all, it was her own fault that her legs were rubbed raw. When she had looked out at the dawning day and had beheld the hot sun beating mercilessly down upon the township of Brunswick and the surrounding countryside, sucking the last bit of moisture from an earth already parched, she had decided not to wear her stockings, but to go barelegged and barefoot for the day.

Flipping her heavy blond hair off her neck, she turned quickly into Front Street, where she could take advantage of the shade beneath the black gum trees lining the pond. She walked as close to the water as possible, hoping for a hint of cool air, batting impatiently at the mosquitoes swarming up from black water cluttered with cypress knees, duckweed, and curdled scum.

Without a care for who might be watching—as an indentured servant she was considered trash by the locals anyway—she pushed her kerchief deep into the bodice of her gown, wiping the prickly sweat from between her breasts. Her actions did not go unnoticed by several old men working at the clay pit beside the pond.

"I'll help ye," one toothless old duffer cackled.

"Just pull 'em out and let my hot looks dry 'em off," another called longingly.

Shona tossed her head. "Don't slobber on the clay, boys," she said with a good-natured laugh. "You need all your spit for your 'baccy."

She wriggled her hips enticingly as she passed, knowing how it pleasured them. This was something she did every time her chores took her by the clay pit, for she had always felt she had nothing to lose by fueling the decrepit old-timers' dreams of lost passion. Though she knew her father, God rest his soul, would thrash her hindside red if he could see her coarse behavior, she pushed that awareness from her mind. She was no longer the beloved, sheltered daughter of a proud Scottish clansman: that was all in the past. Now, she had to survive. She reasoned that she would be old some day, and in need of a soft word and an understanding smile. Besides, the old men had been kind to her, in their way.

But today her flippant behavior was provoked by the knowledge that this would be the last time she walked past this spot! Tomorrow, she would have traveled several miles on her way to freedom.

Freedom! Her strides lengthened as a bubble of excitement gurgled in her chest. Then the saliva dried in her mouth, and her lips stuck together like two pieces of cotton wadding. She had forced herself to live each moment as it came this morning, deliberately pushing aside all thoughts of the morrow. Now that the damn had burst, she no longer had the self-discipline to stop thinking of the plans she had so carefully laid. Still, she must control her excitement for she was nearing the smithy. Jephtha Clemmons knew her moods too well, and he would be sensitive to any changes in her behavior. He had been after her to wed him but his proposals had not been hard to refuse. Though he had been her only friend in the year she'd spent in Brunswick, and he was good-hearted, she had no desire to live out her life in this insect-ridden, foul-weathered tract of land on the coast of Carolina.

Her father had passed on to his only daughter his burning desire for her future: marry a man of substance, whether you love him or not; if you are lucky, that will come later. Though her grandfather, with his romantic turn of mind, had railed and fumed over such a cold-hearted appraisal of her future, his words had fallen on deaf ears. Shona was a product of her father's early teaching, and though he lay dead and buried these past two years, she did not intend to fail him.

Besides, she was not about to spend the next five years yoked to a blacksmith while he labored to buy back her freedom. After all, Jephtha had just finished his own term as an indentured servant. She did not wish to burden him further; for a man, even a strong one like Jephtha, could bear just so much. She would run away, and find a man of substance, a man who would respect her and treat her as an equal, a man who would give her a position of honor in life. Then, if her present owners should be lucky enough to trace her, she would have the wherewithal to tell them to go to hell.

She skirted the Quince house, swung the pot to her other hand, and turned toward the smithy across the path. She could hear the clang of the hammer on the anvil, and the acrid smell of the fire in the forge stung her nostrils, bringing a hacking cough to her throat.

"Jephtha!" she called. "Jephtha! It's Shona!"

The smithy threw down his hammer and raced to grab her close. "Aw, Shona, girl," he crowed, "you've come in answer to this heathen's prayers." He held her away and looked her up and down, one giant black eyebrow traveling in an arc up to his low hairline. "You've come to finally accept my proposal of marriage, have you?"

She shook her head and tapped his chin with her finger. "All you think about is marriage, Jephtha Clemmons." She laughed. "There's other things in life too, you know."

He threw back his head. "Like what, by God?" he roared. He looked down at her from his great height. Her golden hair, tumbling free to below her waist, was burnished copper-red by the sun and little wisps were clinging to her wet forehead. Her amber eyes were swimming with brown flecks, like a cat's. Her full lips were pouting in what he took to be an invitation, and her breasts, those twin peaks of perfection, were rising and falling in what he hoped was desire. "Like what?" he repeated, pulling her into his arms.

She ducked out of his embrace and stood back, hands on hips. "Enough," she said. "You're sticky and dripping with sweat and besides, I've come on business for my mistress!" She picked up the broken pot she had dropped. "You keep your hands to yourself or I'll crack that rock-hard head of yours with this iron."

He knew her well enough to realize she was deadly serious. He shook his head and stepped backward. "Why didn't you just say you was here on business in the first place?"

"Because you didn't give me a chance, that's why. You came out here and grabbed onto me like the bear you are without giving me a breath to speak my piece."

"So speak it," he growled low in his throat.

Shona was instantly contrite. She did not wish her last encounter with her best friend to end on a sour note. "I brought a pot for Mistress Curry. The bail's broken and she wants you to replace it."

"That's easy enough done. When does she want it?"

Shona grimaced. "Right now, of course. But I told her you were busy doing work for the ships at the dock so she said she could wait a day or two at most."

"That's right nice of her," he said, his deep voice dripping with sarcasm.

"You know how she is, Jephtha, she's used to getting her own way—and she usually does."

He scowled. "I can't bear the way she orders you about, always wanting you to do the dirty, impossible tasks. Wed me, Shona, and I'll work off your indebtedness. In two years, no more, you'll be free!"

"I can't wait two years!"

He recoiled from the anguish in her cry. "What are you thinking of doing? Running amok into the woods to hide like an animal gone to hole? You'll get lost and rot in those woods, girl. Or the Injuns will get you and have their fun with you. Can't wait two years!"

"I just meant it wouldn't be fair to you, Jephtha," Shona soothed. "After all, you just earned your own papers, you've been given your fifty acres and your fine gun, and now you have your own business. You don't need a wife to drag you down into servitude again so soon. Now I've got to go," she said, glancing over her shoulder. "Turn around and look behind you. Mistress Quince is looking out her window at us. In another minute, she'll be on her way to the Currys' and I'll be in trouble for dallying. I don't want to feel Master Curry's rod across my shoulders again!"

Jephtha glared at the Quinces' cottage. Sure enough, he could just make out Mistress Quince's prunelike face beside the sacking at the front window. "God damn that sneaky bitch!" he muttered.

"I have to go now, Jephtha, you know that!"

"Yes, I do know it, but I still say, God damn her for being the witch she is. And I want you to tell me if that little bastard Curry lays a finger on you. I'll kill him if he so much as touches you."

"You can't hurt him, Jephtha. They'll hang you if you do. He won't touch me, I promise." Shona backed away. "You will mend the pot, won't you? I'll try to get back for it in a day or so," she said, the lie falling easily from her lips.

11

"You be thinking about wedding me, Shona Cameron," he shouted as she turned and ran back toward the pond. "I'll ask you again proper when you come for the pot!"

Master Curry did not lay a rod to Shona that evening, for, unknown to Shona, Mistress Quince had been too down in the back with the lumbago to make the walk to the Currys'. But Master Curry did rail throughout the long evening. He was extremely upset over spending good money to see his youngest daughter wed a *farmer*. If he could not talk Elspeth out of this alliance, he would have to meet with the rector of St. Philip's, and that was a very uncomfortable prospect indeed! The rector served both St. James in Wilmington and the Currys' parish in Brunswick, but because the two towns had been feuding for years over the wooing of new settlers, the rector finally had had his fill of their dissension and had sided with the Wilmington parish, which happened to be much larger and, consequently, wealthier. This would make any discourse unpleasant.

After dinner, Master Curry sent his wife to bed early; then he stormed at Elspeth Curry for over an hour, reminding her of the precarious health of her mother, of their strained finances, of her duty to the family and her obligation to follow in the footsteps of her obedient older sister who lived with a maiden aunt in Wilmington, and of her great debt to her father in particular. He regretted that this accursed wedding was imminent after such a long, unusually hot summer!

Shona looked on in disgust, sloshing soapy water over the greasy trenchers as she listened to the argument. She knew who would win. Elspeth always got everything she desired, given a little time and a great deal of finagling. This would be no different.

She wiped the trenchers, drained the leather jacks used for milk and gave the table board one last wipe with a linen cloth. By the time she had hung the cloth on its peg, Elspeth was smiling her tight little smile of victory and Master Curry's shoulders were slumped in defeat. "I suppose we can manage it then," he told his daughter. "But you'll have to use Shona as much as possible. I don't want to burden your mother after her last attack of the fever."

"Of course, Papa dear," Elspeth crooned. She gave Shona a bright smile. "I'm sure Shona will be only too happy to help. After all, a wedding is always a happy time, isn't that true, *dear* Shona?"

Shona ground her teeth together, lest she give vent to her true feelings. "I'll help in any way I can, *dear* Miss Elspeth," she replied.

The girls' gazes locked, their true feelings masked, neither caring one whit what the other thought. They were still glaring at each other when it was time to snuff out the candles and retire for the night.

Shona lay on her pallet until the only sounds coming to her ears were the droning of the cicadas and the night rustlings outside. She had not bothered to undress, for she intended to make the final preparations for her flight. She pushed herself to her feet and felt her way to the place where she had hidden her bundle, behind a powdering tub filled with salted beef. For once she was grateful she had this little corner of the storage room to call her own. Out here, away from the house, no one would hear her or wonder where she was going on such a dark, moonless night.

She grabbed her bundle and opened the door carefully, lifting it up a bit to keep the heavy leather hinges from squeaking. When she stepped out into the night, the air was so humid she felt as though she were diving headfirst into a lake of suffocating, warm water. She waited for her eyes to become accustomed to the darkness, then made her way slowly toward the trees at the far side of the clearing. She stepped between the trees silently, feeling ahead with her bare feet lest she step upon a snake or a night-prowling varmint. She walked through the forest for several hundred yards, then stopped before a large oak tree. She smiled as she tucked her bundle into the hollow trunk, for she remembered being told as a wee lass that oaks were very lucky trees, almost as lucky as holly. The next time she visited this place, she would be on her way to freedom!

Her linen shift was soaked with sweat and night vapors by the time she returned to her room. She whisked it over her shoulders and threw it on the floor. She wanted to bathe, but knew that was impossible now; she would have to live with her own smell for a while longer. Tomorrow, when she was miles and miles away, she would spend hours in the river, washing away the odor and filth of servitude.

As she groped through the dark for her bed, something suddenly snaked itself around her wrist. She let out a gasp, but before she could scream, a hand was clasped over her mouth.

"Don't be noisome, Shona girl," came a whisper in her ear. "That could cause a mite of trouble."

She nodded her head slowly and the hand was removed. "Jephtha!" she hissed. "What are you doing here?"

She felt his body shake and knew he was laughing. "I figure if he can't woo the chicken out of the henhouse, then the rooster has no choice but to join her," he said softly.

"Well, this rooster is out of luck," she spat. "You get yourself gone from here before Master Curry takes a long gun to your hindside."

Jephtha pulled her onto her pallet, his hands traveling quickly over her bare flesh. "He don't know I'm in this here henhouse," he whispered, his breath rising rapidly in his throat. "And I'm not aiming to tell him."

Shona felt the thick carpet of hair on his bare chest prickling her flesh, and the altogether too familiar feeling of panic caught her up, choking her throat with icy fingers and turning her sweat into a frigid wash that enveloped her trembling body.

"Oh, you're an impossible man," she groaned. "What can I do? . . ."

His lips stopped the words dead in her mouth, but her thoughts raced like a full-rigged vessel before a gale wind. Shona had grown up in the surety that she would save herself

14

for the man she wedded and the devil take anyone who tried to convince her otherwise. But that was before that butcher, Cumberland, had pained her so horribly as he'd held a knife to her throat and robbed her of her most priceless treasure—her virginity. All the more reason why she would not now give herself freely like some ill-bred lass from lower Scotland. She was highland through and through and as proud as any queen on any throne in the world! She jerked her mouth away from his. "Let me go!" she hissed. "Not you nor any man will ever take me against my will again!"

"Aw, God, Shona," he groaned, his lips seeking her breast. "You'll not be one of them what only teases, surely!"

"Teases!" She wrenched away, her panic turning to rage. "You'll not call me a tease when it was you who laid in wait for me here!" She groped about for her shift, her breast heaving with anger.

Jephtha reached for her arm, but she eluded him and thrust her damp shift down over her hips with a triumphant smile. Though it was ridiculous to think that such a thin piece of cloth could give her protection, she knew she was once again in control of the relationship and if she had not been concerned for his feelings, she would have laughed aloud.

"You're like all men, Jephtha Clemmons. You think because you're aching to rut, every female within a league feels the same way. I've told you time after time, no man will have me until I'm wedded."

"Then wed me! You know how many times I've asked you!"

"I can't marry you. I have to talk to you, Jephtha, and you have to listen to me."

"Not if it's about you not wedding me. I'll not listen to that."

"But you must hear what I'm about to say. And you can't interrupt me 'til I've finished. You have to promise me that. Please!"

A chuckle sounded deep in his throat, much like the rumbling of a bear. "Don't I always? It's impossible for me to refuse you anything, you know that. I'll let you have your say."

Shona looked up at him. She could just see the outline of his face above hers. She blinked back the tears threatening to blind her. "I never meant it to be like this," she whimpered. "I don't want to hurt you."

"Then say you'll wed me. I'll talk to Master Curry tomorrow morning. He won't say no, not with what I'll offer him."

"Oh, Jephtha, you don't understand. I'm . . . I'm going away tomorrow. I'm running away, as far away as I possibly can. I've thought about it for months now. I have everything planned."

He rose up on one elbow and stared down at her. She could see the whites of his eyes, could feel the rapid rise and fall of his chest. "What do you mean, you're running away? What are you talking about?"

She winced at the pain in his voice. "Just what I said. I've been planning to run away for a long time. I can't stay here for another five years. I'll die if I have to stay. I'll just wither up and die!"

"You've never talked like this before. What made you decide to run away now?"

"I didn't decide just now. I told you, I've been planning for a long time. When I first came here to the Currys', I thought I could work for my papers, but now that Elspeth's getting married, things have turned sour. You know how mean she is. She'll insist I help her all the time, and I can't bear the thought of bowing to her in her own home. It's bad enough having her order me about without her folks' knowing, but if she tries to lord it over me openly, I'll either kill her or die myself!"

"But what about me? I'll not let you die! I'll watch after you and take care of you, and you'll be my woman! My wife!"

She squeezed her eyes shut as tears flooded down her cheeks, dripping off her chin. "I can't stay!" she sobbed. "You don't understand, Jephtha. I can't be a servant for another day! I wasn't raised to serve people. Where I come from, I was

16

treated like a princess. My people were lairds in Scotland until that bastard Cumberland defeated them at Culloden Moor and laid waste to the land. Oh, Jephtha, mark well the date of the fall of Scotland. Just two years ago, April 14, 1746, I lay hiding with other daughters and wives beside that field and watched Cumberland's men kill my father and all three of my brothers—James, Matthew, and Donald. Jamie was the last to die. I held him in my arms. He was only fourteen, little more than a child. Then Cumberland slaughtered everyone and everything. He laid the mansions of the chiefs and the huts of the clansmen to the torch until there was nothing but gray ashes. He starved the people, laughing at the children whose bellies were swollen from eating grass from the fields—the only food they could find—and all the time he was holding me prisoner in his house at Inverness, taking his pleasure with me. Then, when he tired of me, he sold me into servitude for seven years! Seven years, Jephtha! It's not the work, you ken. It's the humiliation. To the Currys, I'm a thing, not a person. I can't go on living like this, so I'm leaving tomorrow! And nothing you do or say can stop me!" She collapsed against his chest, her body heaving with her sobs.

Jephtha was speechless. Shona had never shared her past before, but he had heard of the great battle of Culloden and he knew from her agonized recital that she was telling the truth. He had also been a victim of the English system of justice. He'd been arrested and thrown into debtors' prison because he could not pay for a casket for his dead mother, who had been a God-fearing, parish-supporting woman. He would have rotted there if it had not been for the sympathetic gaoler who'd told him he could sell himself into servitude. He had done so, exchanging his debt and his passage to the new world for ten years of labor. He had paid off his debt only six months ago, and though he was a young man of twenty-five, he felt as old as sixty. Yet all he possessed was fifty acres of land, a rifle, and his smithy tools. Starved past rational thought for love and family, he sighed and pulled Shona close.

17

"I understand," he said, his voice husky with emotion. "If you want to go, I won't stop you. But you'll not journey alone. I'm going with you."

"But you can't! You have a business here. And you have your land! You worked too hard and long for it all!"

"It won't mean anything to me if I don't have you. I've spent a lifetime wanting to be close to someone. Oh, I've bedded whores, but they sold me their bodies. I'm hoping someday you'll give me yours as a gift. I know you don't love me the way I love you now, but maybe someday you'll look at me with those sparkling eyes of yours and say, 'Jephtha, old man, I love you.'"

"But what if that never happens? I don't want to hurt you!"

"Then I'll not be your lover. But I'll protect you and cherish you and be your friend—forever."

Thus it was that Shona Cameron and Jephtha Clemmons sat side by side upon her pallet far into the night making plans. They both knew Jephtha was taking a fearful chance, for by aiding and abetting her escape, he was endangering his own freedom, should they be caught.

"I've hidden boys' clothing for myself," Shona told him. "I took some of the master's old breeches and altered them to fit me. And I stole a shirt off the Quinces' line one day last May. I've also got a knit cap I made from scraps I took from the mistress's yarn basket. I couldn't find any boys' shoes to fit, so I'll have to go barefoot."

"You'll have a hard time looking like a boy," Jephtha said with a laugh. "No amount of clothing can hide those curves."

"I'm going to tie myself down. I've saved linen ribands to do the job. And I'm even willing to cut my hair if I have to, though I may get by with just pushing it up under the cap."

"Don't you dare cut your hair!" he said much too loudly. He picked up a strand and let the silkiness slip through his fingers. "It feels like spun gold," he whispered, "so I'm a rich man."

"Then I'll not cut it," she promised. "But I still don't think we should travel together until we put several miles behind us.

18

We might run into someone who knows us, and that could provoke questions."

"I suppose you're right. But I want to keep you in my sight. I never want you far from me again."

"Then I'll keep to my original plan and leave when the Currys are all at St. Philip's talking to the rector about the wedding. They are supposed to meet him there at eleven, and after that they are to meet with Emmett's mother and father to discuss the service."

"Plain, skinny little Elspeth Curry's marrying Emmett Dobbs?"

"Yes. And as far as I'm concerned, they deserve one another. He's got an empty head and she, an empty heart."

"I'm just nockered by the Currys allowing her to wed a farmer's son."

Shona grinned. "For the first time Elspeth showed good sense. Master Curry raged and hollered when she said she wanted to marry Emmett, but she told her father straight out that it was highly unlikely anyone else would ask for her hand. And, though he wanted her to hold out for someone with a higher position in life, he finally agreed."

"But shouldn't you leave by night? That way, it would be hours before they knew you was missing."

She shook her head and her hair rustled against his bare shoulder. "I can't do that, Jephtha," she said softly. "I promised Master Curry that if he would let me have the storeroom for my bed, rather than make me sleep on the floor in the kitchen, I would never run away at night."

"But a promise made like that can't count!"

"I promised and I will not go back on my word. Besides, they'll be at the church for hours. As soon as I see them on their way, I'll run into the trees and change. I'll cut back through the woods, cross the Southport Road when I can, and meet you by the river on this side of Orton Plantation."

"You'll do nothing foolish to put your life in danger!"

"Of course not. Stop fashing yourself. I've been planning

19

this for months. Nothing can go wrong." Shona ignored the way her heart pounded as she said the words aloud.

She would have to alter her plans and allow Jephtha to accompany her. She did not love him, but she was fond of him, and he had been good to her. She sighed softly. She used to be far too strong willed to allow anyone to change her mind, but life since Culloden had weakened her. She could only hope that some day she would find the man she knew was waiting for her, and that she would have the strength to put Jephtha from her life. She pushed him off her bed.

"Now you have to go. It's almost daylight. We can't have someone see you leave and raise a ruckus."

She watched him fumble with the buttons on his breeches. Though it was still dark, she could see the outline of his massive body. His hair was falling down over his forehead and his chest glistened with sweat, for the night was still oppressively hot. He gathered his shoes and stockings in one hand and pulled her close with the other.

"I'll wait just inside the trees by that little bend in the road just onto Orton property. I'll be there early and I'll wait until dark and past, if I have to. Just be careful."

She patted his cheek. "I'll be there as soon as I can. You be careful, too."

She stood by the door and watched him until he disappeared into the trees. Whatever had she gotten herself into? She had planned her life around no one except the marvelous man she was going to find some day, the man who would be wildly handsome like her uncle, Donald Cameron, with thick thews and gentle hands. He would have the strong, wise mind of her grandfather, the sharp eyes of a hunter, the light heart of a bard; be rich as a king with vast lands—and he would give her everything she ever wanted, especially the freedom to be herself. Most important of all, he would ask nothing in return but her loyalty.

Now, instead of seeing the fulfillment of her dream, she was saddled with a bumbling hulk of a man who had nothing to offer except his devotion. She sighed and shook her head. She had really gotten herself into a pother. Knowing Jephtha, she would have the devil's own time trying to shake him from her heels once they began their journey.

She looked out into the night. Perhaps she should just up and start out before the family awoke. She sighed deeply and turned away from the open doorway. She had done some rotten things in her life, but she was not a liar. She would do exactly what she had promised, even though her misgivings almost made her believe she was gifted with second sight. But that was impossible, for she was not the seventh daughter of a seventh daughter.

Deep stirrings within her began to surface, bringing with them a frantic desire to fall to her knees in prayer, but she did not allow herself to give in to the feelings. She had lost her faith in God that afternoon beside Culloden Moor as Jamie's broken body lay cradled in her arms. She had prayed to Jesus, to all the angels in heaven to save her brother's life, but God himself and all of heaven had turned deaf ears to her pleas. Jamie's blood soaked his kilt and her own skirt through, and he died drained white and in agony, the last son of the proud Cameron clan.

She wished it were Friday so she could force a sneeze and know, because it was Friday night and she had sneezed, on the morrow she would see her lover—if she could call Jephtha her lover. But it was Tuesday; a sneeze that night would mean she would kiss a stranger. Then she wished there was a speywife around to read the tea leaves, for she had a bad feeling about the morrow and there was no one to turn to for reassurance. She suddenly laughed aloud. Though she had been surrounded by such superstitions all of her life, she had never once believed any of them and she knew she did not believe them now. Her thoughts only reflected her anxiety. She sighed deeply and turned on her side.

Sleep was a long time coming and her dreams were filled with memories of her lost family. She sat at the feet of her

21

grandfather and listened once again to his words of wisdom. She felt her father's strong arms about her and breathed in the familiar, clean fragrance of leather and sweat. She rode with her brothers across the strath, their exultant whoops of glee echoing in her ears. She heard the soft lilt of her mother's voice reciting Gaelic children's tales of misty moors and brave highland warriors. Her cheeks were wet with tears as she slept.

Chapter 2

The pearly gray dawn was shattered by a wild burst of crimson as the sun thrust its sizzling body above the horizon. The Cape Fear River was transformed into a sheet of molten gold. Farther to the east, beyond the outer banks, the Atlantic Ocean flamed orange and then deep blue beneath a sky showing little wisps of promising clouds. The stubbled corn and hemp fields around Brunswick lay steaming like noggins of hot ale, and the birds were silent as they scratched listlessly beneath shady tree branches for fallen seeds. Only the drone of the cicadas interrupted the silence of yet another morning born too early, one much too hot.

Shona rinsed her face in a bucket of tepid water outside the kitchen door. Her skin was already sticky, and she dreaded stirring the fire to make the breakfast of fried fish Master Curry always insisted upon eating on weekday mornings. She rubbed the small of her back and stretched. She had dozed fitfully, and her bloodshot eyes and the unusual pallor of her skin betrayed the strain she was under as she faced the unfolding of her final day in Brunswick. She did not understand why, but she felt in the marrow of her bones that something tragic would take place before the day was spent.

"Shona! Get in this house and stop your dawdling!"

Mistress Curry's whine grated on her eardrums, and hot

anger stirred just beneath Shona's ribs. "Damn your miserly heart," she muttered beneath her breath. Then she reminded herself this was the last morning she would have to suffer degradation. She pushed the door open and entered the kitchen with her head held high.

"Why are you always late when I need you most?" Mistress Curry questioned with a sniff. A thin stream of mucus always ran from her beaklike nose, and this morning was no exception. She wiped her nose on her sleeve and then straightened her mobcap over her limp curls. "Get busy, girl," she ordered. "You know we've an appointment with the rector soon. I want you to help Elspeth get ready after we've breakfasted. You'll need to help her wash her hair, and I'm afraid you'll have to use the crimping iron. You know how poorly Elspeth's hair behaves on humid days like this, but I want her fringe to lie crisp on her forehead."

"Yes, mum."

"Why are you smiling at me like that? Have you lost your senses?"

"No, mum."

"Mama!" Elspeth's wail from the bedroom interrupted another sniff and wipe of the nose on the sleeve.

"I'll see to the fire. You help Elspeth."

"Yes, mum."

"And stop that infernal smiling. Anyone would think you were demented."

Shona turned toward the bedroom, the smile on her face broadening. She had just experienced one of those rare revealing flashes. She felt like a child again, planning innocent revenge on her brothers, knowing her father would snarl but his eyes would be bright with laughter when the boys told on her. This morning she would push just as far as she could without stepping over the edge into flagrant disobedience. It would be fine sport to see just how far she could go.

She enjoyed herself so during the next few hours that she quite forgot about her premonition of danger. She "ac-

24

cidentally" tweaked Elspeth's back when she laced her into her morning gown; then she "accidentally" pulled a small handful of hair from the unfortunate girl's head when she caught the comb in a snarl of hair. She was afraid she might have gone too far when she "accidentally" tipped a cup of hot tea into the master's lap as she served him breakfast, but though he sputtered and cursed and stomped about, insisting she had burned him half to death, he was much too concerned about his scheduled meeting with the rector to take her to task too severely.

However, as the hour of eleven approached, her enjoyment waned and the seeds of fear she had felt since the night before blossomed into full-blown panic. Something would go drastically wrong this day. She sensed it. She *knew* it.

Mistress Curry shooed her daughter and husband out the front door and then turned to give Shona last-minute instructions. "I see clouds out there, so I don't want you to start the soap making after all. A drenching rain would just put out the fire and ruin the lye. Instead, I want you to take all of these sugar papers we've saved over the last year and put them into a pot of water. Simmer them carefully. Don't burn them on the bottom of the pot, you dreadful girl. Elspeth is going to use the blue dye for a very special woolen gown."

Shona nodded her head, wishing Mistress Curry would leave so she could see for herself if the sky truly promised rain.

"After that, you are to scrutch those flax bundles. If you do a good job, I'll give you the tow flax for another gown. And don't glare at me so, the hard work will drive the meanness out of your bones."

Again Shona nodded as she bit her tongue to forestall telling Mistress Curry exactly whose bones needed the meanness worked out of them. Her mistress stared at her with beady little gray eyes; then, with a final swipe at her nose and a swish of her skirts, she went out the door to join her family in their walk up Cross Street on the way to St. Philip's.

Shona waited until they were well around the bend of

Second Street before she moved. She started to toss the sugar papers into the fire, but on second thought, she smoothed the lovely blue sheets with her hands and placed them in her apron pocket. She had coveted these papers herself for an entire year, having watched Elspeth remove them carefully from each new sugar cone as it was brought from the dock. She would take them with her, and some day she would use the dye to make *herself* a special blue gown.

Her hands shook as she gathered the food she needed for her journey: a loaf of cornmeal bread sweetened with honey, a packet of herbs she had secreted in a drawer, a large piece of salted beef and the last perfect orange from the basket of precious fruit Elspeth kept by her bed.

She stood in the doorway and looked out at the gathering clouds. If anything, the morning was even more humid than the preceding night had been. Surely it was going to rain! She wondered if that had brought the aching cramp to her stomach. Would the Currys be able to track her if it rained? Not if she got a good head start. She knew the rector was a long-winded bag of bones, so if she started right now, even if it rained her footprints would be washed out of the black clay within moments of her passing.

She raced to her room, grabbed her bed sheet, emptied the food treasures from her apron into the center of it, and tied the corners together. Then she walked quickly toward the trees, glancing about in terror lest someone take note of her departure. But no one was in sight. As she hurried on, legs trembling, cursing her own timidity yet knowing she should be rejoicing, she could not quench her feeling of impending doom. She had not felt this unsettled before the battle of Culloden, but that morning, of course, her father's bright, confident smile had warmed her with its glow.

When she reached the oak, she stripped off her apron and gown, then pulled the scratchy breeches over her legs. Ignoring the buttons, she fastened them at the waist with a piece of linen riband. She left the buttons at the bottom of the

26

breeches undone also, to free her legs for running. Then she wrapped her breasts, making them as flat as possible, with another piece of riband. She hated the constricted feeling, but she donned the shirt quickly and then began to push her luxurious mane of hair up into the woolen cap. By the time she was finished, sweat was pouring down her cheeks and stinging her eyes.

When she twisted to place the blue sugar papers beneath her waistband, a sudden muffled boom of thunder startled her and she dropped the papers. She watched as they fluttered toward the ground like bright blue birds settling for a feed upon the acorns. Then she scooped them up and crammed them into her waistband with trembling fingers. Another boom of thunder sounded, this time much louder. She grabbed her bundle and headed into the woods, proceeding southwest toward the Southport Road.

By the time she had traveled several hundred yards, she knew the booming was not thunder. It was coming without interruption now, harsh and cruel to her ears. She looked up at the sky and saw black smoke drifting low over the treetops. She recognized those booms. She had heard them echo across the moors as the British troops leveled their cannon on the Scottish clans and sent grapeshot slicing through the air, decapitating, disemboweling, dismembering, slaughtering.

Her breath became a sob. She threw her bundle down and shimmied up into a large white oak tree. She climbed quickly, tearing her fingers on the harsh bark, ignoring the pain in her frantic need to see what was happening. She climbed as high as she dared, until the branches bent and swayed beneath her weight. Then she turned toward the southeast and shaded her eyes with her hand.

Her heart stopped beating for a fraction of a second, and when it resumed, it was only another muffled roar added to the sound of the cannon booming from the waterfront. Three strange ships, flying flags of blood red emblazoned with golden crosses, their canvas white against the blue-black of the sky,

27

stood off in the middle of the river. She recognized those flags. The Spanish were attacking! Their guns were belching red flashes of doom directed toward the docks and the ships moored there. She could see people scurrying about the pier, racing here and there, with no apparent destination. They sometimes ran pell-mell into one another, then scrambled to their feet and began to run again. During an occasional lull in the shelling, she could hear their screams. The skin at the nape of her neck prickled. She remembered screams like those, and the memory brought the bitter taste of bile to her mouth.

The townspeople were pouring out of their homes now, their arms laden with whatever valuables they could grab and carry. Men toted guns and children; women, food and babies. Shona turned to look for Jephtha's smithy shop. At that instant, it crumbled in a puff of black smoke, the victim of a direct hit. Her scream was cut off in her throat by a sudden fusillade of shots coming from south of the docks. She could see little white puffs of smoke, and she knew that the Spanish had landed just below Orton Plantation.

Jephtha! He had said he would wait in the woods for her! Thank God he was out of the smithy long before now. He would be as anxious as she to leave. But if he was hiding in the woods below Orton, he was in more danger now than if he were still in town. She slid down the trunk of the tree, tearing her breeches in several places, scraping her cheek on a protruding limb.

She did not stoop to retrieve her bundle. All that mattered now was finding Jephtha. She tore through the woods, dodging yaupon trees, crawling through scratchy thickets on her hands and knees. Her breath came in sobs, and her bound chest heaved with the effort of trying to draw an unencumbered breath. The knit cap was yanked from her head by a prickly ash stem, and she retrieved it, cramming her hair back under it as she ran.

When she reached Southport Road, she found it filled with moaning, terrified people, all moving as one body away from the town. She could see Master and Mistress Curry and Elspeth in the middle of the crowd. She ducked her head, but they were not interested in a ragged boy standing at the side of the road. They were intent on escaping slaughter and rape at the hands of the Spanish.

Shona pressed into the throng of people, wriggling through them in her attempt to get across the road. She could see fear in their faces, could smell the sweat provoked by terror, but she did not feel scorn. Her own fear took the form of a bitter taste in her mouth and a pounding heart which threatened to leap out of her chest at any moment. The crowd carried her along as she scrambled and pushed and shoved her way to the other side. When she finally stumbled into the ditch, her clothes were torn and her shins and elbows were raw from kicks and bumps she had received.

She stood at the side of the road for a moment to catch her breath. But the constant peppering of shots from the Orton Plantation soon urged her to double back to the road leading to Orton. She did not stay in the middle of the track, but dove into the trees and tromped through bushes for several hundred yards, knowing that every step took her closer to the gut-twisting peril she had been dreading all morning.

She slowed and dropped to her knees when she saw the banks of the Cape Fear River. She could still hear sporadic musket shots through the booming of the cannons but they sounded far off to her right. She hoped the Spanish landing force had already penetrated the woods and was well on its way into the northern end of Brunswick. She did not care that she was wishing even more peril upon the unfortunate inhabitants of the town. All she could think about now was her dear friend Jephtha and his safety.

She crawled on her hands and knees to the side of the track, then parted a yaupon bush and peered out. The track was deserted. A large drop of rain splattered onto her nose. She turned her face up, but that lone drop was all the sky was willing to part with for now. She rubbed her hands across her eyes and lurched to her feet. Taking a deep breath, she plunged across the track, diving for the cover of the bushes on the other side. For a moment she lay on her stomach, her heart thudding in her ears, her nostrils burning from the acrid smoke hanging heavy in the air. Then she wiped the sweat from her eyes and peered through the bushes into the woods, hoping against all hope that she would see Jephtha's huge body secreted behind a tree trunk or bush. But the woods were empty.

She fought against the tears brimming in her eyes. She had to find Jephtha, she had to! She rose slowly to her feet and began to move cautiously through the woods, keeping as close to the river as she dared. As she walked, the booming of the cannons and the sharp sounds of rifle fire softened, and she became bolder. Soon, she was walking upright, calling Jephtha's name softly over and over.

The sharp crack of a limb to her right stopped her dead in her tracks. She held her breath, lest her ragged panting give her away. When she heard the crackle of broken twigs and the rustle of disturbed leaves, she squatted and pressed her back against a tree trunk. Terrified by the knowledge that she was out in the open, away from the cover of the bushes, she shrank back against the trunk as the rustle of leaves came closer and closer. She prayed it was an animal, even a bear, but not a Spaniard, please God, please Jesus, not a Spaniard, only a bear.

Jephtha stepped out into the clearing in front of her. He saw her the same moment she recognized him. He pulled back his huge arm and rushed toward her, brandishing a tree limb large enough to crush her skull.

"Jephtha!" she screamed. "It's me, Shona!"

He dropped the limb and ground to a halt, just feet in front of her. Then he was grabbing her up from the ground, hugging her and rocking her back and forth.

"God, Shona, I gave you up for dead!" he exclaimed as he crushed her to his chest. "I was sure them bastard Spaniards took you!"

Shona's tears mingled with the sweat pouring down her cheeks. "Oh, Jephtha, I'm glad you're safe."

"Don't move, either of you!"

The harsh, accented voice grated through the air. Jephtha's body stiffened and Shona's heart dropped like a rock to the bottom of her stomach.

"You will move apart, very slowly, with your hands where I can see them at all times."

Shona turned stricken eyes on Jephtha's face. He had blanched, and his brown eyes were now smudges above taut, stark white cheekbones. She could feel the wild pounding of a heart but did not know whose it was.

"I said to move apart!" the voice barked authoritatively.

Shona could not move. She felt her knees begin to buckle.

"Stand up and step away, *boy*," the voice said harshly.

Jephtha stepped back away from her, his hands held out to his sides, his eyes boring into hers, pleading, demanding, ordering her to obey. She moved her arms out slowly, showing her empty hands. Jephtha's steady gaze stopped the trembling of her fingers, and she suddenly felt very calm.

Three foreigners stepped out into the clearing. That they were sailors was obvious, for two wore white breeches and brightly colored shirts. The third was garbed in black, and he had a wickedly curved cutlass tucked in his waistband. But they did not look Spanish. Two were blonds, and the one with the cutlass had fiery red hair. Didn't all Spaniards have black hair and swarthy skin?

"That's better, *hombres*." The redhead favored them with a tight smile.

He moved closer, his eyes glued to the huge hulk that was Jephtha, his movements sure because his companions' muskets were pointed at the giant.

"You Colonials are a strange lot," he said in his husky, accented voice. "Do all of your males greet each other with embraces much like lovers?"

Jephtha shook his head from side to side. "He's my brother," he said quickly. "I was afraid he was killed in the fighting."

31

The Spanish leader moved closer. Shona could smell the stench of spirits on his breath as his pale eyes raked over her body, and she fought to control her trembling, knowing from his lustful leer that he was not fooled by her costume.

"So," he breathed out slowly. "Your younger brother, huh? Strange, you don't look a bit alike. One so dark, and one," he ran his tongue over his lips, "so fair."

"My brother favors my mother's side of the family," Jephtha mumbled, his fear for Shona thickening his tongue.

The leader poked his gun into Shona's chest. "Has he got a tongue, this brother of yours, or is he a mute?"

Shona cleared her throat. "I can talk," she said in as low a voice as she could muster.

A slow, lazy smile spread over the Spaniard's features. "Excellent," he said. "I do not like to take prisoners who are mute." He squeezed Shona's arm painfully between his fingers, his tongue once again wetting his lips.

"Let him go!" Jephtha urged. "He's only a boy! Take me instead, I'm strong, I'll work for you, I'm a smithy, I can help you on your ships! Just let him go!"

The Spaniard barked a short, harsh laugh. "You are a fool," he spat in Jephtha's direction. "We will take both of you. You can work, and your brother can entertain me. I have always preferred young boys, they are so tender."

When his meaning became clear to her, Shona gagged and sagged to her knees. The Spaniard jerked her roughly to her feet. "Don't be *too* tender," he barked at her. "Boys who are too tender are useless. They soon wind up as food for the fish."

She glanced at Jephtha, her eyes pleading that he not cause any trouble. She could see tears glisten on his lashes, but he nodded his head slightly.

"Come!" the Spaniard said harshly. "Our landing boat is just beyond those trees."

He started walking, jerking Shona roughly along beside him. She felt her cap slipping and she pulled it down with one shaking hand, praying it would stay in place long enough for her to think of a way to escape. Dear God, he thought she was a boy, and he liked tender boys! Bile rose in her throat, threatening to choke her. She swallowed quickly, willing herself not to vomit. She did not want to do anything to anger this beast of a man striding along so impatiently beside her.

He pulled her down the riverbank, not taking any precautions about being seen. When they reached the river, she could see why. Several Spaniards stood beside a beached boat, their long guns in their hands, their faces watchful. The leader barked orders to the men, and Shona was pushed into the boat. When he stepped in after her, the boat was shoved out into the water.

"Jephtha!" Shona screamed.

"Silence!" the Spaniard barked. "Your brother will be taken to the ship later."

Shona huddled low on the seat, her hands clenched together, her body shaking with silent sobs. They were going to kill Jephtha, she knew they were going to kill him. She steeled herself for the sound of the shot. But all she heard was the soft hiss of the oars being pulled through the water and an occasional shout from the town. She looked up at the Spaniard.

He sat studying her with narrowed eyes. "We do not kill our unarmed prisoners," he said stiffly. "You will see your brother later today."

She looked away quickly lest he see the tears of relief spilling down her cheeks and making pale rivers through the grime.

There was no hint of a breeze, and the sun beat down upon the bright surface of the water. It was stifling. Shona closed her eyes and fought the darkness threatening to overcome her. She heard a low buzzing in her ears; then her head felt as though it would float away all by itself.

She was shocked awake by a splash of tepid water in her face. "I have told you not to be too tender," the Spaniard snarled. "If you know what is good for you, you will heed my orders. I am Captain Vicente Lopez of the sloop *Fortune*. I am a privateer bearing letters of marque from King Fernando VI of

Spain. I am the commander of these invading forces, and when I give an order, I expect it to be obeyed, *pronto!*"

Shona looked at him wide-eyed. The commander of the forces!

As her thoughts registered on her face, his stern look dissolved into hearty laughter. "I can well imagine that you wonder why I would leave my ship in the command of others while I go out on a petty raiding party. Well, I enjoy the battle—the smell of the smoke, the cries of victory. And, believe me, I leave my ship and my men under the command of the only other man capable of doing the job: Esteban de Larra! You fear me, but I must tell you he is much more ferocious than I! Don't ever cross de Larra if you value your life, for he is driven by the devil himself and all the demons in hell ride his coattails."

Shona shuddered. She could picture this Esteban de Larra, his nostrils breathing fire, his eyes sparking red death everywhere he looked. She hoped she never had an opportunity to put to the test Captain Lopez's warning.

They neared the largest of the three Spanish vessels. The gun ports were silent now, but Shona could hear sporadic gunfire and hair-raising screams floating across the water from the town. She wondered if she would scream when Captain Lopez touched her. She was sure she would. Though she had always prided herself on her control, there was nothing so incomprehensible and thus terrifying to her as a man who liked young boys! But of course, he would discover that she was not a boy, and he would discover that very quickly. What would he do then? Would he kill her in a fit of anger, of disappointed rage? She remembered the way he had licked his lips in anticipation. Surely, he would not allow her to go unpunished for thwarting his planned rape of a young male body!

The boat scraped against the side of the *Fortune.* "Climb!" Captain Lopez ordered.

Shona looked at the rope ladder. She was certain that she could not climb it to the deck. She would fall off into the river and drown, and the Spanish sailors would laugh as she took deep gulps of water into her dying lungs.

"There is no other way," the captain said more gently.

As Shona reached for the rope, she felt a steadying arm on her elbow. She put her bare foot onto the rope, and slowly she began to climb. She was terrified when the rope began to swing out over the water, but her terror prevented her from letting go. Slowly, slowly, she pulled herself upward. At last, she reached the top and helping hands eased her over the railing onto the deck.

Captain Lopez climbed swiftly, surely. In seconds, he was standing beside her. The deck was almost deserted, but all of the men present quickly stiffened to attention and saluted their captain. Lopez returned their salutes with a cavalier wave.

He began to speak rapidly in English to one of his officers. Shona was furious at what he was saying about her, and when the officer grinned and smirked at her, she felt her spine stiffen. The insufferable bastard! She was about to give him a good piece of her mind when Captain Lopez gripped her elbow and began speaking in strident tones into her ear. "Behave yourself, boy, or I will turn you loose among my men after I take my own pleasure with you. Come. I want you to meet my second in command. We will go to my cabin."

His fingers ground into her arm as he led her toward an open hatch. She kept her eyes downcast, for she could feel the sailors' gazes upon her and she knew what they were thinking. Her face burned with shame; her breast was afire with hatred.

Lopez pushed her down a ladder into a companionway, and forward down a dark, narrow hall. He paused before a closed door. "Remember what I told you about de Larra," he hissed into her ear. "He eats little boys for dinner." He threw the door open and shoved her inside.

Shona was momentarily dazzled by the splendor before her. The captain's cabin was lit by a magnificent crystal chandelier ablaze with slim red tapers. Works of art adorned the walls, all

35

set in enormous heavily gilded frames, and a massive, ornately carved desk rested beneath the large galley window. At that desk sat the second in command, Esteban de Larra.

He leaped to his feet and stiffly saluted Captain Lopez. A rapid exchange of Spanish followed. Shona took advantage of the conversation to study this man who was in league with the devil. His voice was deep with a husky quality, which at any other time, she would have found provocative.

He was tall and slim, and powerfully built, though he lacked the robust sturdiness of Jephtha. Instead, he was rock hard. His thews strained the upper sleeves of his black coat and bulged against his tight, black pant legs. The froth of lace at his throat and wrists and his white stockings were the only bit of his attire that was not black. Her gaze traveled up past his broadly set shoulders to his firm, clean-shaven chin with its deep cleft, then to his straight nose and high cheekbones. Again she was startled by his coloring, for his curly hair was blond, tied at the nape of his neck with a simple black riband, and his eyes were the deepest blue she had ever seen, deeper even than the sugar papers in her waistband.

He reminded her of someone she had once known very well. As she studied him, trying to bring to mind that other familiar face, his eyebrows rose and fell with maddening insolence as his own gaze raked over her from head to toe. She remembered instantly. Donald Cameron of Lochiel, her uncle and the clan leader! Though de Larra was much younger, he had the same coloring, the same narrowness of bone, and the same haughty expression as that great Scottish leader who had fallen at Culloden. Perhaps this man was in league with the devil, but she remembered a saying she had heard as a child, "They that deal wi' the de'il get a dear pennyworth." That memory added to his resemblance to Donald Cameron removed her fear of Esteban de Larra. She met his gaze with candor. Did she imagine it, or did she see a startled flicker of appraisal darken his azure eyes? She felt a smile begin and did not try to quench it.

"I trust you will leave us alone now?" Lopez asked his second in command in English.

De Larra's right eyebrow shot up. Then his face eased into a lazy grin. "Of course, Vicente," he drawled. "But I will bring you wine. I'm afraid I have depleted your stores."

Lopez smiled and slapped de Larra on the back. "Fine, fine, Esteban. Trust you to know the right thing to do. And, please order some hot water. This young scallywag could use a good scrubbing."

De Larra's eyes narrowed as he studied Shona. "And he could use some manners too, I'm afraid," he said very softly. Before she knew what he was about, he jerked her cap from her head and her hair tumbled about her shoulders. As she heard Captain Lopez's harsh oath, she caught her breath. She was certain that de Larra and his devils had just deliberately signed and sealed her death warrant.

Chapter 3

Esteban de Larra stared in amazement at the mass of coppery tresses cascading below the waist of the remarkable creature standing before him. His breath caught in his throat as the golden strands sparked red in the flare from the candles overhead. The girl's yellow eyes were wide with terror, and her breath escaped her mouth in gasps.

Vindictive Spanish expressions spouted from Vicente Lopez's twisted mouth, but Esteban gripped his commander's arm and squeezed tightly. "Easy, Vicente," he soothed. "This *vagabundear* is not worthy of your anger. She is only a worthless Colonial. I will get her out of your sight before she does further damage to your senses."

"No!" Lopez screamed. "I will have her flogged for her deception!" His eyes narrowed suddenly, and a tight grin slashed across his features. "Better yet," he crooned huskily, "I will have that giant *hombre* she was with flogged and then drawn and quartered before her very eyes!"

"Oh, God, no!" Shona screamed. She dropped to her knees and pressed her face against Lopez's legs. "Please don't punish Jephtha," she moaned. "He was only trying to protect me."

"He is your lover!" Lopez spat out. "And a liar!"

"No," Shona gasped. "He is only a friend. He wanted to protect me from you. He was afraid you would . . . you

39

would . . ." She could not continue, but fell back, her hands pressed over her face in agony.

"Rape you?" Lopez sneered. "And what of you? Do you prefer to be raped as a boy, is that it?"

Shona dropped her hands and turned to look up at de Larra. "Please don't let him hurt Jephtha," she begged. "He is innocent. This is all my fault."

Lopez stiffened with rage. "I am the commander here!" he screamed. "I am the one you must plead with! Are you begging, little slut? Are you on your hands and knees groveling before me? I am the only one who can save you and your lover, and don't you forget it!"

Esteban watched the girl's eyes. They were wide with terror when Lopez began his tirade, but by the time he finished, they were narrow slits filled with hatred. The little tramp had courage, but this was not the time to display it. He felt pity when he thought of what the future held for her.

Lopez was also aware of the transformation. He brought back his hand and lashed the girl savagely across the face.

Shona saw his fist coming, but she could not avoid it. Her head snapped back from the force of the blow, bright pinpoints of light exploded before her eyes, and her vision clouded. She felt the harsh nap of the rug burn her cheek and knew she had fallen. When she struggled to sit up, her body refused to obey, and she lay in a daze, eyes closed, awaiting with resignation the blow that would end her life.

De Larra stared at his commander. After her first twitching, the girl lay motionless. Had the blow killed her?

Loud footsteps rang in the corridor outside. The door was pushed open and a Spanish sailor rushed into the cabin, his face flushed with excitement. *"Capitán!"* he shouted. "The Colonials have mounted a resistance! They are firing upon our landing party!"

Lopez stiffened and his face froze into an angry snarl. "We shall see about that!" he snapped. He turned to De Larra. "Esteban, you will take command of the sloop we captured this morning. Move her upriver out of the range of their guns at once. We will put down their puny resistance and join you by sunset."

De Larra snapped to attention. "At once, Capitán," he answered briskly.

Lopez marched to the open doorway, then whirled and pointed a stabbing finger at the girl lying on the floor. "And I order you to take that piece of filth with you! Do anything you wish with her, kill her if you desire, but do not let me set eyes on her again, is that understood? Never again!"

De Larra saluted. "Yes, Capitán," he said.

Lopez left the cabin without another word, trailed by the sailor. Esteban stood by the door listening to the sounds of gunfire drifting over the water from the town. Then he shook his head and pounded his open palm with his fist. A pox on safety! He wanted to be in the thick of the battle! He sighed and shook his head. Such was the price he paid for being second in command to his father's best friend. Vicente had always been too protective of the son of Don Manuel de Larra.

He walked over to Shona and stood staring down at her with distaste. What would he do with such a piece of trash? He prodded her with his foot. When she did not respond, he bent and picked her up, his mouth set in a grim line. As he flung her over his shoulder, the stench of sweat wafted from her clothing. He strode from the cabin, fighting with himself over what her fate should be. His first impulse was to toss her into the river and be done with it, but he knew he could not do that. If she were a man, he would kill her and laugh as he performed the deed, yet he could not take a woman's life, no matter if she was a worthless Colonial.

He climbed to the deck and walked quickly to the railing, dodging gun crews racing to their stations. He confronted a sailor who had just climbed up the rope ladder. "Take me to the captured sloop," he barked. "And see that enough ammunition is taken over to her to stand off an attack from shore, if necessary."

41

The sailor saluted and stood back as de Larra went over the side, his movements hasty despite his burden.

Shona bit her tongue to keep from crying out when she was dumped unceremoniously into the bottom of the longboat. She did not move when she felt the boat glide through the water, though she wanted desperately to relieve her throbbing jaw. She lay quietly, hatred burning in her stomach, her teeth gritted against the exultant words she wanted to hurl at that beast de Larra. So the township was fighting back! She smiled grimly at the boards beneath her face. Good! She hoped every bastard Spaniard was shot or run through by a steel blade, and it couldn't happen quickly enough to satisfy her!

Moments later, she was yanked upward and once again flung like a hopsack of potatoes over that broad shoulder. She opened her eyes slightly and tried to see what was taking place as de Larra pulled himself up onto the deck. But she could not turn her head lest she give herself away so all she could see were the bleached deck boards. She knew from the shouting, heavily accented voices around her that the ship was manned by a Spanish crew. Damnation! She was surrounded by the whoring heathens!

"Take me to the captain's quarters!" de Larra ordered. Shona wondered why he continued to speak in English. Could he be aware that she was not truly unconscious? She did not know that Vicente Lopez's crews were made up of an elite force especially trained to attack the English Colonies, and that they had all been ordered to learn English and to speak it when engaging the enemy. Lopez felt that this enabled his men to better understand the minds of the Colonists.

Shona almost groaned aloud at the pain in her ribs as de Larra walked across the deck. Would the bastard never put her down? She closed her eyes tightly and bit her lip in frustration and anger. Moments later, she heard a door open and close, and suddenly she found herself falling. She went limp, expecting another harsh encounter with a floor, but this time her fall was broken by something much softer.

42

"I want a guard placed at this door," de Larra said harshly.

"Yes, sir!" came the reply.

Footsteps moved away, a door slammed, and she prayed she was alone. She lay very still for a long time, sure that this was some sort of trick, that the Spaniard was standing at her side, waiting for her to move before he performed some unspeakable act upon her defenseless body. At last, she turned her head slowly to one side and opened her eyes. All she could see was the closed door. She lifted her head slightly and looked around, her breath frozen in her chest. She was alone!

She closed her eyes briefly and when she opened them again, tears glistened on her lashes. "Oh, God," she breathed. She sat up slowly, her head spinning, and when she touched her jaw, she winced. Her eyes sparked with hatred. "Damn that bloody bastard Lopez to hell!" she said aloud. The words, even though spoken to an empty room, loosened the tight coil of hatred threatening to choke her. She looked down at the bed beneath her. The coverlet was clean, except where her dirty face had smudged it, and two plump bolsters rested invitingly just inches from her hand. She refused to yield to the temptation to lie down and sleep the rest of the day away. She had to escape!

She slid from the bed and looked around. The cabin was roomy and clean, though not as luxuriously appointed as the captain's quarters on the Spanish sloop.

"The Spanish are a bunch of whoremongers!" she said under her breath.

She walked over to the desk anchored to the wall and fingered the book lying open before her. Though she read both Scots and Gaelic, Cumberland had not taught her to read English well, and her eyes were gritty with fatigue. She left the book where it lay and walked swiftly to one of the portholes. Before she could look out, she felt the ship begin to rock and she knew they were moving her upriver as the commander had ordered. She pressed her face against the glass. The wharf was moving out of view behind her, but she could see smoke from the town. The Spaniards were burning houses and business

43

places after their pillaging.

"Kill them!" she whispered, wishing she could join the Brunswick forces which she was sure were under the command of Captain William Dry. She lost herself for a moment in a vision of herself wielding a gun and a knife, cutting at and firing into a mob of Spaniards, watching each face fill with surprise as she hacked away life after life with bloody precision.

As the shore of Orton Plantation came into view, she caught her breath, wondering what had happened to Jephtha. Had they taken him to the command ship? Or had they waited until she was out of hearing before placing a gun barrel to his forehead and blasting away his brains? She closed her eyes and staggered to the bed, fighting the vomit hot in her throat.

"Oh, Jephtha," she cried. "What has happened to you?" She lay on the bed for many moments before she was able to bring her sobs under control.

Finally, she wiped her runny nose on her shirt sleeve and sniffed one last time. Somehow, she would get away, and when she did, she would find Jephtha and, together, they would leave this place of horror and go where they could live in safety. Her grand dream of finding a handsome benefactor lay in fragments about her feet, but she still would not abandon it. Somewhere lived the man she sought. Until he and she found one another, she would content herself with Jephtha. She had not survived Cumberland only to give in now. After all, she was a Cameron. She thought of her father's broad, handsome face. She shook herself. First she had to escape. She rose quickly and tiptoed to the door. She could not hear anything outside. She grasped the handle and twisted. It would not budge. That bastard had locked her in! She aimed a kick at the door but dropped her foot just in time. It might be dangerous to call attention to herself now. De Larra had not harmed her so far but she might not fare as well with one of his sailors. The thought of an encounter with the crew made her chest heave and her breath fight for release. She was suddenly overcome by the need for air. She

44

tore the shirt from her shoulders and untied the knot holding the linen ribands in place. She almost sobbed aloud with relief as the ribands dropped to the floor and her breasts popped upright, marked with heavy lines and throbbing—but free!

The fragments of the torn shirt drifted to the floor and the heavy, scratchy breeches were soon added to the pile. She lifted her arms and arched her back, reveling in the freedom of her naked body. But her hair still rode like a heavy blanket upon her sweaty shoulders. She grabbed a piece of discarded riband from the floor and stooped, flinging her heavy mane forward. Quickly, she wound her tresses into a huge coil which she tied deftly atop her head. When she straightened, the room spun for a moment before she realized she was so thirsty there was no saliva in her mouth. A quick look around the cabin turned up an opened jug of flat ale. It would be better than nothing. She sat on the side of the bed, sipping the ale slowly, savoring the earthy taste of malt upon her swollen tongue.

It was then that she realized the ship was no longer moving. She walked quickly to the porthole and looked out. They were anchored in a cove lined with black gum and cypress trees. Her heart quickened. Surely, she could swim to the shore and escape! As she watched, a huge alligator moved lazily up the bank, the sun sparkling on his wet, knobby back. She shivered involuntarily, her skin prickling. Even if she could escape the ship within the next few hours, she was not sure she was brave enough to dive into these waters!

She returned to the bed, the ale now turned sour on her tongue. Forcing herself to face her situation, she began to chuckle bitterly. Life in Brunswick had been filled with humiliation and hard work, but she had never been in danger of dying, and she had always known that even if she had to serve out her full term she would be free after five more years. Now, she had no such assurance. She should have stayed with the Currys! Why did life always treat her so shabbily? She would never have been captured by Cumberland's men if she had not insisted upon watching her father and brothers go into a battle they were certain they would win, and she would not be sitting naked in this locked cabin, aboard a ship resting in alligator-infested waters if she had not decided to run away from the Currys. She snorted at the thought of God smiling in satisfaction as the Spanish planned their attack and then slipped into the harbor just as she was donning her escape disguise!

What was de Larra really like? Lopez had said he ate little boys. What did he do to grown women? She shuddered and fell back upon the bed. She closed her eyes tightly, but she could not do away with the memory of azure eyes raking over her, of sinewy muscles rippling over flesh and bone. Her fear was suddenly transformed into mind-numbing panic which raced through her body, casting breath and reason to the wind.

Esteban de Larra stood on the deck, surveying his men at work. A casual observer would have thought that he was completely relaxed, but his nonchalance was a calculated pose. His every nerve, every muscle, was screaming for action. The sticky air made breathing difficult, and his body strained for release from the heavy woolen clothing that sealed the sweat to his burning skin. He walked to the railing and looked longingly down at the water. It was muddy and surely filled with poisonous snakes and alligators, but it looked inviting. Valencia, where he'd spent his boyhood, could hardly be called a cool environment. Nonetheless, the heat there had been different, dry and bearable, not this sticky, suffocating blanket which stopped your breath in your chest and irritated your skin. If only it would rain!

He slapped at the mosquitoes buzzing around his face and looked up at the sky. The clouds were heavy, black with smoke from burning buildings and cannon fire downriver. Where was Lopez and why had the firing intensified rather than abated? At least four hours had passed since he had ordered the anchor hoisted. Why had the fates decreed that he not take part in this

46

battle? What was happening?

He was aware of a familiar sensation, anger building inside him, and he knew himself well enough to realize it would soon grow into a full-blown rage. He bit the inside flesh of his lip and clenched his fists. He had worked too hard to be appointed second in command for this voyage to allow the entire battle to go by without his having fired a single shot, without even knowing the pleasure of setting foot upon this foreign soil. Of course, his share of the spoils would be the same as if he were fighting, and surely, after this journey, even Inez would be satisfied with his wealth and would honor him by becoming his wife. Yet, the thought of riches was not enough. His mind and body both screamed to be in on the battle!

"Capitán, the men have finished their tasks. Do they have your permission to refresh themselves?"

De Larra turned quickly and looked at his lieutenant, his eyes dark blue with anger. "That depends upon what you mean, Perez," he said with deceptive softness.

Perez knew his commander. "No spirits," he said hastily. "I only meant, could they break into the water casks and wash the sweat from their bodies? The *insectos*—I mean insects—are driving them mad."

De Larra nodded coldly. "Only two at a time," he ordered. "We must be in constant readiness in case we are needed."

"Yes, sir." Perez saluted and quickly turned away.

De Larra returned to his musings. Inez . . . As usual, the thought of her fragile, white skin, of her huge black eyes and raven tresses, was enough to cool his anger in seconds. How he longed to feel that soft, silken skin beneath his fingers, to explore the secret treasures of the tantalizing body thus far denied him. His breath caught in his throat. Ah, bedding Inez would make all of this a small price to pay. He recalled their parting kiss, the way her lips had softened beneath his, her tiny gasp when his tongue had penetrated the recesses of her honey-filled mouth.

He felt a stirring in his groin. *Madre de Dios*, would the night ahead be yet another filled with taunting dreams which left him weak and spent in his lonely bed? He groaned and turned from the railing. He would go below and see if that filthy Colonial had wakened. He would not bed her, of course, for his need was not great enough to overcome her stench. But he might derive pleasure from baiting her, from seeing those large yellow eyes widen with fear. He began to chuckle as he climbed down the ladder to the lower deck.

Smoke, still trapped in the narrow passageway, burned his nostrils, bringing tears to his eyes, and by the time he reached the captain's cabin, his anger had returned. Impatiently, he unlocked the door and kicked it open.

The girl lay naked on the bunk, her arms clasped about her body as though to protect her from monsters peopling her dreams. Though he made no attempt to soften his footsteps, she did not awaken when he strode into the room and walked to where she lay. He looked down at her, his nostrils flaring in distaste. Her stench had filled the entire room!

He quickly opened the porthole covers and returned to stare down at her. She had attempted to tie her hair on top of her head, but the riband had slipped and masses of coppery curls fanned out over the coverlet, framing her profile with burnished gold. Sooty lashes swept her bruised cheeks on which trails from her tears stood out white against the grime. De Larra stepped back, fighting the sudden twinge of pity which threatened to destroy his common sense. She looked so young, so vulnerable.

His gaze traveled over her body. Her legs were drawn up, but he did not miss the shapely turn of her ankles and the ripe curve of her thighs. As his gaze lingered upon the wedge of golden hair resting at the base of her belly, he felt again that stirring in his groin. He quickly turned his gaze higher. Her waist narrowed above a womanly swell of hips, but it was her breasts which made his breath catch in his throat. They lay nestled on her arms, their ripe fullness evident. Their nipples were dark pink flowers opened wide to the warm air. De Larra was struck by a sudden desire to stroke them and watch them close into tight buds. But the thought of touching that filthy body brought a loud curse to his lips.

Shona awakened instantly. As her eyes opened and she looked up, she uttered a stifled scream and groped to pull the coverlet over her naked body.

"Do not attempt to cover your dirty flesh," de Larra said coldly. "I have seen more enticing meat at the beef market."

"Beast!" she croaked.

She reached for the bolster but his hands imprisoned hers. She struggled to free them so she could scratch at his face, but his grip was unyielding as steel.

"Let me go!" she screeched, kicking and writhing.

His laugh, low in his throat, sounded so like an animal's that Shona panicked. She brought back her knee and kicked out at him, catching him a hard blow in the stomach.

He dropped her hands and lurched backward. "Bitch!" he gasped as he doubled over. "Filthy, stinking *puta!*"

Shona yanked the coverlet over her body and struggled to her feet. "Bastard!" she screamed. "Bloody whoremonger!"

Lashing out at him with her closed fists, she laughed shrilly when she felt solid flesh beneath her pounding hands, but her victory was short-lived. Once again those hands of steel imprisoned hers. As he forced her to her knees, her lips clenched over a scream of pain.

Shona fought the tears welling up behind her tightly closed eyelids. She could not cry! She *would not* cry! Suddenly, her hands were freed and she slumped to the floor, swallowing bile and panting for breath.

"You Spanish pig!" she gasped. "I hope the Kelpie lures you into that river and devours you!" His laughter spurred her on to more vindictiveness. "I hope the alligators catch you swimming and snap off your bod in one bite, though I'm sure it's so bitter, they'd spit it out in a trice!"

"Bod? What are you raving?"

She gestured disdainfully toward the bulge at his crotch.

49

"That puny little thing," she said.

Her head was jerked back as he pulled on the ends of her hair. "Perhaps a taste of my manhood would assure you of its size and sweetness," he said, his voice steely soft. She watched, not breathing, as he dropped to his knees beside her. His eyes were staring, probing, demanding. His gaze kindled a molten flame deep within her belly, and her eyes widened as she felt an unfamiliar passion growing within her quivering body.

He pulled her into his arms and his mouth claimed hers fiercely. She could feel his teeth grating against hers as his tongue entered her mouth, exploring hotly every secret crevice. Her own tongue reached out to twine with his, and she could taste his lust. She choked when her own body responded violently to his probing tongue and caressing fingers. No, this could not be happening! She could not allow herself to succumb like this, not after all of her plans, her vows to save herself for her marriage bed—not to this arrogant bastard of a foreigner. But she was powerless to stop the desire overwhelming her. She could not control her desire for him to take her, even though she knew it would end in panic and humiliating pain.

He pushed her down to the floor, his hands kneading her breasts so hard that she wanted to scream, but the discomfort only increased her need for him to possess her. His hands moved over her belly, then downward, and she uttered a small scream when his fingers began to stroke her, but not because he was causing pain. His fingers were gentle, probing, rubbing, exploring. He pressed her thighs with the backs of his hands, and she opened her legs.

She moaned with disappointment when his hands left her, but when she opened her eyes, she saw him struggling with his clothing. In seconds, his coat, waistcoat, and breeches lay in a pile upon the floor, and his hands returned to her. She arched her back and received him as he thrust himself deep within her.

Then she felt her breath leave her body as the usual panic began. She wanted to respond, but her muscles stiffened as his lips sought one nipple and then the other, his tongue caressing them into hard nubbins of tingling flesh. Her panic grew as he thrust into her with savage stabs, and she closed her eyes, fighting back tears of disappointment. Cumberland's terrible rage had scarred her forever. She would never be able to give herself completely!

When his thrusts slowed, she looked up into his face. He was frowning, as though perplexed that she was no longer responding to him. Then he smiled slightly as his fingers sought her secret place of desire. Gently, slowly, he touched her. Her body began to tingle again, and she felt her hips moving in response. She pushed her hips against his, matching his rhythm, losing herself in the hot, slow, agonizing glory of their coupling. As she did so, his lips returned to hers, and his gasping breath mingled with hers as their mouths sought to complete their frenzied union.

The panic was gone. Shona felt blood surge through her. She grasped his shoulders, raking her nails over his flesh, feeling his blood well up beneath her fingers. She heard him groan, but she knew it was not from pain. Then he began to tremble and his breathing became ragged. She begged him silently to keep from spending himself, but he had been too long without a woman. Her body screamed out in disappointment, and an ache spread through her bringing the pain of unfulfillment.

He collapsed atop her, his breath hot upon her face. "Well, *puta?*" he gasped. "Was it bitter? Or the sweetest you have ever tasted, for you are certainly no virgin!"

Shona did not want to argue—not then. Flushed from the harsh sting of his challenge, she wriggled out from under his body. "Did that disappoint you, Spanish dog?" she taunted. "Do you always rape your captives and ask questions later?"

He leaped to his feet and stood glaring down at her. "I don't have to ask questions!" he said. "You have whore written all over you." He turned his back and pulled on his breeches. "Your smell and the dirt on your body were all I needed to tell me what you are."

The insolence of his words enraged her. She scrambled to her feet and pulled his waistcoat from his hands.

"I am not the *meirdreach* you keep calling me, Spaniard," she hissed. "And your smell is no better than mine. If you had been in the battle, instead of safe aboard your ship, you would be as dirty as I."

He jerked his waistcoat away and put it on, his fingers shaking.

"I do what I am ordered," he said.

"Oh," she crooned, "and were you ordered to take me by that revolting Lopez who prefers little boys? Or do you prefer boys too?"

She did not have time to duck his blow. His open palm caught her across her bruised cheek and she dropped to the floor as though shot.

"Don't you ever talk about Vicente in that way again!" she heard him say through her pain. "He could have had you killed. Instead, he ordered me to take you away so he would never see you again! You should thank whatever god you pray to that he is a civilized man!"

Shona struggled up. "Civilized?" she gasped. "And I suppose you also consider yourself civilized. Well, where I come from a man is civilized when he treats a woman with kindness, not like an animal he can rut with at his pleasure. You are no better than that butcher, Cumberland. In fact, he was more civilized than you! He made no pretense at being a gentleman!"

De Larra stood with his back to the door, one eyebrow raised in disdain. "I don't know who this Cumberland is you are spouting about, but I can assure you, I would meet him on any field of honor and prove myself the better man."

"He was the first beast who took me, Spaniard!" Shona spat. "You are right, I did not come into this cabin a virgin. I lost my virginity when I was sixteen, to a man who butchered hundreds of my people and then stood back and laughed while their blood soaked into the soil of Scotland till the trees and heather shriveled up and died."

"Don't play the martyr with me!" he said. "You enjoyed our coupling as much as I! In fact, I would say more, for I was simply relieving the pressures of forced abstinence. Women do not have such needs."

Shona stared at him, her eyes wide with pain. Then she looked down, and he could see her shoulders tremble.

"You are right," she said in a low voice. "I did enjoy it, and it shames me."

Her simple confession stunned him. What kind of woman was this, who could act the wild harlot one moment and feel shame the next? His eyes narrowed as he studied her. She was young, and fine boned beneath all that filth. And when she was not cursing him, there was a quality to her speech, unexpected in a Colonial. But she had said she was from Scotland, perhaps that explained it. He had a sudden desire to go to her and offer comfort. He pushed the feeling aside.

"I will have someone bring soap and water so you can wash, and also some clothing. In the meantime, be good enough to cover yourself. I do not want you seducing my men." He turned and left the cabin, closing the door softly behind him.

Shona stared at the floor for a long time. She was not only feeling shame, she was deeply confused. How could she enjoy coupling with a beast of a Spaniard? How could her body respond to his when she knew he was a marauding privateer bent upon murder and booty? Tears welled up in her eyes and coursed down her cheeks, but she did nothing to stop them. Perhaps they would cleanse her of the filth she was certain contaminated her very soul.

Esteban de Larra paced the deck, ignoring the sporadic cannon fire in the distance, his forehead creased in thought, his hands clenched behind his back. *Madre de Dios,* what was happening to him? Not only had he given in to his base desires, but he had enjoyed it far more than anything he had ever

53

experienced! He stopped and stood looking out over the water. What he had done was inexcusable. He had used that girl for the whore he'd called her without knowing, despite his brave talk, whether she was a slut or a decent child of decent parents. He would have to make penance and work hard to cleanse his soul, but first he would see that the girl was released and returned to her home.

Suddenly, an explosion so great that it ruffled the air about him boomed up the river from the town. Within seconds, the shock sent waves hurtling against the ship's bow and she bucked back and forth at the end of her drag anchor. As pandemonium broke out on deck, de Larra screamed orders to his men, his heart drumming in his chest, his stomach sick with dread. He had heard only one other explosion like that, and he knew from that experience what had happened. The Commodore's sloop, the *Fortune*, had blown up in the water.

Vicente! He swallowed the vomit in his mouth and urged his men on until at last the *Nancy*, the captured ship Vicente had given him, was moving back down the river toward Brunswick. "Why?" his mind screamed. "Why Vicente?" He forced his thoughts away from pictures of Vicente Lopez visiting his home in Valencia when he was just a little boy, of the pride he had felt when the officer had told him all about his adventures. He shook himself. He could not allow his thoughts to dwell on such things. He was needed now, and perhaps . . .

The *Nancy* tacked down the river, her sails full and white against the black, smoke-filled sky. Her captain paced the deck, shouting orders to the gun crews who were hastily readying ammunition. They realized, captain and crew, that they were not prepared to launch an attack of their own. They did not have enough men or cannons. De Larra felt waves of goose flesh prickle his body as they passed Orton Plantation. Just one more bend in the river, and he would know!

He did not have to wait that long. The *Nancy* began to shove her way through debris before her stern had cleared the plantation banks. Planking, scorched bits of sail, an entire section of the Spanish colors, all floated lazily on the black water, not carried upriver by the current, but by the force of the explosion, a blast so devastating that nothing remained of the *Fortune* but small, charred pieces.

"*Dios, Vicente,*" Esteban murmured. He forced himself to walk to the bow where he strained to see through the smoke-darkened sky.

Suddenly, cannon fire flared in the sky and a tight, satisfied smile lit up his face. Captain Munroe of the *Loretta*, sister ship to the *Fortune*, had hoisted her bloody colors and opened fire upon the town! Good! He hoped every Colonial—including that little bitch in his cabin—would go straight to hell!

As though in answer to his thoughts, he was astounded to see the girl making her way quickly across the deck toward him. She had washed and garbed herself in rough sailor's breeches and shirt, but this time there was no mistaking her for a boy. Even from a distance, he could see the swell of her full breasts. "What are you doing here?" he shouted. "Get back to the cabin at once!"

"But what was that noise?" She grasped his arm. "What happened? Please tell me! I thought the world had blown to bits! I've never heard a sound like that before in my life!"

He shook her hand away and turned to watch the *Loretta*. "It is no concern of yours," he said harshly, fighting the desire to push her off into the water, to punish her for what had happened.

"I have a right to know!" she declared.

He turned and looked at her. At any other time, he might have been amused by the stance she had taken—hands on hips, shoulders squared, head thrown back—but not now. Oh, no, not now.

"I said go below," he snarled. "At once!"

"Not until you tell me why they are still firing on the town, and what that noise was!"

They stared at one another, eyes narrowed, chests heaving. Suddenly, de Larra reached out and grabbed Shona's shirt front. He pulled her close.

"So you want to know, do you?" he asked, his voice low and deceptively soft. "All right, I'll tell you!"

Shona licked her lips, but there was no saliva in her mouth and they felt dry and cracked to her tongue. She nodded slightly.

"The *Fortune* has blown up," he said in a husky whisper. "And, of course, all hands were lost, including Vicente Lopez."

Shona's eyes widened. Then a broad smile burst across her face. "Good!" she shouted exultantly. "That's wonderful! There's less of you bloody Spaniard bastards to sully the world!"

De Larra's vision clouded. He had never felt such rage in his entire life. He grabbed the girl around the neck.

"You are too terrible to live," he hissed. "I am going to kill you myself and send your mutilated body to the townspeople as a warning. The *Fortune* will be avenged!"

Chapter 4

The pain in Shona's throat was excruciating, the panic at not being able to breathe overwhelming. She could offer no resistance. Though her eyes were wide open, she could see only a black curtain shot through with bright pinholes of light. She felt herself sinking into a dark abyss, a hole with no bottom, and she knew that for her life was ending.

But, through her pain and fear, she thought of Jephtha. Was he safe aboard the other Spanish vessel, or had his life been snuffed out in one horrible instant? She had an intense need to know his fate. She felt responsible for him. Somehow, she had to live long enough to find out what had happened to her friend.

She tried to move her legs, but they would not obey. Twisting her body was futile, so she used her hands. She brought them up before her, groping blindly through the black curtain for de Larra's face. She felt flesh beneath her fingers and she dug her nails into it, scraping, gouging. But she knew it was too late when her hands numbed and the lights before her eyes flickered and went out. Too late . . . She sank to the deck.

De Larra stared down at the girl slumped at his feet. Bright ribbons of blood trickled down his cheeks. His heart was cramping, stifling his breath and bringing on pain so great, so consuming, he doubled over and retched. He had killed the girl! By all the saints in heaven, his anger had finally bested him! He had murdered the girl in cold blood!

He dropped to his knees and cradled her head in his lap. Her face was dusky blue, her eyes half open and staring, their dancing lights extinguished. No! It could not be! He could not bear to go through life knowing he had lost complete control of his actions! She could not be dead; he would not allow it! He bent and placed his mouth over hers. He began expelling air, forcing it between her lax lips.

"Live!" his mind screamed. "Breathe!"

Time after time he breathed into her mouth, until his own chest burned and his body tingled as if stung by a thousand bees. "Live!" his mind demanded over and over. She had done nothing to deserve death. She had only voiced her feelings, feelings natural for a Colonial. He raised his head and looked down at her. Was he imagining it, or was a faint pink replacing the blue of her flesh? He pressed his lips to hers once again, forcing air into her lungs. He began to feel lightheaded and did not notice when her hand twitched and her eyes closed.

Again, he raised his head. Suddenly, she gasped and he could feel her chest rise and fall beneath his own. A sob of relief broke from his lips. She lived!

He watched her anxiously for several moments, oblivious to the sailors standing around him. He was unaware that the cannon fire had ceased, that the *Loretta* had hoisted white and was moving slowly downriver, followed closely by the Spanish merchant ship and the three vessels they had captured, leaving his ship alone and undefended. Nothing mattered at this moment but her. He studied her delicate features, delighting in the healthy pink returning to her cheeks, exultant that he had been fortunate enough to restore the life he had come so close to snuffing out.

"Capitán."

The soft voice sounded unnaturally loud and he looked up angrily. His lieutenant stood at his side, his hands clasped before him, an apologetic smile upon his wide face. "I am sorry, Capitán, but I need your orders. The *Loretta* has given up the battle and is leaving."

"Leaving?" He mumbled the word, confused for a moment by a world much broader than the one he had just left. He looked down at the girl, reluctant to interrupt the closeness they had shared. But he knew he must. He lifted her head and gently lowered her to the deck.

He pulled himself to his feet, his body tired and his spirit spent. But when his eyes rested upon his men standing expectantly around him, his mind returned instantly to his command. He squared his shoulders as his gaze swept each face. What did he read on those familiar features? Pity? Contempt? No. His men had served under him long enough to know that they must veil their true thoughts lest they fall victim to his rage. Their faces were impassive.

"Mendoza!" he barked.

One of the older men stiffened and saluted. "Yes, sir!" he answered sharply.

"Carry this girl down to the captain's quarters and see that she is made comfortable. And be gentle with her. I will hold you responsible for her safety."

"Yes, sir!"

De Larra turned to his lieutenant. "Perez, get this vessel under sail. We stay with the *Loretta!*"

"Yes, sir!"

The captain turned on his heel and strode quickly toward the bridge, not seeing the smiles of relief his men were giving one another behind his back.

Shona opened her eyes slowly. She could see nothing but a gray mist. Had she died? She struggled to rise, but an agonizing pain in her throat stopped her and she groaned, adding a burst of fire to the pain.

"Do not try to move, *señorita*," said a voice near her side. "You must rest."

She turned her head toward the voice. A face swam before her eyes, and she blinked until the haze clouding her vision lifted and she saw the man clearly. His face was as rosy as a child's, but lined with many years. White stubble pebbled his round chin, and white tufts of hair stood out from his eyebrows like the wings of an angel. His nose was like a blob of unmolded clay, his eyes were kindly, and his lips were trembling. "Who are you?" she whispered.

His face lit up with a gentle smile. "I am Fernando Mendoza," he said. "But you are not to talk. I have placed cold salt compresses upon your neck. They will draw out the pain."

She shook her head slowly. "I thought I was dead."

His smile faded and his eyes clouded. "No, *señorita*. Capitán de Larra, he breathed the breath of life back into your body. He did not allow you to die. He is a good man."

She turned her head away and gritted her teeth, her aching throat working convulsively over the words of denial she wanted to scream aloud. "He is a bastard," she finally whispered.

She heard the seaman's sharp intake of breath and knew she had shocked him. Good! It was about time somebody knew what kind of a man he followed blindly into battle against innocent victims!

"You must not talk like that," Mendoza admonished quickly. "I do not know what you did to provoke our *capitán*, but it must have been *tremendo* for him to have lost control of his actions. He has always had a terrible anger, that one, even as a child. You must learn to soothe him, not add fuel to his temper, if you wish to survive to return home."

Home. Soft green hillsides and lavender heather beneath misty skies. Rivers filled with fat silver trout and rushing white water. Cool breezes rustling the dry moss on high crags standing sentinel over the land. A wave of homesickness washed over her, bringing a yearning so great she could barely tolerate the misery.

"I want to go home," she moaned.

Of course Mendoza thought she meant Brunswick. "That is impossible now. We are joining the *Loretta* downstream, but later there will surely be an exchange of prisoners. You will go home then."

"Prisoners? Do you know who they are? Have you seen one called Jephtha?"

A violent burst of coughing tore through her throat and she almost fainted from the pain as she fought for breath. She was aware that a wet cloth moved over her face as Fernando wiped away the tears streaming down her cheeks.

"Please, *señorita*," he begged. "No more talking. The *capitán* made me responsible for you. He will have my skin if you are harmed. No more talking."

She nodded her head. It was no use. She was sure the entire crew was so frightened of de Larra, they would follow him into hell itself if he so ordered. She closed her eyes and, moments later, drifted into a deep, dreamless sleep.

De Larra paced the bridge. They had dropped anchor beside the *Loretta* just out of sight of the town and he had sent the longboat for Captain Munroe. It was finally dawning upon him that the total responsibility of this venture now rested upon his shoulders. With Vicente dead, he as second in command became the commodore. His forehead creased as he stared off into the distance. What should he do? There were not enough cannons, nor was there enough ammunition to retake the town. They had captured three other vessels in addition to the *Nancy*, but all were only small merchant ships. With the loss of the *Fortune* and her ten six-pounders and fourteen swivels, it was hopeless to think of renewing the battle. The *Loretta* carried only ten light cannon and twelve swivels, and the merchant ship was lightly armed. Since the loss of the entire crew aboard the *Fortune*, the Spanish forces were much too thin to hope for victory.

He scowled. There was only one course of action left to him.

He must send a flag of truce ashore, stating that if they were allowed to leave with all of the captured vessels in tow, they would inflict no more damage upon the town. His chest burned at the thought of asking for anything from those cursed Colonials.

Captain Munroe was brought to the bridge, where the two men conferred for a long time, arguing in strident tones, scowls on their faces, their words harsh. Munroe wanted to bombard the town with his cannons, to inflict as much damage as possible in retaliation for the loss of the *Fortune*. Though he knew the commander's ship had been blown out of the water by her own overheated cannons, he was furious at the loss and blamed the Colonials entirely.

But de Larra would not be swayed from what he knew to be the only prudent course of action and, as commander, his judgment was final. A small delegation of sailors, led by Lieutenant Perez, was lowered in the longboats. They were bearing a white flag of truce and a document hastily prepared by de Larra, stating his demands.

The two captains watched the boat move slowly against the current on its way to Brunswick. "What about the prisoners, Esteban?" Munroe asked suddenly. "I have over fifty aboard the *Loretta*, and many of our men did not return from their raid upon the town. Are you going to arrange for an exchange?"

De Larra nodded his head slowly. "I must, though I would rather just kill them all and be done with it. But I cannot consign our own men to sure death at the hands of those heathen Colonials. This entire encounter has been unsatisfactory. Our king should have heeded Vicente and allowed us to strike first at the French in Louisiana. They never offer as much resistance as the English."

Munroe gasped at his bold censure of the Spanish monarch. "Lower your voice, Esteban," he hissed. "Such talk could cost you your head."

De Larra chuckled and patted his companion's arm. "Do not worry, Joseph," he soothed. "I know that you, an Englishman

62

yourself, agree with me. If I were standing before Fernando at this moment, I would say much the same."

"And lose your head immediately," Munroe said quickly.

"I don't think so. He shows no signs of his father's insanity. You must remember, the de Larra family has been instrumental in securing many riches for the crown. I am not so sure Fernando would not agree with me now, though he was adamant about not attacking Louisiana first when we met with him so many months ago."

"Why did he want to attack this coast first, Esteban?"

"I'm not sure. He does not have a military mind. Perhaps because so many of our own citizens have settled in Louisiana, he was reluctant to endanger them. He doesn't realize how strong they are. They would not allow themselves to be punished for our raids upon the French. I know they would resist successfully!"

"Then Louisiana is our next objective?"

"Yes. And after this disastrous fiasco—though we have taken much booty—we will force the French to their knees!"

Munroe sighed deeply. "I sincerely hope you are right. After losing the *Fortune*, I am reluctant to continue with our commission."

"We must! We cannot return to Spain with our holds half empty! We will not set sail for home until we can be sure de Somodeville will be pleased with the results of our venture. We must not disappoint our new minister of war."

"Ha!" Munroe's lips turned down in a sneer. "Your Marquis of Ensenada is much too involved with high living to care about how well we fare. All he thinks about is living like a Frenchman and keeping his own wealth."

"That is not true!" Esteban said hotly. "You do not know our minister. True, Zenon is devoted to the French style of living, but he is fiercely loyal to the crown. Don't forget, he was instrumental in the peace treaty drawn up at Aix-la-Chapelle between France and Spain which ended the fighting in Italy."

"So you think he cares about Spain?"

"I know so! He has shared his dreams with me many times. Zenon wants our country to prosper, and we must do all we can to assure his success!"

Munroe shook his head. "Well, I have to say that you Spaniards are a hot-blooded lot when it comes to patriotism. I only hope you're right about de Somodeville. But now, I must get back aboard the *Loretta*. We have had trouble with one of the prisoners, a huge brute of a man. We had to put him in irons away from the others because he kept inciting them to escape."

"Flog him. That will cool his ardor for freedom!"

"You're cold-hearted, de Larra. You can't tell me you wouldn't do everything to escape if you were in a similar situation."

Esteban grinned. "Perhaps you're right. These Colonials are not the spineless worms we were led to believe they were." He leaned against the railing and looked out over the water. "We will just have to wait here until we receive an answer from the Colonial commander. Pray it is the right answer. I have no stomach to resume the fighting now that Vicente is gone. This part of our commission was doomed from the beginning. Return to your ship. I will send word as soon as I receive an answer."

Munroe saluted and turned away reluctantly. Something more than the reply to the Spanish demands was bothering his new commander, and he wanted desperately to know what it was. But de Larra was a haughty bastard, unapproachable and quick to anger. He would just have to wait and see what the day brought.

Esteban continued to stare out over the water. He was restless, but he forced himself to stand perfectly still, calling upon the discipline he always invoked when upset by something he could not control. His body was still, yet his mind was racing; and his thoughts were not concerned with the outcome of this venture. He was thinking about the girl.

64

He could not believe he had come so close to killing her. True, he had lost control of his anger before, but never had he harmed a woman! After all, he had been trained since infancy, both by word and deed, that women were to be treasured and protected. Did his father not protect and worship his mother? Did not Tía María demand her rightful place high on the pedestal of womanhood?

He had known for a long time that his emotions were volatile, yet he had thought he could call upon his years of training to bring them under control at any time he wished. Now, he knew this was not true. Another moment of fury and he would have had to live the remainder of his life with the gut-twisting knowledge that he he choked to death an innocent girl, and a captive at that!

His mind leaped back to their encounter in the cabin, and his face flushed at the memory of her sensuous body beneath him. She had wanted him, he was sure of that! She had made little moaning sounds, had pressed her throbbing body close to his. His flesh twitched as he remembered how it had felt to plunge himself deep into that velvety cocoon. He could never remember rising to such heights before. The ensuing explosion had robbed him of thought and speech for some time. And when he had finally regained control of his voice, what had he said? He had accused her of being a whore! *Por Dios*, he was turning into the heathen all foreigners considered a Spaniard to be!

He straightened and turned to look over the deck of the ship. His men were busy following Perez's orders, preparing his ship for another journey at sea. Though no one was looking his way, he felt as though all eyes cast derisive glances upon him. He would have flogged one of his men for doing what he had done to that girl. Had he lost the respect of his crew? He slapped his palm onto the railing. No! He would not allow that to happen. He had worked too hard, waited too long for a command to allow anything to take it away from him. He had to make this venture a success. He had to return to Inez with riches enough to convince her he was able to care for her properly. They had been betrothed as children. Then her parents had perished in a cholera epidemic, and though she lived in splendor on the Muñoz estate, her brother Francisco had instilled within her a terrible fear of poverty.

Francisco Muñoz. Esteban shuddered. There was something innately evil about the man. Like Inez, Francisco's hair and eyes were black as ebony and his skin was white as milk. But there the resemblance to his sister ended. Where Inez was gentle and childlike, Francisco was ruthless and cruel. Esteban could recall the first time he'd become aware of Francisco's cruelty. Don Muñoz had purchased a fine white Andalusian stallion for his son in honor of his twelfth saint's day. The animal was high spirited and filled with life when delivered, but after only two days, he stood in his paddock with his head down, his sides bloodied by sharp rowels, his lovely spirit broken forever. Francisco had beaten him almost to death for rearing at the feel of the harsh quirt.

Esteban himself had been schooled by the gentle Dominican priests, but Francisco had insisted upon sitting at the feet of the harsh Jesuits, those relentless authors of the Inquisition. And he had indulged in studies of the fine art of torture. Esteban could recall spending many boyhood hours arguing with Francisco about the cruelty of the Inquisition and the rights of the Jews and Moors to practice the religion they embraced, but Francisco would not be swayed. The older he became, the more stringently he embraced the Jesuit order.

It was only natural to all those who knew him that he would enter the priesthood. Then something had happened, something so terrible that even the Jesuits would not reveal it. Francisco Muñoz had been dismissed from his studies. Though the power of the priesthood was now out of his grasp, his convictions were not altered. He joined the Spanish forces as a naval officer, and it was often whispered about Valencia that he was so cruel, his men called him Capitán Diablo behind his back.

Esteban knew Francisco had warped Inez's thinking. First, he had tried to turn her heart from her betrothed with whispered accusations of infidelity. But when Inez was not swayed by these falsehoods and refused to withdraw from her pledge, he'd cleverly changed his tactics and had begun to insidiously plant one thought in her mind—that de Larra, though he was the only son and was in line to inherit all the de Larra lands, was a pauper in his own right. After all, Don Carlos de Larra was still in excellent health, and it would be many years before Esteban inherited. Francisco told Inez that Esteban would never amount to anything, that he would not be able to keep the family home for her, that she would wear rags and eat pig swill. These threats had worked whereas the others had failed. Inez was spoiled, and with the death of her parents, who had always seen to her every need, her fear of poverty was very real. She had insisted that Esteban prove himself by bringing home riches. Then she would decide upon a time for the marriage banns to be read.

Esteban grimaced. He would not allow Francisco to win this time. Inez was so lovely, so fragile, so unapproachable, almost like the Virgin Mother herself. Not at all like that girl in the cabin . . .

The stirring in his groin angered him. Why should he be so drawn to that tramp? Though he felt remorse about the way he had treated her, he knew she was no lady. After all, she was not a virgin and there was no reason to believe her story of rape. She used language only a man should use, but she was a voluptuous young woman with a face and body any man would want to possess and the defiant sparkle in her eyes intrigued him. He had been long without a woman to bed. Perhaps he would not allow her to go with the rest of the prisoners.

He heard a hail from the water and watched the longboat approach. The dour faces of his men told him all had not gone well. He paced the deck impatiently while they tied the boat fast and climbed to the deck.

"Capitán."

"Well?"

Perez looked down, unable to meet his commander's gaze. He regretted that he was the one to bring such bad news to Capitán de Larra. He would be lucky to keep his skin after what he had to relate. He swallowed hard and looked up.

"The commander of the Colonials, a Capitán Dry has sent his reply to your demands."

"And . . ."

"He . . . he said that he would not consent to our carrying away anything other than our own vessels, that he would let us go without another shot fired if we would return the captured vessels, all we have taken from the town, and the prisoners we hold." The last was said in a whisper, so great was the lieutenant's fear.

The men within hearing held their breath, their eyes drawn to the face of their commander. De Larra stood rigid as a statue, his nostrils flared, his mouth a slash across his tanned face, his eyes dark as the river beneath them and completely unreadable.

When he spoke, his words were so soft only those nearest him could hear, but his crew saw the grim smile upon his face and quaked in terror. "So, they want it all back, do they?" His smile widened, but his eyes were dark with rage. "Do they think all Spaniards are cowardly dogs? Do they think we will put our tails between our legs and run? Do they . . ." He paused and fought to control the rage burning his bowels. "Bring Captain Munroe to me at once!" he barked. He whirled about and made his way blindly toward his cabin.

By the time he reached the cabin door, he had controlled his violent shaking, but his heart still beat madly in tune with the pounding of the blood in his temples. He stood at the door for a moment, his eyes closed, his teeth clenched. He was the commodore now, and the dilemma was his. He would solve it in his own way. He opened the door and stepped inside.

Mendoza sat beside the bed, dozing. He jerked awake when the door slammed. "Capitán!" He scrambled to his feet, knocking the chair over in his haste to salute.

De Larra ignored Mendoza's salute as he walked over to the bed and looked down. The girl lay sleeping on her back, her hair fanned out in a golden halo about her head and shoulders. She was still pale, but there was a faint blush of pink upon her high cheekbones. He almost gasped aloud at the dark bruises circling her neck. It was true, he was a *bastardo!*

"She sleeps, Capitán," Mendoza whispered. "She will recover."

De Larra did not reply, but continued to stare down at the girl. She looked so young, so touchingly lovely, so innocent. His breath caught as she moaned and stirred slightly. Her eyelashes fluttered for a moment, then lay like tiny golden wings upon her cheeks.

"She is beautiful," Mendoza whispered. "Like the Madonna herself."

"You are a crazy old man," de Larra said. "She is as much like the Madonna as a sparrow is like a dove." He tore his gaze away and walked over to the desk. "You will have to move her, Mendoza. I am expecting Captain Munroe. We have decisions to make, and I must have my cabin to confer in."

"But there is no place for her, young master," the old man protested. "And I am sure it would do her no good to move her at this time. Look, she sleeps so peacefully, if not like the Madonna, then surely like an angel. Please don't move her, Esteban!"

"Enough!" de Larra barked. He instantly regretted his harsh tone, and looked at the girl. She stirred, but again her sleep deepened. "You have forgotten yourself again, I fear. I know you have been with our family since before I was born, but aboard this ship, I am not your young master, I am your captain. And I am sorry, but I must insist that the girl be moved. Go prepare the mate's quarters. If Perez gives you any trouble, tell him it is by my order. He can bunk with the rest of the men for a while."

Mendoza bowed his head. He knew this young man better

than any other, and he recognized the steel in his voice. "Yes, sir," he answered with a heavy sigh. "I will go at once."

The old man left the cabin, and de Larra was alone with the girl. He was frustrated by the feelings he had for her. Why did she attract him so? It would be simple to assume it was because he had enjoyed her body more than he had ever enjoyed any other, yet he knew it was far more complex than that. She intrigued him. She was both a harlot and the Madonna Mendoza had called her, and he wanted to know her better. He wanted to hear the story of her life, to know where she had learned her exquisite English, to know why she used such foul language when angered, and to learn who she cared for. Ah, perhaps that was the fascination. Whom did she love? Vicente had mentioned a lover. Perhaps he was one of the prisoners held on the *Loretta*. Esteban chuckled deep in his throat, but there was no humor in the sound. Maybe he would bait her with that lover, make her beg for his life.

No. He had done her enough harm. He was not the monster she thought him to be. He was a Spanish gentleman, and from here on he would conduct himself like one. He paced over to the desk and threw himself down in the chair, knowing he would have to let her go and fighting the pain that thought brought to his mind and body.

Mendoza interrupted his mental battle. "Capitán, I have prepared her quarters. If you would care to inspect them? . . ."

"No, I am sure they are fine. I will carry her."

"But you should not have to do that," the old man protested. "I am much stronger than I look. I can—"

De Larra squeezed the old man's elbow tightly. "I know you are, Fernando. Please just do as I say. I am in no mood for another argument."

Mendoza nodded. "Yes, Esteban. I will go before you and open the doors."

Esteban got heavily to his feet. He felt as though the world rested upon his shoulders. Decisions, decisions, all important, all affecting lives. He scooped the girl up tenderly, making sure

70

her head rested against his shoulder. Though she murmured, she did not awaken as he carried her carefully out of the cabin and down the passageway toward the door Mendoza held open. The fragrance from her newly washed hair wafted in the air about him as he walked, and he was amazed at the difference it made in his feeling for her. Without that awful stench of sweat, she became a precious burden, no longer the *puta* he had so scathingly called her. When he laid her on the small bunk, her eyes fluttered open, but he could tell she did not see him, for there was no recognition in her gaze. Then her eyes closed and her breathing slowed.

"Go on deck and wait for Captain Munroe. When he boards, show him to my cabin and make sure we have wine and glasses—and make up that bed."

"Yes, Capitán."

Once again, he was left alone with her. Though it was dusk, the air was still warm and sticky, so he did not cover her with a blanket. He poured a cup of water and placed it upon the table where she could reach it without rising, and he lit a candle. Then he walked to the porthole and looked out. He did not see the water. Instead, he was seeing her on that other bed, her naked body curled on the mattress, her breasts cradled against the coverlet, her legs drawn up like a child's. His breath quickened and desire flooded through his body. He had to feel her passionate embrace once again. He had to know she desired him as much as he desired her. He had to run his fingers through that glorious hair and taste the honey upon her lips.

He thought momentarily about Inez, and how different the two girls were. But he pushed the memory of Inez's dark beauty aside quickly as though he suddenly found it distasteful. Then he whirled and strode quickly from the cabin, his mind made up. He would not release the girl with the other prisoners. He would take her with him!

Chapter 5

The silence was complete. No moans, no cries for help, no gurgling breath struggling through blood-filled lungs. Nothing moved. It was as though time had expired and spread its final black curtain over the battlefield called Culloden. Only a faint stench of blood and vomit remained to remind the girl sitting at the edge of the moor that over one thousand of Scotland's finest had screamed and fallen and died here. Her anxious eyes searched through the night for a glimpse of movement, but the darkness was a black void reaching off into infinity.

Suddenly, there was a harsh glare of light and she looked up to see a full moon riding high, its surface ablaze with the light of a hundred suns. She looked away and shielded her eyes with a trembling hand. The light shone about her so brightly, she expected to see the face of God himself upon the surface of the moon, yet when she glanced upward again, it was not God's face she beheld, but the maniacal, grimacing face of William Cumberland! She gasped and tried to struggle to her feet, knowing that the light would consume her if she did not escape.

She could not move. A dead weight rested upon her legs. Jamie. A sob tore at her throat and she screamed, but the scream came forth as a low moan born in her very soul. Then the stillness was broken by wild laughter, and she knew that the moon was laughing—Cumberland was laughing—and she could not breathe.

She twisted and turned and struggled. The weight pressing her into the blood-soaked earth would not yield. Suddenly the pipes began to skirl about her, their familiar, discordant reeds calming her need to escape. She saw dark shapes rise up from the earth as the men of the clans threw off their mantles of death and began to dance to the pipes. The burden was suddenly lifted from her legs as Jamie joined the dancers. Kilts flared bravely in the white light, reds, greens, and blues blending as trew-clad legs flashed to keep up with the swirling, skirling pipes.

She saw Donald Cameron dancing beside her father and brothers. His blond hair shone almost white in the blinding glare of the moon that was Cumberland's face and she could see the excitement sparkling in his blue eyes. Suddenly, he stopped and raised his hand. The pipes were silenced with a soft wheeze, and the men about him stood at attention. He raised his face to that face in the sky and stood for a long time, a grim smile hardening his handsome features into stone. At last, he lifted his arm and thrust it toward the moon, and out of his throat, and out of the throats of all of the clans came one mighty shout, *"Chlanna nan con thigibh an so is gheibh sibh feoil!* Sons of the hounds come hither for flesh!"* It rose as a roar which filled the sky and bounced from ben to corrie, over strath and loch, from sea to sea, until all of Scotland reverberated with its awesome sound.

But Donald Cameron was no longer Donald Cameron. He was Esteban de Larra and he stood alone in the center of the moor. The Spaniard glanced sadly back at the men of Scotland ringing the moor as he raised his great broadsword before him. Then he swung it in a wide arc, and the clans all dropped to the earth once again, unmoving and lifeless as they would be throughout eternity. De Larra nodded and looked back at the girl who once again held her Jamie in her lap. His right eyebrow arched and his eyes sparked daggers of light as he touched his

74

lips to his sword and raised it to her in salute.

He pulled his arm back and released the broadsword high into the sky. The girl watched it slice through the air, higher, higher, until its razor-sharp blade split the moon that was Cumberland's face in half and the light exploded in a brilliant blaze. Fragments of light turned into a shower of falling stars which arced across the black sky until, after what could have been either a breath or an eternity, the last one blinked out.

De Larra stood in the center of the moor, his black-clad body bathed in a soft glow. He turned and walked slowly toward the girl, and she gently placed her burden, her Jamie, upon the earth and rose to meet the slayer of Cumberland. De Larra's smile fell softly upon her, his azure eyes filled with pain and knowing. Within the deepest recesses of her heart, she knew he was one with her. He reached out his hands, and she touched his fingertips with her own. Then he dissolved into a vapor, leaving her alone with her dead and the awful stillness.

Shona struggled up through the heavy blanket of sleep pressing her deep into the mattress. Her throat convulsed as she fought for breath, and the pain brought her instantly awake. She gasped at the pain—not the pain in her throat, though that was bad enough, but the pain brought by the pictures her nightmare had painted upon the backs of her eyelids. Tears gushed down her cheeks as she rocked back and forth upon the bed. Sorrow for the fallen clans, grief for her dead father and brothers, agony over the loss of her Jamie, and a renewed sadness at the loss of her mother who had died when birthing Jamie—all overwhelmed her, making her wish for her own death. Almost an hour passed before her tears were spent and the nightmare began to fade into a haunting memory.

Though she was exhausted, she was afraid to lie down again, lest the nightmare return. She looked over at the stub of a candle sputtering in its holder; then panic flooded her. The candle was almost spent, and she could not bear to be in darkness now! She leaped to her feet. Ignoring the giddiness brought on by her sudden movement, she began to rummage

75

frantically through the drawer in the table beside the bed. Her hand closed around a fat candle and she sighed aloud with relief, paying no more attention to the pain in her throat. She held the wick over the dying flame until it caught, but when she held the flaming candle high, her relief was extinguished. She was not in the same cabin!

She walked quickly around the room, knowing that it was night and that she was still aboard a ship, but which ship? When she spied a Spanish sailor's uniform hanging from a peg against the wall, she knew she was still de Larra's captive. Why hadn't de Larra killed her? She fingered her neck, wincing at the soreness of the bruises there. She seemed to remember a funny little man telling her that the captain had actually saved her life. Preposterous! Yet, she still lived.

She sat on the side of the bunk and closed her eyes as the memory of his enraged face appeared before her. She could feel his hands clamped about her throat. Maybe she *was* dead! She was so totally alone, with no sound, no indication that anyone else was around. Perhaps the papists were right and this was purgatory. She staggered to her feet and stumbled to the door. She had to know!

The handle turned easily beneath her trembling fingers. She pulled the door open and looked out. A lantern hanging on the wall illuminated the long, narrow passageway with flickering light. She looked longingly at the nearest ladder. If she were not in purgatory, she would take this opportunity to escape. But when she turned to make her way down the companion-way, a sudden harsh, barking laugh interrupted her stride, freezing her heart in her throat.

She whirled and looked at the closed door near the end of the passageway. It looked familiar. She was certain it was the door leading to the cabin in which she had been held captive before. Snatches of a loud conversation came to her. She could not contain her curiosity and tiptoed down the hallway to stand outside the door, pressing her ear to it.

"It is a foolproof plan." She recognized de Larra's voice.

"I'm not so sure," came the reply.

"It cannot fail. We have the girl to use as a hostage. This Captain Dry of the Colonials will have no recourse but to accede to our demands."

Girl? Shona repressed a gasp. Could he mean *her*?

"I hope so. But where did you find a girl? We have only male captives on the *Loretta*."

"Vicente found her on his forage to the plantation up the river. It was a mistake, really. She had disguised herself as a boy. He didn't know her sex until he took her aboard the *Fortune*."

Shona heard a harsh, barking laugh. "And I'm sure he wasn't pleased with his discovery. I'll wager he had plans for his 'boy' captive!"

Flushing, Shona fought to keep from throwing the door open and telling both men exactly what she thought of them. When she realized she was missing de Larra's reply, she pressed her ear to the door again.

". . . don't think you should talk like that about the dead. We all know Vicente's weakness, but he was a fine commander."

"You are right, of course. So, we are to move our ships down the river to the place they call 'Bald Head' and tomorrow morning, you will send a message to Dry that you are ready to negotiate for an exchange of the prisoners."

"Yes. I want those captive merchant ships moved with us. The night hours should give us ample time to remove their cannons, arms, and anything of value from their holds. There is no reason for us to take those ships with us. They are too small, and with the loss of the *Fortune*'s crew, we are too shorthanded to man them on our journey to the Louisiana Territory. But there is something I feel it is important for us to do. I want you to bring some of your captives to me. Having prisoners on this ship will give me an opportunity to stall for time. I do not intend to return this vessel. It is perfect for our needs."

"I agree. And after the exchange, we will stall until nightfall tomorrow, then set sail under darkness—without returning the booty we took from the town."

"Exactly, Joseph. I have no intention of returning those riches."

"Nor I. You will be a very wealthy man when we return to Spain, Esteban. But what of the girl? When will you release her?"

Shona held her breath. The silence lengthened. Why didn't de Larra answer?

"I'm not sure yet," he said at last. "Perhaps we will put her off on that point of land at the mouth of the river, or we can set her free in a small boat any time before we reach the sea."

"Well, you have convinced me. Now I must return to the *Loretta* and ready her for the sail down river. And I will see that Captain Gomez is informed of your plans. He will need to take the bulk of the booty aboard his merchant ship."

When Shona heard the shuffle of feet, she leaped away from the door and stood in the passageway, her eyes darting to the nearest ladder. Did she have time to climb it to the deck? If she did, what would she find? Sailors would be stationed there. She moved quickly back to the cabin she had left earlier. She had no chance to escape now. She slipped inside and pushed the door to, leaving it barely ajar so she could peek out.

A man she had never seen before left the cabin. She wondered if he was the captain of the larger Spanish ship, the one they called the *Loretta*. De Larra stepped out on deck, but he did not follow the other man up the companionway.

"I'll see you tomorrow, Joseph. Be sure to tell your men it is imperative that they work quickly. After all, they have much at stake in this venture."

"Rest easy, Esteban, I will."

De Larra stood outside the cabin, watching the other captain climb the ladder. Shona tingled with a strange sense of excitement as she watched him. Her dream had been so real. He was so tall, so muscular. He looked like some sort of god as the lantern light flickered on his blond hair, turning it to the color

78

of the ripe moon. She froze when he turned his eyes in her direction. She was sure he could see her, for he frowned and that damnable eyebrow rose in its haughty arc. But she could not step back now; he would be sure to see the movement. He did not move toward the door, but stood staring at it with a bemused expression on his face. She watched him, her heart pounding in her throat, her mouth dry. Why did he affect her so? He was only a man, and a Spaniard at that!

Yet, there was no denying that he attracted her. She remembered the gentle touch of his fingers upon her flesh, and she could scarcely breathe. Did Esteban de Larra somehow figure in her future? That other man had said that he possessed great wealth, yet no matter how she tried, she could not erase the memory of the dream in which he had saved her from Cumberland.

Suddenly, he began to walk toward her. She backed into the room and groped her way toward the bunk, quickly blowing out the candle. She felt the hard frame against her legs and lowered herself gently onto the mattress just as a shaft of light penetrated the darkness. She closed her eyes and slowed her breathing, trying to still the wild pounding of her heart. Soft footsteps approached. She heard the rasp of flint and in seconds, despite her closed eyelids, she sensed that the room had brightened.

Esteban stood looking down at the girl, at the glorious mass of curls that spread out over the pillow, at the exquisite curve of waist into hip, at the rise and fall of her ripe young breasts. He stood there for a very long time before he turned and quietly left the room.

Shona lay very still after she heard the door close. Though she knew he was gone, he had left an aura of peace behind, and she basked in its soft glow. He could be harsh and cruel and demeaning, yet he was capable of great passion and, she hated to admit it, tenderness.

She opened her eyes. He had left the candle lit and the corners of the cabin were bathed in shadows; but this time she did not find the dark areas menacing. What should she do? He was holding her as some sort of hostage, though she did not understand that part of the conversation she had overheard. How could she have any value? But of course, he could not know that here in America she was only an indentured servant. He must think her the daughter of an upstanding citizen of Brunswick, a very valuable commodity. She smiled. He had a surprise in store for him if he thought the townspeople placed any value upon *her* life!

But would they know who he held? She had never given him her name; indeed it had never been asked. Surely some of the townspeople were still afraid to return to their homes. Perhaps Captain Dry would assume she was just what Esteban de Larra thought she was. If that proved to be true, she would be released after all of the other prisoners. Since she still intended to run away, that meant she would never know what had happened to Jephtha!

She sat up. There had to be some way to know whether he still lived. She rose from the bunk and began to pace the cabin. Perhaps if she went to de Larra and told him she was an indentured servant and was of no value to the townspeople, if she begged for information concerning Jephtha, he would take pity. No. She could well imagine what his response would be to *that* sign of weakness! She went to the porthole and pressed her forehead against the cool glass. What would be the best way to gain information from her captor? Certainly not by being spiteful. Her bruised neck bore witness to that folly. She resumed her pacing. Perhaps a bold offer would suffice. She could go to him and tell him that if he allowed her to watch the other captives being sent on their way to freedom, she would not cause him any more trouble. That way, he would not know of her interest in one prisoner, and he would have no reason to become angry.

But she was not supposed to know an exchange of prisoners was in the offing, or that she was to be a hostage! She chewed on her knuckle and searched her mind for an answer.

Suddenly, the ship began to rock and shudder, and she knew they were setting sail for Bald Head. She would have to come up with a solution before morning, but she was much too tired to think tonight. She lay back down and closed her eyes.

Shona did not have time to find a solution the following morning. She had just awakened and washed her face in the bucket of stale water when de Larra himself entered the cabin carrying tea and bread.

He stood just inside the doorway, his face expressionless. As they stared at one another, Shona wondered if he felt as she did . . . afraid and more than a little uncomfortable. But she could not look away, nor could she break the silence.

It was de Larra who did both. "I thought you would be hungry," he said as he placed the food and drink upon the table beside the bed. "I know it isn't much, but it should give you strength."

"Thank you," she said in a low voice.

He was staring at her again. Her breath caught in her throat.

"Is your . . . is your throat better?"

Her hand went to the bruise. "Yes," she said quickly. "Much better."

"Did you sleep well?"

"Oh, yes, very well, thank you." Why didn't he go away? Why did he continue to look at her?

"I will have Mendoza bring you something more suitable to wear. I am sure we can find a gown in what we took from the town."

"No!" Her vehement refusal startled her, but she hastily gave an explanation he might accept without telling him the real reason she wanted to keep the boy's clothing—it would be easier traveling in it once she was released—for she had no intention of returning to Brunswick once she was off this ship. "The clothes would be recognized when I go home. I wouldn't want to cause hard feelings."

81

He smiled, and she thought it was a tired smile. "I don't understand. How could there be hard feelings from your family and friends? I should think they would be delighted to see you free."

She tossed her head back and smiled wickedly. "But I have no family—and no friends. I am alone in the world."

His startled look brought a loud laugh to her lips.

"Surely you did not think to gain more riches from my family before releasing me?" she taunted. "I'm delighted that you thought so highly of me, Captain de Larra, but, you see, I am merely an indentured servant!"

Shona waited for his angry outburst, but to her surprise, he threw back his head and his laugh filled the cabin. She stomped her feet and pushed her lower lip out in a pout, not at all pleased to have lost the advantage so quickly.

"Ah," he chuckled, "I should have known. The beautiful girl with the easy command of the English language who enjoys bandying about barnyard words. It all makes sense now. You are not a lady of quality. You are a servant!"

"And what if I am?" Shona spat. "You are a Spanish bastard!"

He nodded his head. "You are probably right, little one, and even if you are wrong, it gives you such pleasure to call me that, I will not dispute you this time." He shook his head and laughed again. "No wonder you were in such a state of filth when Vicente found you. I would wager all I own that you were running away!"

Shona flushed. "Of course!" she said. "You would run away too if you had five years of servitude to look forward to!"

"Again you are probably right," he said, the humor suddenly gone from his voice. "But what is your name? What do they call you?"

"Shona. Shona Cameron."

His eyes narrowed as he studied her before he answered. Was he wondering if she were telling the truth? "That is a very beautiful name," he said at last.

She was instantly on guard. "I was named for a Scottish island. But I have to admit, it is much easier to say than your name . . . Esteban. My tongue trips when I try to say that."

"It means Stephen in your language. I was born on Saint Stephen's day."

"Then I will call you Stephen. But you are mistaken. In my language, the Gaidhealach of the Heilands, you would be called Stiabhan." She stopped and looked at the cross he wore about his neck. "You're a papist?" she asked suddenly.

He smiled grimly at her question. "Of course. Does that offend you?"

She nodded her head. "Yes, I suppose it does. The Roman church was outlawed in Scotland years ago. We have been taught that papists are little better than heathens."

"And is that what you think I am?" he said coolly. "A heathen?"

Though his voice was velvety soft, she decided to soften her statement. After all, if she wanted information about Jephtha, she would have to stay on his good side.

"Perhaps not you," she replied cautiously.

"But you are undecided?" There was, once again, a glint of humor in his eyes.

"I believe I have been told that indecisiveness is a very feminine trait," she answered lightly.

"That may be true." He chuckled. "But it is almost impossible to view you as a female as long as you are garbed in those ridiculous clothes. Please change your mind and accept a gown."

"Perhaps I feel safer if you don't view me as a woman," she said firmly. "Though I do appreciate your offer."

His eyebrows rose. "Is it me you wish to guard yourself against—or your own desires?"

She turned crimson. "Why, you son of a pig, you forced yourself on me!"

At his harsh laugh, she leaped at him, wanting nothing less than to tear the flesh from his cheeks which already carried her marks, but he was quicker. He grabbed her arms and pinned them to her sides. As he pulled her into his embrace, his body pressed hard against hers, and before she could say another word, his lips were crushing hers, his tongue probing her mouth.

Shona fought against the languid warmth threatening to engulf her. This time she *would* not, *could* not give in! But her body ignored the frantic signals sent by her mind and quickly acquiesced to the throbbing in her veins. She groaned as she began to return his passionate kiss, drowning in his taste and in the feel of his hands running over her back. She wanted him. Her flesh screamed out for him to take her, but after what seemed like an eternity, he pulled his lips from hers.

"You taste like sunshine," he said huskily, "and orange blossoms."

She stared up into his face, her body quivering with strange delight as his fingers trailed lightly down her buttocks. "Please let me go," she whispered.

He cupped her chin and raised her face to his, brushing his lips softly across her eyelids, her cheeks, her forehead, her chin; and her breath caught in her breast as he buried his face in the hollow of her throat. His lips trailed over her burning flesh, their touch as gentle as the soft flutter of a butterfly's wings, and she found herself melting deeper into his embrace, all thought of escape wiped away by the sensations claiming her body. His lips sought hers again and she drank deeply at passion's well, her tongue probing the sweetness of his mouth, her breasts throbbing against the hard crush of his muscular chest. He moaned deeply as her fingers lightly touched the small crescent scar on his cheek, then moved to entangle themselves in his curly hair, pulling him even closer.

She gasped as he suddenly pulled away, his eyes deep blue and vibrant with desire. "You are a *sirena*—a lorelei," he said. "You drive away all thought of duty—of my command. You will ruin me, yet I am powerless to escape your enchantment."

She wanted to laugh. *Her*, a siren! Enchanting! Tears

suddenly pricked her eyelids as he gathered her close and rocked her back and forth, his ragged breathing filling the room. He was the one who had woven a web about *her*. His rugged, beautiful body filled her with such desire that she could scarcely breathe as he gazed down at her. She realized with a start that though he had just given her the opportunity to plead for release, she could not. "It is I who am under your spell," she whispered.

For a moment he grasped her face between his trembling palms and stared deeply into her eyes. Then he pulled her toward the bed, pressed her onto the mattress, and covered her body with his own. He reached beneath her shirt and her nipples rose and tightened beneath his touch and as he pushed aside the material and then took one into his mouth, his tongue teasing, suckling, bringing a deep, tingling throb to the secret recesses of her helpless body. She arched her back, pressing against his hardened manhood. As his fingers trailed down beneath her waistband to her bare belly, she moaned, her entire body and mind consumed by the desire to ease the burning ache between her thighs.

"I do not want to rush," he said raggedly. "I want to spend hours and hours drinking from the sweet fountain of your body."

His ensuing groan was interrupted by the sound of bells and harsh shouts from the deck above. He pulled away and sat on the side of the bed, a look of pain crossing his face.

"And we do not have hours now. I am needed on deck to supervise the transfer of the prisoners."

His words splashed across her like a bucket of cold water. She pulled her shirt down and sat up, wanting to be angry, yet unable to feel anything other than disappointment.

"Of course," she said. "I momentarily forgot your lofty position," she added, her voice heavy with sarcasm.

He took her hand and pressed her fingers to his lips. "But there will be time later for us to enjoy the fruits of our passion."

His self-assured tone fueled the tiny flame of anger burning in her breast, and she bit her tongue to stem words of bitter recrimination. She pulled her hand away.

"Of course," she repeated. "You must go."

She watched as he stood and ran his fingers through his hair, then tucked his shirt firmly into his waistband. "I will return as quickly as I can," he said. "Be patient."

She ground her teeth together, all vestiges of passion swept away by his self-confident tone. What a fool she had been! She had allowed her body to deceive her into indulging in feelings she had no right to enjoy. She had temporarily forgotten her need to escape—to find Jephtha! Her only chance lay in her opportunity to get on deck.

"Please let me go up on deck, Stephen," she pleaded. "I need some air or I will die!"

He smiled. "Only if you take the offer of a gown. You do not want my crew to believe you are a strumpet."

Her mind raced. She did not want to change. Encumbered with heavy skirts, she would have the devil's own time trying to escape! But she had no choice. This time, he held the high cards. She smiled.

"All right. But please make it something light . . . it is very warm today."

He nodded. "Yes, it is. And there are black clouds overhead. I am sure there will be much-needed rain before nightfall."

"I hope so! This land has been dryer than a drunk without— I mean, we need the rain," she added lamely, noting Stephen's astonished look.

"Wait here and I'll have Mendoza bring everything you need. And after you have refreshed yourself with a bath and have changed into a gown, please feel free to come up on deck."

She lowered her head so he would not see her expression of disgust. "Thank you, Stephen," she said softly.

He put a finger beneath her chin and raised it. "And don't think you will escape once you are on deck," he said firmly. "My men are well trained, and there are alligators in the river—lean and hungry alligators."

"You are a suspicious man. Why, I don't even know how to swim," she lied.

He bowed. "Until later, *querida*."

She waited until he had had ample time to climb the ladder before she threw the teacup at the door. It burst into small slivers and she frowned as they showered about her. Damn! That tyrant was more maddening than all of the Currys put together! She threw herself down on the bed and cradled her chin in her hand, the throbbing, unfulfilled ache between her thighs taunting her with the reminder of how that bastard of a Spaniard had stirred her emotions. Then she bit her tongue and forced her mind to the task at hand. Now, at least, she would have a chance to find out what had happened to Jephtha—if he was one of the prisoners transferred to this ship. She closed her eyes tightly and concentrated with all of her might. Oh, God, please make it so!

Chapter 6

When Shona answered the light rap on the cabin door, Mendoza stood in the passageway, his pale eyes lit with an impish smile, his blob of a nose twitching with pleasure.

"I've a gift for you, Madonna," he said shyly. "And it's the palest of *azul*—blue—as is befitting your beauty."

Shona eyed the bundle he held out to her. "A gift? Why should you be bringing me a gift?"

He chirruped like a happy child. "Oh, it's not from me, *señorita*, it's from the capitán. It is the gown he promised."

Shona made a face.

"You are not pleased?"

She could not bear the way his features sagged with disappointment. "Of course I'm pleased," she lied. "Won't you come in?"

"Oh, no, I could not do that. The *capitán*, he says to me, 'Fernando, deliver the package, then come back up on deck, *muy pronto.*'"

Shona smiled at the way he rolled his eyes. "I gather that means immediately," she said as she took the bundle from his hands and fingered the material. Perhaps it wouldn't be so bad after all, for it did seem light and airy. "Thank you."

When he did not make a move to leave, she patted his arm. "You had better obey your *capitán* before he loses his temper. I can testify to what he does when displeased."

Mendoza stepped backward, deeply alarmed. "Oh, Madonna," he said hastily, "you must remember what I told you before. Do not do anything to anger the *capitán*. He has much on his mind now, for they are going to begin the exchange of the captives shortly. Already, they are bringing some of them over from the *Loretta*."

Shona was startled. "Already? I must get dressed then, thank you again."

She closed the door quickly before he could continue the conversation. "Damn the bloody world!" she spat out as she whirled about and began to tear off her breeches and shirt. She took precious seconds to secrete the sugar papers in the drawer of the table. They were her only possession aside from her clothes and she was determined not to lose them. As she eyed the bundle, she thought it was just her luck that the gown had been delivered so late. Now, she might miss Jephtha!

When she tossed the gown across the bed, she filled the air with a spate of invectives. What was that madman of a captain thinking of? She had expected a practical gown, something like those worn by Mistress Curry, but what had he sent her? This bit of froth was as light as the spindrift from the sea, and as useless. She picked it up and shook it. A small package fell out. She unrolled it and gasped aloud. A lawn shift! Her displeasure turned to delight as she brushed her fingers over the soft material. She rubbed it lightly over her cheek. She had not felt such softness since she'd left Scotland!

She washed quickly, not taking time to dry herself properly for she feared she was going to be too late to see Jephtha. When she slipped the shift over her head and smoothed its softness over her hips, her mind reeled with memories, but she pushed them aside. This was no time to think of the past. She donned the gown, then pulled the bodice together and fastened it, smoothing down the piece of shift showing above the low, square neckline. Pale blue flowers entwined with green leaves and stems adorned the panels that ran down the front edges of the gown, parting to show the lightest of dimity across the front. She could not imagine who had owned this dress. It was far too fine for anyone she knew, and she was sure no lady in Brunswick had the nerve to wear something this fragile! It must have been taken from Mistress Moore's pressroom at Orton. The sleeves hung full and long and she bit her lip in frustration. Though it felt marvelous to be dressed in soft materials again, she knew this was the worst possible attire in which to effect an escape. The gown was one of the newest sack-back styles, with a soft flowing drape hanging from the neckline to the hem at the back. How could she possibly run with so much material impeding her?

She looked down at her bare feet and grinned. She would present quite a picture of elegance appearing on the deck without shoes! She dashed to the table and began pawing through the drawer, but she could not find a comb for her hair. She leaned forward and caught the long curls up in her hand, gave them a deft twist and then tucked the ends into the large coil she had made. The hairdo wasn't any more practical than the dress, but it would have to suffice. She must hurry!

She could hear shouts and loud voices as she made her way up the companionway ladder. When she reached the deck, she was astounded to find the morning sky almost as black as night. Threatening rain clouds hung low over the ship, the furled sails popped against their bindings, and the deck pitched as the wind scudded across the top of the water, leaving choppy waves in its wake. As a violent gust swept across the deck, she pushed her billowing skirts close to her body, muttering to herself that dressed as she was, she would probably be blown off the vessel and float away like a miniature ship under full sail!

A sudden blast tore her hair loose from its coil. "Damnation!" she said loudly. She heard a gasp at her side and turned quickly.

Mendoza stood looking at her, his mouth hanging open, his eyes wide. *"Madonna!"* he said in a shocked voice.

Shona never apologized for her vocabulary, but she made an

91

exception this time. "I'm sorry, it just slipped out," she said.

He shook his head slowly. "Such a lovely picture you make, you must never allow such words to sully those pure lips."

She found his distress comical, though she did not allow him to see her amusement. Pure lips, indeed! "I'll mind what I say from now on," she said.

He looked at her for a moment, eyebrows knitted together across his wrinkled forehead. Then he smiled and motioned her to follow him. "The *capitán*, he said you are to stand over there out of the way, and I am to stay with you for protection."

Shona bit back an exclamation of dismay. She had hoped to have the freedom of the deck, but she now found she was to have a guard. She followed Mendoza to the spot he indicated, just in front of the taffrail. "But I can't see much from here," she complained. "Can't we go a little closer?"

"Oh, no, Madonna. You might be harmed by one of those captives. After all, they are ruffians and they might hurt you."

She almost choked as she tried to control her laughter. Hurt her indeed! She had been in Brunswick for over a year, and she knew every man in town. Likely or not, they wouldn't even recognize her, dressed as she was in fine dimity and lace.

She stepped to the other side of Mendoza and peered amidship. She could see several men standing with bowed heads at the railing, their hands tied tightly behind their backs. But there was no giant form in that group. Jephtha was not one of them.

"Are they all here? Have they brought all of the captives aboard?"

Mendoza smiled patiently. "No, there is another boatload coming over in a minute. The river is tossing and turning like a serpent in the wind and the last boatload almost capsized. They are bringing them over in smaller groups now."

He could still be coming then. He had to be!

But Jephtha was not in the next boatload, or the next. Shona watched intently as each man was helped up the rope ladder onto the deck. She would not give up hope. Then a familiar

92

form struggled over the railing. She gasped. Master Curry! How had he been taken prisoner? She could not repress a smile of satisfaction as she watched his obvious discomfort. He huffed and puffed as he pulled himself on deck. Then he almost fell, but he was jerked rudely erect by a sailor. She was not sure because of the failing light, but it appeared that he had been crying. Though she wanted to spit on the deck, she did not, knowing Mendoza would surely faint at such unwomanly behavior. But where was Jephtha?

She was too absorbed in watching the activity to see Captain de Larra climb down the accommodation ladder from the quarter-deck and start in her direction. She did not see his eyes rake her from head to toe, nor did she see the look of appreciation on his face. He stopped at her side and made a bow.

"Señorita Cameron, I am amazed by the transformation."

Shona whirled about. "You startled me," she said coldly.

His right eyebrow rose dangerously. "Are you so intent upon watching the townspeople you told me would never miss you? I should think you would feel only disgust at the way they have treated you."

"You can't know how I have been treated!" she protested. "Most of those men were kind to me. It was only a few—"

"And your master? Is he among the captives?"

Shona's eyes instantly sought out Master Curry. Should she tell de Larra? No, she could not. She did not know what the captain might do if she pointed out her master to him.

"No," she said. "He must have escaped your raiders."

De Larra's eyes bored a hole right through her, and she knew she had not fooled him. Then his eyes narrowed as he looked over at the group of disheveled men. "Is it that one, the tall skinny one with the plain black coat?"

Shona giggled despite herself. "Lord no!" she exclaimed. "That's the rector. I doubt he'll ever leave Wilmington and St. James after this!"

"Then might it possibly be the short, squat man with the

balding head, the one who is sweating in fear?"

Shona froze. How had he known? But perhaps he was just baiting her. "No," she said. "I fear not."

De Larra grinned. "You are a poor liar, Shona. Shall I fetch him and make him kowtow to you? Would it make you feel better if he bowed at your feet for a change? Perhaps I could find something menial for you to tell him to do."

She gasped. "Don't you dare!" The moment the words were out of her mouth, she regretted them. She should know better than to dare a man like de Larra.

His grin widened. "Oh, but I do dare! After all, I am the commodore."

Before she could stop him, he had walked over to the group and singled out Master Curry. He grasped the man's bonds and pulled him roughly over the deck toward Shona. She wanted the ground to open up and swallow her. What would Master Curry think?

De Larra halted his captive in front of her. "I believe you know this lovely young woman," he purred.

Master Curry raised his head. He gasped and recoiled as though burned. "Shona!" he said. "Dear God, what are you doing here, and dressed like that?"

Shona did not have time to reply. De Larra jerked Master Curry's hands back and the terrified man almost fell to his knees. "Miss Cameron is my guest," the captain said harshly. "I don't remember giving you permission to call her by her Christian name."

Master Curry's face waxed white and beads of sweat dripped from his forehead and rolled down his pudgy cheeks. "I . . . I'm sorry," he whispered.

Suddenly, Shona realized she was enjoying Master Curry's predicament enormously. Hadn't he demeaned her at every opportunity? Hadn't he cuffed her about the shoulders with his cane when she displeased him? Hadn't he threatened her time after time with bodily harm?

She looked over at de Larra, tossed back her head, and

94

smiled broadly.

He knew immediately what she wanted.

"Kneel!" he demanded.

The hapless captive groaned as he was forced to his knees. "Please . . . please don't hurt me," he babbled. "I didn't mean to treat her poorly. I fed her well and even gave her a bed in the shed, I haven't hurt her too badly, have I Shona . . . I mean . . . Miss Cameron?"

He looked up at Shona, his tiny eyes almost hidden in the folds of his quivering cheeks.

When she looked down at him with feigned disdain, not replying, his shoulders began to shake and within seconds, he was sobbing openly. Immediately Shona was ashamed of herself for tormenting this pathetic fool, no matter how much he had humiliated her in the past.

"Let him go," she said quickly. "He's harmless."

So, de Larra thought, the little baggage has a heart! He pulled Curry to his feet and shoved him back across the deck to the other captives. When he returned to Shona, she was staring out over the black water.

"You did not like to see him suffer."

"No."

"Yet you have dreamed many times of degrading him as he has degraded you?"

"Yes."

"Then why? . . ."

She whirled about, her eyes wide, tears on her lashes. "Oh, just go away. You've had your fun."

"*My* fun? My dear Shona, I believe it was *your* fun I was engineering."

She turned and glared at him, but refused to let him bait her.

Stephen smiled softly. "You are so beautiful when you are angry. Your eyes sparkle like golden sherry, and your lovely bosom heaves with indignation. I have never found you so desirable."

Shona began to sputter. She wanted to slap his arrogant face, but even in her anger, she knew that would be suicide. "You are insufferable," she hissed.

De Larra looked at her with mocking eyes. "Perhaps you would like to go below? I have a few minutes before my men arrive from the town. . . ."

"No! You promised me I could come on deck. It's much too hot in that cabin." Dear God, he couldn't send her below now. Then she would never know about Jephtha!

"You mean he has not come aboard yet?"

Shona's eyes darted to his in alarm. "Whatever do you mean?"

"Why, your lover, the one taken captive with you. But I suppose he's not aboard because I remember that he was supposed to be a giant, and I made sure that only the shortest of the men were transferred here from the *Loretta*. A shame; now you will have to wait to be reunited."

Shona felt as though she were about to faint. "Then he's alive?"

Stephen watched her carefully, oddly disturbed by her concern.

He shook his head. "I do not know. I remember Vicente mentioning that your lover was a giant of a man, but Captain Munroe has said nothing about such a prisoner."

"Jephtha's not my lover!" Shona insisted. "He's just a friend, one of the few people who've been kind to me, that's all."

"Then why do you care so much what has happened to him?"

"Because I don't know whether or not he was on the ship that blew up," she admitted in a low voice, reluctant to remind him of that disaster.

He exhaled slowly. "So . . . Then I am afraid you must prepare yourself for the worst. No captives were taken from the *Fortune* to the *Loretta* before she blew. And there were no survivors."

Shona reeled and would have fallen if he had not caught her.

96

He pressed her face to his chest so he would not have to witness her tears of grief. Then he ran his fingers over her hair until her sobs quieted.

"You cared for him much, then?" he asked as she stepped from his arms.

She looked down at the deck and nodded her head.

"But he was not your lover."

She threw back her head and met his gaze squarely. "Must you be lovers to be fond of someone?" she asked hoarsely.

"No. But your grief is great."

"Of course it is! Jephtha was the only one in that town who cared about me. He listened to my problems and he felt my pain right along with me. And I killed him! It is my fault Jephtha's dead." She twisted away, and he caught her before she could run from the deck.

"What do you mean? You had nothing to do with that explosion!"

"You just don't understand," she cried, new tears rushing down her cheeks. "He was helping me run away! If it wasn't for me, he would be safe in the town right now. He would never have been at Orton! It's my fault he's dead, I tell you!"

De Larra shook his head slowly and forced her to turn to face him. "Men choose their own fate. Your friend chose his own path through life, you did not choose it for him. No one is that powerful, only God himself."

"Don't speak to me of God. There is no God. Or if there is, He sits up there and mocks us by allowing us to love, and then tearing our hearts out by destroying everything we care about."

Stephen grabbed her close and shook her. "You must never say that again!" he said. "You must not blaspheme God! He will surely punish you!"

She jerked away and stood glaring up at him, her breast heaving with emotion. *"Punish me!* How could He punish me more than He already has? I have lost my mother, my father, and my brothers! He has taken away my home, my

97

Scotland . . . my freedom, and now my only friend! What further punishment is there?"

She stared defiantly at Stephen.

"You are overwrought," Stephen said, not unkindly. "I will have Mendoza take you back to your cabin."

"No! I want to stand here until I am released . . . or don't you intend to release me with the others?" she taunted, knowing full well the truth.

"Of course I do. But it will take time to effect the transfer. You must rest and recover from the shock you have sustained."

"You are a liar," she said scathingly. "I overheard your conversation with that other man in your cabin. I know you intend to keep me as a hostage!"

"Well, well," Stephen said slowly. "So you are a spy, too."

"A spy? Perhaps. Better a spy than a liar. Oh, I know all about your little plan. That is why you wanted me here, all decked out in splendor for Captain Dry to see. I am the assurance you will get away with stealing everything you took from the town. Why you're nothing more than a pirate or a common thief!"

Stephen grabbed her arm. "Mendoza will take you below and lock you in your cabin. You will be released when I say so and not before."

She spat on the deck, and his fingers tightened on her arm until she cried out in pain.

"I assure you that I am at the end of my patience with you," he said. "Now, you will follow Mendoza quietly across the deck and hope that no one has seen the spectacle you have made of yourself. We will continue this later if you wish. Go!"

He gave her a shove and she staggered against the taffrail. She was so angry, she did not see Mendoza step up beside her, nor did she see the tears shining in his eyes. Her rage gave her the strength to stay upon her feet as the little seaman led her gently toward the hatch. She would get even! By God and all that was holy, she would have her revenge!

98

Chapter 7

The air was rancid with sweat and vomit, the darkness unrelieved by candle or lantern. Lice burrowed deep beneath clothing, bringing even more misery to the captives crowded into the darkest corner of the hold.

Jephtha Clemmons shook his head and quelled the bellow burning in his chest. It would do no good to make a row. He had tried, and that had only earned him the iron chains biting into his ankles and wrists. What was happening on deck? He could hear stomping feet and an occasional shout over the groans of the men crowded shoulder to shoulder in the darkness. But at least there was room to move an arm or a leg now that they had taken some of the captives away. Where had they taken them? And what lay ahead for those who remained?

Though he was miserable, his own safety was not paramount to Jephtha. One agonizing question returned time after time to his weary brain. What had happened to Shona? He closed his eyes so tightly he saw dancing spots of light, and his heart felt as though it were going to burst open with grief. He would not allow himself to believe that she had been killed in the explosion which had rocked the great ship. She must have been removed to another vessel before the renewed firing. She could not have been killed!

But what had the heathen Spaniards done to her? He

99

groaned loudly. His precious Shona, with the golden hair and the yellow eyes. Why had he ever considered helping her escape? If they had not been away from the town, none of this would have happened. Oh, he might have been captured anyway, but at least she would be safe with the women right now, away from the danger.

He slammed his fist against the planked wall in frustration, but the pain did nothing to lessen his agony. Spaniards were heathens. Spaniards raped women and did unspeakable things to them, everyone knew that. If they had touched Shona, if they had harmed her, he would spend the rest of his life tracking them down and he would slaughter them with relish.

He had never thought himself capable of feeling as much admiration for a woman as he did for Shona Cameron. She was so filled with life, so positive about her future. Even harsh servitude had not broken her spirit. Surely Shona Cameron was everything God had intended when He had made woman. No, the Spanish couldn't have hurt her. That would be too much. He began to plan his next steps. He was sure he would be released soon, for there had been talk among the last captives brought to the hold of an exchange. He would go to the Currys the moment he was released and, together, they would find her. It no longer mattered that Master Curry was a selfish prig. All that mattered was that he would be as anxious as Jephtha to find her.

And if he did not find her immediately? Jephtha leaned against the wall heavily, ignoring the chains biting into his ankles. Then he would spend the rest of his life searching for her.

Chapter 8

Night was falling and the last of the prisoners had been exchanged. Commodore de Larra stood at the taffrail looking out at the longboat carrying its final load upriver toward Brunswick, his blue eyes glowing with excitement. Though lightning slashed the sky to the south and thunder had boomed all day, the storm had not yet broken. It must hold off for another hour. He turned and watched another jagged arc light up the sky far away. In one more hour the darkness would be complete and the Spanish ships would sail. No returned booty. The *Nancy* under the Spanish colors. And Shona Cameron his!

He smiled broadly. The attack upon the English Colonists had not turned out so badly after all. The ships he had returned to Brunswick had been stripped of everything of value, their cargoes replaced with crates of ballast taken from his own vessels. He had lost only ten men, not counting the crew of the *Fortune*. His smile faded. He would miss Vicente Lopez. The man had had strange sexual preferences, but he had been a commendable commander. God grant that *he* himself would be as good a leader.

And the girl . . . His pulse quickened. They would share many nights before they reached the Louisiana coast. He would woo her, and he would win her. He was sure she would be a very willing captive after the first day or so. Every woman loved beautiful gowns, and he had trunks full of them with which to ply her. He also had a fortune in precious stones. Ah, yes, Shona Cameron would be his to bed at will. He closed his eyes as he remembered the loveliness of her slender body. Her full breasts, ripe and mature, appeared before his eyes.

"Capitán."

The soft voice at his side startled him, and he turned quickly.

"Fernando, what do you want? Didn't I tell you to stay with the girl? What are you doing here?"

Fernando faced his commander with more than a little trepidation. Esteban would not like what he was about to reveal, and no one knew better than he what bad news could do to this proud young man. But then again, no one knew better how to handle de Larra. After all, Fernando had known Esteban when he was an infant at the breast of his wet nurse. He had held him upon the back of his first pony and had soothed away his tears of frustration at not being allowed to attend the court in Madrid with his parents.

"You told me to see that she wanted for nothing, Capitán. But I fear I am unable to give her what she wants most . . . her freedom."

"Freedom! Of course you cannot give her that!"

"But she insists that she is a captive, and thus should be released as all of the other captives have been. She tore the lovely gown you gave her into little shreds of cloth, and then she stomped what was left of it into the floor. She insists she will wear only the seaman's clothing until she is given her freedom. Her anger is a match for no other I have seen . . . except yours, Capitán."

Esteban laughed harshly. "What? You are afraid of the wrath of a woman? You, who have faced Tía María with valor, who have remained unscathed even when she repeatedly vented her spleen upon your unfortunate head? You, who have stood beside me valiantly in battle? What has the girl done to you, Fernando? Has she taken away your manliness?"

Fernando blushed at the mocking tone. "I am not afraid of her, Capitán," he said very formally. "I only promised to tell you of her wishes. Nothing more."

"Tell me of her wishes?" Esteban's eyebrows rose. "You are her agent then, sent to deal with her captor? Is that it?"

"No! I am a human being, as she is a human being. And, if you will only take time to remember, you are also human. She grieves for her friend who has died. And it is not right to keep her captive when you have released all of the others. You must release her, Esteban. You must not allow your passion to—"

"Enough! Who are you to tell me what to do? I am no longer a child wearing skirts. I am a man, and I am your commodore. I will release her when I wish and not before!" Esteban turned his back and looked out at the river. "How does she grieve?" he asked after a long silence. "Does she weep?"

"No, Commodore. But her eyes are as large and as deep a yellow as those of the cat you used to keep in the stables. She hurts deeply. I can tell."

"I remember that cat. I also remember how it purred and rubbed against my legs when I offered it tidbits. Will she also purr, Fernando?"

"Esteban!"

Fernando's shocked voice made him smile again. "Do not pretend to be shocked, my old *amigo*. We have seen much, the two of us. The girl will be tamed in time."

"Then . . . then you do not intend to release her? You mean to take her with us?"

Esteban turned and met the old man's gaze squarely. "Yes. She goes with us. See? It is already beginning to rain. Soon there will be a storm, and we must be well under sail when it breaks with all of its fury. It will be much too dangerous to set her ashore then. She might drown. You would not want that, would you?"

Fernando's gaze did not waver. "Of course not, Commodore," he said, once again stiff and formal. "I am sure that Señorita Muñoz will be pleased when you return from your

103

travels with a young woman friend for her."

Esteban clenched his hands. "You have said quite enough," he said softly, his voice silken with controlled rage. "You may return to my cabin and prepare it for two. And on your way, post a guard at the girl's door. She has enough spunk to try to escape, even in the midst of a storm."

"Yes, Commodore."

Esteban watched the old man walk stiffly away, his head held high, his back ramrod straight. He knew his old friend's cheeks were quivering with indignation, and he was sure he would be the object of many a prayer before the night was over. Fernando Mendoza was a true and faithful son of the Church, and his piety had just been tested to the utmost.

Fernando had not exaggerated Shona's tantrum. The fruits of her anger lay in shreds upon the floor, dirtied by her feet and the spittle she had so liberally showered upon each piece. But for now, her anger was spent. A deadening numbness was beginning to invade her body. Jephtha was dead. She was once again a captive. And she knew that this time, her servitude would exact a much harsher toll than it had in Brunswick.

She closed her eyes, trying desperately to stem the tears streaming down her face. Damn! She wiped her sleeve furiously across her face. Tears would not buy her freedom. Nor would sitting here feeling sorry for herself. She could certainly do with a champion at this moment, but as usual, she had only herself to rely upon. Well, that Spanish bastard would not win!

She leaped to her feet. That funny little Mendoza had been gone for a long time, and she was sure he had failed in his mission to gain her freedom. But she didn't need him. She would do it on her own!

She looked about the cabin, seeking something dark to put over her breeches and shirt. A dark blue blanket was all she could find, but it would do to hide her in the deepening twilight. She threw it over her shoulders and tiptoed to the door. Though she could hear shouts above her, there was no sound in the corridor outside. Had a guard been posted? She tried the handle and it turned easily. When she opened the door slightly and peeked out into the passageway, it was deserted.

She did not take time to make a plan for her escape. Though she knew the river was the home of alligators and poisonous snakes, she was sure death would be better than what she faced if she stayed. Intuitively, she knew it was now or never. She chose the ladder at the far right at random, and raced down the passageway. Ascending the rungs quickly, she paused for a moment when she reached the open hatch to pull the blanket up over her hair. Then she raised her head and looked through the opening. A light rain was falling. She could see the outlines of men scurrying about through the darkness, but no lanterns lit their activity. She crept up onto the wet deck and hunched down. Where was the nearest rail? To the right, or to the left? There was no time for debate, for she could hear footsteps coming toward her out of the darkness. She crawled away from the sound, her heart pounding madly in her throat.

She bumped her head upon something hard and bit back a curse. A muffled laugh close by her left side almost turned her stomach inside out. She froze. A voice speaking softly in Spanish slowly faded across the deck. She swallowed and drew in a deep breath.

Her trembling fingers felt the wood in front of her. She was at the rail! She slowly rose to her feet, keeping the blanket over her head, and suddenly, a brilliant arc of lightning leaped across the water before her, illuminating the way to freedom. She knew being in the water during a lightning storm could be dangerous, but she did not hesitate. She scrambled over the side and leaped into space just as a huge clap of thunder exploded over the ship.

She hit the water feet first. Though it was warm, it was still a shock to her sweating skin, and she swallowed a mouthful of the dark liquid before she could clap her lips together. She felt herself plunging down and threw out her arms to slow her descent. Then she kicked her legs and slowly began to bob toward the surface. When her head popped out of the water, she lay on her back, gasping in the sweet-tasting air. She was safely off the ship. She had escaped!

She opened her eyes as another bright flash of lightning sparked across the surface of the river, and to her horror, she found herself looking directly up into the face of Esteban de Larra who stood at the railing. She allowed herself to sink deeper into the water, and as soon as she was completely submerged, she began to swim in the direction of the shore. She forced herself to remain underwater until her lungs were bursting and her head buzzing, surfacing only long enough to take in several gasps of air, then plunging under again, pulling as hard as she could with her arms and kicking her feet frantically. She could not allow him to catch her now, not when she was so close!

The water became warmer, and she smiled as she came to the surface again. She must be getting close to the shore. She took several breaths, not taking time to see if she was being pursued before she submerged again. The next time she stroked upward, her feet touched the muddy river bottom and she knew she had won!

She pulled hard along the surface for several strokes, then allowed her feet to drop. Again, they sank into soft mud. She pushed her streaming hair back from her face as she peered through the darkness, but the shore was hidden by a soft curtain of rain. Suddenly, she heard a splash to her right. God! Had that bastard followed her? She allowed herself to sink until her head was submerged and then she began to slog slowly through the mud toward the shore, trying to move as cautiously as possible lest she disturb an alligator. But she had not taken a proper breath and was soon forced to bring her head out of the water. More splashing, this time much closer. Panic erased all thought of caution. She stood waist deep in the water and frantically began to wade toward land.

A sudden burst of lightning lit up the sky and she found herself only a few yards away from the largest alligator she had ever seen. His eyes were glassy balls beneath knobs of glistening black skin, and as she watched, he thrashed his giant tail through the water. Then he opened his mouth wide to show white gums and teeth so large and sharp that she panicked completely. She turned and began to stroke wildly away from the shore, her arms and legs out of control now. Her mouth tasted bitter as gall, and her body was covered with goose flesh. She felt something grab her arm and she screamed, swallowing water.

"Don't fight me!"

She heard the voice, but it made no sense to her. She pulled and writhed, trying to escape the grip on her arm.

"I said don't fight me! Let me pull you! Just kick your legs!"

It was a man! She grasped the hand holding her and clawed frantically, trying to put more room between herself and the alligator.

"*Madre de Dios*, stop fighting! Do you want to kill us both?"

The harsh words finally registered. *De Larra!* She stopped struggling and allowed him to pull her close. Sobs racked her body, and she swallowed more water.

"I am going to swim," he gasped. "Don't try to help. Just allow me to pull you along."

"Alligator!" she choked. "He'll follow!"

He did not answer, and she felt herself being pulled along the surface of the water. She tried to kick her legs but they were as numb as wooden sticks and would not obey. She began to sink.

Her hair was jerked and a hand cupped her chin. "Turn over on your back and rest. I will do all of the work."

She tried to obey, but her limbs would not function. She felt herself being pushed under the water and she tried to fight, but again, her arms and legs ignored the frantic signals her brain was sending. Suddenly, she was flipped over and she gulped air into her starving lungs.

107

"Perez! Over here!"

De Larra's voice came from a distance, and she knew he had left her to die, to be torn in two by those sharp white teeth. But she was too tired to care. She closed her eyes and allowed herself to drift, the water caressing and supporting her exhausted body. She was aware of a light, but she did not question what it might be. She was dying, yet she was at peace. *God, if there is a God, let the alligator kill me in one bite.* She drifted in what felt like circles, around and around, the light behind her eyelids fading slowly into total darkness.

Then a loud explosion forced her eyes open. She wanted to scream because the British were killing her brothers . . . no, the Spaniards were killing Jephtha . . . but she could not make a noise.

"It is all right, Madonna. You are safe in the boat now."

Madonna. Someone had called her that. She tried to wipe the film away from her eyes, but her hand would not obey. Then a familiar face swam into view. Fernando, he called her Madonna! But why was Esteban de Larra's face above her? She struggled to sit up, but a hand pushed her down.

"You must lie still. We will be back aboard the ship in moments. You are safe now. Perez has shot the alligator."

"The storm is breaking upon us, Capitán."

"I know. Make haste. We must sail as soon as we board."

Shona struggled to sit up. "No!" she groaned. "Let me go! I don't want to sail!"

Firm hands pushed her back. "Lie still," de Larra said. "If you capsize this boat, we'll all be food for the alligators."

Shona closed her eyes in defeat. The Spanish bastard had won. She was once again a captive. It seemed that Shona Cameron, last proud member of the decimated Cameron clan, would never taste freedom again.

Chapter 9

The *Nancy* tossed and writhed in ocean swells whipped into foam-capped mountains by the howling wind. The deck was awash, and the sails snapped and tore at their ropes, adding to the cacophony of sound. As the rain pounded down in thundering sheets, de Larra stood braced beside the helmsman. Even though he ran a hand across his face, it was impossible to make out their course. He was relieved that the winds, which had been blowing them southeast when they'd hoisted the sails, had continued to blow in that direction. A slight deviation to the east and his ship would have been ground to death upon the rocks of Cape Fear.

But they were upon the open sea at last and he had altered their course to the south. He grinned broadly. They had done it! The Spanish ships had escaped without a single Colonial sail at their heels! He threw back his head and savored the beating rain upon his face. It felt cool and clean, and it quickly washed away the last remnants of his frustration. Another hour or so and his ship would have enough sea between it and the shore. Then he could turn the command over to Perez.

They were many days away from their destination. Days . . . and nights. Though he knew Perez could not be trusted completely, under the watchful eye of Fernando, he was an excellent lieutenant, capable of commanding the *Nancy*

109

when his captain needed a rest. That would allow time to spend with the girl.

Shona. His breath caught in his throat, and his blood began to race through his veins as his imagination conjured up a vision of her exquisite body lying naked on the bed before him, her arms raised in eager supplication, her full lips trembling with desire, her sparkling yellow eyes mirroring his own passion. . . .

Fernando Mendoza held tightly to the ropes stretched across the deck for hand holds as he made his way from the main hatch toward his *capitán*. Mendoza's dark mood was not caused by his drenching, for the rain had cooled the air, and soaked clothing was an improvement over the sticky sweat which had pricked him for so long. It was the girl. And the *capitán*. They were both possessed by devils of discontent, and he, Fernando Mendoza, was caught firmly in the middle of their battle for supremacy.

He growled low in his throat. How could a woman with beauty as radiant as the sun have such a foul temper? He shuddered and paused for a moment to collect his wits. He had only taken her the bed gown his *capitán* had given him, but by all the saints above, she had thrown a fit so dark, so violent, he had been tempted to retreat from the *capitán*'s cabin at a dead run.

He sighed deeply. That cabin was another source of trouble. He was sure the *señorita* would not have been so angry if she had been taken to the mate's cabin she had occupied before. She had actually accused him, Fernando Mendoza, of being a party to her seduction!

He wiped at the water on his face and continued across the deck. He had tried to explain that she was being placed in the *capitán*'s cabin for her own comfort, that he had made up the bed with the softest of sheets, just for her, but she would not listen, not even when he raised his voice in order to be heard over her harsh words. He flushed at the memory of their shouting match. Never in his entire life had he used such a tone of voice when addressing a woman! His shoulders slumped as he made his way up the ladder to the quarter-deck. Esteban would also shout when he heard her demands. Oh, sweet Mother of Jesus, what was a poor man to do when dealing with two people with such violent tempers?

As he drew nearer, he saw Esteban standing at the side of the helmsman. His dark blond hair was plastered across his forehead and his soaked black coat and breeches clung to his body like a second skin. Though Fernando could not see the expression on his superior's face, he quelled the impulse to beat a hasty retreat and plodded stoically on. This was his capitán. He would be brave and face whatever the fates had in store for him. Pray Esteban was in a gentler mood than the weather!

Shona tried to pace the confines of the cabin, but the pitching deck made walking impossible. She threw herself down upon the bed and sat with her hands braced against the roll of the ship. "Damnation!" She knew that soft-hearted old fool Mendoza would not present her demands for a private cabin and clean, dry seaman's clothing to his "capitán" with any more authority than a child trying to cajole a treat from a recalcitrant parent. She smiled as she recalled his angry shouts. Perhaps he would succeed after all.

Her smile was fleeting. De Larra would outshout him, and she would be forced to stay in this cabin, as a plaything to be toyed with whenever the fancy took that insufferable boor of a captain. She looked down at the gauzy film of a gown she had been forced to put on. "Either wear it, or nothing," Mendoza had shouted. Well, the gown was so transparent, it was little better than nothing! She looked down at the hard nubbins of her nipples pressing against the thin material. She knew what a sight like that would do to de Larra. She didn't stand a chance of escaping his passion.

She thought longingly of the other cabin. If only he would

111

agree to her staying there, she could have the privacy she longed for. But here she would be available anytime he chose, and she was certain that would be often. She pushed herself to her feet and stood swaying, eying the door. Was it locked? She did not remember hearing a key turn in the lock when Mendoza left. She lurched over and turned the handle. The door swung open. The passageway was bathed in the ghostly dancing light of the swinging lantern. She stepped out of the cabin and made her way cautiously forward.

The door to the cabin she sought was firmly closed. She saw immediately why the captain had insisted she use his cabin. There was no lock on this door! She eased it open and stepped inside into total darkness, but the dark did not worry her, for she knew her way around. She walked unerringly to the table and opened the drawer. Her hands closed over the candle and flint. She withdrew them, struck the flint on its box, and lit the candle.

Suddenly, she heard a rustle beside her and her breath froze in her throat. She was not alone! She set the candle in its holder, turned—and found herself staring directly into a pair of gleaming black eyes. She gasped and whirled, but not fast enough. A hairy hand snaked out and grasped her arm.

"Let me go!" she gasped. She twisted and turned, trying to escape the firm grasp.

"But you have just arrived, *señorita,*" answered a purring voice. "Surely you came to taste the fruits of love which Perez has in such abundance. I will not disappoint you."

"God! Let me go!" She pulled until her arm throbbed, but the hand was unrelenting. "Please!" she gasped. "I didn't know you were here! Please let me go!"

The answering laugh was filled with malice. She whirled about and grabbed a handful of black hair.

His laugh turned to a scream. "*Puta!*" He lashed out, knocking her to her knees with the back of his hand. Then he grabbed a handful of material and tore her bed gown from bodice to waist. "I will bed you!" he hissed. "You cannot come

112

in here flaunting your half-naked body and leave without fulfilling me."

Shona cringed on the floor at his feet. "I didn't know you were here," she moaned. "I thought I was alone."

"You lie! I have seen your eyes upon me before. I have not had a woman for months! Now, I will take what you came to give!"

She scrambled away from his grasping hands and reached the door just as it was thrown open.

De Larra's tall body was outlined in the doorway, his clothes dripping, his hair plastered across his forehead. She pulled herself to her feet and threw her arms around his waist. "Help me!" she panted. "He's trying to rape me!"

His arms did not open to offer comfort. Instead, he stood with his hands upon his hips, his eyes blazing with fury. "Perez!" he barked. "Clothe yourself this instant!"

She buried her face against de Larra's wet shirt, her body convulsing with shivers. "I didn't know he was here," she babbled, unable to control her tongue. "I came here to be alone. Please believe me, I didn't know he was here."

His eyes were cold when he looked at her. "You really are a *puta!*" he snarled. "But I did not think you would stoop so low as to seduce my own lieutenant."

Shona felt her face flush with rage. "You beast!" she screamed.

She raised her fists to strike out at him, but he grabbed her wrists and held them tightly.

"Your insults will not sway me this time, Señorita Cameron," he said very softly. "I should have known you could not be trusted. Are all Scottish women so hot they will bed anyone? You knew I would return. Couldn't you wait?"

This time, he had said too much. Shona lost all control. She kicked and bit and fought against the hands imprisoning her wrists, her breath coming in gasps, her eyes spitting fire. But her strength was no match for his. He held her away easily, his mouth twisted into a cruel smile, his azure eyes as cold as the deepest loch—and as unreadable.

Perez, fully clothed and very red of face, faced his commander. "She lies, Capitán," he said. "She came in here to lure me to bed. Look at what she is wearing! It is as if she wears nothing!"

De Larra eyed the torn gown. "And it appears that even that flimsy bit of cloth was too much," he drawled.

Shona wanted to scream out that Perez had torn the gown, but she was so angry, she could do nothing but strain against the bonds holding her and sputter.

De Larra ignored her. "You will report to the deck immediately and take command, Lieutenant Perez," he ordered. "And we will talk about this little incident later. You have much to explain."

Perez drew himself up to his full height and saluted. "Yes, Capitán!" he said briskly.

De Larra pulled Shona out of the way and Perez sidled past, his face twisted with anger.

When she heard his footsteps ringing on the ladder, Shona returned her attention to her captor. "You must make him tell you the truth," she insisted. "I thought the room was empty. You have no right to slander the good name of the Scots. We are an honorable people."

"And honorable people go parading about clad in transparent gowns? Come, my dear, Señorita Cameron, I am not a fool!"

Shona jerked her hands away and stood rubbing her wrists. "You sent this gown to me!" she said hotly. "I would rather be clothed in nothing!"

The moment the words were out of her mouth, she regretted them. She watched his face as the flinty steel in his eyes melted into desire and his lips parted in a smile. "I shall grant your wish," he said.

Before she could move, he slipped the shredded gown from her shoulders and it dropped to the floor in a frothy puddle of white. Though her mind screamed at her to run, she could not obey. She was amazed when he stepped backward. "Go if you wish," he said, ever so softly. "I will not follow."

But Shona could not move. She felt that she was drowning in the depths of his blue eyes, his pleading, caressing eyes. She looked at the cleft in his chin, at the small crescent scar on his cheekbone, at his right eyebrow, arching dangerously; but no matter how she fought it, her eyes were drawn back to his. They offered understanding, warmth, passion.

He stepped backward again, until several feet separated them. She felt herself tremble as a longing warmth spread through her body. He is a liar! she reminded herself. He only wants to use you! Then he'll discard you as he discarded the gown when it got in his way.

A small sob escaped her lips. She had to escape him. He would ruin her life! But the moment that realization hit her, he raised his hands and held them out before him, beseeching.

Instantly, the passageway was transformed into Culloden Moor. Once again, she stood in a darkness lit only by the stars. And once again, the slayer of Cumberland stood before her with his arms outstretched. She recognized the knowing in his eyes—the understanding—and she moved forward as though in a dream, her feet barely touching the rough boards, until her fingertips touched his.

This time, he did not disappear, and she did not awaken from her dream. His hands closed over hers, his slim, strong fingers promising warmth and sanctuary from the world which had abused her. He pulled her slowly to him until her body was pressed tightly against his. Then he lifted her into his arms and carried her to his cabin.

His caresses were gentle, his fingers alive upon her bare flesh. His storm-chilled body soon warmed in her embrace, and his lips, touching her neck and shoulders, were soft as gossamer webs. "Let me love you, *querida*," he whispered. "And give me your love in return. God meant us for each other."

She closed her eyes, and her answer was a ragged sigh, born

of a longing too deep to be denied. She reached up and placed a fingertip in the deep cleft of his chin, then touched the scar on his cheekbone before she moved her fingers up to fondle his damp hair.

He groaned and bent to place his mouth upon hers, his lips moving gently, softly, until her lips parted and his tongue entwined with hers. She knew she was losing herself, but she was helpless as a babe in his embrace. A glorious fire spread through her and she pressed her body against his, wanting nothing less than to become a part of him.

His lips touched her eyelids, her cheeks, her chin and forehead, the tip of her nose. *"Mi amora,"* he whispered. "My love."

His fingers trailed down to the peaks of her breasts, leaving shivers of delight in their wake, and he stroked her nipples until they stood erect. Then he bent and licked each bud until she thought she would die with pleasure. When his hands moved down along her belly, to the golden triangle waiting so impatiently to be stroked, some awareness returned to her.

"Please, Stephen," she pleaded. "Please . . ."

"I want to feel and taste every part of your captivating body," he breathed. He gently turned her onto her stomach and lifted her hair from the nape of her neck, his lips and tongue working their fiery magic over her helpless flesh. "I cherish you," he said huskily as his fingers brushed her buttocks, leaving waves of delicious goose flesh in their wake. He moved down on the bed and lightly kissed the backs of her knees, then he delicately stroked the back of each calf until his lips were nibbling at her toes, evoking a cry of delight from her. He kissed each toe, each instep, each ankle, then his hands traveled up, up, over her thighs to her dimpled buttocks, tracing delicate circles over and over again while his lips nipped at her earlobes, his warm breath tantalizing her until she felt she would surely die if he did not claim her immediately.

She began to whimper and he turned her, gathering her into

116

his embrace, his hard manhood throbbing against her thigh. She reached down and grasped his hard, hot flesh between her fingers, caressing him until he groaned and buried his face in the hollow of her neck, his urgency matching hers.

Then he raised his head and stared down at her, his handsome face suffused with a smile so dazzling, so radiant, she felt tears prick her eyelids and slide down her burning cheeks. He caught a tear on his fingertip and stared down at it, his eyes strangely tender.

"I cannot believe this," he whispered raggedly. "I have waited all of my life to love you."

She smiled up at him. "I, too, have waited a lifetime," she breathed.

He rose over her, and she parted her legs, guiding him with trembling fingers. He entered her slowly, gently, until she felt her body consume him completely. A sob caught in her throat for she felt no panic, only warmth and completeness. She moved in rhythm with him, her back arching as she sought to hold him deeply within her, not willing to allow him to withdraw even for one second. He thrust into her, his fingers stroking, fondling, bringing her closer and closer to the brink of that delicious, deep chasm. She pressed her arms around him, pulling him even closer. She could not get enough of him, of his touch, his smell, his taste. She wanted more, even more.

He leaned over and sucked on one nipple, then the other. Then his lips claimed hers and his tongue invaded the sweet recesses of her mouth. She accepted his kiss eagerly, moaning as his fingers gently kneaded her mound of desire. She knew she was drowning, yet she gladly plunged headlong into the glorious sea of their shared passion.

Then she felt him shudder and cry out. Her own body reached the same chasm and she plunged over, falling, falling, while the stars exploded in the skies and showered her with glistening bits of light.

When he rolled over and pulled her into the warm circle of his arms, she smiled and gave a soft sigh of contentment as his lips fondled her earlobe. He picked up a strand of her hair and twined it around his finger.

"You are my *tesora*, my treasure," he whispered.

He looked down at her, his eyes devouring each feature. She stared up into his face, bursting with words she could not utter. He was the most handsome man she had ever beheld, and his body had worked magic she had never known possible. She wanted him again and again—and again.

He must have read her thoughts, for once again his fingers began to explore her body. He kissed, he nibbled, he caressed, he stroked, he lipped and fondled until she felt as though she would die if he did not make them one once more. Her breath caught in her throat as he moved between her legs, his tongue flicking, flicking, his warm lips moving over her defenseless flesh, bringing renewed, delicious waves of desire.

She caressed him, moving her hands over the deep dimples in his muscled buttocks, her fingers trailing down his hard thighs, then firmly stroking his throbbing manhood.

This time he entered her with one quick, fierce thrust, and she cried out in delight, her warm, moist flesh encompassing him eagerly, her breast heaving with ragged breaths, her cheeks burning with the hot flame of her passion. He moved rapidly, then slowly, teasing her by withdrawing and then entering her with exaggerated, lingering strokes, his eyes sparkling with laughter. He kissed her, and she nibbled lightly on his tongue, then caught it between her teeth, biting down until he stepped up his thrusts to match her growing need.

Suddenly, he rolled over, pulling her on top. She rode him hard, unable to believe the delicious sensations washing over her entire body. When she bent low, he pressed her breasts together, nibbling on the nipples as if they were one. Then he arched his back and she pulled him into herself completely, their mingled cries filling the cabin. She wanted to hold back, to prolong the ecstasy, but she could not. She was impaled on his flesh, and she was rising to such heights, she knew she could reach out and touch the stars.

Desire suddenly exploded into a brilliant, glorious, shower of light, and their cries became one as he joined her in her rapturous journey.

When she collapsed across him, her hair fanning across the bolster like strands of spun gold, he gently moved her to one side, his face suffused with light, his eyes as blue as the deepest sea. His fingers brushed the corners of her mouth.

"You belong to me now. I will never let you go," he said.

She was filled with wonder, for she felt no fear, no resentment. This was the man she had always known she would find. Stephen de Larra had truly slain Cumberland. He had erased all the years of suffering, of degradation. Indeed, she now questioned whether they had ever truly taken place. She finally knew what it meant to be a woman—a woman who was loved. Stephen had given her the greatest gift she had ever received. She belonged to him.

"I don't want you to," she answered. "Ever."

Chapter 10

The soft light suffusing through the cabin told Shona it was dawn. She stretched luxuriously, then ran her fingers lightly over the empty place beside her. Had it all really happened? She smiled and lay back down, fanning her hair out over the pillow. Yes. It was true. The icy dam within her had finally melted, allowing her to give freely of herself.

Stephen. She remembered being kissed awake while it was still dark. "I will return later, *mi amora*," he had said softly. "Close your eyes and dream of me." But she could not recall dreaming at all. Her body felt warm and more relaxed than it had ever felt before. She wriggled her toes and burrowed deeper beneath the covers. What kind of spell had he cast over her? How had he erased all those years so quickly? She closed her eyes and imagined his fingers trailing over her flesh, and a moan escaped her lips. Why had he left her? And when he returned, would it be the same?

Esteban took the cup of wine Fernando held out before him. "Thank you, *amigo*."

"You look rested, my *capitán*. Are your worries over?"

Esteban grinned. "Just some of them, old friend, just some."

Fernando cleared his throat and shuffled his feet.

His commander recognized his discomfort. "What is it? Are you again a harbinger of bad news? I am sure you don't come to me with more demands from the *señorita*, for I have left her sleeping soundly."

Fernando's wrinkled face turned crimson. "You should not tell me that, Esteban," he admonished. "That is your private life, though . . ."

The right eyebrow rose. "Though what?"

"Though there is talk."

"Talk? What talk? What are you raving about now?"

Fernando's back stiffened and his bushy eyebrows lowered. "You have commissioned me to be your eyes and ears," he said stiffly. "I am only fulfilling my duty."

Esteban sighed and shook his head. "All right, then, out with it. What have the men been talking about this time? Do they want more wine? Fewer duties? Women?" His eyes narrowed at the telltale flicker in Fernando's eyes. "Ah, so that's it! They want women! So how is this something new? Do my crew ever talk about anything else for long? Why are you bothering me with this gossip now?"

"It is not gossip, Esteban. This is serious. Your validity as a commodore is at stake."

"My *validity?*"

Fernando grasped the railing and fingered the wood with his callused fingers, drawing strength from the familiar feeling. "The men are whispering that the *señorita* is . . . that the *señorita* has . . . Oh, my *capitán*, they think that the Madonna is a *puta* sent here by Satan himself to tempt you!"

He looked down at the deck, steeling himself for the explosion sure to follow his disclosure, but there was only silence. He looked up quickly. Esteban was staring at him in disbelief. "It is true!" he said quickly. "Perez has filled them with tales of her going to his cabin last night. He has convinced them that she is bent upon destroying our mission! He has even hinted that she is a Colonial spy!"

"Spy!" Esteban hissed. His face had lost all color. His chest

122

rose and fell rapidly as he fought for control.

"We know that is not true," Fernando said quickly, "but you must do something to convince the men that what Perez says is a lie."

"I will kill him."

The words were spoken so quietly, Fernando was not sure he had heard them correctly. But one look at his commander's set face told him that he had. "You cannot!" Fernando said. "What about your plans? You have known since we began the voyage that Perez is a spy employed by Francisco Muñoz. But you have told me time and time again that you will control him, and thus thwart any plans Muñoz has to destroy this mission. You have said that you enjoy watching him squirm when he is torn between his loyalty to Muñoz and his greed for the gold we are sure to take. If you kill him now, you will never know what he plans, who else he has in his employ. Please, please listen to an old man! Forget about killing Perez. Just do something to convince the men that what he says it not true. That will shame him, and he will lose control over those who might believe more of his lies!"

Esteban shook his head. "I don't know what to tell them."

Fernando grasped Esteban's arm. "Tell them the truth! I have not even heard it from your lips, but I can guess what it is. I know the Madonna was not happy in your cabin. I am sure she went to Perez's cabin to escape from you. She did not know he was there. Am I right?"

Esteban nodded.

"Then tell that to the men. And tell it to them in front of Perez. But if you are wise, you will realize that when you do, you will be making a lifelong enemy of him, for he will never forgive you for shaming him before the others."

Esteban patted Fernando's hand. "Thank you, *amigo*." He sighed. "As usual, your wisdom surpasses mine. I will do as you say . . . and I must tell you that what you guessed about last night is the truth. How could you be so sure?"

"I may be an old man, but I have lived far too long to believe that the Madonna is a *puta*. She has much to learn about controlling her temper, but we all have faults. She is true and loyal, and from the look on your face this morning, as good in bed as she is good to look at."

"She is even better than that." Esteban chuckled. "Now, I want you to call the crew together. Rouse Perez from his bed. I want him to hear every word I have to say. Then, find a decorous gown for the Madon—a gown for Shona to wear and tell her to prepare herself to come on deck. Warn her that if she allows one foul word to escape her lips, she will be transferred to one of the other ships."

Fernando recoiled in horror. "No! If you want her to behave, you tell her. I have taken enough abuse from her tongue."

"Very well. But first, call the men."

Esteban de Larra was every bit the commodore as he addressed his crew. The sullen clouds parted suddenly and vivid sunlight shone on his white ruffled shirt front, and the truth sparkled in his azure eyes as he outlined what had happened the night before. He did not spare Perez, but vehemently denounced his behavior.

"As my lieutenant, I would expect Perez to behave as a gentleman," he concluded. "But you have just heard an account of his actions. He is no better than the lowest of the low. He took advantage of a frightened, helpless woman, a woman completely at his mercy, much like one of your own sisters would be under the same circumstances."

Several of the men grumbled and cast derisive looks at Perez who stood sullenly to one side.

"I know none of you would have debased yourselves as he did. But I feel the shame he is being put to now will suffice as punishment. Just remember, I expect my crew to behave like the Spanish ambassadors you are. We will reach Louisiana before long. Once there, we will fill our holds with all the

124

French have—and you will be allowed to find your women, but only the women willing to be found."

He laughed with the men.

"Now, I must tell you that Señorita Cameron is our guest. She is to be treated as you would treat one of our women . . . with the greatest respect. She has endured many hardships and has been separated from her country and those she loves. I am sure I can count upon you to convince her that the Spanish are honorable and, at all times, gentlemen. You are dismissed."

Perez waited until the quarter-deck had cleared. Then he stormed up to Esteban.

"Why didn't you just break me?" he snarled. "The men will never follow my orders now. You have ruined me."

De Larra studied Perez. Rage had turned the lieutenant's face a dull red and the pockmarks on his cheeks stood out white and ugly. His small black eyes were bright with hatred and his thin lips were trembling.

"I did not break you because you are too good a lieutenant to lose. But a good lieutenant will remember one thing. Loose talk always returns a hundred-fold. There are many riches to be obtained in Louisiana." Esteban saw the lust for gold leap instantly in Perez's small black eyes. "As my lieutenant, you will receive a large share. Don't anger me again. You are dismissed."

But Perez could not allow de Larra to think badly of him. After all, he had his commission. "I want Esteban de Larra to die somewhere in the New World," Francisco Muñoz had told him. "It is up to you to see that it happens." Now, he had to make one more attempt to convince de Larra that the girl had lied.

"But, Capitán," he said softly, "you believed me last night. Surely you don't take the word of that *pu*—, of that *señorita* over my own?"

De Larra stared at him with steel in his eyes. "I did not believe you last night. I was trying to allow you to save face.

125

But your loose tongue was your undoing. If you had kept your own counsel, I would never have mentioned it. But you lied and in lying, you undermined my authority as commodore of this mission. I believe I have already dismissed you."

He did not remain to watch Perez leave, but he did not have to see him to know that he had made a very vengeful enemy. Perez would have to even the score. He just prayed his animosity would be directed against himself and not Shona.

Chapter 11

"No woman of mine is going to use a sword!"

"I'm not going to use it, I just want to know how! For protection!"

Shona's eyes blazed as Esteban turned his back and walked to the cabin door. "Don't leave!" she shouted. "I want you to teach me!"

She rushed after him as he stepped out, but he closed the door in her face. When she heard the key turn in the lock, she screamed, "Stephen! Let me out of here! Stephen, come back here you . . . you . . ." She pounded on the door, then kicked it, but her bare foot smarted and she hopped back, cursing under her breath.

"Stubborn son of a Spanish whore," she muttered, forgetting that in his presence, she had quickly returned to the ladylike language of her childhood. Now, here she was, using the gutter language she had picked up since her capture by Cumberland. She limped over to the bed and threw herself down. What had gone wrong? The past few days had been the most glorious of her life. They had spent the nights making love, and Stephen had shown her the gentle, yet wild, side of his nature. Their mornings had been spent sharing remembrances of their lifetimes.

She had recognized early on that Stephen was kind despite

his show of pride and his haughty demeanor. He'd spoken with loving devotion of his parents and of his younger sister, Juana, who lived on the family's estate outside of Valencia. And he'd told her of his boyhood, his schooling at the feet of the Dominican monks, the tutoring in swordsmanship by his father, the gentleness of his mother, and the constant remonstrations by his Tía María, who was somewhat of a rebel, that women were special and deserved more than an occasional fling in bed. He also had shared with her his hopes for the future of Spain, his unbending patriotism.

And he had listened as she'd poured out her bitter story of defeat. He'd comforted her when she'd told of the death of her mother in childbirth, and of the staunch support she had received from her father throughout her young life. He'd laughed when she'd told him about her grandfather, the old man of the highlands who was filled with a monumental pride and rabid patriotism. Tears rose to his eyes as she recounted the battle of Culloden, and told of the degradation of the Scots at the hands of the British. His face blanched as she recounted her year with Cumberland, and he held her body close to his until her trembling ceased.

Now this! How could he be so blind? She threw herself down upon the bunk and pounded the bolster in frustration. She should never have told him that she was well schooled in the use of the dirk. She should never have shared her memories of the stag hunts, when she had ridden as hard and as fast as any man and had often taken the first game. She should not have explained that in Scotland, it was not unusual for women to accompany their men anywhere they chose, even into battle.

She closed her eyes and groaned. She should have noticed how quiet he became when she mentioned riding bareback over the moors and across the straths. She should have recognized the hostility sparking in his eyes when she recounted the mock battles she had entered into with her brothers. After all, the women of Spain were not allowed such freedom. But she had been blind to all but her memories.

When would she learn? It had taken her only two days to recognize how to handle Stephen de Larra. Be loving. Be passionate. Be proud. Be demanding, even. But never, never push!

But she was bored and her monthly was upon her, bringing her emotions to a peak. The weather had alternated between squalls and clear, brisk days, and though she had been allowed on deck that first morning out, Stephen often talked now about the danger they faced in these waters, even though they were flying the Colonial flag. Because of the danger, he had allowed her on deck only that one time.

Though he had plied her with beautiful gowns and breathtaking jewels, she felt trapped in this small cabin—a prisoner of love, perhaps, but still a prisoner.

Yes, she was bored. She had never taken delight in beautiful clothing. Though she enjoyed the feel of softness next to her body, and bright colors entranced her, she could get as much enjoyment from a brilliant green shirt and breeches as she could from a delicate gown. That was another thing she and Stephen disagreed upon. She had always preferred to wear men's clothing, finding it allowed her more freedom to move about, but he was shocked by her request for seaman's clothing.

"You are a woman!" he had protested. "Women do not wear breeches, except under the most unusual circumstances."

"But I always wore my brother's breeches," she had answered hotly. "And I have even worn their trews. They are much more practical than these full skirts. You don't understand. You don't have to hobble about, encumbered by yards and yards of material!"

"I've a good mind to keep you naked," he said, advancing steadily, his eyes gleaming with desire. The disagreement had ended in bed with long kisses and loving embraces.

Now, Shona smiled and threw back the covers. Her breakfast tray would soon arrive and she was famished! She dressed quickly, then combed her long hair until each strand glimmered dull gold. As she made the bed, she realized that Fernando would be bringing her breakfast as he always did, and she decided to try to cajole him into teaching her to use the sword.

But when she approached him with the proposal a few minutes later, he recoiled as though she had slapped him. "Madonna! You are a lady. Ladies do not have to wield a sword. They have other wiles much sharper than any blade."

She laughed and wrinkled her nose. "You have a honeyed tongue, Fernando, and if you will not teach me swordplay, there can be nothing against your teaching me to speak your language, can there?"

His eyes crinkled at the corners as he laughed like a pleased child. "There is nothing at all wrong with that, Madonna. If you wish to learn Spanish, I, Fernando Mendoza, will be most happy to teach you. But I must warn you, it is a difficult thing, learning a new language. I spent many years perfecting my English. Perhaps you do not have the gift of the tongue."

"I already speak three languages. I was raised speaking the Gaelic and the Scots. I spoke very little English until . . . until a few years ago. So if I can learn English, I can surely learn Spanish. Come, we will start this instant."

Esteban found them late that afternoon, deep in study. He watched them, both too intent upon their work to know that he had stepped into the cabin. The white head bent close to the golden one presented a contrast he fervently wished he could capture on canvas.

"Plotting some evil scheme, are you?" he asked lightly.

They both jumped apart, Fernando's wrinkled face flushed. "Capitán! I did not hear you enter."

Esteban pulled Shona to her feet and planted a kiss on her upturned lips. "Mmm, that tasted like nectar from the sweetest Valencia orange," he said.

Shona wrinkled her brow, deep in thought. Then she smiled brightly. "Orange. Naranja."

Esteban's eyebrows rose in surprise. "What's this? You

130

spoke that like a native."

Her smile broadened and her yellow eyes sparkled, their brown flecks turning dark with delight. "Oh, Stephen, Fernando's teaching me Spanish. Isn't it wonderful? In no time at all, I'll be able to speak your language. Aren't you proud of me?"

"But . . . orange? Isn't that a strange place to start?"

Fernando picked an orange from the basket on the table. "I decided to start with everything in this cabin, Capitán," he explained. "It is more practical that way."

Esteban took the orange and tossed it into the air. "You are always practical, Fernando," he teased. "But you did not seek my permission to teach Shona Spanish. Have you forgotten your position aboard this ship?"

Fernando's flush deepened, but his pale eyes were steady as he studied Esteban. "I will never forget my position, Capitán," he answered seriously. "I beg your forgiveness for my oversight. May I take my leave now?"

Shona threw herself into Esteban's arms. "Oh, don't blame him, it was my fault!" she cried. "I wanted something to pass the time. I forgot all about his other duties. Please don't punish him, Stephen. If you must take it out on someone, take it out on me."

Her trembling lips were so desirable, Esteban had to restrain himself from kissing her deeply. Instead, he pulled her close and stroked her back. "There, there, I am not going to punish anyone." He raised her chin and kissed her lightly upon the tip of the nose. "I think it's an excellent idea. I was only making light with you."

She jerked away and stood glaring up at him, hands on hips. "You are insufferable, you . . . you . . . ." His right eyebrow arched dangerously and she finished weakly, *"Hijo* of . . . of Don de Larra."

He threw back his head and laughed. "Yes, I am the son of Don de Larra, though I have never heard it put exactly that way." When tears rose to her eyes, he hugged her to him and

131

mumbled into her hair, "I am very, very proud of you, *mi amora*. You may continue your studies with my blessing."

"Oh, Stephen, you are wonderful! I will study very hard. Every day!"

"Your studies must end for now, *querida,* for I have come to take you up on deck. I have flagged the *Loretta* to our side. The merchant ship with her full hold is lagging far behind. The *Loretta* has much more sail and is having a hard time staying back with us. I am going to instruct Munroe to go on to Louisiana at his own pace. He can snoop around the shore and wait for us to catch up. And then, together, we will wait for the merchant."

"But, won't that be dangerous?" Fernando asked. "We will all be at the mercy of the British and French without escorts."

Esteban sighed and shook his head. "It was a hard decision to make. But I feel it is the right one. Both the merchant and the *Nancy* are of British design. With English-speaking crews we can bluff our way through an encounter with the enemy. But the *Loretta,* with her high quarter-deck, is obviously a Spanish ship. She must have room to maneuver. With her large number of cannon, she can take care of any problems, short of being completely surrounded by enemy ships."

"Then you intend to continue flying the Colonial flag?"

"Of course. And I have further instructed our crew to don the Colonial clothing we took. There is no reason to fear for our safety. I have taken every precaution."

"Then I must go and change my clothing. Do I have your permission to retire, Capitán?"

Esteban nodded. "Of course. Oh, and Fernando, you may spend the mornings and early afternoons instructing Señorita Cameron in Spanish. But I trust you will not reveal any secrets concerning my boyhood. I know you have a long memory."

Fernando saluted. "Of course not, Capitán," he said briskly. But as he left the cabin, his broad grin belied his words of promise.

Shona hugged Esteban and rested her head upon his chest.

"Oh, you are wonderful," she said. "I thought I would go crazy with nothing to do all day. Now I can keep busy."

"Just as long as you are not too tired to welcome me warmly when I return to the cabin every evening."

"I have worked hard all day with my first lesson. Do you want me to prove how warmly I can welcome you?"

"I would like nothing better." He sighed. "But I am afraid it will have to wait until later, dear one. Right now, I have a surprise for you."

"Another surprise? Oh, Stephen, I don't need another gown. And if you give me any more jewels, I will be so weighted down I will not be able to walk."

"It's a different kind of surprise. Sit down here and listen to me."

He took her hands and looked at her seriously. "Remember how we argued about you not learning to use the sword?"

She nodded and opened her mouth to speak, but he hushed her.

"Not now. Hear me out first. I have been thinking about what you said. I fear a sword would not offer you the protection you seek. A man's arms are much longer, and he is able to endure a long duel with more ease than a woman. But I am going to give you a skill no man would suspect of a woman. I am going to teach you to use a *pistola*."

"A pistol! Oh, that's marvelous! I have always wanted to use a firearm!"

He pulled her to her feet and patted her on the bottom. "Your first lesson will take place tomorrow afternoon. But now I want you to come on deck with me. The *Loretta* will be sending a longboat, and I want you at my side."

"But won't your crew object? I mean, I have always heard that having a woman aboard is supposed to be bad luck."

"They were all so entranced by your beauty, I have been bombarded with questions as to your next appearance. And besides, my men are not superstitious. They put their trust in God, where it belongs. Now, wipe that smudge of ink from your

133

cheek and come. We must make haste."

When Shona stepped out onto the deck, she was delighted to find the sun shining. As she followed Esteban across the deck, a soft breeze played with her hair, teasing the little curls about her face. She caught the admiring stares of the men and, for one of the rare times in her life, became flustered with embarrassment.

The *Loretta* lay a quarter of a league off the starboard bow, and she was breathtakingly beautiful, her white sails standing out against the soft blue of the sky. Shona could see the longboat making its way across the sea toward them. Small white horses rode the crests of the choppy waves and Laughing Gulls swooped over the sea, their raucous "ha-ha-ha's" punctuating their flights.

Shona gazed at Esteban, her heart swelling with happiness. He had never looked more handsome. Beneath the black coat, his shoulders were square and strong, and the ruffles at his throat and cuffs were sparkling white. His slim breeches and snowy white stockings accentuated his wide-legged stance, and his blond hair, caught back by a narrow black riband, was ruffled by the breeze. When he turned and smiled down at her, she was reminded of her first impression of him. Devil indeed! Oh, he was proud—haughty even—and he could be cruel, but never with those he loved. And love shone deeply in his azure eyes as he looked at her. No, Esteban de Larra, commodore of the Spanish mission to the Colonies, bearer of letters of marque from King Fernando of Spain, was no devil.

A feeling of love washed over her, causing her to tremble. His smile vanished.

"Are you cold, *querida?*" he asked, frowning. "I will have Fernando fetch your shawl."

"No, I'm not cold, Stephen," she answered breathlessly. "I just realized how much you mean to me." She gasped at what she had just revealed. What had happened to her plans for the future? She could not be in love—she would not allow it, for it was not in her plan! She was astounded when a look much like

134

pain passed over his features.

"You are fast becoming my life," he said so softly that she could barely hear the words. Then his look of distress disappeared and they were caught up in activity as Captain Munroe and his men were hauled aboard the *Nancy*.

As the two captains conferred at length, however, Shona could not forget that look. What had it meant? Did Stephen regret becoming involved with her? Was he having second thoughts about being entangled with an indentured slave? He had made her understand that he did not appreciate her lapses into vulgarity when she became angry. Was he thinking that he could not tolerate the time it would take her to learn not to express herself in that way? And how would she feel if he pushed her aside now?

She stood looking out over the sea as the men talked, her mind a welter of confusing, painful thoughts. She had never imagined that she could fall so hopelessly in love so quickly. After all, he was her captor! And a Spaniard! He was proud. He was ruthless. He was the enemy! A picture of her grandfather's wise face swam before her eyes. "You canna marry for ought but luv," he had told her often. "Marriage wi'out luv is like brose wi'out sugarolly, it'll stick in your thrapple, no pass further, 'til you're forced to spit it oot."

She was in a predicament, for she could not ignore what she was feeling for Stephen. He was passionate and capable of infinite tenderness. He was extremely intelligent, and loyal to his country and its causes. And he loved her, she was sure of that.

The wind shifted, and she was able to hear some of the men's conversation. Curious, she sidled closer, hoping since they were looking out at the sea toward the *Loretta*, that they would not turn and discover her presence. She was startled to hear her own name.

"When are you going to get rid of Miss Cameron?" Captain Munroe asked Stephen. "Or have you changed your mind about putting that little piece of baggage ashore?"

Shona's hand flew to her mouth. She held her breath, desperately wanting to hear Stephen's reply, yet dreading it.

De Larra sighed deeply. "I don't know. I have half decided to wait until we reach Louisiana. It would be cruel to land her in Spanish-held territory."

"You think she'll fare better with the French? Or have you, perhaps, decided to take her back to Spain with you? I seem to recall hearing something about a certain Spanish beauty . . ."

Shona did not wait to hear Stephen's reply. She whirled about and stumbled toward the hatch, her heart beating a frantic tattoo, her eyes blinded by tears.

Stephen did not see her leave the deck. He was too incensed by Joseph Munroe's prying questions. "None of this is your affair!" he barked harshly. "What I do is none of your concern!"

Munroe backed away from de Larra's stabbing forefinger. "Whatever you say, Commodore," he said quickly. "If there is nothing more to discuss, I will take my leave. May you have fair winds and calm waters. I'll see you in Louisiana."

De Larra's return salute was stiff. Since he had not given vent to his bitter rage, his lips were a thin slash on his pale face as he watched Munroe climb down the rope to his longboat. His knuckles were white as he gripped the railing, cursing under his breath the English captain who had inadvertently opened the door to a decision he did not want to face. He stared out over the sea, presumably watching the departing longboat, but in reality, seeing nothing.

What had happened to turn his entire life into a tangled web of confusion and indecision? What had become of that other Esteban de Larra—proud, sure of himself, dead set in his determination to fulfill his solemn vow to return to Inez with enough wealth to convince her once and for all of his love.

Worst of all, what had become of that love? Though he could still recall Inez's pale, composed face with affection, the memory of the promise lurking behind those slightly pouting lips no longer filled his body with the same burning desire.

136

Now, another face pushed the pale one aside. Shona. *Dios*, he was completely under her spell! While life with Inez would be serene, he now found himself wondering if her piety would come between them in their bed. He could never imagine Inez allowing herself to indulge in the wild abandonment Shona brought to their lovemaking. How could Inez, that sheltered pious girl, ever allow herself to lose the genteel training that had been drummed into her?

And even more important, Inez did not possess one small part of Shona's inquisitive, devil-may-care nature. Life with Inez would be predictable, dull even, but life with Shona would be one adventure after another.

He sighed deeply. It was obvious he would have to make a decision soon. He was not being fair to either woman as things stood. But he had known Shona for only a few weeks. He had loved Inez since he was a child. . . .

Shona paced the confines of the cabin, her hands clenched, her chest heaving with sobs. That bloody Spanish bastard! He had been playing with her all along, intending to put her ashore when he tired of her! He had never loved her, it had all been a sham, a convenient way for him to have a good toss in bed! She threw her bolster to the floor and stomped it. Would she never learn? Why had she allowed herself to be duped? And by a proud, haughty, evil, heathen Spaniard, at that! Her father had been right, and she had been a total fool!

She eyed Stephen's clothing which hung on pegs. Suddenly, she raced to the wall and jerked the uniforms into her arms. "I'll show you, you bastard!" she screamed. "I'll show you that you can't treat a Cameron that way! You'll never touch me again!" She opened the door and threw the clothing into the passageway. Then she scooped up his books and the ship's log and added them to the pile. She searched frantically through the cabin, tossing all of his belongings out into the hallway until it was strewn with everything he owned.

When she could no longer find anything else to throw, she slammed the door, turned the key in the lock, and stepped over to the porthole. She removed the cover, wanting the breeze to cool her sweating face. Her entire body trembled, and her legs felt as though they would give way any moment. The violent activity had burned her anger into a tiny cinder flickering uncertainly inside her heart. It was being replaced by a pain so great, she doubled over. Why? Why had he made her believe he cared? She stumbled over to the bunk and collapsed, burying her face in the mattress. He would pay! Oh, by all that was holy, she would make him pay! If only she had a knife, she would use it to cut out his heart as he had cut out hers!

Suddenly, she sat up and lurched to her feet. She would use his cutlass, the one she had thrown into the passageway! She turned the key and threw open the door.

Stephen stood just outside, his eyes wide as he viewed the destruction about him.

"Shona, what the hell—?"

She immediately tried to pull the door closed but she could not match his strength. He forced the door open and grabbed her arms. "What is going on?" he demanded. "What are you doing?"

His fingers dug into her arms, but she did not feel pain, only the warmth of his touch. No! She would not allow herself to melt into his arms. He had used her. He had toyed with her like a cat toys with a mouse. She kicked at his legs and writhed, trying to escape his grasp.

"Let me go, you bloody bastard!" she screamed. "You vile pig of a Spaniard!"

His cheeks blanched as though they were white flesh over bone, and he released her arm and drew back his hand. Yet she stood facing him resolutely, her chest heaving, her eyes blazing.

"Go on," she prodded. "Hit me! Or would you rather choke me again? You seemed to enjoy it so much the first time!"

She was totally unprepared for his reaction. His hand

138

stopped in midair, then dropped to his side. *"Mi amora,"* he said, "I vowed by the Virgin never to touch you again in anger, and I almost broke my vow."

His reaction startled her so, her anger disappeared completely. It was replaced by a dark, aching void. Though he offered a safe, comfortable harbor, she could not allow herself to be charmed by him.

"Don't touch me," she whispered. "You have betrayed me. I heard what was said on deck. Please leave me alone."

At the pain in his eyes, her first impulse was to offer him comfort, but she stood firm, determined to salvage what little there was left of her pride—of her dignity.

"You wanted me to believe your lies until the very last." She was amazed at how calm her voice sounded, how controlled.

He reached for her, but she backed away, shaking her head.

"No. Your little game is over. The mouse has decided not to nibble at the bait any longer."

"Allow me," he said gravely, with just a touch of irony, "a chance to explain."

She turned her back and walked slowly to the bunk. Wondering all the while at the calmness which had settled over her, she sat, folded her hands in her lap, and raised her eyes.

"Then speak," she said. "And this time, I hope you will have the decency to tell me everything. I deserve the truth."

He stood for a moment, his head bowed. Then he raised his chin and his eyebrow rose imperiously. "I did think about putting you ashore when we were back at Brunswick," he said evenly. "It is not my custom to take female prisoners, no matter what the circumstances. But I delayed and then the storm came, and we had to sail with the tide." He began to pace the room, his hands clasped behind his back. "Then I toyed with the idea of putting you on one of the offshore islands, but the opportunity never presented itself. And the longer I delayed, the more impossible it became to send you ashore. So I began to think about taking you with me to Louisiana." He stopped pacing and whirled to face her. "I know you think it

139

was selfish, but I . . . couldn't bear to think of never seeing you again."

He stopped before her. "I suppose I've grown to love you, Shona," he said simply. He reached for her hands and pulled them to his chest. "I have put off time and time again making the decision, but I still cannot bear to lose you."

When he pressed his mouth to the back of her hand, she pulled away and clasped her fingers tightly in her lap.

"And the Spanish 'beauty'?" she asked, her voice choked by the wild beating of her heart. "Is she your wife?"

He looked up, surprise glinting in his brilliant blue eyes. "My wife? No! What kind of man do you think I am? I may do many things that are wrong, but I am not that despicable!"

"Then who is she? And what does she mean to you?"

After a moment, he replied. "While I was growing up in Valencia, there was an adjoining estate, belonging to the Muñoz family. There were two children, a son Francisco and a daughter Inez. Though Francisco and I were childhood friends, something happened when we reached manhood and we became bitter enemies. Then Don and Doña Muñoz died during an epidemic, and Inez was left alone because Francisco had joined the Spanish Navy. It was only natural that I was thrown together with her, even more natural that I should become very fond of her . . . she is a beautiful, gentle, shy girl."

Shona nodded. At last, she felt he was telling her the truth, and even though it was painful, it was better than lies.

"So, Inez and I became betrothed. But when Francisco heard of it, he was adamant that we not marry. He planted worries in Inez's mind about my lack of money, even though she knows I will inherit the family estate some day. That is why I embarked upon this mission. To prove to Inez that I could care for her by returning with enough gold to satisfy her fears. Do you understand?"

Shona nodded. Oh, yes, she understood. Wasn't that her own goal, to find a man of substance, one who would ensure a

140

good future? She nodded again, signifying that he should continue.

Stephen looked up at her, and she recognized the deep pain mirrored in his eyes. She did not draw back when he reached out and stroked her cheek.

"And then I met you. You were so beautiful, under all that filth, so young and filled with life; and you were so brave. I did not mean to take you that first time—I still regret forcing myself upon you—and then I almost killed you with my bare hands!"

Suddenly, he pulled her into his arms. She did not pull away, for a great peace was beginning to settle itself over her.

"I don't understand how you can love me after what I did to you," he groaned.

"Don't," Shona soothed. "I do love you, with all of my heart." There, she had said it! She had taken that first step; she had committed herself to a course that she had been taught was wrong, all wrong.

"I did not want to fall in love with you," he said. "I fought hard not to, but I could not help myself. You are everything I have ever wanted in a woman. You are brave and proud. You are passionate and so filled with every womanly quality, I carry a picture of you painted on the backs of my eyelids all day, every day."

Shona did not want to ask, but she knew she must. "And Inez?" she whispered, choking on the sobs filling her breast. "What about Inez?"

"She has paled to a mere ghost in my memory," he replied. "But I cannot do what I wish without telling her first."

"What you wish?"

He held her against him, and she could feel the wild beating of his heart. "I wish to take you back to Spain with me. I wish to present you to my parents and to Juana as my dearest beloved betrothed. I wish to have the banns announced in the cathedral in Valencia, and then . . . I wish to make you my wife."

Shona gasped as his lips met hers. His wife! Her father's words of caution echoed through her mind. "Marry a man of substance. If you are fortunate and love comes later, so much the better, but remember, beloved daughter, marry a man of substance!" She groaned as his tongue entwined with hers. By Stephen's own words, he had no wealth of his own. But he had position . . . and when his parents died . . . She pulled away and looked up into his face, her heart swelling with the love she could not control even if she wished. Perhaps her father had been wrong. Perhaps her grandfather, that wise, craggy old man of the Highlands had offered the best advice: wed for love and love only!

Stephen led her to the bed, his hands pulling impatiently at her clothing. As he undressed her, she suddenly realized that she was on her own now—it no longer mattered what the men in her family had advised, for one was dead and the other as lost to her as though he were dead also. She found her own trembling fingers fumbling at Stephen's shirt laces, and she knew with a certainty there could be no turning back. She was committed. She could never bear to part with him. She loved him far too much.

Love welled up in her breast until it took complete control of her mind and body, and she found herself the aggressor. She slipped his shirt over his head and peeled down his breeches, then lay for a moment, savoring the sight of his magnificent body. The muscles of his chest rippled over his lean flesh. She ran her fingers lightly over his tight belly, then tangled them in the curly hair at his groin. She caressed his aroused manhood, the flesh hot and pulsing inside her palm. He groaned as she fondled him, her other hand moving in lazy, enticing circles over his buttocks.

Then his lips sought hers, but she pulled away, shaking her head with a slow, flirtatious smile. Her lips lightly caressed his forehead, his flushed cheeks, his cleft chin. Then she nibbled delicately on his earlobes before thrusting her tongue, in soft little stabs, into his right ear.

"You are a *bruja*—a witch!" he gasped.

She laughed, delighted. "Of course," she purred wickedly. "And I am weaving a spell you can never escape."

She rubbed her hands down his arms, his chest, his thighs, brushing ever so lightly over his manhood, and she followed her trailing fingers with her tongue, flicking it in and out over his flesh until his entire body was flushed and burning with desire. Then she loosened her hair from its riband and allowed it to ripple over his chest and belly as she moved her head back and forth, the curls slipping and sliding over his taut flesh in delicate circles as her fingers worked their magic.

Finally, she positioned herself over him, moving her golden wedge enticingly over his throbbing manhood. Then, with a triumphant cry, she lowered herself onto his hot, velvety lance.

When his hips thrust upward, she cried out with utter rapture. She leaned over and crushed his lips with her own, her tongue stabbing into his mouth to match each thrust of his hips. When he embraced her, trying to regain the initiative, she suddenly pulled away, grinning wickedly as her circling tongue replaced the moist, warm inner flesh of her body. He groaned loudly, his hands grasping at her elusive breasts, as she sucked lightly on his throbbing flesh, her tongue flicking in and out in maddening circles. When she felt a tremor run through his body, she mounted him again, guiding him inside, riding, riding until her own flesh turned to liquid gold, melting, running hot in sensual streams of wild passion.

Again she forced herself to withdraw. Again she enticed him with her tongue until his gasps broke the silence of the cabin. But when she mounted him this time, she allowed the sensations washing over her own body to control her movements, maneuvering rhythmically until she felt herself rise to heights always before out of reach.

The volcanic torrent building inside her erupted violently, spewing rivers of exquisite delight throughout her entire being. She felt herself arch backward as she cried out, realizing

143

with only a tiny part of her mind that Stephen's cry was blending with her own. Then she collapsed over him, her limbs twitching, her breath coming in gasps.

He softly caressed her, his whispered endearments guiding her gentle return to reality. "I will never escape your spell, nor do I wish to," he murmured.

He slid out from beneath her and cradled her in his arms. "May I take what we have just experienced as an answer to my proposal of marriage?"

She smiled and snuggled closer. "Of course," she said simply.

He closed his eyes and soon his chest rose and fell with the gentle breath of slumber. But as sleep fought to claim Shona, the specter of Inez rose before her eyes, nebulous and undefined, but she pushed it aside and returned her thoughts to Stephen, and to their future together. Shona realized now that she had never felt so fulfilled in her entire life. She smiled softly. Perhaps there was a God after all. Perhaps he sat on his great white throne chuckling even now. Perhaps this had been his plan all along.

Chapter 12

The following days were so filled with activity and happiness, Shona seldom thought about Inez Muñoz. Fernando was an excellent tutor and within two weeks, Shona was putting entire sentences together in Spanish. Her only regret was her own reluctance to ask Fernando to teach her phrases she could use to show her love for Stephen. Instead, she decided to copy what he was saying, but this proved to be a problem.

"You are my *querida*," she said one night as they lay entwined upon the bed.

She was hurt when he raised up on one elbow and began to laugh. "I should hope not," he said.

"But you call me that all the time! Surely it isn't something nasty. I always thought you were saying something loving."

He pulled her close and nuzzled her cheek. "I am. I am calling you my darling. But you have used the feminine ending. If you want to call me your darling in my language, you have to change it to *querido*."

She bit his lip and pulled away, but not quickly enough to escape his grasp. *"Querido, querido, querido!"* she mimicked. Then his lips claimed hers and the Spanish lesson was forgotten as their passion overcame them.

Stephen was quick to keep his promise to teach her to use

the pistol. The first time, she was uncharacteristically shy when she realized all of the crew were watching her. But her discomfort was replaced with concentration as the lesson began. To her delight, she proved to have a natural eye, and in no time she was placing the balls squarely in the middle of the red pennant fluttering from the taffrail. Every time she hit the mark, the men raised a mighty shout, and her cheeks flushed at their approbation.

"You are changing my men's thoughts about what a woman is capable of," Stephen told her one night. "They have been raised to believe a woman can only bear children, keep a household in order, and attend Mass. I am afraid they will all return home expecting their women to be excellent marksmen."

"Is that so bad? Isn't it about time women were recognized as having many of the abilities men have always thought were theirs alone?"

"Of course it isn't bad. The only problem is that most women don't share your talents."

"Scottish women do."

"Why haven't I known about this before? I would never have wasted my time mooning about over Spanish women."

Shona caught her breath. Was he still thinking of Inez?

He must have seen the worry in her eyes, for he embraced her instantly and his lips were quick to bring reassurance. When their kiss ended, he removed his signet ring from his little finger and placed it on the ring finger of her left hand.

"I have been meaning to give you this token of my love for some time."

Shona turned her hand, admiring the heavy gold band with three circles entwined upon it. "What do the circles mean?"

"It is the family crest, and is so old I don't think anyone really knows anymore. My father always says it means unity . . . oneness."

"As we are one?"

"Yes, *mi amora*, as we are one, and will always and forever be one."

As the *Nancy* approached the coast near St. Augustine, there were only two clouds to mar Shona's life. The first was Lieutenant Perez. Though he kept to his own quarters when not on duty, he was always on deck when Stephen gave her the promised pistol lessons. She could feel his cold black eyes watching her every move. At times her discomfort was so great, she called upon all the self-control she possessed to prevent turning and discharging the ball directly at him. He hated her and she knew it; and she was powerless to overcome her foreboding of evil. Lieutenant Perez was biding his time. She was sure he would not allow the voyage to end without taking revenge for his shame.

The second dark cloud was a literal one. The fog. Every night, as darkness settled over the sea, a heavy blanket of moisture blinded the helmsman, making progress fraught with danger. At first, Stephen left the cabin and paced the deck, slapping his fist into his palm as he railed at the fates. But after a week of such nightly fogs, he relaxed and ordered the ship to heave to until dawn. Granted, they could not make the progress he wished, but at least the fog hid them from the British who were making great inroads in plying the waters off of this Spanish-held territory.

It was after one such fog-shrouded night that Shona's blissful world was turned upside down. Stephen left the cabin earlier than usual to make sure the ship would be well on its way as soon as the fog lifted, and shortly after his departure, Shona was awakened by a loud commotion on deck. She hurriedly donned a gown. Then, without thinking why, she grabbed the pistol she had been using for practice and raced to the ladder. When she reached the deck, the men were all standing quietly at the port railing, staring out over the sea

147

through wisps of white fog.

Esteban saw her and motioned her to stay where she was. She hid the pistol in the folds of her gown and stood still, hugging her arms against the early morning chill, resenting his order. She wanted to see too! Moments later, Fernando made his way to her side.

"You must not come to the railing, *señorita*," he said with great seriousness. "There may be trouble."

"What kind of trouble? What's going on? What are the men looking at?"

Fernando's eyes were troubled as he met her gaze. "It is the *Loretta*. She is drifting just off our port side, her sails tattered, her cannon still exposed in her gun ports. She has obviously been involved in a battle."

Shona gasped. "A battle! But Stephen told me the Spanish held this territory! And what of her crew?"

He shook his head wearily. "We do not know. It is true we Spanish hold this coast, but the British have been trying for years to take it from us. As for the crew, the *Loretta* appears to be deserted. There is no sign of life upon her decks."

Shona pushed him aside and started across the deck to see for herself, but he quickly grasped her arm and pulled her to a stop. "Please obey the *capitán* this time," he said urgently. "He has enough on his mind right now. You will only be in his way."

Shona gritted her teeth—Oh, why did she have to be a woman—but she obeyed Fernando. This apparently was a very serious situation, and she did not want to distract Stephen from his duties.

He was deep in conversation with Lieutenant Perez and several of the older men, and Shona watched them intently, aware that they seemed to be having an argument.

"What are they talking about, Fernando? They can't seem to agree."

"They are talking about whether to approach her now or wait until later."

148

"But if she's deserted, there can't be any danger, can there? Surely they must see if there are any survivors!"

"It could be a trap."

"A trap! By whom? You said yourself there was no one on deck!"

Fernando sighed deeply. "That does not mean she is unmanned, *señorita*," he said with great patience. "If she was overcome by the enemy, by the British or the French, for example, they could be hiding below decks, just waiting for us to board her."

"But where is their ship, then? They couldn't have appeared out of nowhere."

"That is why there is the argument. The *capitán*, he wants to wait and approach later in the morning. The others insist that he should board her immediately in case some of the crew might still be alive."

"What do you think, Fernando? Should they wait or board now?"

He sighed again, his forehead wrinkling with doubt. "I do not know. But I am inclined to agree with Esteban. He has an uncanny knack for knowing what to do when trouble strikes."

"Why don't they just ready the cannon and then board? Stephen has told me many times that the *Nancy* is well armed."

"The cannon would be useless in such a situation. You see, they must have range to be effective. No, once we board her, it will be only pistols and knives."

Shona shivered. Pistols and knives. Thank God she had brought her pistol with her! But she realized she must keep it hidden at all costs. If Stephen knew she was armed, he would insist she return to the cabin, as would Fernando should he see her pistol. She wanted to stay with Stephen.

The clutch of men broke up and she realized that Stephen must have won the argument, for the others wandered back across the ship, shuffling their feet and whispering amongst themselves. All but Perez, who still stood at the railing. Suddenly, he turned and looked squarely at her. She could not believe the arrogant hosility of his gaze. When he smiled, she shivered uncontrollably. His smile was a sneer expressing absolute hatred.

She was still trembling when Stephen made his way to her side. The small crescent scar on his cheekbone stood out stark white against his tan skin, and his eyes were so dark they no longer appeared blue.

"Fernando has told you?"

"Yes. What are you going to do?"

"We are going to wait awhile, prepare our cannon in case it is a trap, and then move in. Once we get close, the cannon will be useless, of course, but we must try to save this ship. I will prepare my crew for any eventuality. And I will lead them."

The pistol dropped from Shona's numb hand as she threw herself into his arms. "Stephen, you can't!" she wailed. "You are too valuable! Don't take any chances. Let that dreadful Perez lead them."

"What are you doing with that thing? *Por Dios*, Shona, can you not leave the fighting to the men?"

She grasped his hands and pulled his arms about her. "Not if you are going to be in danger. I'm going to fight with you!"

He pulled away and scooped the pistol from the deck, sticking it into his waistband. "You will not!" he shouted, oblivious to the stares of the men on deck.

"But you said we were one! If we are one, I cannot allow you to fight without—"

He reached out and muffled her words with his palm. "Come. We will talk in the cabin. Must you air our private life in front of my men? You will make me the laughingstock of the entire crew."

He half-dragged her to the hatch and pushed her down the ladder. Under normal conditions, she would have reacted with an anger unmatched even by his own, but these were not normal conditions. She was frightened—not of Stephen, but *for* Stephen. She allowed him to pull her into the cabin, where he threw her into a chair and stood over her.

"Now we can talk. And when we have finished talking, I trust you will allow me to resume command of my ship!"

She was instantly contrite. He was right, of course. He was the captain, the commodore, and she was taking up his valuable time with her caterwauling. She resisted the tears that threatened and raised her face to his.

"I'm sorry, Stephen," she said quietly. "I didn't mean to embarrass you before your men. I was only concerned for your safety. You can have me flogged, if you wish."

He stared at her for a moment, his eyes wide with surprise. Then he smiled faintly. "*Querida*, it is I who must apologize. I have taken my frustration out on you, the one person in the whole world I least want to hurt."

Again, she fought against tears. He must not see her cry—not now. "I understand," she said.

Then his arms were around her, his lips seeking hers with more hunger than ever before. But when the kiss ended, she knew he must leave, and she choked down her fears.

"Go with God," she said, forcing herself to stand back.

His smile was tender. "Then you do believe in God."

"I have enjoyed the bounty of his blessings for weeks now. How could I not believe?"

He took a small gold-embellished pistol from a drawer in his desk and handed it to her. "This is for you. It has what we call the *a las tres modas*, or what others call the Miquelet lock. And here are two powder horns. The silver one is filled with the fine powder for the pan. The other has the larger grains for the barrel. You cock it by pulling this ring toward you. Then you prime the pan and flip the frizzen, this little bar, back over the pan. That done, it is ready to fire."

"But why are you giving me this now? It is far too beautiful for me! I am only a beginner!"

His smile was twisted. "You are already a better shot than many of my men. But you must remember one thing. This pistol is small, and you must not be far from your target."

She nodded, the lump in her throat choking down her words

of gratitude for the priceless gift.

"I want you to lock the door from the inside," he said sternly. "Do not open that door for anyone but me . . . or Fernando. If anyone else tries to get in, shoot through the door."

"Then you believe you are walking into a trap!"

"No. But I will not take chances with my own life. And that is what you are—my life."

He kissed her once again before leaving. She could hear his boots ringing on the ladder. Only when his last step faded did she give in to tears. She threw herself down upon the bed and sobbed uncontrollably. She had seen the lie in his eyes. He *did* think it was a trap.

Moments later, her tears spent, her face ravaged with pain, she rose from the bed and stumbled to the porthole. There she was, the *Loretta*. Would that broken, seemingly deserted ship mark the end of everything that meant anything to her? Would she have to stand at this porthole and watch the life snuffed out of her beloved?

Her eyes opened wide. Not if she had anything to do with it. Stephen had said he was taking time to prepare the cannon for firing as they sailed close to the *Loretta*. And surely in the heat of the battle—God, please don't let there be a battle—she could sneak unnoticed to the deck and place herself in a position to cover any danger Stephen might encounter.

She picked the pistol up from the bed and began to review the steps of loading and firing. Then she grabbed up her bandolier of balls, strapped the powder horns to their hooks and raced for the door. On her way down the corridor, she prayed that Perez was not in his cabin, for she planned to borrow some of his clothing.

Chapter 13

Esteban's mind was in turmoil as he raced up the companionway ladder. Though his entire life had been a preparation for leadership, he had never known he would be so overwhelmed by the magnitude of command. On the one hand, it was his responsibility to see his ship and crew safely through any adversity they might encounter before returning to their home port. But added to this burden was his consuming fear that something might happen to Shona. He knew the fear was irrational, yet he could not relieve it with logic. She was his woman—his life—and, as wrong as it might seem to the military mind, her safety took precedence over everything and everyone else.

His face was grim as he walked quickly around the gun crews, watching closely as they manned their cannons. His eyes darted from cartridge, wad, and shot being loaded to the wire being dropped down the vent to make sure the cartridge was rammed home correctly. He heard the order "Run out," and watched the men haul at the side tackles, the guns moving forward until their muzzles protruded beyond the gun ports. He watched the cannons primed and the pans closed just before the order "Point" was screamed by the gun-crew captain. But as the handspikemen and side-tackle men trained to the left or right to adjust the elevation, his mind wandered and he was transported back to his own cabin, Shona in his arms.

Madre de Dios, he could not bear the thought of Shona

153

injured—or dead! He shivered as darkness covered his soul, blotting out the shimmering sun and the men scurrying about the deck. He had never believed it possible that any one woman could so completely control his every waking thought. He had imagined himself in love with Inez, but that had been a simple boyish infatuation compared to what he felt for Shona. He closed his eyes, and instantly a picture of her leaped to his mind: the sunlight playing upon her golden hair, sparking it with highlights of copper; her yellow eyes, darkened by brown flecks, dancing beneath winged brows; her straight nose, the nostrils slightly flared with desire; her full lips parted, waiting breathlessly for the touch of his own; her body trembling as it poised for his touch; but strangely, even more important, her bright, inquisitive mind seeking and probing for information. He had never known that a woman could have such a mind. It fit his own as a comfortable glove fits the hand of its owner. He groaned and threw back his head. Was there something more he could have done to assure her safety? He looked at Mendoza handing out powder and shot and took a step in his direction. Then he stopped and whirled about, his eyes seeking the derelict *Loretta*. It was no use. If he sent Mendoza to stay with Shona, he would be short one more man on deck, and he needed every man he had. If his fears proved correct, they were heading into a trap, and the *Nancy* was not as heavily armed as the *Loretta*.

He raised his glass and studied the derelict's powder-blackened sails and the cannons still standing in their gun ports. Then he ran the glass over each mast, each sail, hoping to find a clue as to what had happened. But, other than the tattered sails, there was no sign of damage. He knew it was a trap. He smelled it, he felt it in the marrow of his bones. But there was nothing he could do that he had not already set into motion, nor could he leave a sister ship to the mercy of the seas without investigating the fate of her crew.

*   *   *

154

Shona's hands were shaking as she wound her braided hair about her head and donned a heavy woolen cap. She was tempted to run back to her cabin to check her image in the mirror, but she did not have time. She looked down at the hastily rolled up breeches and the shirt hanging below her hips. Even though Perez was not a tall man, his clothes were much too large for her small-boned body. She tied a kerchief around her neck and knotted it high under her chin. She knew her pale complexion would stand out among the suntanned faces of the crew like a flea on a shaved dog! She wet her hands in the bucket of stale drinking water, then wiped them quickly on the floorboards. Gritting her teeth in disgust, she smudged the dirt across her cheeks and forehead, not forgetting her chin and the tip of her nose.

She was priming her pistol when a sudden lurch sent her reeling against the bunk. The ship was moving! She braced herself against the wall and carefully primed each cartridge of her bandolier with an explosive charge sufficient for one shot. She cursed the time this took, but she knew it was necessary to be prepared to discharge the pistol more than once.

Oh, God, if there was just some way to know that everything was going to turn out all right! She took up her bandolier, tucked her pistol into her waistband, and tore down the companionway.

She chose the aft ladder, having decided there would be less activity around that hatch than the one farther forward. She climbed slowly, her heart in her throat, her breath coming in gasps. What if one of the men recognized her? Worse yet, what if Stephen saw her? She gulped as she stuck her head out into the open, her muscles coiled for a quick retreat, her eyes darting around the deck.

She needn't have worried about discovery. Every man was at his station and far too engrossed in preparation for battle to be looking about. The gun crews knelt on the deck beside their cannons, their captains pulling the trigger lines taught, ready to jerk at the command to fire. The rest of the crew lined the

155

rails, armed with pistols and knives.

She chanced a quick look at the quarter-deck, but Stephen was nowhere insight. It was Perez who stood beside the helmsman, his legs set apart, his shoulders stiff with pride, his face grimacing in what she supposed was a smile. Where was Stephen? She crept frantically up onto the deck and crouched low, searching for those broad black-clothed shoulders which would stand taller than any other.

Then she saw him. He was pressed into a crowd at the bow, his glass trained upon the *Loretta*. She spied a cluster of powder monkeys standing just behind him and gathered herself for a dash across the deck to join them. But at that instant Stephen turned and threw out a hand to Perez. The helmsman whirled the wheel sharply to the port and the ship slowed and began a wide circling turn.

The silence on deck was complete, the tension in the air so palpable Shona could feel it wrap itself about her chest like a tight wire, making it difficult to draw a breath. She crouched, frozen to her spot.

When she heard noises overhead, she looked up and saw men deftly reefing sails to slow the ship's headlong plunge. Then the *Loretta* hove into view and she gasped at the blackened holes in the once-proud ship's canvas.

Suddenly, her eyes widened in disbelief. As she watched, the Spanish colors were struck from the *Loretta*'s mast and a leering skull and crossbones was hauled up in its place. Stephen was right! It *was* a trap!

On the *Nancy*, the gun crews hauled their now useless cannons back in and armed themselves for hand-to-hand battle. As Shona readied herself again for a dash across the deck, she was stopped by a grating jar as the two ships collided. Thrown backward against the ladder housing, she felt her breath leave her in a rush. Momentarily stunned, she rubbed her aching ribs and readjusted the bandolier across her shoulder.

The boarding net was lowered and grappling hooks were

156

tossed and secured. Suddenly, the deck erupted into pandemonium. As screaming, rushing men fought to be first over the rail, Shona leaped to her feet and ran forward, her hand reaching for her pistol. She rammed a cartridge into the barrel as she ran, trying to keep her eyes upon Stephen who had disappeared onto the deck of the *Loretta*. But when she reached the side, she was pushed backward by a burly sailor brandishing a long knife.

"*Alto!*" she heard him shout as she fell. Her pistol was knocked from her hand, and she scrambled for it. Scooping it up, she reached for her powder horn and pressed herself against the planking to steady her hands as she primed the barrel. She heard gunfire and hair-raising screams, and her heart leaped into her throat. Stephen was in danger!

She pulled herself to her feet and scrambled over the railing onto the *Loretta*'s deck—right into a scene from hell. Filthy, ghastly-looking men brandishing knives and pistols were pouring up onto the deck from the open companionways. They screamed and shouted, "*Arm! Arm!*" as they fired and hacked their way across the planking. Shona pressed into the crowd of men, her pistol in her hand, as she frantically looked for Stephen.

Suddenly, a man beside her gurgled and dropped, bright red blood gushing out of his throat to splash her face and shoulders. Bile rose to her mouth, but she clenched her teeth and pushed forward, intent only upon reaching Stephen's side. There was a loud explosion, then another man fell against her, knocking her to her knees. She heard a triumphant shout and looked up just in time to see a huge curved knife poised over her head. She raised her pistol, but before she could pull the trigger, the knife and hand disappeared as one of the *Nancy*'s crewmen brought his own knife to bear. A red haze washed before her eyes as her rescuer plunged his knife deep into the throat of the attacker.

She smiled a grim smile of thanks when she realized that she was looking into the horrified gray eyes of Mendoza. His mouth formed the word "Madonna" just before he was shoved violently away.

Shona pulled herself to her feet. There had to be some way to reach Stephen's side! She backed away and began to skirt the mass of men locked in combat, her pistol ready, her finger on the trigger. Her arm was jerked to one side and she whirled, ready to fire.

"Madonna!"

Mendoza was pulling her backward, away from the battle!

"No!" she screamed. "I must find Stephen!"

"Please!" Mendoza screamed. "For the love of God! Please, Madonna, come away!"

Shona jerked her arm away and whirled, ready to continue her search. Then she heard a loud explosion and as she looked back, a crimson splotch appeared on Mendoza's shirt. He sagged slowly to the deck, his hands still reaching out to her. She heard an exultant cry and found herself staring directly into the black eyes of Juan Perez!

"So!" he screamed. "One protector is dead! Now for de Larra!"

She looked at the smoking pistol in his hand. Perez had killed Fernando! She raised her pistol and aimed it directly at his face.

At that instant, she was knocked from her feet by another falling body, and her pistol discharged. When she regained her feet, Perez had disappeared into the mass of men locked in combat.

She retched as she pulled herself over to the railing. He'd said he was going to kill Stephen! She gulped in great gasps of air, and a strange calm fell over her as she reloaded her pistol. Her hands were steady as she pulled back on the ring and primed the pan, her heart frozen with purpose as she rammed the shot into the barrel. Perez would not destroy the only one she had left in the world. She would see him in hell first!

She tripped over the bodies of the *Nancy*'s crew as she made

158

her way toward the bow. She realized then that the *Loretta* was crawling with pirates! And they must be winning, for there were far fewer men left to do battle. She made her way carefully forward, her mind clear as she avoided the fighting men, intent upon saving her next shot for Perez.

When she reached the bow, she saw Stephen. He held a pistol in one hand and a dirk in the other, and he was using both with abandon. One of the powder monkeys crouched at his feet, loading one of his two pistols as quickly as he emptied it. She should be the one doing that! She made her way toward him, her eyes feasting upon the grace of his motions, upon his blond hair ruffled into curls by the wind.

Suddenly, Stephen saw her and his face blanched. He took a step toward her. Then she heard a hoarse, triumphant shout and tore her gaze from Stephen.

Her heart stopped beating. Perez was standing at the rail, his pistol trained on Stephen's chest. But at that instant, a pirate lunged toward Stephen, his knife raised. As Stephen parried the thrust with his own knife, Shona's scream was cut off by the sound of a loud explosion. She watched in horror as Stephen jerked backward, his hand going to his chest. A searing pain pierced her own breast as he fell, the pistol and knife rolling from his hands.

She scrambled forward, unaware of the shouts of surrender, unaware that, without their commander, the brave Spaniards, greatly outnumbered, were giving up the battle. She clawed her way through the men clustered around Stephen, and when she reached his side, she dropped to her knees and stared at the bright red stain covering his chest. She could not breathe. She could not think. She could only feel—and what she felt was her own heart being torn from her breast.

His eyelids fluttered; then he looked up at her, his eyes filled with surprise. His lips turned up in a ghost of a smile as he whispered, *"Querida."*

Suddenly, he gasped and clutched at his wound. His eyes

159

clouded and closed, and he sighed deeply.

Shona looked at the pallor of his skin, at the light brown lashes resting in half-moons upon his cheeks. She took one of his hands and pressed her lips to his palm, unaware that his blood was smearing her lips. She kissed his hand and was bending to press her lips against his when she was jerked violently backward. The cap was yanked from her head and her braids dropped over her shoulders.

"So! A lass!"

The man's voice was victorious, exultant. She stared up, into the leering face of the giant who stood over her. She was not aware of his features, only that his eyes were deep green, and that his smile was so cruel, he looked like one of the gargoyles she had seen on a castle wall.

"Bonny too, once we wash off some of that dirt." He bent over her. "Come, lass. Dinna shed any of your tears for that spawn of the devil. He's deid as a boot."

The pirate was mistaken, for Shona was not weeping. Her eyes felt as dry and hot as burning pokers, and a strange numbness was creeping up over her body, rendering her motionless and mute. She looked at the huge hand clamped over her arm, but she did not feel the fingers biting into her flesh. He dropped her arm and straightened.

"I said, get up!" he roared. "The battle's over! The Daonine Sith have left their shians and come to help us! The heathen Spaniards are defeated!"

Her numbed mind could not comprehend what he was saying. She knew he had referred to the Wee people populating the Scottish braes, but his words held no meaning. She stared up at him, her eyes glazed.

"Get up, I say!" he roared again. "I've a fancy for a braw lass like you—you've the look of the Scots about you. You'll be mine!"

"You wouldn't want her," a harsh voice broke in. "She's nothing but a *puta!*"

160

"*Puta. Whore. She lies, Capitán. She came in here to lure me to bed.*" The ice around Shona melted in a gush. She jerked her head around. Perez leaned against the railing just a few feet from her, his cruel slit of a mouth twisted into a leer.

When he met her gaze, he laughed harshly. "She's a spy!" he shouted. "And a whore! Give her to me. I know how to handle her. She'll sell herself to anyone for a peso."

"No! That is a lie!"

Shona turned toward the familiar voice. She watched in amazement as Fernando stumbled toward her, his hand pressed over the red stain covering his shoulder. "She was betrothed to our *capitán*," Fernando said, his voice a hoarse whisper. "She is a good woman . . . an honorable woman."

Joy burst through her veins in a flood. Fernando was not dead! Oh, dear God, she was not completely alone!

The giant above her was saying something, but it was not important. She had only one mission to accomplish. She placed her left hand beneath her right forearm and raised her pistol. She saw terror flicker in Perez's eyes and knew he would try to move. But he was too late. Her finger was already squeezing the trigger. His mouth opened in protest just as a tiny hole appeared between his eyes. His body jerked once as it catapulted back over the rail.

Shona lowered the pistol to the deck and stared down at Stephen's lifeless features, waiting hopefully for the giant above her to end her life so she could join Stephen. They would never be separated again.

But her death was not on the pirate's mind. He roared with laughter and slapped his leg with his huge palm. "She's got spunk, yon lass!" he shouted to his men. "She'll make me a fine woman!"

He reached down and hauled Shona to her feet. Drawing her to his hairy chest, he ground his mouth against hers. Even when her lips would not yield and her teeth remained clenched against his probing tongue, he did not lose his good humor. He

161

raised his head and laughed again. "After I've washed the heathen blude from her lips and cleaned her barkit face, I'll tame her!" he crowed. "It's better to have a lass with spunk!"

He motioned to one of his men. "Keep her cheek for chow. I've a ship to run."

Shona was pulled rudely into the grasp of the other man. Her arms were pinned harshly to her sides, and she was jerked away to a place at the rail.

The giant strode to the ladder and climbed effortlessly to the quarter-deck. There, he struck a leering, wide-stanced pose, his fists doubled on his hips, his head thrown back. "Put the longboat from their ship into the water. We'll set adrift all of these Spanish heathens what still live, just as we done to the first crew. Then take aw of value from their hold. After we've tossed all of those dead bodies into the sea—for the sharks are hungering for another meal—we'll cast off and blaw their bludy ship out of the water!"

Shona heard only a portion of what he was saying. They could not toss Stephen into the sea! She would not allow it! She pulled and writhed, trying to escape the hands imprisoning her. When she could not, she twisted around and brought her knee up into the man's groin. He uttered a shriek and dropped her arms instantly as his hands went to his throbbing member.

Shona dashed across the deck to Stephen. She knelt and lifted his head into her lap, shielding his body with her own.

But the pirate leader's rough hands soon made a mockery of her effort. She was lifted from the deck and pulled off to one side, her flailing arms as ineffectual as a bothersome fly. "He's deid!" the giant shouted at her. "We can't have him stinking up our ship!"

"Don't throw him into the sea! Please!" Shona sobbed. "He's a Christian. He deserves a decent burial."

"He's a Spanish heathen, that's what he is!" the huge man bellowed. "He's not even good enough for shark meat, though I've no other choice."

Shona would not give up. "Wait, I can prove he's a

Christian. He wears a cross around his neck. Please look. Just look, that's all I ask."

She stared up at her captor's face, her eyes wide with pleading. She knew she had won when his eyes clouded with doubt. "Please," she whimpered. "Just look for the cross. It's on a chain."

His eyes narrowed as he looked down at her. Then he nodded his head at one of his men.

In seconds, the man held the cross out to his leader who grunted and took it with a harsh laugh. "What does this prove?" He sneered. "It's probably some booty he took from a puir Christian lady he raided."

"No!" Shona exclaimed. "His mother gave it to him. He told me. Look—it has his family's crest etched into the back."

The pirate grunted again and pressed the cross into Shona's hand. "Who cares?" he asked. "You maun have it. It will na' do him any good where he's going."

Shona watched numbly as several of the pirates gathered around Stephen's body. They picked him up and dragged him across the deck, his boots making a muffled sound on the boards. When they lifted him over the rail, Shona broke away with a violent twist and went running toward him. She was too late. She watched in horror as Stephen's body plummeted into the water, sending a spray into the air.

She tried to leap after him, but was pulled backward and imprisoned once again by those huge hands. The sky began to darken, and the sounds of voices became the drone of a thousand angry bees. Shona slipped to the deck, unconscious, a vision of blood-red sea water carved into her soul.

Kenneth MacKenzie left the railing to kneel at Shona's side, a satisfied, smug smile wreathing his broad face and making his red beard jut out at a jaunty angle.

Both he and his men were unaware of the feeble struggle for life taking place in the sea beside the ship. The cold water shocked Stephen, and his eyes flew open. He gasped, sucking in water, as a tight band of panic and pain encircled his chest.

Then he writhed beneath the water and struck out with his hands and legs, trying for the surface.

Light flooded his eyes as his face broke the water. Shona. He had to get back to her! He retched as he grasped the boarding net and then floated onto his back, his sudden burst of energy waning. The sky turned black and the sound of the surging waves faded into oblivion.

Chapter 14

The *Loretta* rocked gently against her sea anchor, riding the soft swells with barely a creak of her timbers. The glint of the sun shining on the water reflected arrows of light against the porthole, sending dancing patterns of pale yellow across the walls of the cabin. Shona lay on the bunk staring at the guttering candles sputtering in the chandelier overhead. Red wax dripped down the tapers, filled the saucers, and collected into bloody tears which swayed above her head. Yet she could not shed tears.

She blinked her burning eyes, willing the dam holding back her tears to break. It was useless. Her tears lay like granite stones in her breast, their weight threatening at any moment to stifle the beat of her aching heart.

Stephen is dead. She mouthed the words without sound. She could think them, but she could not speak them. Clenching her hands, she winced. Then she lifted one hand and stared at the golden cross resting in its palm. She should throw it away. She had been right all along; there was no God. There was only pain, and death and loneliness. But she knew she would not discard the cross. It had belonged to Stephen. He had worn it beneath his shirt, nestled against his golden skin, above his beating heart. She raised her head, slipped the chain around her neck, and then lay back down.

She should try to escape while the ship still rode at anchor, while she could still attempt to join Stephen in his watery grave, but she was too tired to rise. She felt as though an implacable hand had pressed all the vitality from her body, making movement impossible.

A sudden, loud explosion rattled the chandelier, snuffing out the last of the candles. Another explosion rocked the ship, then another. They were blowing the *Nancy* out of the water! She had to watch—she had to pay her last homage to Stephen.

She rolled slowly to one side and pulled herself up until she was sitting on the side of the mattress. When she attempted to stand, the room spun around so she groped her way from the bed to the wall and then to the porthole. She grasped the latch to keep from falling and looked out as the *Nancy*'s main mast splintered and crashed to the deck in a confusion of canvas and ropes. A round of shot tore into her quarter-deck, another into her bow, leaving a gaping hole. Several more balls found their mark and the *Nancy* began to list, then to sink, water gurgling up the sides of her hull until only her bow remained out of the water. Seconds later, that, too, disappeared, and only the boiling sea marked the spot where the once-proud ship had stood.

Suddenly Shona's head was too heavy to support. Her shoulders slumped and she slid down the wall until she was huddled in a ball upon the deck, her cheek resting upon the boards. It was all done—all over. Her dream had ended.

She was still lying on the floor when the door was flung open and then slammed violently.

"What's this?" a voice roared. "I thought you had spunk! Come on. Up, up lass, there's wark for you to do!"

Rough hands grasped her under the arms and lifted her to her feet. She swayed and would have fallen if those same hands had not held her. It was the pirate leader. She recognized his gravelly voice, his stench. She opened her eyes and looked up at him. He was as large as Jephtha, and as solidly built, but his hair was as red as Jephtha's had been black, and his eyes were the green of new spring grass. She stared up at him, willing him to kill her and be done with it.

Instead, he shook her until her teeth chattered. "I said there's wark for you to do," he said, his voice so loud the chandelier rattled overhead. "There's wounded to be tended, and the surgeon needs your help."

Wounded? He expected her to tend his wounded? A spark of hostility flickered in her mind.

He shook her again. "You look strong as an *each*," he roared. "As a horse, in case you're a Lowlander and dinna ken the talk of a *Gaidheal*."

The spark flamed into a full-blown fire, searing Shona's brain until she exploded into action. She wrenched free and backed away, her hands clenched before her. "Don't profane the good name of the Scots," she hissed, her eyes narrowed with disgust. "I'll not tend your wounded, now or ever!"

She expected him to strike her. Instead, he placed his hands on his hips and laughed uproariously, his head thrown back, his mouth opened wide. "Aw, that's more like it," he sputtered when he had control of himself. "Why, lass, I'd never gie my ain wounded to you. You'd most likely kill them where they lay. It's a Spanish heathen that hae need of you, though I'm afeared he's too auld to last long."

Spanish heathen? Then one of Stephen's crew remained on board! "What's his name?" she asked quickly.

"I dinna ask names of dying men," he growled. "But if you're Shona Cameron—and that's as good a Scottish name as I've ever heard—he's calling for you. You'd best jump to it, *Nic*, and stop acting like a *naoidheanan*."

Shona recoiled. "I'm not your daughter and I'm not acting like a child," she shouted. She tossed her braids behind her back. "Now, take me to him, if you're going to. I'm tired of all this talk."

His bulky body blocked her way. "Well now, isn't that too bad?" he mimicked. "The wee bairn is tired. Do you know who you're talking to, lass? Well, I'll tell you! You're talking to

Kenneth MacKenzie, descended from the Brahan Seer himself, and captain of this ship!"

Shona saw the pride in his face, but she would not give him the pleasure of noting her surprise. The Brahan Seer! Her grandfather had raised her on tales of that first Kenneth MacKenzie and of his uncanny way of predicting the future. Did this giant of a Scotsman possess those same powers? She raised one eyebrow, and her features froze into steely disdain. "The name of the captain of this ship is Joseph Munroe," she said firmly. "You are a beast and a vicious killer. You bring dishonor to the name MacKenzie."

His eyes registered his amazement. It was obvious he had expected adulation. His lips pulled back into a snarl, and before she could react, a huge palm cuffed her across the cheek. She fell against the wall, her ears ringing, but she pulled herself up quickly. She would not allow herself to fall at this monster's feet.

"Did you enjoy that?" she whispered. "Or would you prefer that I bleed for you?"

She was unprepared for his reaction. Instead of sparking his mercurial temper, she had only succeeded in amusing him again. He roared with laughter until tears streamed down his ruddy cheeks, soaking his beard. Then he grabbed her arm. "Come, lass," he choked out. "You're like a fresh breath of wind across the straths. You're just what's needed by the wounded."

Shona followed him willingly, though her heart still lay like a dead lump in her breast. He pulled her down the companionway and pushed her up the ladder ahead of him, his hands lingering caressingly upon her buttocks. When they reached the deck, she pulled away and strode purposefully toward a group of men lying beside the taffrail. The surgeon, a tiny, bent-backed figure of a man, knelt beside one of the wounded. His hands were gory with blood, and when he looked up in surprise as she approached, she saw that his eyes were yellow and rheumy with age and probably from many a friendly bout with the bottle.

"This lass is here to help with that Spanish heathen," MacKenzie roared in a loud voice that Shona was beginning to realize was entirely normal for him. "Gie her aw she needs," he called back as he walked away.

The surgeon's appraising look was filled with weariness. "There's not much you can do for him," he said with a sigh. "His wound's clean and the ball damaged only soft tissue—no bones—but I can't stop the bleeding."

He indicated a prone figure several feet away. "At his age, he won't last long. Can't you help with some of the younger ones?"

Shona ignored his whining plea. She recognized the Spaniard at once. It was Fernando! She knelt by his side and placed her palm lightly upon his forehead. It was clammy and his skin had the pallor of one who has already passed into death. But at her touch, his eyelids flickered and opened. He did not appear to recognize her, for his eyes closed; but they popped open again and his stubbled cheeks began to quiver.

"Madonna," he whispered.

"Don't talk, Fernando," she said. "Just lie very still. I'm going to take care of you."

His lips turned up in a shaky smile. "Alas," he whispered. "It is too late."

Shona straightened and pulled his shirt aside. "It is never too late," she said firmly, "not as long as you are still breathing."

She removed the blood-soaked wadding. The surgeon was right. The wound did appear small and was located in the fleshy portion of the chest, just below the collarbone. It was bleeding freely. She raced to the pile of gauze wadding stacked beside the surgeon and quickly returned to Fernando's side. Folding a piece into a pad, she placed it over the wound, pressing until Fernando groaned with pain.

"I'm sorry to hurt you," she said, "but I must stop the bleeding. I'm going to put as much pressure on this as you can bear."

"I am dying, Madonna," Fernando quavered. "It is useless."

She pressed harder. "Nonsense. You are not going to die. I need you. You will not leave me alone."

He groaned as she placed her other hand over the wadding to add weight. "I am an old man," he whispered. "I can give you nothing."

She wanted to reassure him with a smile, but her lips would not cooperate. Instead she frowned.

"You are my friend," she said, her voice falling harshly on her own ears. "You can give me companionship. You are all I have left in this world. And you can give me all you remember about . . . about Stephen. I will live on those memories, for everything else has been taken away."

Tears pricked her eyelids, but she did nothing to stop their flow, knowing they would come no further. They swam in her eyes and blurred her vision, refusing to relieve her agony by slipping down her cheeks.

He sighed deeply and closed his eyes. "Then I will try very hard to live," he whispered.

Fernando did live, and Shona sat on the deck long after the *Loretta* was under sail, pressing upon the wadding covering his wound until her hands became numb and her arms felt as though they were wooden pegs fastened to her aching shoulders. She would not allow the surgeon to move him, even when he insisted that leaving the patient out in the open on a moonlit night would bring certain madness.

"Everyone knows that sleeping under the moon causes insanity," he whined. "And even if he lives, he will become a raving maniac, though I'm not so sure you could tell, him being a heathen."

Shona fought to control her temper. "That is one superstition I do not believe in at all, nor should a man of

170

healing such as yourself," she said firmly. "The bleeding is under control. If you move him before morning, it will only open the wound and he will surely die."

The surgeon threw up his hands and shuffled off across the deck. "Don't say I didn't warn you," he called over his shoulder.

Shona watched him move wearily away, his back bent, his arms hanging loosely at his side. Perhaps she should not have been so hard on him, but people like him made a mockery of the art of healing. He should have known about applying pressure to a wound to stop bleeding; she had known that since she was a bairn. She knew he could not have spent so much time on one patient without losing others, but she pushed that thought from her mind. Better to hate the man.

She looked down at the wadding she had placed over Fernando's wound. It was still the same dingy white it had been when first applied. She released one hand and watched closely. No change. She removed the other hand and held her breath. Still no change. The bleeding had stopped.

She threw back her head and rolled it around, easing the cramp in her neck. Then she wrapped her arms around her body and looked up into the sky. The moon rode the starry night like a majestic white sun, flooding the deck around her with soft light. Why couldn't the night before have been so bright? If it had, none of this would have happened. It was the fog, that treacherous, wet, salty blanket which had betrayed the *Nancy* and all of its crew.

She shivered and sat listening to the sounds of the snapping sails and to the soft gurgle of their wake. There were so many unanswered questions. What had happened to the crew of the *Loretta?* How had they been taken? And where was Mac-Kenzie's own ship?

She did not have long to wait for the answers. She heard footfalls on the deck and looked up to see the pirate captain making his way toward her. In the moonlight, it was easy to see that he had tried to make himself more presentable. His fiery hair sparkled with drops of water and his beard was combed. He had even donned a clean shirt and breeches, and he wore polished boots. For her? She looked away, her chin held high.

She was startled when a soft blanket was draped over her shoulders. "Canna hae you catching your death," MacKenzie said. "Night vapors can be the daith if you aren't accustomed to them."

She threw her head back and glared up at him. "And what makes you think I'm unaccustomed to night vapors?" she questioned, her voice dripping with scorn. "Or do you suppose all the women of Scotland are delicate flowers?"

He dropped to the deck beside her. "You're more like the heather," he said huskily. "Hardy, sweet smelling, and much better to look at than a garden full of roses."

"Roses have thorns."

He chuckled, a rumble deep in his throat. "And I suppose you dinna? You're prickly, all right. But I still say you're more like the heather."

This sort of talk made her uncomfortable. "Where are we going?" she asked. "Where are you taking me, and where is your own ship? Or did you and your crew walk on the water to take the *Loretta*?"

The chuckle turned into a full-blown laugh. Shona was suddenly struck with the surety that this man never did anything by halves. He lived his life to the fullest, taking what he could when he could, and he gave no quarter.

"You're full of questions tonight." He laughed. "But how's your patient? I thought he'd be feeding the sharks lang syne."

Feeding the sharks. Stephen's body falling, falling, splashing into the sea; a red-stained wash appearing on the surface. Shona felt faint.

He reached out and grasped her arm. "What's the matter? You're as white as a thirled winding sheet."

She turned her head away. She did not want to see the concern mirrored in his eyes. She did not want him to care about her.

"I have stopped the bleeding," she whispered. "Fernando will live."

"Fernando, is it? How did you come to be on a Spanish ship? Was that bastard you shot right about you? Are you really a bizzem?"

His booming voice brought a groan to Fernando's lips. Shona pulled away from him and bent over her friend. "It's all right," she crooned. "Go back to sleep now. I'm here." She took the blanket from her shoulders and tucked it around his body. He smiled slightly and began to breathe deeply again.

She turned and glared at MacKenzie. "If it is possible, please keep your voice lowered to a shout," she hissed. "He needs his rest if he is to recover."

"Who is he?" MacKenzie demanded. "Why were you on that ship?"

Shona looked back at Fernando. "He is a friend," she answered softly. "A very dear friend."

"And? . . ."

"I don't see that it is any of your business. You have taken us prisoner, but that does not give you the right to pry into our private lives."

"By God," he grumbled, "you're as bad as that Captain Munroe. He was as close-mouthed as a *gilidhe* with a full stomach."

"And, like a trout, he wouldn't take your bait?"

"Don't look so smug. He wouldn't tell me anything, but he didn't have to. After I set him adrift with his crew, I went through his cabin. And right there, in his desk, was a book—a book with some very important writing in it. So I scuttled my own ship and waited . . . it was like taking the virginity of a young bizzem, it was that easy to lay my trap."

"But how did you take the *Loretta* in the first place? She is surely more heavily armed than your own ship!"

He laughed again. "Oh, she is that," he gurgled. "And my taking her was a pure accident . . . a little piece of the luck of the Daoine Seth. It was the fog I'd been cursing night after

173

night what done her in. There we were, drifting with only a drag anchor, when my mate comes to me and whispers he's seen the outline of a ship right off our port bow. So I tippy-toed up on deck, and sure enough, there she was, pretty as a picture. It was the easiest job I've ever done. Took her without a shot."

"But the sails! I saw the holes in them!"

"Oh, I did that afterward. Just before I scuttled my own ship. Wanted to prime the bait just so, wanted to make a pretty puzzle out of her. What had happened? Where was her crew? And it worked, though your captain had more sense than I gied him credit for. He must have smelled a ratton, being ready for battle the way he was. Only he didn't figure on me having such a big crew, and that mistake done him in."

Shona leaped to her feet, her face flushed with anger. "You're a beast!" she hissed. "You're a vulture, feeding on dead bones!"

He sat on the deck, grinning up at her. "I'd say I was more like a chicken hawk," he countered, "with a great big haul of tender chicks in my belly."

She watched, wide-eyed, as he got slowly to his feet. She could see the lust in his eyes and the rapid rise and fall of his massive chest. She looked frantically about, seeking a place to hide. But before she could move, his hands reached out and he pulled her close, wrapping his hands in one of her loosened braids. "You're my kind of lass," he said huskily. "I'll see you have some new cloes, something to fit you better. You sew, don't you? You can make over some breeks to wear. I always like a woman better in a pair of breeks . . . I like to see the outline of their *hurdies*, sweet and sassy, just asking to be pinched."

She pulled her hand back to slap his face, but he was quicker. When he grasped her wrist and pressed, she screamed in pain.

"I can snap that wee bone without any effort at aw," he purred. "I dinna take kindly to being slapped. Always brings the anger ower me."

"Let me go!" She tried to bring her knee up to his groin but

174

he side-stepped neatly, dragging her along with him. "Just the way I like a woman," he laughed. "You'll be the best toss in bed I ever had or I'll say my name isna MacKenzie!"

"No!" Shona screamed. "No! You can't do that to me! I'll cut out your bloody heart and roast it on a fire!" She fought and pulled against his grip, but it was as if she were a gnat wrestling with a drone bee. She became desperate. There was only one avenue left to her. If he was as superstitious as most Scots . . . She stopped struggling and dropped her voice to a hoarse whisper. "I'll put a hex on you! I'll put a curse on your family that will last till eternity! You might be a relative of the Brahan Seer, but my mother was a daughter of the Earl of Strathmore!" The lie came easily to her lips.

She saw a flicker of fear cross his features, and added more fuel to the fire she had sparked. "You know about the Strathmores, don't you?" she continued. "How every now and then they give birth to a vampire? Well, I'll answer your question now about what I was doing on that Spanish ship. I was sent to ruin their mission but you stopped me! Now, I'll have to make you my victim unless you leave me alone!"

He dropped her hands and backed away, his face blanched white in the moonlight. "You're lying," he whispered. "That's only a tale."

"Like the Brahan Seer is a tale?" she asked with a grim smile.

"Na! That is the truth! He foretold the battle of Culloden, you ken that! And many other things, too! Why, he wouldna hae been put to deith if he hadna told that woman why her husband was dallying so long in Paris!" He licked his lips nervously. "Even if you're telling the truth, the Strathmores always keep their monster behind locked doors."

"But you've already forgotten what I said," Shona countered. "My mother was the youngest daughter of the Earl. My father stole her away from the castle. I was born on the Isle of Shona."

His forehead creased as he sought to digest her explanation.

175

Shona knew the time had come to be bold. She stepped forward and pointed her finger in his face. "Bed me!" she demanded. "Bed me so I can suck your blood from your body and feed myself. It's been a long time since I've supped on good Scots blood!"

His eyes looked like round green beads. Drops of sweat popped out on his forehead, and he backed away. "Na, na," he babbled. "I muanna want to bed you. I've changed my mind. There's much for me to do. We're making for our island. I canna bed you now!"

She took another step toward him, and he whirled and ran heavily across the deck as though the devil himself were fast upon his heels.

Shona stood rooted to her spot until he disappeared down the main hatch. Then she began to shake. Her body was convulsed with shivers, and she felt as if she could not get her breath. She stumbled to where Fernando lay and collapsed into a heap beside him.

"Oh, God, what have I done?" she moaned.

"You've just acted a part better than I've seen them do at the Prado," Fernando whispered.

She sat up and looked down at him. "You heard? Oh, Fernando, I didn't think he would be a fool enough to believe me!"

"You even convinced me!" Fernando laughed weakly. "I had shivers running up and down my body like I was dying with the ague."

Shona grasped his hand and squeezed it. "But he surely won't believe me for long . . . not when he stops to think about what I said. No one could be that stupid."

"Then you'll have to play your part until we can escape," Fernando whispered. "Make him sweat every time he comes near you."

Shona shook her head. "It won't be easy. I even frighten myself when I talk like that."

Fernando coughed, and she quickly checked the wadding

covering his wound. It was still clean. She pulled the blanket up over his shoulders. "Go to sleep, old friend," she said fondly. "You're right. I'll have to keep up this act until we can escape."

She watched until his breathing slowed and deepened. Only then did she succumb to her terror. She had always been as honest and as straightforward as she possibly could, and the ease with which she had fallen into the lie frightened her. It would not be easy to pretend to be something she was not—but she had to do it. If that monster so much as touched her again, she would die. She still belonged to Stephen, in life or in death, and she would never bed another man as long as she lived! She spent the remainder of the night recalling all of the old Gaelic superstitions she had heard.

Chapter 15

The sun leaped over the horizon, flooding the dark blue sea with streaks of orange, and Shona trembled with fatigue as Kenneth MacKenzie took his place on the high quarter-deck. When she saw his gaze turn in her direction, she threw back her head and forced a loud cackling laugh from between her parched lips. Though she was too far away to read his expression, she knew he was still pondering her warning, for he turned abruptly and studied the sea far ahead of the plunging ship.

She sighed and blinked her salt-caked eyelashes. Her legs were cramped, she had little feeling in her bare feet, and her shoulders felt as though they bore the weight of the world. She longed for the comfort of a bed and a long draught of cool, clear water!

She was startled and more than a little convinced that MacKenzie possessed the divining powers of his grandfather when one of his men approached her almost immediately, offering to carry the wounded Spaniard "heathen" to her cabin. Tears pricked her eyelids, but she blinked them away and coldly informed the seaman that, though she agreed that Fernando must be moved, it must be done with the utmost care, for though his burden might be Spanish, the man was definitely not "heathen."

She was sure that MacKenzie had told the crew about her professed powers, for the pirate picked Fernando up with the care a mother would show an ailing infant, all the while eying her anxiously for approval. Shona struggled to her feet and followed woodenly, biting her lip against the pinpricks needling her feet and legs.

She had just settled Fernando on her bunk when the surgeon appeared, bearing a chest of ointments and salves. "You've a touch of healing in your hands," he said as he bent over the Spaniard. "I didn't give him another hour when you took over."

Ignoring his compliment, Shona rummaged through the medicine chest, choosing only fresh wadding, a handful of bruised scabious, and a packet of tobacco with which to dress the wound.

The surgeon watched her carefully. "I've a decoction of nettles and wine in my quarters," he said eagerly. "Perhaps I should fetch it?"

She arranged her supplies on the table beside the bed. "There's no rotting of the wound," she said. "The tobacco will draw out any of the poisons." She saw his shoulders slump and knew he was as exhausted as she, having been up all night tending his own wounded. "But thank you anyway," she said softly. "I'll let you know if I need it later."

His lined face brightened. "You be sure to do that," he said eagerly. "I'll check in on you later."

She watched him shuffle toward the door. "Wait," she said suddenly. "Have you a sharp knife?" She bit back a smile at the look of fear crossing his face.

"Whatever do you need a knife for? Your teeth will do to tear the wadding."

She glanced down at Fernando. A small tic at the corner of his mouth told her he was conscious and hearing everything. She walked slowly toward the surgeon. "I don't need a knife for the wadding," she said in a hoarse whisper. "I need it for the nail parings."

His mouth dropped open. "Nail parings?" he squeaked. "Whatever do you mean?"

She leered at him. "I pare the patient's nails," she intoned breathlessly, "then I wrap the parings in a piece of his clothing, wave it three times around his head and hide it in an unknown place. It never fails to cure."

He grabbed the door handle and twisted it violently. "Never heard of such a pagan practice," he gasped as he threw the door open. "Pagan, that's what it is!"

Shona bit back the comment that he was no one to talk for he had raved the night before about a full moon causing insanity. Instead, she smiled knowingly and nodded her head.

"Pagan it might be," she said, "but creatures like me know what to do, and when to do it."

He whirled about and shuffled down the corridor without another sound.

Shona's smile disappeared instantly. Pray God he related all of this to MacKenzie, for if he did not, it would be wasted. She closed the door and had just returned to Fernando's side when there was a timid rapping on the door. She was amazed to find the surgeon standing outside. He stared at a spot on the floor. "I forgot to tell you that there will be a man bringing you a mattress to sleep on," he said in a whisper. Then he turned and retreated hastily.

"Did you count to ten before you returned?" she called after him.

He hesitated, but did not look back. "Did I what?"

She cackled ominously. "If you forget something, and don't count to ten before you return, it will bring you very, very bad luck," she said.

He paused for a moment, then ran clumsily down the corridor without a backward glance.

Shona's laugh was genuine as she pulled the covers from Fernando. "You should have seen him run," she said.

Fernando opened his eyes and smiled. "You're laying the groundwork well, Madonna. He will be telling everyone about your dire warnings."

She shook her head. "I only hope he tells the right person," she answered. "If MacKenzie doesn't hear, it will be for naught."

"He will tell him. These pirates are a superstitious lot. You were so convincing, you brought shivers of dread to me, just as you did last night."

Shona studied his wound. Though it was angry and red, there was no sign of putrefaction. She smeared a mixture of scabious and tobacco on a new dressing and gently tied it in place. When she stood back, she was frowning. "I racked my brains all night for all of the horrid tales of bad luck I could remember," she declared. "It wasn't easy, for I've never held any of the superstitions to be true so I've forgotten them."

"I am happy you do not believe any of them," Fernando said gently. "God in his heaven will take care of you. You need fear nothing when he and his angels are watching over you."

She uttered a loud oath and paced to the porthole where she stood looking out over the tumbling water. "Don't speak to me of God, Fernando," she said when she was in control of her emotions. "Stephen is gone. My dreams died with him. There is no God."

Fernando did not argue with her. He had seen the agony in her eyes, had recognized the raw wound she had suffered, far more serious than his own fleshly one. Instead, he closed his eyes and offered up a prayer to the God he still believed in with every fiber of his being.

Kenneth MacKenzie was in a quandary. He should never have shared the lass's words of the night before with Evans, his first mate. The conversation had spread like wildfire through the crew, and now, what with the tales the surgeon had added, his men would not go near Shona's cabin. Did he himself believe her to be the Strathmore vampire? He did not know. Like Shona, he had been raised upon tales of the supernatural.

After all, there was his own grandfather, the Brahan Seer. He knew his grandfather's gift was real, for too many of his prophecies had come true for it to be discounted as mere superstition.

Then, to add to his growing fear, there was his experience in Dunphail, at Rait Castle. He himself had seen the ghost of the young girl with no hands, wearing a blood-stained gown. Granted, it had been the most fleeting of glimpses in the midst of a heavy fog, but it had been enough to convince him to leave Scotland far behind in search of someplace where ghosts did not appear holding their heads in their hands as the ghost of Lady Anne Douglas did regularly at Drumlanrig in Wigtownshire.

What should he do? There was always the possibility of dumping the lass overboard to drown, but he could not do that. She was too bonny, too filled with fire. He wanted to bed her too badly to do away with her; his loins ached with longing even now. What if all she'd said was mere blather? He paced the confines of the quarter-deck, his face creased with indecision. If he did dump the lass overboard, and she was telling the truth, she would not die. Instead, she would return to make short shrift of him! He imagined her sharp teeth biting into his neck, and he winced at the thought. By all the gods, he was in a fankle and could see no way out, short of biding his time. In the meantime, there was no man aboard his ship who would set foot near her cabin, and she was in need of a mattress, food, and drink.

There was no way out. He would have to risk taking her what she needed himself. Signaling to his first mate, he turned the command over to him. Then he walked quickly across the deck, determined to rot in hell before he would allow her to see his fear. But, unlike his grandfather, he could not foretell the future; thus, he did not know how miserably he would fail.

Shona heard the knock on the door and turned quickly to

183

Fernando. He winked and nodded his head. She began to chant loudly all of the Spanish words Fernando had taught her, mixing them up, mispronouncing them, not making any sense, reciting them as they came to her mind. As she chanted, she waved her hands over his prone form, fluttering her fingers like butterflies' wings.

She heard the door open and close behind her, and she lowered her voice to a hoarse whisper as she continued reciting the nonsense.

"Damnation, lass, I'll not stand here and listen to such blethers," MacKenzie roared.

Shona did not miss the slight quiver in his voice. She stopped chanting, stilled her hands, and lowered them gently to her lap. When she turned to face him, her eyes were cold and her face impassive.

"You are a brave man, Kenneth MacKenzie," she said.

His eyes darted from her quiet hands to her expressionless face. "What do you mean? I dinna ken you."

She smiled grimly. "Only a very brave man or a fool would interrupt my incantations."

His face flushed an angry red. "Are you calling me a fool?" he shouted.

Again she smiled. "I called you a very brave man," she reminded him quietly. "But perhaps I was mistaken."

He swallowed noisily and nodded at the tray in his hands. "I brought you some food and drink. There's no reason to chap me."

This time, Shona's smile appeared sweet and genuine. "Thank you. I will not forget your kindness."

She watched his eyes narrow and knew she had addled him. Good. Let him spend time attempting to figure her out; then perhaps he would be too confused to try to force her into his bed. She rose and walked swiftly toward him. She did not miss his agitation when she took the tray from his trembling hands. "I would appreciate some light wine," she said as she placed the tray on the table. "And some soap and water. If you would be so kind."

She poured water into a cup and held it to Fernando's lips. The silence behind her was deafening. After Fernando had drunk his fill, she refilled the cup and drank deeply of the sweet water, relishing the feel of its coolness sliding all the way down to her empty stomach. When she had drained the cup, she turned and smiled at MacKenzie again. "If you don't mind," she said, "I could use that soap and water now. I'm badly in need of a bath."

Lust leaped into his eyes, and she knew he was imagining her naked before him, her body glistening with soap and water. She gritted her teeth and inwardly cursed her lack of judgment. "Also, I could use a twig for my teeth," she purred. "I don't like them to become dirty. It hinders my work."

Instantly, the lust was replaced by fear. He backed away until he stood against the door. "I'll fetch them now," he boomed out. "And . . . and, I'll bring you a mattress . . . and blankets . . . and some clean cloes."

Before she could say another word, he whirled and threw himself out the doorway, his face a mask of panic.

He did not return. Instead, a toothless old seadog brought the things she had requested. Shona did not know how MacKenzie had bribed the old man into doing his dirty work, for it was patently obvious the poor old fool was overcome with fear. His hands shook as though he suffered with the palsy and his voice cracked. His prominent gullet bobbed up and down in his many attempts to swallow. He did not enter the cabin, but stood in the doorway, placing the pail of water, soap, sacking, and blankets on the floor at his feet. When she approached to collect them, he stepped far back into the companionway, his eyes darting from side to side as though he were awaiting for an untoward move on her part, which would spur him into beating a hasty retreat.

When he brought the mattress, Shona found his actions just as comical. He shoved it into the cabin and watched it uncoil like a snake about to strike. Then he whirled about and without a word, ran awkwardly for the nearest ladder.

Fernando chuckled from his bunk. "It appears you have gained a reputation," he said. "And you must retain it if you are to survive this journey."

Shona grimaced. "You're right, of course. But I have to tell you, I'm not enjoying it."

She bathed Fernando's face and hands and fed him some of the tepid gruel and a piece of scorched scone. After he had eaten his fill, she helped him into a clean shirt, then pulled the blankets up under his chin.

"Time for you to rest," she said. "Your color is much better, but you've a lot of healing to do before we reach land."

"When will that be, Madonna? Where are they taking us?"

She shook her head and sighed. "I don't know. MacKenzie mentioned something about an island. With this act I'm putting on, it's hard to question him. I don't know what they mean to do with us."

"I'll rest now. I must be well and ready to travel when we get to that island. We must escape as soon as possible."

She sat by the bed until he had fallen into a deep sleep. Then she propped a chair under the door handle, rigged a blanket across the cabin and removed her filthy clothing. The water was cold, but she did not mind. The soap was some they had taken from the *Nancy* and she felt her throat tighten when she smelled the familiar fragrance of orange blossoms. Valencia. Stephen had intended to take her to his home. He had described the rows and rows of orange trees heavy with the scent of delicate white blossoms. She closed her eyes and tried to envision the scene he had painted with words, but only one picture leaped into her mind, sparked, perhaps, by the scent of the soap—she and Stephen making love the last time.

It had all started so innocently. She had merely made a comment about the impossibility of taking a long, luxurious bath aboard a ship. She should have been warned when Stephen's eyebrow arched dangerously, but instead she prattled on about how wonderful it would feel to use his delicately scented soap in a proper bath. She was startled when he left the cabin abruptly, without even an explanation of where he was going. But when he returned much later, her fretting turned to instant delight. He was carrying a large tub and behind him were several seamen burdened down with buckets of hot, fresh water.

She watched with wide eyes as they emptied their buckets into the tub, filling it almost to the top. Yet, even then, she was too thrilled with the prospect of a relaxing bath to give any thought to the seamen's secretive smiles as they filed silently from the cabin with occasional winks and knowing grins.

Stephen stood before the closed door, his hands placed firmly on his hips. "Well?" he asked.

"But where did you get the water? Surely we can't waste it on a bath!"

When he did not reply, but only continued to stare at her, she dipped her fingers into the tub, swishing them lightly through the hot water, her face beaming. It suddenly did not matter that fresh water was very scarce. She would have a good, long soak; then she would wash her hair! She tore at the fastening on her gown.

Stephen brushed her hands away. "Surely you will allow me the honor of undressing you!" he exclaimed.

"Of course!" she laughed. "Only hurry, I can't wait to dive in!"

He cupped her chin and lifted her face to his. "Nor I," he purred.

Still, her delight with the bath did not allow her to see the dark blue of his eyes, or how his lips were twitching. She stood patiently as he unlaced her gown, his hands lingering over each movement. Then he slipped the gown off over her shoulders and slid it down over her hips slowly, his lips brushing her soft undershift on the way down. When the shift had joined the gown on the floor, he cupped her bare breasts in his hands, caressing them lightly, his fingers kneading her placid nipples into tight buds before he kissed each one lightly, lingering only long enough to bring shivers to her bare flesh.

He pulled away and bowed. "Are you ready milady?" he asked, offering his arm. She placed her hand lightly on his wrist and curtsied. "I'm ready!" she exclaimed.

He led her to the tub and balanced her while she stepped into the warm water, her gasp of pleasure bringing a smile to his face. But when she started to slide down, he caught her arm and shook his head. "Not yet," he said quickly. "This rarest of pleasures must be enjoyed to the fullest."

He bent down and cupped the water in his palms, releasing it in pleasant trickles down her thighs and then over her breasts. She gasped with delight as even more warm water cascaded down her shoulders.

He kneeled beside the tub and pulled her down into the water. But when she reached for the soap, he took it from her, and lathering his hands, he soaped her cheeks, her forehead, her chin, her neck. He lingered over each ear, stroking it as though it were a delicate sea shell found only on some faraway, illusive shore. She shivered with delight as he cupped fresh water in his palms and rinsed away the fragrant soap. Then his hands were moving over her shoulders, her upper back. She started to protest that he had forgotten her breasts, but he was already lathering her belly, his hands deliberately ignoring the wedge of golden hair that usually enthralled him. He washed her thighs, her calves, her ankles, then each toe, all the time smiling broadly and humming beneath his breath. She closed her eyes and leaned back in the tub, holding her heavy mane of hair away from the nape of her neck with one hand.

"Are you enjoying your bath?" he whispered.

She murmured a long, "Mmmmm," and sighed contentedly.

"But the best part is yet to come," he said.

She opened her eyes, ready to protest that nothing, absolutely nothing in the world, could be any better. His face was only inches from hers, his eyes so deep a blue they appeared almost black. His nostrils were flared, and the corners of his full lips were tilted as he smiled broadly.

She stared up at him, fighting down a bubble of laughter. Then she splashed water all over him, trying to pull him into the tub fully clothed. He pulled away and tore out of his clothing. Leaving a dripping pile—shirt, breeches, stockings, and shoes—beside the tub, he slipped into the water in front of her, cramming his long legs between hers.

"I thought you would never ask me to join you." He chuckled.

"There isn't room!" she shrieked. "You're smothering me!"

"You have never complained before."

"This is different! Really, Stephen, there isn't room in this tub for both of us!"

He answered by grabbing the soap and liberally lathering her breasts. He worked slowly, his hands moving in ever-tightening circles, his fingers tweaking each nipple. She moaned and shook her head as the familiar tingling began in her groin. "It's no use!" she exclaimed. "You are too clever."

"Not clever," he countered, "only hungry. Do you realize how beautiful you are? Your body is the tawny color of orange-blossom honey. Your lips and enticing nipples are as pink as the first blush of sunrise in the dawn sky." He licked a bit of foam from one nipple. "And you taste like the sweetest clover kissed by the Valencian sun."

"I taste like soap. But don't stop. You sound like one of the bards who used to visit our home to lighten the long winter nights with pretty words and songs of love."

"I trust you will allow me to do more than recite pretty words?"

She gasped as his fingers gently explored her secret place. "I will die if you don't," she sighed.

His hands continued their soft message of love while his lips moved over her breasts. He sucked on each nipple, twirling his tongue in delicious circles until she cried out in delight. Then he soaped her buttocks, massaging her muscles, before he concentrated on that golden wedge of hair he had neglected before. He soaped and rubbed, soaped and rubbed until she felt that she would die with ecstasy. She gasped as his finger entered her and stroked slowly in and out, rippling the water in soft waves.

Then he pulled her onto his lap and her breath caught in her throat as his hard, velvet shaft penetrated her. She matched his rhythm with her own, rising and falling until her entire body burned with passion. When his lips closed over hers and his tongue probed the inner recesses of her mouth, she tasted the sweetness of oranges as her hips rose and fell with his. Unheeded, the water spread out from the tub in ever-widening circles as they moved in unison with their desire.

He grasped her so tightly that she could scarcely breathe but breathing was no longer important for the flame building inside her was all-encompassing. It blazed, then burst into a raging inferno, igniting her entire body. She soared on the hot winds of passion until she heard him cry out and once again she was consumed completely by the flames.

At last, she collapsed against him, her breath coming in ragged gasps, and he held her tightly, whispering her name over and over again, his body trembling against hers. When she opened her eyes, she found him looking at her, such a dazzling smile on his face that she almost wept for joy.

"My dearest Shona," he said. "You mean more to me than life itself!"

The memory faded instantly, the mind pictures replaced by the scene which had haunted her for days. "More . . . than life itself." The sea turning red with Stephen's blood.

She rubbed her eyes and toweled her chilled body briskly. She had no idea what she would do with her life now. Perhaps she would return to her original plan—to find a wealthy man and make him fall in love with her. But she could never return that love. She knew that she had tasted the only love she would ever experience and now that was over.

She pulled on the clean breeches and shirt, making a face when she realized they had been washed in sea water, for they were stiff with dried salt. Then she placed a blanket over the

190

mattress and lay down with a deep sigh. In seconds, her eyes had closed and she was fast asleep.

Fernando healed quickly. In three days, he was sitting on the side of the bunk and within a week, he was leaning on her arm as they walked about the cabin. MacKenzie did not make another appearance and this perturbed Shona. Though she was relieved that she had to playact only occasionally to keep the toothless seaman in line, she wanted to see MacKenzie just long enough to gain permission to walk about on deck before she succumbed completely to a debilitating case of cabin fever.

Fernando was quick to note her increasing edginess. And, true friend that he was, he took immediate steps to ease her unhappiness. He began to share his memories of Stephen.

Through his eyes, Shona watched the infant Esteban take his first wobbly steps toward his adoring parents. She saw him lose himself in the orchard groves at the age of three, felt her heart swell with pride when he was found striding manfully in circles, his tiny face streaked with dirt, but not a tear in evidence. She thrilled to the story of his first pony and was pleased by the care he had taken to retain the tender mouth of his charge. She giggled with Fernando over the ten-year-old Esteban's insistence that he be allowed to wear long pants to cover his knobby knees and scratched shins. And she listened with tear-filled eyes to the tales of his tenderness toward his little sister Juana, of his love for his mother and his adoration for his Tía María.

Shona ate little. Instead, she filled her body and soul with Fernando's tales of Stephen. She lost weight until her eyes filled her thin face and became so striking that Fernando could not keep his gaze from the brown flecks floating in those huge yellow pools. She seldom smiled and when she did, she looked as though the attempt pained her. Fernando began to pray that they would reach the island soon, for if they did not, he was sure she would gradually pine away until she died.

His prayers were answered toward the middle of their third week aboard the *Loretta*. The journey had been uneventful, with placid seas and brisk winds. The weather had gradually warmed and the air in the tiny cabin became stifling at midday.

Shona sat on her mattress, her shirt pulled up and tied beneath her breasts, her breeches rolled above her knees. She had insisted that Fernando remove his shirt, reminding him that the bandage about his chest was all that modesty required. As she looked at him now, dozing, his chin bobbing as he dropped deeper into sleep, her own eyelids began to droop.

Suddenly, there were loud shouts, and she could hear feet racing about on deck. She leaped up and ran to the porthole. "Fernando!" she cried. "Come, look! Land!"

He joined her at the porthole, and together, they looked out on the first land they had sighted since leaving Brunswick. Off in the distance, they could see broad white beaches graduating upward to dense forests of varicolored trees. "Where are we?" Shona cried. "I've never seen such a tangle of green colors."

Fernando shook his head slowly. "I do not know. It has the appearance of the tropics. I have only seen forests like those where there are jungles."

"Jungles?"

"There are areas of the world where vast tracts of land are covered with every kind of tree imaginable. There the vines grow much higher than a man's head, with leaves larger than a ship's sail. There are snakes and birds of the most brilliant color, and insects which bite and fly into one's face most boldly."

Shona shivered. "I don't like the sound of that. I have never been fond of snakes or insects."

His throat rumbled with a chuckle. "I share your feelings," he said. "I have seen snakes with bodies large enough to swallow a pig! And mosquitoes—yes, mosquitoes as large as birds!"

Shona turned away from the porthole. "I hope you're wrong," she said fervently. "I don't relish the thought of

192

escaping only to find ourselves surrounded by snakes and mosquitoes as large as you describe."

"Do not lose heart." He patted her arm. "Perhaps I am wrong. After all, we are still too far away to be sure that is jungle."

But the closer they sailed to the shore, the surer Fernando became that they were approaching an island close to the shores of South America. As he eyed the densely forested slopes of the island, he shared Shona's fears that escape would be next to impossible unless they could somehow steal a boat and make their way north to the Spanish-held territory.

The sun was setting, casting long, dark shadows over the peacefully undulating waters of the bay when they dropped anchor. Shona had untied her shirt and had allowed it to hang over her hips, for the evening was chilly without the warming sun. She sat upon her mattress, her chin resting upon her drawn-up knees, her eyebrows lowered in a frown. She fought hard to retain the hope that they might somehow escape from their captors, but she knew she was fighting a losing battle.

She had lost her pistol and bandolier somewhere on deck, but she had a pewter spoon, a bone comb, and two leather sneak cups. Not much of an arsenal. Her fingers sought the golden cross lying between her breasts. It felt warm to her touch and, somehow, comforting. Perhaps God . . . She dropped the cross and slapped the mattress. No! There was no God. If she and Fernando were to escape, they would have to rely upon themselves.

She got up and crossed to the porthole, watched the flames of a bonfire flickering near the edge of the softly lapping water. What had happened to her since Stephen's death? She was ready to give up. It all seemed so useless now. For the third time in her life she had been taken prisoner. Perhaps a life of servitude was her fate. Maybe she was one of those unfortunate ones who would never know what it meant to live a life of freedom.

She turned and looked at Fernando. He sat upon his bunk, his white head bowed, his eyes closed. She knew he was praying. Anger flooded over her. Why was he wasting his time? With all of his years, didn't he know that God was just a myth—a fairy tale thought up by some imaginative master to keep his slaves in line, a hope to keep the downtrodden alive with dreams of an ever-illusive tomorrow?

She knew that even if she were to find a way to escape her captors, she would never be free again. For the rest of her life she would be bound to Stephen by the fragile chain of love which had enslaved her heart.

She turned her back upon Fernando and returned her gaze to the shoreline, but she could no longer see the fire. Tears were spilling from her eyes, pouring down her cheeks in endless hot streams. Her throat convulsed and she choked, the sobs she had been harboring since Stephen's death bursting forth, sending her to her knees. She rocked back and forth, her grief bringing such pain she did not think she could survive the agony of her loss. "Stephen, Stephen," she moaned, "oh, Stephen, I can't live without you!"

She felt hands upon her shoulders as Fernando kneeled at her side. "Cry, Madonna," he murmured. "Allow the tears to wash away your grief. I was afraid you would never allow the tears to fall. Cry, Madonna."

Shona fell into his arms and he rocked her, whispering words of encouragement, his hands bringing warmth to her icy fingers. She relived each moment with Stephen, felt his hands upon her flesh, saw his azure eyes smiling down at her, tasted the honey from his lips upon her tongue. His warm, manly smell was in her nostrils. His words, "You are my heart," came to her, and her own heart felt as though it would burst from her throbbing breast. She relived the horror of that moment, frozen in time, when the bright red stain appeared on his chest and his mouth opened in surprise, then he fell to the deck. She watched his body flying through the air toward the water . . .

194

saw it strike . . . watched the dark blue sea turn crimson with his blood. But a new picture came to her, returning again and again until it wiped out all others: Stephen standing before her, his full lips turned up in a welcoming smile, his eyes dancing with blue lights, and that damnable eyebrow cocked as though daring her to refuse him. *"Don't give up,"* he was telling her. *"You belong to me now and forever. Never give up."*

She began to smile through her sobs, and soon she was hiccuping with laughter. Stephen was not really gone. He would never leave her. She would have her memories of him forever. His face would be before her wherever she went. His hands would reach out to encompass hers whenever she felt alone. He would strengthen her resolve when it failed. Stephen was not gone.

Chapter 16

Shona slept poorly. She expected that she and Fernando would be pulled from the cabin and taken ashore at any moment. Though she heard scuffling overhead on the deck and men shouting as they emptied the *Loretta*'s hold, the door to her cabin remained closed all night long. When she finally fell into a deep slumber in the early hours of the morning, she dreamed that she was running through a tangle of brush and trees, pursued by a red and green snake carrying a pig in its mouth. She screamed, but no sound came from her lips. Then she tripped over a root and sprawled face down in the tall grass. When she tried to rise, the snake curled itself around her legs, slowly undulating its huge coils around her body. Shona grabbed a knife lying beside her and stabbed again and again at the snake, sending blood shooting high into the air. Suddenly, the snake turned into Kenneth MacKenzie, and the pig became a snarling black dog held tightly between the Scotsman's teeth. The dog's saliva was blood and the blood was dripping upon her face.

She awoke with a start and sat up, her heart racing madly, her breath coming in gasps. She wiped her forehead, expecting to find blood on her palm. Though her hand came away wet, it was only sweat. She hugged her knees and sat shivering in the dark, trying to draw meaning from the dream. Was it foresight? Was she going to escape on the island, only to be pursued and captured by MacKenzie, perhaps with the aid of a snarling black dog? She sat perfectly still and concentrated upon calming her racing heart. If it happened, it happened. It would do no good to worry now.

As the dawn's first light crept into the cabin, she rose, stretched, and splashed her face with water. Fernando was still sleeping, his mouth agape, a soft gurgle fluttering his lips. She smiled down at him and pulled the blanket over his bare feet. Let him find peace in sleep while he could. The day to come was sure to be filled with problems that neither of them wished to encounter.

She tiptoed to the porthole and looked toward the shore. The bonfire had been extinguished, but she could see men scurrying about upon the sand, their figures black against the pearl gray of the dawn. As she watched, a boat was pushed off from shore and the bow was turned toward the *Loretta*. As it neared, she recognized the huge figure plying the oars. It was MacKenzie. He was clad only in a pair of breeches and sweat glistened on his straining thews as he propelled the craft through the sea. Did she just imagine it, or was his face set determinedly? Was he coming for her? She clasped her hands together tightly.

"Stephen, give me strength," she whispered.

She quickly bundled their belongings together in a blanket and propped it beside the door. When she touched Fernando's hand, he woke with a start.

"What is it?" he mumbled as he rubbed a hand over his face. "Is something wrong?"

"No, I thought it was time for you to awaken. MacKenzie just came back aboard."

His gray eyes grew large with knowing. "Turn your back, Madonna," he said quickly. "I will dress."

When he had finished donning his shirt and breeches, he sat on the bunk and pulled her down beside him, grasping her hand tightly. "Are you ready?" he asked in a hoarse whisper.

198

She nodded.

"Do you have a plan?"

She shook her head. "No. We'll just have to take advantage of any chance that comes along. I'm sure he'll have us well guarded."

"We must be together!"

"I know that, but I don't know how to make it happen. I know he'll want to get me alone. I'm sure he's just been biding his time."

Fernando's brow wrinkled. Suddenly, he dropped her hand and slapped his knee. "I know a way!" He leaped up and began to pace the cabin, his cherubic face lit with joy. "It is your turn to be sick, Madonna." He gestured impatiently for her not to interrupt. "You are pale and very thin. It will be easy for you to appear ill . . . very ill . . . perhaps unto death."

"But that won't work! It will just put me completely at his mercy. He'll only push you aside and insist the surgeon take care of me. I can't bear the thought of that butcher touching me!"

Fernando stopped pacing and bent low to whisper in her ear. As he revealed his plan, she began to smile. Fernando was a genius. When he had finished, she raced to her bundle and removed her comb. If only the tines were sharp enough! This had to work!

Kenneth MacKenzie strode purposefully across the deck toward the main hatch. He had stalled long enough. The time had come. He swallowed the last remnant of fear as he climbed down the ladder and turned toward her cabin. The wench had been lying, he was sure of that now. If she was the Strathmore monster as she claimed, she would have made her escape long before now. He grinned widely. He had special plans for that bonny lassy! He would take her to the Bastard's Lair and there, in that large, soft bed which he claimed as his when in port, he would take his fill of the sweetness too long denied him. Saliva

199

spurted into his mouth and his member stirred and leaped erect.

He did not bother to knock, but threw the door to her cabin wide and strode in, his head thrown back, his bearded chin jutting out in defiance.

Once inside, he stopped and his mouth flew open. The room was lit by a single candle stub, sputtering in its holder on the table. The Spaniard knelt beside the bunk, his hands clasped before him, his shoulders shaking. And on the bunk, lay the girl. MacKenzie stepped closer.

"What's going on here?" he roared.

The Spaniard leaped to his feet, and held trembling hands out in supplication. "Oh, *señor*," he gasped. "I am so grateful you have come. We must take the *señorita* to the shore at once."

MacKenzie pushed the pleading man aside and leaned over the bunk. He could not believe what he saw. The girl lay as though dead, her face a pale blur upon the pillow, her golden hair framing her pathetically thin face. Two drops of blood lay like crimson tears upon her cheeks. The pirate grabbed her hand and groaned aloud at its icy touch.

"What have you done to her?" he growled. He began to rub her cold hand briskly.

"I have done nothing, *señor*," the Spaniard babbled. "She has willed herself to die! She wishes to leave her body here so she can return to Scotland unencumbered with the flesh you hold captive."

MacKenzie felt hot anger spurting through his veins, but underlying his anger was an awesome fear. Was he going to lose her? He could not bear the thought! He dropped her hand and whirled to confront the old man.

"Why dinna you tell me she was ailing?" he demanded. "I must fetch the surgeon. He'll know what to do."

The Spaniard backed away, his hand over his mouth. "Oh, no," he moaned. "You will kill her if you do that! I am the only one who knows how to restore her to health. You must allow me to tend her, but first, you must take her ashore."

MacKenzie fought hard to control his anger. He could not strike the man, for if he rendered him helpless, should the Spaniard be telling the truth, he would be consigning the lass to her death as surely as if he had stabbed her through the heart with his own hand.

"How do I know what you say is true?" he snarled. "This could be another Spanish trick."

Fernando gestured toward the girl. "Does that look like a trick, *señor?*" he asked softly. "She is dying, I tell you. If you don't act quickly, it will be too late. I only pray you have what I need to heal her."

MacKenzie looked down at the pale face. He suddenly felt as though someone had pushed a knife into his gut. She *was* dying! No! He could not lose her! He had waited all of his life for someone like her to warm his bed, to birth his sons! "What do you need?" he asked. "I will gie you aught!"

He thought he caught a glimpse of triumph in the Spaniard's eyes, but the heathen's face was lost to his view as he stepped to the girl's side.

"Later," the old man admonished. "First, you must take her ashore. Here, I will wrap her in the blanket. She must not catch more chill in the morning air."

MacKenzie pushed the Spaniard aside impatiently. "I'll do it," he growled.

He pulled the blanket from her and looked down in horror at her thin body. Then he quickly lifted her and laid her upon the blanket which he wrapped tenderly about her. She was so still. Was she living? He placed a finger beneath her nostrils, and though he was relieved to feel her breath, he was horrified at how lightly it fluttered against his finger. He picked her up and cradled her head upon his shoulder.

"Open the door," he ordered. "Then gae before me up the ladder and tell one of my men to get the boat ready."

As Fernando scrambled to obey, he forced himself to frown. He could not allow the pirate to see his glee at the success of his

201

plan. He threw the door open wide and hurried down the companionway, ignoring the twinge of pain in his shoulder. He had to take advantage of the giant's fears while he could.

He climbed the ladder rapidly, not taking time to look back. MacKenzie was following. But when Fernando stopped a seaman and boldly ordered him to prepare the longboat, he was greeted with a boot to the rear and a hard cuff to the side of the head.

"Spaniard!" the seaman hooted. "Trying to escape are you? I'll run you through and laugh while you gurgle your last breath."

Although his shoulder was racked with pain, Fernando pulled himself slowly to his feet and gestured behind him.

"You had better do what I said," he gasped, "or you will wish yourself dead."

The seaman grinned and raised his knife.

Suddenly, a booted foot appeared out of nowhere and knocked the knife from the upraised hand. The seaman grabbed his wrist and screamed. Another boot caught him in the small of the back and sent him hurtling across the deck onto his face.

MacKenzie roared like an enraged bull. "Prepare the boat, you bastard, or I'll feed you to the sharks!"

The seaman scrambled to his feet, clutching his injured wrist. "Yes, sir!" he shouted. "Right now, Cap'n!"

Fernando kneaded his throbbing shoulder while the boat was pulled alongside. Then he stood beside the railing as MacKenzie climbed down the ropes, cradling Shona in his strong arms as though her body were no encumbrance at all. When he had scrambled down and cradled her head in his lap, MacKenzie put his back to the oars.

As they glided across the water, Fernando had to remind himself that Shona was pretending. Her face was so pale, and she lay so still, she almost convinced him that she was, indeed, at death's door. Only when her fingers pinched his knee was he jolted back to reality.

When they approached the shore, he was astounded to see that what they had thought was clean white sand, was actually a filthy beach covered with human refuse and teeming with huge blow flies. MacKenzie beached the boat and roundly cursed the seaman who did not drag the craft onto the sand fast enough. Fernando was puzzled by the way this huge man could be so vehement at one instant and then cradle the girl in his arms with such tenderness in the next. He shook his head as he followed the pirate leader up the beach.

The stench assailing his nostrils brought bile to his mouth as he trotted at MacKenzie's heels. Animal offal was mingled with human excrement everywhere he looked. As their steps led them up a sandy track into the trees, they passed decaying grass huts with gaping holes in their roofs. Filth and refuse tumbled in wild profusion from the open doorways, and ragged children, ranging in color from tan to jet black, scratched at lice and clutched the wasted legs of their dark-skinned mothers, their eyes dull from too little food and too much idle time.

Fernando blinked back tears. Only man could defile such a natural paradise as this. Why had there been no fishing boats plying the placid waters of the bay? Where were the goats and pigeons, the racks of drying fish? Why did the women they passed shrink back into the shadows and look out with terror-stricken eyes? Why were the only animals in evidence a few runty hogs rooting about in the refuse with obscene-sounding grunts?

He realized he was lagging far behind MacKenzie and ran to catch up, taking heart that the pirate had not insisted a guard bring up the rear. Perhaps escape would not be too hard after all! If they could find a boat, that is, for he had seen none in the harbor.

MacKenzie turned onto a broad track lined with wooden buildings, the first evidence of true civilization Fernando had seen. But the condition of the ramshackle structures, unpainted, with splintering boards and broken steps, soon convinced him that the European occupants of this island were no more civilized than the natives. The street was crowded with shouting, shoving men all moving in the same direction—toward a large two-storied structure fronted by a peeling wooden fence that enclosed a sandy, weed-infested yard.

MacKenzie pushed his way toward the building, shouting curses and obscenities at the top of his voice. Fernando noted how quickly the crowd melted before the roaring giant. The old seaman who had brought food and water to their cabin now raced ahead of his captain, pushing the gate open with a frenzied gesture. "You're getting old and slow, Jack!" MacKenzie bellowed as he elbowed his way past the trembling seaman and mounted the steps. "Ho, Smitty! MacKenzie's here! Where are you, man?"

Fernando panted for breath as he climbed to the top of the porch, but his eyes quickly took in the faded sign beside the open doorway: The Bastard's Lair. Food, Drink and Women. Above the lettering, a leering skull had been painted in black. It seemed so appropriate that Fernando began to chuckle as he entered the dim, sour-smelling interior.

A grossly overweight man waddled toward them, wiping his hands on his greasy apron. "Aw, Captain MacKenzie," he fawned, his tiny eyes bright with greed, "they told me you had put in! And with a new ship! But you bring your own woman! Lucinda will be so disappointed—"

"Enough of your blethering!" MacKenzie bellowed. "This lass's feeling poorly. We'll need water and . . ." He faltered and turned to Fernando. "Tell Smitty what you need, man!" he ordered. "I'll take her up tae my room."

"I will see her settled; then I will tell you what I need," Fernando answered firmly.

MacKenzie nodded and strode quickly to the stairs. He paced through the gloom down a long hallway and paused outside the last door.

"Open it, fool!" he roared.

Fernando sidled past him and threw the door open. The

stench of cheap perfume struck him as he stepped inside.

"Pull back those blankets," MacKenzie ordered.

Fernando moved to obey, but his way was suddenly blocked by a woman of color who moved from the shadows to stand before him, her hands on her hips, her black eyes blazing.

"Don' touch that bed!" she spat out.

Fernando was pushed violently to one side as MacKenzie confronted the woman.

"Get out of here, bitch!" he bellowed, lashing out at her with his boot and catching her in the hip. She crumpled into a heap on the floor, but was up in seconds, her face twisted into a hideous snarl, her hands snatching at the blanket covering Shona.

"You bring another woman to your bed? Lucinda will kill her!"

Fernando grasped the furious woman's wrists and pushed her away, ignoring the sharp pain in his shoulder. He tied the mosquito netting to one side and pulled back the bed covers. The sheets were dingy gray and streaked with filth. As he watched, a large black beetle scrambled across the pillow. He brushed it onto the floor and squashed it. He pulled the blankets up again.

"Put her on top," he said to MacKenzie. "The sheets are dirty."

MacKenzie placed Shona tenderly on the bed. But when he reached out to remove the blanket covering her, Lucinda launched herself at him, scratching at his face with her long fingernails. Though Fernando had been embarrassed by Shona's use of expletives, they were nothing compared to what this woman was screeching.

Her tirade, however, was short-lived. MacKenzie brought back his fist and hit her full in the face. Instantly blood splattered from her smashed nose, and she dropped to the floor as though dead.

"Smitty!" MacKenzie roared. "Come up here!"

Fernando bent over Shona. He marveled that she was able to

remain so still throughout all of the ruckus. The drops of blood
had dried into two black tears upon her cheeks. Her eyes were
closed and her face was so pale, her breathing so light, that he
felt a stab of fear. Was something really the matter with her?
He bent over her and pressed his ear to her breast. The steady
thum-thum of her heart reassured him, but he forced himself
to frown.

"She is sinking," he said in a whisper. "I fear it is too late.
There has been too much confusion."

MacKenzie pushed him away and frantically grabbed
Shona's hand. "It canna be! She canna die! You canna let her
die!"

Fernando was spared an answer when Smitty came puffing
into the room, his dirty face streaked with sweat and his
chubby cheeks crimson red with exertion.

"What's the matter, Captain MacKenzie?" he gasped.

"Get that bizzem oot of here!" MacKenzie ordered, stabbing
a finger at the unconscious Lucinda. "Then bring clean sheets,
a new bolster and blankets, and water. At once!"

Fernando could see the unanswered questions in Smitty's
eyes, but the proprietor had enough sense to hasten to do as he
was bid. He grabbed Lucinda's ankles and dragged her from the
room, leaving a streak of blood on the sandy floorboards. He
was back in moments, burdened with stacks of clean linen and
a jug of fresh water.

Fernando grabbed a towel and wet it in the jug, but before he
could bathe Shona's face, the towel was snatched from his
hand.

"I'll do that," MacKenzie said in the quietest voice Fernando had ever heard him use. "You make a pallet on the
floor. We'll move her there while we change the bedding."

An hour later, Shona lay naked between clean sheets,
covered by sweet-smelling blankets. Though Fernando had
tried to dissuade MacKenzie from removing her clothing, the
pirate would not listen, so he had prayed that she would have
the fortitude to remain inert. She did not disappoint him.

MacKenzie bathed her body with great tenderness, patting it dry with a touch lighter than Fernando had thought possible. When the pirate captain was about to cleanse Shona's face, he hesitated before washing the blood from her cheeks, and Fernando was exultant. The man was still afraid!

MacKenzie smoothed her hair, the gentleness of his huge hands incongruous. He stood back. "Now, tell me what you need to make her well. I'll move heaven or hell, but I'll get aught you say you hae to hae."

Fernando thought frantically. He had known this time would come, but he had pushed it from his mind. Now, he was at a loss. He knew it was imperative that he request things almost impossible to obtain—that he and Shona needed all the time alone he could finagle. He wrinkled his brow and pursed his lips.

"I will need a fern that has but one branch. Do not bring one with more than one branch, or it will not work. And it must be scraped and the scrapings put to boil in a large pitcher full of water for two hours. Then you must bring some soot, the whites of two eggs, and a little oil of roses. And I will need vinegar, yeast, and honey. And most importantly, I need three gold coins to hide in her mattress and a very sharp knife to place under her bed."

MacKenzie reared back. "Knife! Are you crazy, auld man? I thought you said you would cure her! What good will gold coins and a knife under her bed do?"

Fernando shook his head and clucked his tongue. "You seem to forget, *señor*," he said softly, "that what ails the *señorita* is not so much physical, as spiritual. She suffers from a great darkness of the soul, brought on by her . . . by her captivity. She told me she was captured by her mother's people and kept locked in a dark chamber for many years, and she will not allow herself to live such a life ever again. She will simply leave this body and inhabit another."

MacKenzie stared down at Shona. Fernando could see the battle he was fighting. He wanted the girl, wanted to bed her,

207

wanted to keep her. But if she died, he would lose her completely. He sighed deeply and nodded. "I'll get what you want, but it will take time. Do you want the coins and the knife first?"

Fernando swallowed a smile of victory. "Of course. Then the fern, and after that, the remainder of my list."

MacKenzie took a sack from his waistband and counted out three gold coins. Then he removed his knife. "Is this sharp enough?"

Fernando ran his finger over the blade. "Perhaps after a little honing?"

MacKenzie grunted and walked to the door. "I'll be right back," he promised.

When he had closed the door behind him, Fernando hurried to Shona's side. He pressed his fingers into her shoulder. "Do not move yet, Madonna," he whispered. "He will return shortly."

The knife, sharpened to a razor's edge, was returned moments later. Fernando made sure that MacKenzie saw him place it beneath the bed. Then he shooed the pirate out the door with orders to bring only what he had requested—no substitutions.

"And make sure there are no more disturbances from that woman," he instructed, following MacKenzie down the hallway to the top of the stairs.

When the pirate nodded acknowledgment, Fernando returned to the room. He had learned what he needed to know: there was a guard posted at the foot of the stairs.

He moved a chair over in front of the door so he would have ample warning if MacKenzie returned; then he tapped Shona on the arm.

"You can open your eyes now," he whispered. "We will be alone for a little while."

She came alive with a violent shudder. "Oh, God," she moaned. "I thought I would die when he undressed me."

Fernando averted his eyes, his cheeks burning. "I am

sorry," he whispered. "I could not stop him."

Shona grabbed his hand and squeezed it. "Oh, Fernando, I know you couldn't," she said. "You were wonderful! When I heard you slide that knife under the bed, I thought I would burst out laughing."

"It's fortunate that you didn't," he said seriously. "He is very much afraid he will lose you. I am certain if we carry this through, we will be able to escape. But there are problems. . . ."

"What are they? Surely we can overcome them."

"The first, maybe. MacKenzie has posted a guard at the bottom of the stairs. But there may be another way out of here. The second is much more serious. There are no small boats in the harbor. Only the one belonging to the *Loretta*. I fear we will have to escape over land and hope we can find a craft on the other side of the island."

Shona's smile disappeared. "That's no little problem," she said. She ran her fingers through her tangled hair. "How long do you think we can stall him?"

"I don't know. He is a very impatient man, but he cares for you. Perhaps a few days. Also, we do not know what his plans are, how long he intends to stay on this island."

"If only we had someone we could trust! What about that woman, Fernando? What happened to her?"

"She was MacKenzie's woman! His . . . his *puta*, Madonna."

"I know that. I could smell her perfume the moment I entered the room. But what happened to her? Do you suppose we could convince her to help us escape? She didn't seem to like the idea of my being here."

"That could be very, very dangerous. You couldn't see how she was looking at you. If her glares had been knives, you would be dead."

"But that's just it! Perhaps we could make her understand that if she helped us I would no longer be around to endanger her position with MacKenzie. I couldn't see what happened, but it didn't sound as though she was afraid of him."

Fernando grinned. "She was not. She flew at him like a wild she-cat. But I still think we should wait and try something else. We can always use her as a last resort. I am not so sure she would be willing to tangle with that *hombre* again. I am certain he broke her nose."

Shona frowned. "He's a blot on all Scotsmen!" she said. "But the MacKenzies always were a little odd. It's just my luck to have to tangle with one of them. If only he had put me on that boat with the others . . ."

"Then I should be dead, Madonna, but smiling down from heaven at your escape."

She grabbed his hand. "Oh, I'm sorry! I just didn't think! Don't talk like that, I would die if you were not here with me."

"The men in that boat may not have made it to shore," Fernando mused. "They may have perished without food and water."

"As we may perish even if we do find a boat?" she asked quietly.

He turned and stared at her. "You are right. We must find provisions. Perhaps the woman will help us, after all."

"Then you will feel her out?"

"Yes. I will try to go downstairs later. But that means you will be left here alone with that beast."

Her smile was grim. "I can take care of myself," she said firmly. "Now, hadn't you better hand me my comb? I need some more bloody tears before MacKenzie returns."

"What if he sees your finger?"

"The pricks are not that large. I will open the same ones I used before."

Fernando knelt and felt under the bed. When he straightened, he held the knife in his hand. "I did not think to bring your bundle. Use this. It is much sharper and will not hurt as badly."

Shona pricked her finger and squeezed until she had two large drops which she gently placed upon her cheeks. "How does that look?" she asked as she settled herself for another long stint of playacting. "Convincing?"

Fernando chuckled. "Very."

When he rose to return the knife to its resting place, Shona placed a restraining hand on his arm. "Where will we go, Fernando?" she asked. "And how will we know which way to sail? It's so far to the Colonies."

He patted her hand. "You must try not to worry. I learned much from Esteban. Somehow, God will manage to guide us to the Spanish territories."

Shona's lips trembled. "No. God will not guide us. Stephen will. Stephen will take us to safety."

Chapter 17

Late that evening, Fernando placed a few drops of the juice from the fern upon Shona's lips, rubbed some more into her temples and reluctantly left her in MacKenzie's care. The Spaniard was fighting an inner battle as he made his way cautiously past the drunken bodies littering the hallway. He knew it was dangerous to leave Shona alone with MacKenzie, but he needed to find out as much as he could about the Bastard's Lair. He must try to make contact with Lucinda.

He gagged at the rancid stench of stale cooking oil and spirits as he stepped around more drunks sprawled upon the stairs. Surely every pirate on the island had already imbibed enough spirits to fill the bay! Even the guard lay in a stupor upon the steps. Though the lower floor was a maze of halls and rooms, he followed the raucous sounds of laughter and the shouts, and soon found himself standing in the arched doorway of the great room.

Fernando was not timid, but he was not rash, either. He stood for some time, staring into the densely packed room, every nerve in his body tuned to a fine pitch. Over fifty men were crowded in there, draped over tables and sprawling on the floor. As he watched, he pondered his chances of surviving discovery. Granted, MacKenzie had assured Fernando that he had told his men to leave the Spaniard alone. Still, these rowdy seamen were well into their cups. Would they remember their captain's order when they seemed to be having great difficulty even sitting on the benches?

Fernando's stomach growled with hunger. He had insisted that Shona eat the food sent up for him, assuring her that he would find something later. He straightened his shoulders and eyed an empty spot at a table in a dark corner, mentally mapping out how he would reach it. He would have to chance it. He had to eat now or he would have no strength when the time for escape came.

He stepped into the room, sidled past a group of men engaged in a noisy argument, and turned toward the table, only to find his way blocked by a grinning pirate clad in ragged clothing, a thick bandage on his right wrist. *Madre de Dios*, it was the same man who had booted him across the deck! He knew he was as good as dead.

He stared deeply into the pirate's eyes and fingered the cross about his neck, rejecting the impulse to turn tail and run. Christ had faced the mob which had demanded his death with great strength. If he, Fernando Mendoza, was about to die, he would do so as a man. He threw back his head and straightened his shoulders.

A bellow erupted from the pirate's throat. Fernando had not been aware of the silence of the crowd until that roar echoed through the room. It seemed to bounce off of the walls and floor, gathering strength as it reverberated. When it died, the only sound coming to his ears was the harsh breathing of the man barring his way.

He sifted frantically through his mind for a way to handle the explosive situation. When a thought came to him, it was so simple, he almost laughed aloud. He raised his hand and stabbed a forefinger into the pirate's chest. "You will move, *señor*," he said in a harsh whisper, "or I will bring the curse of the Strathmore vampire down upon your head, and upon the heads of all who occupy this room."

The harsh breathing was interrupted as the pirate caught his breath. Fernando saw movement out of the corner of his eye and realized that several of the men were stabbing their fingers out in front of them, making the ancient sign to ward off the evil eye. He snarled low in his chest and poked the pirate in the chest again.

"I will count to three, señor, then it will be too late."

He raised his hand and his forefinger stabbed the air. "One," he shouted. He raised his middle finger. "Two."

Pandemonium erupted in the room. The pirate blocking his way was grabbed from behind and thrown to the floor. Benches were overturned as bodies hurtled toward the door. Growls, shouts, curses filled the air as the pirates pummeled each other in their frantic desire to quit the room. Fernando stood silently in the midst of the confusion, his face frozen into a hideous grin, his hand still raised, his body untouched by the fleeing pirates. Within minutes, only one pirate remained, and he was lying in a drunken stupor beneath a table, completely oblivious to all that had transpired.

Fernando lowered his hand and shuddered. He had not realized there was such power in superstition! He made his way slowly to a table next to the fire, his soul shrinking from the vile act he had just performed. "God forgive me," he whispered as he collapsed onto the bench.

"You got great power, mon." The woman's harsh whisper startled him and he looked up quickly to find Lucinda staring down at him. Her huge black eyes were surrounded by the whitest whites he had ever seen. She was smiling, her full lips trembling as though she fought to keep from laughing aloud. Her wide nose was swollen grotesquely and he looked away, embarrassed.

She laughed then, a rich, full laugh born of genuine humor. "Lucinda's a real mess, ain't she!" she said with mock dismay. "Her poor nose be smashed all over her black face. Must be real hard for a gen'leman to look at her."

Her implied slur stung and he looked up quickly. "You are a very beautiful woman," he said sincerely. "Even with a broken nose."

Her mellow laugh reached out toward him. "You don' have to lie to this womon," she said. "Lucinda ain' afraid of your power. She got her own." She lowered her face until it was inches from his own. "Lucinda's a *santeria*—a *mambo*," she hissed. "And her loa is the Legba. He be more powerfuller than any ol' vampire."

Fernando felt a stab of panic. *Madre de Dios*, she was talking about voodoo! When The Dominican priests in Valencia had found that he and Esteban were going to the New World, they had spent much time instructing them in the various religious cults they might encounter. And surely voodoo, with its phallic snake gods and chicken sacrifices, was the most bizarre! He turned away and stared into the fire. He could not allow her to know how much her horrid religion frightened him. Despite his reluctance to enlist her aid, he knew that he and Shona needed this woman.

He looked up at her smiling face. "I wouldn't be so sure your god is greater," he said. "There is no way to escape the bite of the vampire."

When her placid features registered no fear, he was suddenly aware that she was baiting him, and enjoying every moment of it. He swept his hand across the table, sending sneak cups and trenchers tumbling to the floor. "Get me some food," he said. "And then we will talk more. I think your Legba and my vampire can benefit one another."

She lifted her chin in disdain, not answering. Then she turned and walked slowly across the room, her full hips undulating voluptuously beneath her bright red skirt. When she disappeared through the doorway, Fernando let out his breath in a ragged sigh before dropping his head into his hands.

What had he started? How could he know she could be trusted? Was her desire for MacKenzie strong enough to spur her into aiding the escape of the woman she thought was going to replace her?

An angry Smitty brought him a trencher of boiled pork and

216

potatoes. "You're bad for business," he whined as he slammed the trencher down, splashing pot liquor across the table. "Eat and get out as fast as you can, and don't come back."

Fernando grabbed a corner of Smitty's apron and mopped at the spill. "I am a guest of Capitán MacKenzie," he said coldly. "I will do what I wish, when I wish." Smitty yanked his apron away and waddled angrily from the room.

The pork was greasy and cold, with globules of fat congealed on top of the juices, but Fernando was too hungry to mind. He applied himself vigorously to the food, using the hunk of bread as a sop and spoon. He ate the meat with his fingers, relishing the spicy taste, sure that he could feel strength already permeating his body. Then he gulped the ale, forgetting that he much preferred light wine, as was the way of the Spanish. Only when he had swallowed the last morsel of bread did he sit back and relax, staring into the flickering fire, his body and mind content.

But his contentment was short-lived. Lucinda glided back into the room, two tankards of fragrantly spiced ale in her hands. She did not ask, but seated herself opposite him, shoving one tankard across the table. "You need this to digest the mess you jest ate," she said with a smile.

It was true; the meal was beginning to churn uncomfortably in Fernando's stomach. He took a sip of the ale, the warm libation of cinnamon and nutmeg soothing his discomfort immediately.

As Lucinda's long fingers caressed her cup lovingly, Fernando shuddered at the memory of those sharp nails reaching out to rake MacKenzie's face.

"We talk now," she said. Her tone was businesslike. Her features had hardened into a cold mask.

Fernando was aware that she would make a formidable enemy. If only he knew how much she cared for MacKenzie!

She leaned forward and stared at him. "That womon upstairs, she will go or she will die!" she said suddenly. "MacKenzie belong to Lucinda!"

"But she wants to go!" Fernando cried. "It's MacKenzie who's keeping her here!"

Lucinda picked up her tankard and gulped the hot contents until the cup was drained. Then she slammed the tankard to the table. "He be a fool!" she spat out. "Always, he seek the one with the golden hair to make his babes." She pulled one round breast from the top of her gown and bobbed it up and down before him. "It will be Lucinda who suckles his seed on her paps, not that pale womon upstairs! You must take her away, mon! You must take her away!"

Fernando sighed and shook his head. "It's no use, Lucinda. MacKenzie has her watched all of the time. Even now, there are men on the stairs. There is no way we can escape."

Her black eyes glittered with hatred. "Then she will die."

He swallowed his fear and leaned closer. "But you can help her escape. With your help, it will be easy."

She threw herself back on the bench and chuckled low in her throat. "Why should I do that, mon?" she asked. "I can kill her more easier."

Fernando reached into his waistband and pulled out two of the gold coins. "For this," he answered softly, holding the coins just out of her reach.

Her eyes widened and her breathing quickened. "Where you get that?" she hissed.

"From MacKenzie," Fernando said. "It is for the woman. He said there would be more later."

She threw her empty tankard into the fire. "He give her gold?" she screamed. "He never give Lucinda gold! Always he promise, but never the gold! Only cloth and glass beads! Never the gold!"

"Help us escape and it's yours!" Fernando watched her eye the coins greedily. Then he placed them on the table and shoved them toward her. But when she reached for them, he grabbed them back and palmed them. "No! Not until you help us escape!"

218

"You might be kill! Then Lucinda do all that work for nothin'!"

"If you agree to help, I'll give you one coin now. Then, when you arrange our escape, I'll give you another."

Her eyes narrowed. He knew she was figuring her chances for success. "It must be a good plan," he added, flipping his hand over so she could see the two gold coins resting in his palm. "We must have a boat, and food and water enough to take us to the Colonies."

Her pink tongue touched her full upper lip. "It be hard," she breathed slowly. "Much work. Much worry for Lucinda."

He turned the coins so they caught the firelight. "But worth it," he said.

Suddenly, she snatched one coin from his hand, bit it, and slipped it into her bodice. "I pray to Legba," she said. "And you must pray to your god. MacKenzie, he be ver' angry."

Fernando smiled. "But that doesn't worry you. You can handle him."

Her white teeth flashed. "You one smart mon," she said with a laugh. "But Lucinda great big smarter!"

"What do you mean?"

She pulled thoughtfully at her heavy ear bob. "This work you have me do, it won' cost two gold piece. Lucinda has friends. She get it done for nothin'!"

Fernando was beginning to enjoy this exchange. He leaned back and chuckled. "That's your business, Lucinda. If you make a large profit on your venture, more power to you."

She leaned forward and stabbed one long-nailed finger at his chest. "You smart like a fox," she said. "You remind Lucinda of a mon on the big island an' Lucinda did not like that mon."

"What big island? Where are you from? Do you mean, perhaps, Cuba?"

"'Course Lucinda mean Cuba! On the big island, Lucinda belong to very, very rich mon. He a leader of all mon."

Excitement welled up in Fernando's chest. "Do you speak

219

Spanish, Lucinda?" he asked.

She frowned. "Maybe Lucinda do, maybe she don'," she answered slowly.

"Does MacKenzie?"

She leaped to her feet. "Wha' for you want to know that?"

"Because if you speak Spanish, and MacKenzie doesn't, we might be able to use that in our escape."

She turned her buxom bottom to the fire and smiled at Fernando. "He don'," she said. "But we don' have to use that talk. Leave it all to Lucinda. She take care—"

She stopped suddenly and held up her hand, signaling Fernando to be quiet. Then she gestured meaningfully toward the drunk moaning beneath a table several feet away.

She pulled Fernando into a corner. "Lucinda know that mon," she whispered. "He no good mon."

"Do you think he heard us?"

She pushed out her full lower lip. "Don' know. But Lucinda take no chance."

She moved quietly toward the drunk. Fernando pulled her back. "What are you going to do?" he whispered.

"Don' touch me!" she hissed. "You don' touch a *mambo* of the Legba."

He dropped his hand. "Excuse me. I did not know."

She walked slowly to the drunk and jabbed him in the ribs with her bare foot. "Hey, mon!" she called softly.

The drunk groaned and tried to turn over.

She kicked him harder. He coughed and rolled over on his back. His eyes were bloodshot and his stubbled cheek was covered with sand from the filthy floor. He rolled his head from side to side.

She knelt by his side. "You know Lucinda, mon?" she crooned. "You know the power in Lucinda?"

He groaned again and tried to sit up.

She pressed him back to the floor and stood up, placing her large, splayed foot upon his chest. "Listen close, mon," she said. "You hear nothin' in this place tonight, hear? You know

220

nothin' 'bout Lucinda and her business with this mon, hear?"

The drunk batted his eyes and retched. She removed her foot and leaped backward as a spew of vomit gushed from his mouth. "Bah!" she exclaimed. She turned to Fernando. "He don' know nothin'," she sneered. "An' if he do, Lucinda take care of that mon. He won' talk."

Fernando stared at the woman. Beads of perspiration glistened like jewels on her black forehead. Her large eyes were narrowed into slits and she wrung her large hands together as though she relished the thought of having to silence the drunk.

"I trust you won't do anything violent? I mean, I don't want any bloodshed on our account."

She threw back her head and her rich laughter echoed through the room. "Don' have to bring blood!" she laughed. "Just make him afraid. Legba do all the rest!"

Fernando felt that his immortal soul was in danger. He knew he had to escape from her evil presence immediately! "When do you think we can leave?" he asked.

"Two days. MacKenzie be very busy killin' hogs. You go then."

He nodded. "I will speak to you later," he said. "You know which room I'm in."

Lucinda watched him walk swiftly from the room. When he had disappeared into the hall, her face broke into a huge smile. "Don' need to bring blood on you either, mon," she said softly. "Lucinda don' need Legba to take care of you an' that womon. Lucinda do that herself!"

221

Chapter 18

Shona was so worried that it was difficult to keep her thoughts serene, to prevent her muscles from twitching. Fernando had been gone for a long time. What was keeping him? Having to lie so still was torture for someone who usually paced off tension. She was sure she would lose control if he did not return to relieve MacKenzie soon.

The pirate's ragged breathing came closer, and she heard a soft rustle as the mosquito netting was pulled aside. She knew he was bending over her, staring into her face. Her nose began to itch, and she yearned to scratch it. God, she could not keep this up much longer! Her foot jumped involuntarily, and she held her breath.

When MacKenzie's hand caressed her cheek, she pressed her head deeper into the bolster, shrinking from his touch, praying he would not notice. She felt his breath on her face and his beard tickled her cheek. She could not bear the stench of spirits and sour sweat assailing her nostrils. She had to do something!

Pushing aside her fear of the agony she knew it would invoke, she desperately concentrated her thoughts upon Stephen. Slowly, his face appeared before her, bringing a pain so acute she almost gasped aloud. Fighting back her rising fear that he would disappear if she so much as blinked her eyes, she studied his dear, familiar features. His dark blond hair was curled and tousled, as though he had just stepped down from the windy deck. His high cheekbones were ruddy and tanned, and his smooth cheeks clean-shaven, accentuating the small crescent scar she had fingered so often. His eyes were dark, dark blue, and they smoldered with the consuming fires of his passion.

He smiled, the corners of his full lips turning upward like the wings of a soaring bird. Then he held out his arms, beckoning her with a toss of his head and a charming tilt of his right eyebrow. When she stepped into the warm circle of his love, his slim, gentle hands caressed her body and his lips trailed across the hollow of her throat, evoking a shiver of anticipation so exquisite she felt as though she would be consumed by her own burning desire. His mouth covered her own, his lips soft, yet demanding. Then his tongue pressed between her lips and entwined with hers, filling her mouth with sweetness. All thoughts of MacKenzie and of her predicament were wiped from her conscious mind as she succumbed to Stephen's vibrant, tangible presence.

She pressed closer until the beating of his heart became one with hers and his taut muscles flexed against her breasts, stifling her breath. Her body melted, like liquid gold being tried in a raging fire as his throbbing manhood pulsed against her most secret places. His hands kneaded the small of her back, then moved down to her buttocks, gripping her even closer to his vital body.

She yearned to hear his deep, throaty voice whispering her name, or crooning the sweet, musical Spanish words of love he used so often; yet her own need was so compelling, she was unable to give voice to her desire. His fingers trembled as he slowly undressed her, devouring her with his eyes, and she tore at his clothing, gasping with the urgency of her need for him. Then he lifted her into his arms as easily as one would pick up a feather, and he carried her quickly to the bed. He laid her down ever so gently and lowered himself over her, teasing her for a moment with a lopsided grin as he pressed his engorged manhood against her stomach.

She grasped his face between her hands and pulled him down until their mouths were joined, their lips and tongues moving, tasting, entwining, giving silent voice to their love. As his fingers brushed over her breasts, her soft nipples rose and tightened into aching buds of desire, and when he pressed his throbbing flesh between her thighs, she opened her legs eagerly, arching as he entered her with one violent thrust. The sensation was so intense, so exquisite, she felt as though she would surely die, caught in the death throes of her own rapture.

They moved slowly, their hips rising and falling in unison to the silent music of their love ballad. As Stephen stared down at her, his smoky gaze devouring her face, feature by feature, she plunged into the dark blue seas beneath his arched brows. She dove deeper, deeper, until she was completely immersed in the burning liquid of his passion.

Then they rose together, soaring above majestic mountains, the vibrant wings of love slicing through the blue heavens effortlessly, eagerly, their bodies buoyed by the hot winds of their passion. Higher and higher they flew, drawn ever closer to the blazing sun. Then, suddenly, they were engulfed by its fiery rays, and Shona yielded to their scorching embrace. As Stephen stiffened and arched beneath her, a deep, answering moan built within her and she was powerless to stop it.

"Shona, lass." MacKenzie's voice jolted her from her imaginings as rudely as the shock of icy sea water. Stephen's image vanished instantly and she had to bite her tongue to keep from screaming aloud in anguish. Oh, God, he had been so close! She had seen him, felt his warm, living body pressed to hers! They had been one for a few fleeting moments of rapture. . . .

She felt MacKenzie rubbing her arms and hands, and it was all she could do not to rise up and scream out her bitter disappointment. But she remained limp, telling herself that she could take it. She must take it.

"Wake up, Shona," MacKenzie breathed close to her ear. "You must get well. I dinna want to live without you. We'll be marrit, lass. You'll not be my captive. You'll be my wife! You'll bear me fine, strong weans, all sons, and I'll take you away to anywhere you want to go! Live, lass, live!"

His *wife!* Revulsion washed over her. She could picture herself, a knife in her belt, standing on the quarter-deck beneath a leering Jolly Roger, ducking musket balls ricocheting off the deck while a runny-nosed, redheaded child pulled at her breeches. She swallowed a snort. His wife indeed! A mosquito buzzed near her ear and she steeled herself, calling forth every ounce of self-control she could muster.

She heard the door open and close, and footsteps neared the bed. At last—Fernando!

"How is the *señorita?*" he whispered.

"No better," MacKenzie growled. "I thought you said you could heal her!"

"You have not brought me the oil of roses," Fernando answered. "Without that, the other ingredients will not bring about a cure."

"I told you, I've scoured the island, even had my men turn the huts inside out. I've sent to the large island for some, but that will take time."

"Then you will have to practice patience. Without the oil of roses, she may hang on to life, but she will not recover."

Shona heard a ragged sigh and felt the mattress rise as MacKenzie stood.

"I've work to do," he said. "Do you need anything more tonight? A mattress to sleep on?"

Fernando's laugh sounded like a short bark. "Sleep! What makes you believe I could sleep with her so ill? I will stay in the chair beside her bed. You must leave now. So much conversation will only bring her distress."

"I'll leave a man posted on the stairs. If you need anything, just tell him."

226

"I will. I know you care deeply for the *señorita*. Please take your leave quietly."

Shona heard MacKenzie open the door and then close it. As his footfalls faded down the hallway, she began to sputter. "Care for the *señorita!*" she hissed, opening her eyes. "What's come over you, that you would pander to that animal, Fernando?"

He placed a finger to his lips and nodded toward the door. "Wait a moment," he whispered. "He may decide to come back."

She waited, watching the door, her heart in her throat. When several minutes had passed, she groaned and stretched her arms over her head.

He sat beside her on the bed. "What happened while I was gone?" he asked. "Was there any trouble?"

She grimaced. "Only once. He kept patting my face. I thought I would explode. But I . . . I . . ." She threw herself into his arms. "Oh, Fernando, I imagined Stephen was here. I wanted to die when I realized he was only in my thoughts!"

He patted her awkwardly. "There, there. I know it has not been easy. But you have been so very brave. If you can only continue for a little while longer, we will escape this horrible place!"

She pulled away and wiped angrily at the tears on her cheeks. "You were gone so long! What happened? Did you talk to that woman?" She was surprised when a look of fear crossed his face. "What's the matter? Won't she help us?"

Fernando's fear was replaced by a weary smile. "Yes, she will. She said she will arrange our escape in two days' time."

"Then why are you afraid? I saw that look on your face. Don't you trust her?"

"No, but that is not my problem." He shook his head. "Oh, Madonna, I fear we have entangled ourselves with a very evil woman. She is a voodoo priestess, and she exudes wickedness with every word, every movement."

Shona plumped the bolster and turned on her side. "Tell me

everything that happened. I want to know every word that was said."

Fernando related his entire evening, making light of his danger upon entering the great room. When he finished, he leaped up and began to pace. "I'm not sure we can trust her, but we have no other choice. This island is crawling with MacKenzie's men. Without Lucinda's help, we will be unable to find provisions and a boat."

"Then we'll have to trust her. You're too afraid of your God's displeasure to think clearly. You're fashing yourself over nothing."

He stopped pacing. "He is your God, too, Madonna, if you would only realize it."

Shona sat up, her face impassive. "I don't want to talk about it," she said firmly. "Turn your back. I'm going to wrap myself in a blanket and walk around. I hope you told her I would need some clothing!"

"I did not think about it. Do not worry, I will be seeing her again."

Two days passed without a visit from Lucinda. By the second evening, Shona was finding it almost impossible to lie still, and Fernando was sure the woman had duped him out of a gold coin. How could he have been so sure she wanted the second? And, more important, would she give them away?

He took only a few minutes to gulp down several spoonfuls of greasy stew in the great room, then made his way back upstairs. Shona was becoming too exhausted by her ordeal to lie still for very long. He paused outside the room to collect his wits. Tonight, he and Shona would have to devise a plan for escaping on their own. When he opened the door and stepped inside, his shoulders were bent and he felt as though he had aged ten years.

MacKenzie greeted him with a broad smile. "The vinegar poultice you put on her chest seems to be working," he said

228

exultantly. "Her color's better already."

Fernando shook his head and pulled a long face, inwardly cursing the pirate's keen eyes. He himself had noticed that the bloom was returning to Shona's cheeks just that afternoon. He had tried plastering her face with egg whites to make her appear pale, but of course, the eggs had dried to a hard mask and he had had the devil's time removing them.

"Don't raise your hopes too high, *señor*," he told MacKenzie as he looked down at Shona. "I have only said I would try to cure her. Everything depends upon whether or not she wishes to get well."

"She moaned several times," MacKenzie said eagerly. "And she even moved her arms and legs when I felt her forehead. I'm sure she's mending."

Fernando humphed, but said nothing. He knew Shona's resolve was dwindling. If they had to remain here much longer, unable to lie still, she would most likely give their charade away.

MacKenzie crossed to the window and looked out. "I'll be busy most of the morrow," he said. "The wind's rising. We're still in the hurricane season and it's time to slaughter the hogs. If I dinna keep a tight rein on my men, they'll get more hog herders than hogs and get roaring drukken while they roast the poor bastards alive on the spits."

Chills coursed over Fernando's body. *Madre de Dios*, no wonder the women of the island looked so haunted! They had to escape this island of infamy, and soon! "I will tend to the *señorita*," he said, forcing his voice to an even tone. "She seems to mend better when you do not spend too much time with her."

MacKenzie whirled about, a scowl on his face. "What do you mean by that?" he roared. "Are you telling me I'm keeping her from getting well?"

"Of course not," Fernando soothed. "I only meant, so much talking seems to agitate her spirit. She appears to prefer complete quiet."

229

MacKenzie relaxed and stomped to the door. "I'll be here sune with the oil of roses," he said. "And I'll expect her to be much improved by tomorrow night." He smacked his lips and grinned broadly as he left the room.

Fernando almost collapsed when the door closed behind the pirate. When would he learn to control his tongue? He crossed to the bed and looked down at Shona. It was obvious why MacKenzie thought her health improved. Her cheeks were rosy, and the food he had been stuffing her with every day had begun to erase that gaunt, gravely ill look.

She opened her eyes. "I can't take much more of this," she moaned. "I don't think Lucinda's coming."

He shook his head. "I fear we must come up with our own plan. I was right about her. She only wanted the gold piece. I told you she was evil."

"If she's evil, she'll want more than one piece of gold. Perhaps she got caught."

"No, I am sure not. MacKenzie would have raised a roar which would have been heard as far away as the mainland if he had found her trying to arrange for our escape." He collapsed into the chair with a deep sigh. "It's no use, Madonna. It is up to us, now. And I don't even know where to start."

She reached beneath the blankets, removed a large wad of sacking and tossed it to the floor. The pungent odor of vinegar filled the room. "Close your eyes. I'm going to get up and then we'll plan. I always think better on my feet."

He sat in the chair while Shona, wrapped in a blanket, restlessly paced about the room, her bare feet whispering on the floorboards the only sound breaking the silence. At last, she crossed to the bed and sat down heavily.

"I can't think of a thing," she said. "We've still got two gold coins, but they're useless to us here. Every time I come up with a plan, it's so badly flawed, I discard it. How about you?"

He shook his head. "The same. If only there weren't so many people about! The way things are, we could not even reach the stairs without being detected."

Shona bit her lip and stared into space. She had thought and thought, but her mind was still a blank. There had to be a way!

Suddenly, she heard a light scratching sound in the hallway. Throwing herself back on the bed, she pulled the top blanket up to her chin, closing her eyes.

She heard the chair scrape and knew Fernando was getting up to investigate. The door hinges squeaked, there were scuffling sounds, and then the door slammed with a loud bang. She jumped.

"Lucinda!" Fernando gasped. "I didn't think you would come."

Shona opened her eyes. A voluptuous black woman stood staring down at her, her hands placed disdainfully upon her broad hips, her black eyes flashing with hatred. So this was the infamous Lucinda! She met the woman's gaze unflinchingly.

"You don' look sick to me," Lucinda spat out. "Who you tryin' to fool?"

Shona pressed her fingers into Fernando's arm to silence his hasty reply. She pulled the blanket about her and stepped from the bed. She wanted to have every advantage, so it was inadvisable to be forced to look up at Lucinda. When she reached her feet, she was astounded to find that the woman still towered over her. Damnation! Why hadn't Fernando told her that Lucinda was a giantess!

She tossed back her hair and raised her chin. "We are trying to fool MacKenzie," she said firmly. "I have no desire to become his woman. You have nothing to fear from me."

Lucinda's rich laughter filled the room. "You! What makes you think you could ever take my place, pale, weak little white womon?" she laughed. She sobered suddenly, and her eyes narrowed to slits. "MacKenzie belong to Lucinda!" she hissed. "He need a real womon!"

Fernando stepped hastily between them. "We know that," he said quickly. "That is why I asked you to help us escape. The *señorita* does not want to replace you in MacKenzie's heart! Or bed." His face flushed and he swallowed noisily. "I thought

231

you had forgotten, and just before you came in, we were trying to think of a way to get away from here."

Lucinda chuckled again, her good humor restored. "You never get away without Lucinda to help." She pushed Fernando out of the way and stood looking down at Shona. "You got a big heart, womon?" she asked suddenly. "You got strong legs an' a strong mind?" She squeezed the tops of Shona's arms and shook her head, not allowing her to answer. "Soon, a big wind come up, womon, an' then the rain come down an' drown the weak ones. You still want to go?"

Shona nodded. "We still want to go. I'm not afraid of a little storm."

Lucinda's eyes widened and she rolled her head from side to side. "A li'l storm?" she hissed. "You don' know what you talkin' about, womon. The wind and rain what come soon will pick up trees an' throw 'em about like they be pieces of grass! The rain come down and fill you nose holes an' swallow the breath out of you! You still ain' afraid?"

Shona's gaze did not waver. "No. I will go through anything to get away from here."

Lucinda motioned to Fernando. "An' you, mon? You ain' afraid?"

Fernando stepped to Shona's side. "I am afraid, but that will not stop me from escaping."

The breath left Lucinda's mouth in a long, drawn out hiss. "So . . ."

She nodded her head curtly toward Shona. "You got clothes, womon? You got somethin' to wear 'sides that old blanket?"

"No. I'll need some breeches and a shirt. And shoes."

"Ha! The res' Lucinda can get, but shoes—no. There ain' no shoes on this island."

"Then I'll go barefoot."

Lucinda bit her full lower lip. "Lucinda will help you, but you must do everything she say, or you will die!"

"We'll do everything you say," Shona said quickly. "When

232

can we leave?"

"You be in one big fast hurry," Lucinda answered. "But Lucinda say you right in goin' fast. MacKenzie be killin' hogs in mornin'. That mean he bein' ready to sail soon. Everythin' ready 'cept breeches an' shirt. That take no time to get." She moved slowly toward the door. "Lucinda be back before night go away. You be ready to go with her."

"Be careful," Fernando warned, "MacKenzie's coming back later to bring some medicine."

Lucinda's smile faded instantly. She grasped the handle and pulled the door open. "Don' never tell a *santeria* what goin' to happen," she said with disdain. "She know everythin'."

When the door closed, Shona collapsed on the bed and groaned. "You were right. I don't trust her," she said. "She hates me and I'm sure she'll do anything to get me out of her way—permanently."

Fernando patted her shoulder. "I do not trust her either, but we have nowhere else to turn. We will have to watch her carefully to make sure she does not lead us into a trap."

"What about the storm? Do you think she was exaggerating?"

"I doubt it. Violent storms can strike until sometime in early November, and since this is late October, we are not out of danger. We will just have to move as fast as we can once we get away from here." He placed the bolster beneath her head and tucked in the blankets. "We only have to get through one more visit from MacKenzie. Are you up to it?"

Shona grimaced. "No. But I'll get through it somehow. Do you think he'll come back soon?"

"I do not know, but we must be ready when he does. Perhaps we should stop talking. Why don't you try to get some sleep. You will need all of your strength for what lies ahead."

"What about you?"

"I will sit in this chair next to the bed, and if I feel like it, I will doze."

Shona settled back and closed her eyes. Suddenly, she

turned on her side and looked over at Fernando. His head was bowed and his lips were moving. "Are you praying?" she whispered.

He raised his head and smiled. "Don't you think I should?"

She stared at him for a moment, then turned onto her back and stared at the ceiling. He had returned to his prayers when he heard her soft reply. "I guess it can't hurt."

She was still staring at the ceiling when she heard steps in the hall. She closed her eyes and steadied her breathing.

The door was thrown open and MacKenzie's voice boomed out, "I've got it! The oil of roses! My man found it on the main island. It came all the way from Spain!"

"Shh!" Fernando admonished. "She is sleeping peacefully. You will disturb her."

Shona heard MacKenzie's steps approach the bed. "You'll have to give her the oil," he said in a much softer voice. "How are you going to do it?"

"That is a secret," Fernando answered. "Now, you must go. I will administer the oil, and you can expect a great improvement in her condition when you return tomorrow night."

Shona steeled herself for MacKenzie's touch. Seconds later, she felt his hand brush her cheek, but she lay perfectly still as his fingers moved over her face. This was the last time she would have to endure his hands upon her.

"I canna' wait 'til tomorrow night," MacKenzie said. "I'll be back before that."

"But you must allow time for the elixir to work!" Fernando protested. "If you insist upon coming back before tomorrow night, do not expect a complete recovery." He sighed deeply. "But, of course, that is up to you. Do what you must."

MacKenzie's hand left her cheek. "I want her well and sitting up in bed ready to welcome me. I'll hold off 'til the night, but I'd better not be disappointed."

"I guarantee you that by tomorrow night, Shona will be

recovered," Fernando replied firmly. "You have my word."

Shona swallowed a smile. Leave it to Fernando to avoid any further lies. Yes, by tomorrow night, she would be completely recovered—and they would be well on their way to freedom!

Fernando dozed as they waited for Lucinda, but Shona could not sleep. She paced the room, flexing her leg muscles and swinging her arms from side to side. She had been idle too long. Would she be able to keep up with Fernando when they made their escape? Though he was well along in years, his body was solid and well muscled from years of hard labor.

She squatted and rose on her toes, stretching her arms toward the ceiling. What worried her most was her certain lack of wind. It seemed like years since she had run through the countryside toward Jephtha who was waiting at Orton Plantation. Thoughts of Jephtha and of his fate made her angry, and a surge of energy poured through her limbs. She worked steadily for another hour, not stopping until she could feel the blood rushing through her veins and her breath came in gasps. Then, she threw herself down upon the bed and lowered the netting.

She closed her eyes and almost reluctantly allowed her memory to call forth Stephen's image. The hurt of allowing him to go was terrible, but the pain of never thinking of him was even greater. She recalled the hours they had lain together in his bunk, sharing their pasts, laughing, devouring one another with their eyes, their mouths. Her face burned and she pressed her cool fingertips to her cheeks. This was not the time to torture herself. She would need all of her resources in a short time. She opened her eyes and watched the sacking at the open window billow into the room. Moments later, she heard the first raindrops on the roof overhead, smelled the heady, warm fragrance of soil and sand absorbing the welcome moisture.

What would they do if a hurricane struck? She had experienced one such storm on the Carolina coast, and her heart shrank from the thought as she recalled the roaring wind, the lashing rain, the rising sea. Should she pray? No, though it was God himself, if there was a God, who controlled the winds. Instead, she very carefully turned her thoughts again to Stephen. He would not allow her to perish. Even now, she knew he was watching over her. He would be with her no matter what the morrow brought.

Chapter 19

Shona sat up in bed, certain she had heard a sound in the hall in one of the lulls between the sporadic bursts of rain. She strained to catch the sound again, but the wind howling around the corners of the building built to a crescendo, drowning out everything but its own banshee shriek. She glanced at Fernando. He sat upright in his chair, wide awake and alert. They waited for a moment, both listening; then Shona dropped back on the bolster just as the door opened.

Lucinda entered the room regally, her shoulders thrown back proudly to accentuate her full, bouncing breasts, her mouth pursed in disdain. She dumped the bundle she carried onto the floor beside the bed and looked at Shona with narrowed eyes. "You make fast hurry, womon," she said. "Lucinda want to get you away quick."

Shona pulled the blanket firmly around her naked body and pushed back the netting surrounding the bed. "Turn your back," she ordered. "You too, Fernando."

Lucinda's eyes glittered like black onyx. "You don' tell *santeria* what to do!" she spat.

"I do if you don't have the decency to respect my privacy!" Shona returned quickly. "I don't know what sort of modesty you demand here, but where I come from, a woman does not bare her naked body to the stares of others."

Fernando stood and whirled about, ducking his head. He was embarrassed by Shona's words. Lucinda shrugged her shoulders and sauntered over to the window where she stood with her back turned, making a pretense of watching the rain. Shona was amused by the woman's attempt to keep control of the situation in order to retain her dignity.

When she shook out the bundle and spread the clothing on the bed, she moaned with dismay. The dark blue shirt and breeches were ragged and dirty. "I can't wear these," she protested. "They're filthy, and probably crawling with vermin."

Lucinda whirled about. "What you want? You want white so you can be seen in the night?" She turned her back again and shrugged her broad shoulders. "You wear that or nothin'. It don' matter to Lucinda."

Shona sighed. The woman was right. She mumbled to herself as she pulled the breeches over her legs, then donned the shirt. The stench of rancid sweat stung her nostrils, and she shivered at the thought of lice lurking in the seams.

"I'm dressed," she said. "But I'd better do something with my hair. Have you a cloth I can tie over it?"

"Perhaps you could use part of the sheet," Fernando volunteered.

"No!" Lucinda hissed. "You need that sheet! Lucinda braid your hair an' wrap it tight."

Her agile fingers made short shrift of the work, and soon a thick braid was deftly wound around Shona's head.

As Lucinda eyed her handiwork a smile of satisfaction softened her lips. "That good," she pronounced. "Now, mon, you tear that sheet an' tie pieces together real tight."

"But whatever for?" Fernando protested. "Surely you do not expect us to climb down to the ground from the window!"

"How else you want to get away? You expect that guard on the stairs to disappear? Lucinda make much magic, but that be too much to expect even from her!"

Shona pulled the blankets from the bed and removed the

238

sheet. "I hope you know what you're doing," she muttered, her hands shaking with agitation. "Surely there is another way out of this place."

"Only the stairs," Lucinda grunted.

Fernando took the sheet from Shona and tore it into narrow strips. "It is a good thing I am accustomed to tying firm knots," he said as his thick fingers turned the strips into a rope.

"What about the other supplies?" Shona asked. "Did you find a boat, and food and water?"

"Of course," Lucinda replied curtly. "Everythin' be ready on other side of island."

"But how will we find it? We don't know our way. We could get lost trying to reach the other side."

Lucinda smiled broadly. "You don' go alone. Lucinda take you." Her smile disappeared as quickly as it had come. "But you make fast, or daylight catch you close an' MacKenzie find you much quick."

Shona looked at Fernando, her eyes wide. He smiled weakly and nodded his head. "I'll tie the rope to the legs of the bed. You open the window wide and be ready to climb down first."

"You should go first."

"No. The rope will hold you with ease, but if it should tear with my weight, at least you will be safely on the ground."

"You could be hurt!"

"I will not be hurt." He eyed Lucinda's large body and shuddered, knowing she outweighed him by far.

Lucinda threw back her head and her body rocked back and forth with soundless laughter. "This womon no' go down that sheet!" she laughed. "Lucinda go down stairs an' meet you outside."

Fernando nodded. "Good. Well, it is tied firmly. It is time to go." He threw the makeshift rope out the window.

Shona straddled the sill and grasped the rope between her hands.

"Let your body slide to the first knot, then loosen your grip until you reach the next knot," Fernando instructed. "That

239

will slow your descent."

She nodded, then lowered herself over the side and wrapped her bare feet around the rope below. The rain spattered her face and the wind tore at her body. When she loosened her grip slightly, she gasped as the sheet whispered through her hands, stinging her palms.

A gust of wind caught Shona and lifted her far out into the air, but the gust died suddenly and she swung back into the side of the building with a loud bang. The breath was knocked from her straining lungs, and her arms felt as though they were being torn from their sockets. She reached the first knot, then grabbed frantically with her feet so she could loosen her hands enough to pass it. Again she slipped toward the ground.

As she reached the second knot, she looked up through the driving rain. She could barely make out Fernando's form outlined in the lamplight at the window. She thought she saw him nod his head. Her hands were throbbing and her shoulders screamed with pain. She gritted her teeth and passed the knot. Seconds later, her feet touched the ground. She dropped to her knees and pressed her stinging palms into the wet earth.

The rope jerked as Fernando's dark shape appeared outside the window. She watched him inch his way downward.

Suddenly, a sharp bang punctuated the air. Shona whirled about and pressed her back against the building. A shaft of light shot across the yard to her right and loud voices, slurred with spirits, came to her ears. She held her breath. God, don't let them see us, she thought.

She twisted about and looked up at Fernando. He was hanging halfway down the building, his body swaying in the wind. She was sure he had heard the voices and was waiting until the danger passed. But as she watched, he suddenly jerked backward and began plummeting toward the ground. The rope had parted!

She stepped aside and he dropped with a loud thud at her feet. Forgetting the voices, the peril, she kneeled at Fernando's side and grasped his body to hers. "Fernando! Are you all right? Fernando!"

He groaned and shook his head from side to side. "Just . . . out . . . of breath!" he gasped.

Shona smoothed the wet strands of hair from his forehead and pulled him into her arms. "Oh, thank God! I thought you were—"

Suddenly, a firm hand dug into her shoulder, sucking the words from her mouth. She almost fainted. They had been discovered!

The hand shook her from side to side. "Hush you mouth!" a voice hissed. "You want them men to hear you?"

Lucinda! Shona gulped in air, trying to calm her wildly beating heart.

The woman kneeled beside them. "You all right, mon?" she asked softly.

Fernando nodded. "Yes. Just winded."

"Then we go fast. Those men goin' to hunt hogs. They all leave soon. We can't stay here."

Fernando rolled onto his side and staggered to his feet, pulling Shona up with him. "Lead the way," he said. "But do not go too far ahead. It is still dark and we need to keep you in sight."

Raw hatred was evident on Lucinda's face as she eyed Shona. Shivers of doubt shot through the girl's body. Was this a trap? Was the woman luring them straight into the arms of MacKenzie? She pushed her doubts aside as she turned to follow Lucinda who was already fading into the darkness at the edge of the clearing.

Fernando pushed her into the brush in front of him. "I will follow you," he whispered. "That is safer."

Shona nodded and pressed through the underbrush, her eyes straining to keep track of Lucinda who was moving swiftly ahead. How could the woman move so unerringly in this darkness?

Shona was soaked to the skin in minutes, but the wind and rain abated as they made their way deeper into the shelter of the forest. But brambles caught her clothing and tore into her flesh, and roots reached gnarled arms across the path to trip her, sending her time and again in a headlong dive to the ground. Her lungs strained in her chest. She could hear her own ragged breathing, feel her blood pounding a steady thrum-thrum in her temples.

They followed the elusive Lucinda for what seemed like hours, until Shona realized that the darkness had melted away and the underbrush surrounding them stood in black silhouette against the graying morning. Her legs were numb and her tongue clove to the roof of her mouth. She felt sure she would die if they did not stop and rest.

But Lucinda did not call a halt. She was always a few yards ahead, her head high, her long red skirt held close to her thighs, out of the reach of the brambles. Shona limped after her, wondering how the woman could walk this far without shoes. Her own bare feet were already cut by sharp stones and prickly twigs, and the calves of her legs screamed for relief.

Noting that the trees and underbrush were beginning to thin, Shona wondered if they were almost at their destination. She had no idea how large the island was, or just where Lucinda was taking them. She forced herself to move faster. Perhaps if she caught up with the large woman, she could convince her to stop for a few moments.

Lucinda appeared to sense, without looking back, that Shona was gaining on her. She lengthened her strides until the girl was forced to trot to keep up.

After a few minutes, Shona had such a painful stitch in her side that she had to stop. Her legs trembled as she dropped to the ground, unmindful of the sharp stones beneath her, cursing her lack of stamina.

Fernando kneeled at her side. "Madonna, you must not give up now," he urged. "Not when we are so close."

"Are we really close?" she panted. "I am certain we've walked a thousand miles."

"We are. There is a clearing up ahead. Let me help you reach it. We cannot lose sight of Lucinda."

He pulled Shona to her feet and put her arm over his shoulder, but she pushed him away.

"No. I can do it on my own. I just needed to catch my breath."

She stumbled along the faint trail, peering through the misty drizzle for a glimpse of their guide, but the woman had disappeared from sight. Shona forced her legs to move faster. Her muscles trembled so, she staggered from side to side. At last, she broke into the clearing. The wind tore at the seared grass, whipping it against her ankles like sharp knives. Out in the open, the rain pelted her face, blurring her vision, but she spied a large tree in the center of the grassy plot and she turned her steps in its direction. She could not go on. She had to rest or she would die!

Fernando clasped her shoulder. "We must rest," he said. She knew he could go on for hours, that he was only trying to accommodate her, but she allowed him to convince her that he, too, was tired. She stumbled toward the tree.

When they reached their destination, they found Lucinda standing beneath the swaying branches, a look of disdain twisting her features. "What the matter, womon?" she sneered. "You don' keep up with Lucinda good. You' puny li'l body tired?"

Shona slumped to the ground, her back against the tree trunk. "No!" she spat. "I just need time to catch my breath."

Lucinda hunkered beside her. "Good for you Lucinda patient womon. Other womon would leave you to find your own way."

"She stopped for me," Fernando said as he dropped beside Shona. "The wound in my shoulder has drained my strength. I need to rest for a few moments."

The look on Lucinda's face told Shona that she had not swallowed Fernando's excuse. She closed her eyes and rested the back of her head against the trunk, shivering from the cold. She was so numbed in body and spirit that she was not sure she could go on.

A sudden vision of Stephen appeared in her mind. He was smiling wickedly, his eyebrows raised, his blue eyes glittering with amusement. "It's not funny!" she protested silently. Still, he grinned at her, until she wanted to reach out and slap him. Then his smile was replaced by a look of deep longing. He lifted his arms out to her. Though she heard no sound, his lips formed one word, and that word seared itself into her brain. *"Courage."*

Her eyes popped open. How much time had elapsed? Fernando was still sitting at her side, and Lucinda stood looking down at her. She shook herself and jumped to her feet, a sudden charge of energy running through her body.

"Come on," she urged. "It's time to go."

Lucinda grabbed her wrist. "You goin' to keep up? Lucinda want to get through the swamp before the storm come."

Shona shook her hand away. "Of course. Get going."

Fernando grasped Shona's arm to stop her headlong rush. "Wait," he said. "How much farther is it? And what is this swamp you talk about?"

"Lucinda don' know how far to tell you. Soon we reach swamp and after that, we get to other side of island and find boat. Then both of you sail into storm or no, whatever you want. You no longer be Lucinda's problem."

Shona quickly followed Lucinda, amazed by her newfound strength. They entered the trees again, but this time the foliage did little to shield them from the brunt of the storm. Their progress was hindered by the roaring wind which drove pelting thongs of rain into their faces, and by broken tree branches littering the path. They skirted giant rocks, composed of what looked to Shona like pure marble. They crawled through thickets of guava and marabu on their hands and knees, the thorns tearing at their clothing. The ground beneath their feet became soft, and even Lucinda's pace slowed as they slogged their way through deep muck, their feet making sucking noises with each step.

The underbrush thinned, but giant ferns and mahogany and lignum vitae trees reached out thick limbs as though to impede their progress. Shona heard a loud snort and stepped back just as a peccary dashed across the path in front of her, its long, dark bristles glistening with rain. Moments later, she heard the sobbing cry of a wildcat, and then a deer plunged out of the swamp in front of her, its tail raised in warning. Dear God, what next? Were there alligators in this swamp, as in Carolina? Or poisonous snakes, their triangle-shaped heads raised, their tongues seeking easy prey? She recalled her dream and wondered if, at this very moment, MacKenzie was on their trail, a snarling black dog racing ahead of him. She wished she had the knife Fernando had tucked into his waistband. If her dream had truly been an omen of things to come, she would feel safer with the knife in her hand!

She quelled her fears, however, and doggedly continued on, Stephen's single word of encouragement still racing through her mind. *"Courage,"* he had said. She would not allow herself to fear what lay ahead. She would take one step, and then another, and soon this horrible swamp would lie behind them.

Her resolve was forgotten when she grasped a tree limb to pull herself along. There, inches from her fingers, lay an enormous snake! She jerked her hand away, realizing even as she did so, that the head of this monster was rounded, and that he was, therefore, not poisonous. She stared at the snake, marveling at its glistening striped body coiled so casually over the limb. "I'm much too large for you to swallow," she gasped out as she plunged on.

Lucinda waited ahead, her hand raised in warning. Shona approached cautiously. The black woman gestured to her right. There, reposing on a hummock of tufted, dead grass, lay a giant alligator! She forced herself to look closer. This one was different from those to which she was accustomed. Its snout was slender and delicate, not broad and thick. But its long tail was just as explosive, and it was every bit as deadly. She shuddered when it opened its giant mouth and roared a warning.

"Follow close now," Lucinda warned. "You' feet go where mine go or you be swallow' up." She smiled broadly and laughed aloud at Fernando who had stopped behind Shona. "Don't worry, mon," she said with a snort. "Lucinda not be lost. Just follow close."

Shona pressed her fingers into Fernando's arm, then turned and made her way carefully in Lucinda's footsteps. They wove their way across hummocks of spongy earth, avoiding the dark, mysterious pools lying on either side. Here, the storm was raging far overhead, snapping tree limbs and showering them with sudden deluges of rain, and the cacophony of sound was even louder than it had been in the open.

Lucinda made her way slowly, turning every now and then as if to assure herself that Shona and Fernando were right behind her. She needn't have worried. Shona was following so closely that, at times, she even bumped into the huge woman, who instantly shrank away. Fernando was right on Shona's heels. He had seemingly given up all pretense of being a gentleman and had placed his hands firmly on Shona's hips.

The water was rising, and Lucinda stopped often now, her black eyes darting from side to side. "This be one big storm," she shouted back at Shona, who could only nod in answer. "We reach that big tree, then we stop for a while," Lucinda added.

Shona grasped the woman's skirt and followed her through ankle-deep black water to a large mahogany tree, the roots of which were firmly anchored in solid soil, far above the roiling water. Lucinda gestured for Shona to sit. She did so gratefully, every muscle of her body afire. She no longer had any feeling in her feet, and her ears rang from the constant roaring of the wind and the grating of tree limbs. Fernando sank to the ground beside her.

"Are we lost?" he shouted.

Lucinda shook her head. "*Santeria* never lost," she shouted in answer. "Water comin' in fast. You wait here. Lucinda find way an' come back for you." She pressed a small package into Fernando's hands. "You eat this."

Shona eyed the package longingly as Fernando unwrapped thick slabs of roasted pork. Her mouth tingled, but she had no saliva to allow her to swallow. She shook her head when he held the meat out to her.

"You must eat!" he shouted. "You need the strength!"

She shook her head again. "No!" she screamed. "I can't swallow without some water. It'll just stick in my throat."

She looked up when Lucinda laughed wildly. The black woman stood before them, hands on hips, her wide face split ear to ear with a leering grin. "They be water all around." She gestured at the black, writhing pools lying close by. "Just don' drink any, or you die pukin' you' guts out on the ground."

Hatred pulsed through Shona's body, bringing welcome warmth. "We know not to drink!" she shouted. "We know about the swamps!"

A look of cunning appeared on Lucinda's face, freezing Shona's anger.

"You give Lucinda gold coin now, mon!"

Shona whirled about, fearful that Fernando would comply. But he was shaking his head vehemently. "No! You will get your other coin when we reach our destination and not before!"

Lucinda spat at her feet, her face a mask of hatred. "Now, mon!" she screamed. "Or Lucinda no' take you any more!"

Fernando's face blanched and Shona knew the turmoil he was undergoing. They were trapped! If they gave the woman the coin, she would disappear and leave them to die in the swamp. If they did not, she would lead them no farther.

Again, Fernando shook his head.

With a barking laugh, Lucinda pulled a long knife from her skirts. She lunged forward, stopping only when the sharp point was pricking Shona's throat. "You best do what Lucinda say," she screeched. "Or this womon, she be crocodile meat!"

Shona felt Fernando move, and knew he was reaching for his

247

own knife. "No!" she shouted. "Give her the coin! We don't have a chance unless you do!"

Fernando looked helplessly at Shona. "But she will leave us here!"

Shona blinked back the tears stinging her own eyes. "I know. But at least we'll be alive!"

Fernando stared at her wordlessly, his helplessness mirrored in his face. At last, he shrugged his shoulders and held out his hands. "All right. Take your knife away. The coin is in my shirt. I will get it."

Lucinda moved one step back, holding the knife menacingly out before her. "Get it!"

Fernando reached into his shirt and removed one of two small packets. He unrolled it carefully and held the gold coin out to Lucinda. She grabbed it, bit it quickly, then placed it inside her bodice. "You got more, mon?" she sneered. "You got more gold in there?"

Fernando showed her the empty paper and shook his head. "No! That is all I have!"

Lucinda smiled and tossed her head. "Lucinda go now an' find the way. You wait. She be back soon."

Shona could not believe her eyes as the large woman stepped behind the tree and vanished from view. She and Fernando leaped to their feet, skirting the tree, hoping to see the way Lucinda had gone. But she had disappeared, leaving them alone except for the howling storm and the rising water.

Chapter 20

A vivid slash of lightning split the sky, followed instantly by a crash of thunder so loud that it shook the hummock Shona and Fernando were sitting upon. As if awaiting just such a signal, the skies opened and dumped a deluge of rain drops so large they formed a solid sheet of water. The swamp was obliterated from view and talk was impossible.

Fernando cradled Shona in his arms, trying to shield her from the water, but she shook him away and tried to smile as she formed the word "no" with her lips. Let the rain fall. Perhaps it would wash away the filth engrained in her clothing and, with a little luck, drown the pesky varmints crawling all over her body. She closed her eyes and ducked her head to clear her nose and mouth.

The wind gusted in giant blasts, and they found themselves slipping from their perch into the steadily rising, writhing water. Fernando signaled Shona to grasp a root and to hold onto his breeches. He slipped his shirt over his head and crawled back up to the tree, dragging Shona with him.

Shona pressed her mouth to his ear. "Shouldn't we stand? The water is rising so fast!"

Fernando shook his head. "No! The wind is too fierce. We must lie down." He looked at the large tree trunk and back at the shirt in his hands. Shona realized now what he was trying to do. She shook his arm to get his attention, and shook her head. "It won't work," she mouthed. She dragged herself up beside him and motioned for him to hold her. Quickly, she removed her own shirt, ignoring his motions of protest. She took hold of his breeches once again and thrust the shirt into his hands. The agony of his embarrassment at seeing her bare breasted was all too evident as he tied the shirt sleeves together.

Shona inched her way up to the slender root he held and signaled him to leave her. She watched anxiously as he grasped the rough red bark, trying to gain a handhold. He handed her one sleeve, then crawled slowly around the tree. He was gone so long, she was sure he had slipped off into the water on the other side.

When she felt a tug on the sleeve, a sob of relief escaped her lips. Seconds later, he crawled back beside her, where he tied a firm knot, making a complete circle of the shirts around the huge trunk. He wrapped one hand around the makeshift life line and pulled her up beside him. She grasped the shirt with both hands.

They lay on their faces, the rain whipping their bare backs like buckshot, their noses clogged with slime. Stephen's cross dug into Shona's right breast, but she did not move. She found the sharp pain strangely comforting.

She had a sudden thought and laughed aloud, choking on a mouthful of mud. She no longer had to fear MacKenzie finding her. Her dream had all come true. The hog and snake she had seen on the path, the knife, and the black dog. How could she have been such a fool? Lucinda was that snarling black beast with blood dripping from its fangs. It did not matter that MacKenzie had not sent her on her evil errand—Shona was sure he had had no hand in this murderous deed—Lucinda had devised and carried out a plan to keep her man.

Shona's hands grew numb with cold, and she could feel the water lapping at her feet. She closed her eyes, trying to conjure up another vision of Stephen. But all she saw behind her

250

eyelids was a grinning Lucinda, the water beading on her satiny black skin. She concentrated on keeping her grasp on the shirt as the water rose to her knees. God, if this storm did not end soon, the water would rise over them and they would drown!

She felt something slither across her back. She tried to rise, but her knees slipped and one hand was torn from the shirt sleeve. She grabbed for it, but her numb fingers would not obey. She screamed and choked as she clawed her way upward, her arm flailing in the air frantically. Then a firm hand grasped her arm, and Fernando guided her fingers toward the shirt. She slipped her palm over the material and willed her fingers to close. When something crawled across the back of her neck, she did not jump again. If it was a snake, and it bit her, so be it!

The weight left her neck and she felt a slimy object force its way beneath her left breast. The blood froze on her veins. No! Not there, where it could sink its fangs into her tender flesh!

She raised up slightly and shook the rain from her face. What she saw brought a bubble of hysteria to her throat and she rocked back and forth, laughing helplessly. There, in the shelter of her breast, sat a tiny green frog, its large yellow eyes staring up into her face. She lay back down, content to grant the frog a reprieve from the pounding rain. It was somehow very comforting to know that her own body offered protection to one of nature's harmless creatures.

The water rose to her hips, forcing her to hold even more tightly to the shirt as her legs bobbed behind her. She felt something brush her side, and when she turned her head, she saw a small deer hauling itself out of the water. The animal went to its knees beside her, its side heaving, its body trembling with exhaustion. "Why not?" she asked herself. She recalled the story of Noah her grandfather had told her when she was a small child. "But this is a mighty poor ark," she breathed to the deer who lay huddled against her, shivers shaking its body.

Suddenly, a large wave swept over her head, choking and blinding her. She reared up, fighting for air. When the wave receded, she used what she was sure was every ounce of her remaining strength to pull herself to her knees, realizing as she did so that the frog and deer were both gone. Damn! They were so helpless, so innocent!

Fernando grasped her arm and she turned toward him. His eyes were wide and his mouth opened and closed like that of a beached fish. He began to pry at her hand, and she pushed against him, trying to make him stop. But he waved his arm wildly, gesturing that he wanted to untie the shirt. She shook her head violently from side to side. Without their life line they would be swept into the water!

Another wave hit. She held her breath, choking on the water, counting the seconds until the wave receded. When it did, only her head was in the clear and the air was so filled with rain, her situation was little better. She looked at Fernando who was once again gesturing wildly. This time he made himself clear. He wanted to untie the shirts and use them to tie her to him. She released her hold and grabbed for his arm, but it slipped from her grasp and she found herself being drawn backward into the water. She clawed wildly, knowing her time had come, but unwilling to give in.

Her fingers gripped something solid, and she held on to it with all of her remaining strength. Water covered her face. She reared her head back and retched. She felt flesh beneath her fingertips and knew she was holding onto Fernando's waistband.

Suddenly, his body moved as they were carried out into the swirling water. She felt herself sink. She kicked out her feet, but they could not find a purchase on the slimy bank. Again she slipped under the water, losing her hold on Fernando.

A firm hand grasped her under the arm and pulled her to the surface. Fernando held her close and shouted in her ear, "Do not fight. Try to stay afloat while I tie us together!"

She nodded and began to tread water. He passed one of the shirts beneath her arms, and tied the remaining sleeve onto his own right arm, pulling the knot tight with his teeth. Again he pulled her close. "Do not fight the waves. Let the water carry us along. Just try to keep your face clear."

She hugged his neck. "Don't leave me!" she screamed.

He shook his head. "The shirt will keep us together. Hang on now, here comes another wave!"

The water hit them in a solid wall, carrying them, within its watery depths, deeper into the swamp at breakneck speed. Shona's hold on Fernando was broken, and the shirt tied beneath her arms tightened until she feared it would choke what little breath she had from her body. She closed her eyes and clawed upward, kicking her legs. When rough bark scraped her side, she grabbed at a tree trunk, but it was torn from her grasp. Pinpoints of light danced before her eyes. Her lungs felt as though they would burst. She opened her mouth for a breath and swallowed water.

The shirt tore into her breast, pulling her upward. But she had no more strength. Her body sagged against the relentless pull. Seconds later, her face broke the surface.

She retched and gagged, trying to get air. At last, a tiny breath reached her starving lungs and she gasped again and again. Fernando's face swam before her eyes. She tried to smile, but her face felt frozen. She felt a firm surface beneath her feet. But when she tried to stand, her numb toes slipped in the slime and she fell back into the water.

She felt the wave gathering strength as it recoiled from its impact with the bank. Oh, God, it was going to wash them back with it! She clawed with her feet, but the water had already taken her away from her foothold.

Fernando pulled her close again. "Do not fight!" he shouted. "Let the wave carry us!"

But she did not want to go with the wave. She wanted to reach solid ground, and all hope of that was swiftly diminishing.

Fernando gripped her arm and squeezed. She looked at him and wondered how he could smile at a time like this. They were caught on the crest of the wave and whisked back through the swamp. Branches and broken roots snagged their clothing. But always, the force of the water tore them away. There was a thrashing in the water beside her. A wildcat clawed futilely at the wave, its body caught in a force it could not control. She watched as it sank beneath the surface. It did not reappear.

The trunk of a tree loomed before her. She lurched wildly to one side, knowing such an impact would kill her, but the tree disappeared from view. Then her foot caught in a submerged bush. She kicked free, screaming at the searing pain in her ankle, and still the rain came down in a solid sheet, blinding and choking her. She clutched wildly for Fernando. His hand closed over hers.

She lost all track of time as the wave carried them along on its mighty crest. Her entire body was numb, even her torn ankle no longer throbbed. Occasionally she retched as her stomach tried to expel the water she had swallowed, and her blood beat loudly in her temples, its wild pulse the only thing she could hear. She closed her eyes, allowing the water to carry her where it willed. It was no use. They were as good as dead and she knew it.

Suddenly, the rope tightened. She opened her eyes. Fernando was staring straight ahead, his mouth open. There, several hundred yards ahead, was a gigantic wave, rushing in their direction! She tried to smile. This was it. She had no strength to fight a wave that large. She would allow it to hit her and drag her into its giant maw; then she would be with Stephen at last. She closed her eyes and waited for it to strike.

Fernando shouted something. She felt him clasp her shoulders. *"Dive!"* he screamed. "Watch! Just before it hits, dive!"

The wild hope in his voice triggered an answering spark. She stared straight ahead, mesmerized by the wall of water rushing toward them. When it was only feet away, its foamy curl towering above their heads, she felt a tug on the shirt tying them together. She gulped in a chest full of air and dove.

Chapter 21

Kenneth MacKenzie stood at the *Loretta*'s rail, his eyes anxiously sweeping the shore. The damage the hurricane had wrought before the calm center had come over them was evident everywhere. Debris was tossed by the swollen waves which still rocked the ship violently from side to side, and the harbor was littered with the bodies of animals, limbs of trees, and even the thatched roof of a shack. The small strip of beach not under water had been swept clean of one set of offal, and covered with another.

By God, he had to know what had happened to Shona! He snapped his eyeglass from its case and raised it with trembling hands, knowing even as he did so that his gesture was useless. There was no way he could see past the trees at the edge of the beach. He could not learn the fate of the settlement.

Had Smitty followed his orders and removed the lass from the Bastard's Lair? Had he taken her to safety in one of the caves littering the spiny ridge running down the center of the island? He pounded the rail in frustration. Damn! He had no way of knowing how long this calm would last, and his first consideration had to be his ship.

He eyed the blue skies with apprehension. Wisps of clouds floated innocently overhead. He wet his finger with spittle and held it into the air. Just a light breeze. But only an idiot would think that the danger was over. He knew from experience that the worst was yet to come.

He growled out a quick order, bidding two of his men to check the drag and sea chains and to make sure the ship was still firmly heading into the wind. Two more were instructed to use poles to push the floating roof away from the ship. Yet another was sent into the water to check the hull for damage, and three more were sent into the hold to make sure the ballast had not shifted during the ship's violent pitching.

He climbed to the quarter-deck, outwardly eying the lashed wheel, the planks cleared of anything that might be blown about. Inwardly, he was raging against the fates. Why, by all the gods, had the hurricane struck today? If it had only held off for another forty-eight hours! He growled and shook his wild mane of red hair. Only forty-eight more hours, and he would have had the lass safely aboard.

He had laid his plans so well. He licked his salt-encrusted lips, tasting instead, his own desire. Without the storm, he would have the hog butchering out of the way, and be headed, even at this very moment, toward the Bastard's Lair. Once there, he would wash, have Smitty trim his hair and beard and then . . . He groaned aloud. It was not fair! He had waited so long!

He closed his eyes, seeing behind his lids the picture which had haunted him for weeks . . . Shona, her golden hair fanned out in splendor across the pillow, her full lips pouting with desire, her slim arms raised in welcome. He was sure the oil of roses had done the trick. She would be rosy cheeked, and the brown flecks in her yellow eyes would dance as she gave herself to him.

And then . . . then he would bed her for the entire night, and leave her in the morning only to prepare his ship for sailing. He would work like a demon, drive his men beyond anything they had ever endured. He would see that his cabin was so clean it squeaked, and he himself would put clean sheets and blankets upon the bed. Remembering what had pleased his

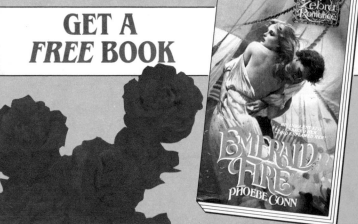

mother, he would send one of his men to gather flowers to place on the table beside the bed, even if he had to threaten the man with death!

Then he would row Shona out to their love nest, and once again taste the sweet nectar of her lips and body. They would sail with the tide the following morning, he and his woman!

A gust of wind pressed his clothes against his body, and he opened his eyes, looking at the sky. Was it starting again so soon? No. There was no sign of pregnant rain clouds on the horizon. He sighed and walked to the railing, this time staring out into the distance toward the sea, his mind once again returning to the lass.

When this storm was over and he had assured himself of the safety of his ship, he would go for her. Though Smitty was devious and lazy, he was much too afraid of him not to obey his direct orders. Shona would be safe. Should he take her back to Scotland? Would she like that? She had never said, and though he thought he had left his homeland and the stigma of being a MacKenzie behind him forever, he would be willing to return if that was what she wished.

But first, with Shona comfortable in his cabin, he would make one more sweep for booty. He would head for the Louisiana territory, where the weak French held onto their land with trembling fear, lest someone stronger take it away. He snorted. He did not want the land. But he did want everything else! He would fight and overcome the French and English ships bringing supplies; then he would raid the settlements, until his hold bulged with riches. Perhaps he would even commandeer another ship, so he could take Shona back to Scotland in style. They could retire there with enough to live on for the remainder of their lives. And, if he returned home with enough gold, even being the grandson of the Brahan Seer would not be a hindrance.

His face flushed as he remembered his humiliating departure from the Highlands. His father had been accepted as a necessary evil by the people, for they regarded him as the son of a national hero and thus overlooked his oafish and stupid behavior. But *his* son, that was another matter entirely. Perhaps it would have been different if Kenneth had inherited the gentle, unassuming nature of his mother. Though he had her fiery red hair and green eyes, there the resemblance ended. He was a giant of a man, as his father was. And, like his father, he possessed a violent nature, given to tantrums and petty revenge. And even more damning, he was not endowed with his mother's keen intelligence.

The young Kenneth had vacillated between craving the people's approbation and damning them for their snobbery. By the time he'd reached his early twenties, he'd been filled with a hatred which bouts of unnatural good humor could not overcome. In one last attempt to win friends, he had begun to pretend he could read the future as his grandfather had. At first, he'd predicted only things which could not fail to come to pass. But as his fame had grown, he'd become careless. His sham had been exposed when he'd overheard quite by accident that a local unwed lass was with child by the local laird. Hastily putting two and two together, he'd proceeded to name names, and to predict the downfall of the laird's holdings. Yet, unknown to him, the laird and the lass had been secretly wed, and when they'd produced their proof to the people, Kenneth MacKenzie had been publicly ridiculed and scorned. He'd fled his homeland in the middle of the night, humiliated and alone.

His eyes swept the horizon again, a frown creasing his forehead. The sky above the sea was turning a dusky gray and the wind was rising even as he watched. He would have to call his crew in to safety. It was about to begin anew.

As he turned, a large object floating in the water caught his eye. He stopped and studied it, trying to pinpoint what it was that had attracted his attention. It was only a waterlogged tree, covered with spiny branches, floating low in the water. But wait, there seemed to be something else. He raised his eyeglass and brought the tree into focus. By God, there were two people hanging onto that tree! He wiped his hand over his eyes and raised the glass again. One white head and one . . . *God!*

He tucked the glass into his waistband as he raced down the ladder. "Lower the longboat!" he screamed.

His first mate, Evans, rushed to obey, then stopped and looked back helplessly. "It's lashed firmly, Cap'n. It'll take time to untie, and we ain't got time!" The first fat raindrops fell as he gestured toward the sky.

Without another thought, MacKenzie raced for the rail. "Man overboard!" he called as he ran. He vaulted over the side and hit the water feet first. Seconds later, he was fighting the bucking waves, his strong arms slicing through the water. His heart beat in his throat and his body felt leaden. He would know that golden hair anywhere! Shona! Was she dead? He choked on a mouthful of water and pushed the thought from his mind. She was alive! She had to be alive!

A wave washed the tree toward him. Frantically, he pushed himself even harder. Another wave, and the tree was almost on top of him. He pressed himself between the branches, his eyes smarting, his chest heaving. He lashed out, working his way toward the trunk. When his hands closed over bare flesh, he shook the water from his eyes, then cursed. It was only the Spaniard.

He heaved himself up onto the trunk and gripped his legs against the slippery sides. His weight pressed the tree into the water until it was completely submerged. Hysteria rose in his throat. Where was Shona? He slipped into the water on the other side and the tree floated free again. There! He scrambled through the branches, a fierce growl coming from his lips. Her chin was barely above the water line. God! Had he drowned her?

He reached out and grasped her under one arm, ignoring the rising wind and the rain obscuring his vision. When her head fell back, he cupped it in one hand as he attempted to free her from the branches. He pushed his feet against the trunk as he pulled on her, but she did not float free. Then his frantic fingers moved down her bare flesh. There seemed to be

259

something tied under her arms. He brought his knife up from his waistband and very carefully worked the tip under her bonds. She slipped free and he pulled her into his arms.

He felt a hand grip his shoulder. "Cap'n!" Evans shouted. "Let me have her. You get the other 'un."

He pushed the hand away. "Na! Leave him be. Help me!"

The mate shook the water from his eyes. "All right. Peters is in the water too. He can take care of the old man."

MacKenzie and Evans cradled Shona's body between them as they swam toward the *Nancy*. The Scotsman would not allow himself to look closely at her face. He did not want to see her lax mouth, the deep scratches on her forehead, the pallor of her cheeks.

When they reached the side of the ship, eager hands helped them up the net. But once he was aboard, MacKenzie would allow no one else to touch the girl. He picked her up gently and waited impatiently for a man to unlash the hatch cover. "If he's still alive, tell Peters to put that Spaniard in chains and take him ashore," he ordered as he descended the ladder. He was so engrossed with his burden he did not even make sure the rest of his crew had sought safety from the storm.

He pushed into his cabin, kicking dirty clothing and discarded scraps of food out of the way. He placed Shona on his bunk and stood looking down at her, his chest tight with fear. She was naked from the waist up, and little remained of the breeches clothing her hips and legs. Deep scratches covered her face and arms, and a large cut gaped wide on her ankle. Worst of all, she lay so still. He could not detect even a slight rise and fall to her chest.

He placed his gigantic hands around her ribs and began to squeeze, gently at first, then harder. Again and again he pressed, encouraged when a small trickle of water rolled down her chin.

She made a gagging sound. She was alive! He turned her head so she would not swallow her own vomit, and began to squeeze again. Water gushed out of her mouth. Then she

260

retched and retched. More water spewed onto the bed. He could hardly believe she could live with so much water inside of her. He continued to press until she gasped and flailed her arms, at which point he bunched a bolster up and put it under her head to ease her breathing.

"Shona! Shona, lass!" He bent over her, his chest tight with unshed tears. He could never remember crying, and he was not about to show such weakness now. "Shona!" He pushed her tangled, wet hair away from her face and gently stroked her cheek. "Wake up, Shona. Wake up, lass, you're safe now."

When her eyelids fluttered, he studied her face intently, willing her to look up at him. But she only sighed deeply, and her breathing slowed and steadied.

As he sat beside her, his mind succumbed totally to the overwhelming adoration he felt for the bonny lass lying on his bunk. In her, he saw his salvation. With her by his side, the people who had ridiculed him and reviled him would be brought to their knees. And if she really was a Strathmore, all the better, for that was a name revered and feared throughout the land. Not that he still believed she was the Strathmore monster, for he had pushed that fear from his mind completely when he'd seen her in the water. But she was bonny, and possessed a keen mind. Better yet, she would stand up for the one she loved.

Kenneth MacKenzie had no doubt that he could make her love him. He had saved her from drowning, hadn't he? She would be eternally grateful and forever in his debt. Not that he would exact any payment, unless you counted gratitude.

Shona shivered, and he lay down beside her, pressing his body against hers. When he buried his face in the hollow of her neck and pressed his lips against her soft flesh, she moaned and threw her arm across his shoulders. He raised up and looked down at her. Her eyes were still closed, her lashes resting softly upon her pale cheeks. He pulled back the blanket and looked at her. That damnable gold cross lay nestled between her breasts. He was tempted to tear it from her throat, but the sight of her dusky rose nipples, softly flared by the warmth, wiped that thought from his mind. He lowered his head and took a nipple into his mouth, gently moving his tongue over its surface.

Shona felt her body respond to Stephen's probing tongue. She caught her breath as his hands traveled slowly downward. He groaned loudly . . . there was something wrong!

She opened her eyes and screamed in horror. That was not Stephen's blond head pressed against her breasts! She wrapped her fingers in the mat of filthy red hair and pulled. Then she screamed and twisted her body, thrashing her legs violently from side to side.

"No!" she screamed. "No . . . no!" This was another nightmare!

As she gave one last violent tug and twisted far to the side, she felt his body leave hers; then she was falling. She hit the floor, and the breath left her lungs. Rolling over onto her stomach, she pushed herself up, gasping for air. She tried to stand, but the floor moved beneath her feet and she reeled against the bunk.

MacKenzie lay on one side, looking up at her with a puzzled expression. "Pig!" she screamed. "Bastard, whore monger, son of a swine!" She scratched his face and gouged at his eyes, her breath coming in sobs, a red haze before her eyes.

She felt his fingers grind into her wrists, but she continued to fight him with her entire body. Throwing herself onto the bunk, she pounded her knee into his belly. He was shouting something, but she was too filled with her own raging anger to understand. He slipped out from under her knee and threw her down, twisting her arms behind her back. She thrashed about wildly, but she could not escape those punishing hands.

"Bastard!" she screamed into the mattress. "Your mother was the daughter of a whore!"

He grasped her hair and pulled her head back. "Dinna talk like that about my mother!" he raged. "She was a lady! She—"

Suddenly, she lunged to one side, throwing herself to the floor. She landed on her back, and MacKenzie threw himself on top of her, his great weight grinding her bare flesh into the splintery planking. Then she spat in his face.

Suddenly the color drained from him, and his lips drew back in a sneer. He raised his giant hand. Shona laughed. Let him hit her. The blow would most likely kill her. Death would be welcome.

The sound of loud rapping on the door halted his arm in midair.

"Cap'n! Come quick! A Spanish trader's limpin' into the harbor and she's laden to the gunnels!"

MacKenzie snarled and rolled off of her. Shona lay panting from exertion as he pulled his breeches and shirt on.

She watched him paw through the desk drawers. Then he whirled and stood staring down at her.

"You'll pay for that, bizzem!" he growled. He dangled a key in front of her and grinned fiendishly. "I'm gaun to lock you in! If the ship goes down, you'll be trapped beneath the water! Think about it, bizzem!"

He threw the door open and slammed it closed behind him. The howling wind drowned out any sound of a key turning in the lock.

Shona scrambled to the door on her hands and knees. Pulling herself up, she tried the handle. It would not move. She crawled to a corner and huddled there, her body shaking uncontrollably. She was in the captain's cabin on the *Loretta*. It reminded her of that pig Lopez's cabin aboard the *Fortune*. Dear God, MacKenzie had somehow found her in the sea and had brought her here! She pounded her fists on her knees, ignoring the pain. How could Stephen let her down like this? She had counted upon him to deliver her from danger and instead . . .

Her stomach muscles tightened and hot vomit spewed from her mouth. She leaned over, retching and gagging until the spasm passed. Then she wiped her hand over her mouth and staggered to the bunk. Stephen was not able to protect her. Stephen was dead! She grasped the golden cross between her

263

fingers, snapped the chain with a sharp tug and threw it onto the floor. Next, she twisted the ring on her finger, but her knuckle was swollen and she could not pull it off. She threw back her head, her face contorted, and she sobbed out her agony.

On deck, MacKenzie ignored the rising wind and roughening sea, and screamed his gun crews into action. Lashings were removed, and cannons run out. A few of the older seamen shook their heads as they worked, certain that the giant Scotsman had finally lost his mind. They could see that the storm would soon unleash its full fury upon their unfortunate heads again.

"Evans, hand out the arms!" MacKenzie shouted. As the first mate jumped to obey, a sudden gust of wind almost sent him to his knees. He looked back at his captain. MacKenzie was staring across the water at the Spanish crew busily reefing the trader's sails. His bearded chin jutted out in rage as he threw himself down the accommodation ladder and issued new orders with a snarl. "Make fast, mates, and quickly. We'll take the Spaniard as soon as the storm blows itself oot."

He watched impatiently as the crew fumbled with lurching ropes and pressed their bodies against the wind in order to remain on their feet. By the time the last cannon had been lashed, the sea anchor at the bow of the *Loretta* was being dragged along the sandy harbor bed by the violent pitching of the ship and the pounding waves. The large vessel, still held firmly at the stern by the drag anchor, swung about, exposing her vulnerable starboard side to the raging storm. She rolled far over on her port side, wallowed, righted herself, then rolled again.

MacKenzie clung to the sides of the ladder. As the ship stabilized, he leaped to the quarter-deck and raced for the wheel. He cursed his numb fingers as he fought with the lashings. When the ship shuddered and dipped sharply, he hung onto the spokes as his feet went out from under him. Damn! He could not lose this ship!

He held his breath as the *Loretta* wallowed once again, letting it out slowly as she righted herself. Then he swung his entire weight onto the wheel, trying to force the rudder to move. But the force of the waves pounding toward the shore made his efforts futile. He screamed for Evans, knowing even as he did so, that his voice could not be heard over the howling wind.

But the experienced first mate was already at his side, adding his own weight to the wheel. They fought the stubborn spokes, their breath coming in loud grunts, their neck muscles bulging with the strain. The rain pounded their faces, making vision impossible. The wind lashed at their bodies, pulling their feet out from under them. Only their grasps on the wheel kept them from being thrown from the bucking deck.

The *Loretta* rolled again, her port rail now under water. Then she shuddered, and her agonized groans could be heard above the shriek of the wind. Another wave hit, and she wallowed deeper, shivering violently from the impact. The wheel began to turn as the rudder lifted in the water. MacKenzie held his breath, his mind screaming encouragement to the gallant lady.

The wave passed, and she slowly came upright. The two men once again threw all of their weight onto the wheel. Slowly, slowly, the *Loretta*'s bow moved into the brunt of the wind. MacKenzie positioned himself more firmly and signaled for Evans to do the same. The storm was not over. They would have to stay at the wheel until it blew itself out.

The Scotsman's hands grew numb. His arms felt as though they had been torn from their sockets and his face was raw from the driving pellets of rain. It was all the lass's fault! He was sure she had tried to escape and had been caught in the storm. If she had not distracted him, he would have sighted the Spaniard himself and taken her before the storm returned.

He cursed and stomped his foot. The lass had cheated him! He had almost had her but she had pushed him away! He would pay her back for what she had done. He licked his lips in anticipation. Perhaps he would strip her and flog her tender back raw in front of his men. . . . No, she would only turn those yellow eyes in his direction and curse him roundly. There had to be a better way to punish her.

His musings were hampered by a persistent twinge of fear. Perhaps she was the Strathmore monster after all! Perhaps she had called up this storm in order to escape. He glowered. No. If she were the monster, she would not have failed, and by damn, even if she were, he would not allow her to go unpunished after what she had done! First he would take the Spanish trader, and then . . . He chuckled to himself.

Shona rode out the storm hunched on the floor, her hands clutching the bunk frame. When the gusting wind quieted and the ship stopped its violent pitching, she climbed up onto the mattress and lay on her back, not bothering to cover her naked body with the blanket; she did not feel the cold. She stared at the chandelier overhead. The red wax once again swayed in grotesque, hardened tears above her head. But this time, there were no answering tears within her. There was only a deep, seething anger.

Stephen was dead. Jephtha was dead. Fernando was dead. She was completely alone again. She and she alone was responsible for her own destiny. From now on, she would use anything and anyone to survive. Never again would she allow herself to care for another human being. Never again would she put her life in another's hands. She would be cold and ruthless. If hurt, she would hurt in return and take pleasure in the hurting.

She raised her hand and looked at the ring upon her finger. When her swollen knuckle had gone down, she would remove the ring and throw it, together with the cross, over the side of the ship into the sea. She wanted no more reminders of what had been. From now on, there was only today—and only herself to care about.

She heard a key turn in the lock and turned her head toward the door. Hatred welled up in her throat, almost choking her. Let MacKenzie try to abuse her body again. Just let him try!

266

Chapter 22

Rosa Gordo's plump hands kneaded the dough automatically for this morning her mind was not focused upon mundane daily chores such as bread making. Her lips pursed and her usually serene brow wrinkled as she groped for the elusive solution to the problem which had been thrust upon her the evening before. Why, oh why, had she consented weeks ago to care for the wounded, half-drowned *marino*, Esteban de Larra, who had been carried, more dead than alive, through the massive cypress doors to the fort by his *compadres?* Granted, she had volunteered many times to nurse soldiers suffering chills and fever from the swamp sickness, but to care for one with such a hole in his chest . . . She clucked to hjerself, wiped a strand of graying hair from her eyes with a floured hand, and attacked the dough even more vigorously. Muttering indignant maledictions under her breath, she invoked El Diablo to shower distress upon the unfortunate head of Comandante Hernandez for placing her in such a miserable state of anxiety.

After all, she was a woman of middle age, widowed, her only son gone long since to the arms of the Blessed Virgin in heaven. She had remained at this Spanish garrison called Castillo de San Marcos in the Florida Territory only because her husband, God rest his lovable old soul—she crossed herself hastily, leaving smears of flour on her forehead and black dress—had breathed his last right here behind these sixteen-foot-thick walls. After a long period of excruciating grief, she had promised herself that the remainder of her days would be spent in placid, homely work, perhaps mopping an occasional feverish brow, but never would she allow her heart to become involved in the welfare of another. And now, here she was, her eyes gritty from too little sleep, her tears threatening to ruin the leaven in her bread.

Why, had she allowed the young man thrust into her care to invade the sanctity of her lonely heart? Why had she expended so much energy, so much devotion on nursing a total stranger? At first, when it appeared there was no way he could survive, she had attributed her fierce determination to see him recover to the fact that he reminded her of her dear departed Pedro, the son born much too late in her life, the son destined to live only a short time upon this earth. Pedro had also been blessed with the bluest of eyes, the fairest of hair which curled around his angelic face in damp wisps as he slept. Yet, she had begun to realize lately that her bond went much deeper than a mere resemblance to a long-dead son.

She pondered her reluctant attachment as she shaped two flat loaves, then placed them in the clay oven and absent-mindedly dusted her hands on her skirt. It must be the mother in her, the unfulfilled instinct to care for, to nurture, to bring that wounded, bleeding body to healthy, vigorous manhood— that must have overcome her resolution to stay uninvolved. She had become a victim of her own emotions, trapped by some demanding, instinctive urge to nurture this gloriously handsome young man. And as she'd become involved in his physical needs, she'd been driven to take care of his emotional needs as well.

She poured a cup of wine and sat on the deep window sill, sipping absent-mindedly, looking over her shoulder at the early morning sun weakly filtering into the room as her mind relived the events of the previous evening when Esteban had stunned her by announcing his decision to leave the fort after the Lord's Day mass and to begin his long odyssey about the territory, seeking some word of his beloved Shona. She felt a stab of resentment toward the golden-haired girl Esteban had called for constantly in his delirium. Surely, if the girl were living—and Esteban would not countenance otherwise—she would want him to recover completely before undertaking such a journey! But such thoughts were unfair, weren't they? Tears filled Rosa's large brown eyes and spilled down her plump, rosy cheeks. She could understand such a love, for hadn't she and her beloved husband shared just such a deep bond, unbreakable even by death? She knew that under similar circumstances, he would have searched heaven and hell to find her. But the boy was much too weak to make such a journey! He was not completely recovered from his terrible wound. He would weaken, sicken, and surely die in some crocodile-infested swamp, alone and in great pain. Somehow, she would use the three days remaining to convince him he must wait at least another fortnight. Surely, there must be a way open to her. She had spent almost the entire night upon her knees beside her cot, imploring the good Virgin to intercede upon her behalf. She finished the wine, her hands trembling on the cup, and stood resolutely. She would walk about the grounds, leaving herself open to any chance encounter, relying upon the Blessed Madonna to lead her to someone who would know what to do.

Esteban paced his room on shaking legs, his breath laboring in his heaving chest. Though the thick walls blocked the steaming heat of the morning sun from the room, his brow was beaded with sweat. He circled the walls one more time, determined to regain his strength, for he had set a goal and only three days remained until his departure. He stumbled and cursed loudly as he returned to his cot. He would not lie down. He would simply sit on the edge of the matress until his breathing returned to normal and the trembling of his limbs abated.

He fingered the red, puckered scar on his ribs just to the left of his heart. So much time had elapsed since he and his men had boarded the *Loretta!* And Shona . . . A picture of her shoving and slashing her way through the pirates to gain his side remained forever etched upon his memory. He groaned aloud as he recalled her slim, lithe body side-stepping, dancing away from danger, the little pistol he had given her held firmly out before her. Despite his earlier resolution to remain seated, he fell back on the bed, covering his eyes with his hand. But nothing could erase his vivid remembrance of the love in her eyes as she bent over him, her tender fingers caressing his cheek, sobs wracking her shoulders.

He groaned again and forced his mind pictures back farther in time, to the happy days they had spent after declaring their love for one another. He recalled her joy in her first Spanish lesson and the opulent green velvet dress she wore so reluctantly. He remembered her arms eagerly reaching out, her trembling lips parted and the pink tip of her tongue delicately touching the corners of his mouth, rousing him to heights of passion he had never thought humanly possible. He smiled at the memory of their shouting, cup-throwing arguments and their glorious coupling afterward. Where was his beloved now? Had she somehow escaped the pirates? She had known he was planning to raid the French in New Orleans. Had she made her way there? Or had she been carried across the seas—no! His pain was so great, he sobbed aloud. Such a thought must never again be allowed to enter his mind.

He rolled over on his side and stared at the doorway. Where was Rosa? Why had she not come to interrupt the agonizing memories which always plagued him when he was left alone? Did she not know how much he needed her? Such thoughts brought a wry smile to his lips, and his right eyebrow rose in a sardonic arc. What an ass he was, still depending upon the stout, motherly little woman to nurse away his fears and fill his hours with pleasant conversation. Rosa Gordo had a life of her own, and it was about time he allowed her to resume it. After all, he would be leaving in three short days. There was little time to wean himself from the constant care she had showered upon him so lovingly. If only there were some way to repay her . . . But of course, he had nothing. He had only fleeting memories of clinging to the anchor rope until the members of his crew the pirates had released in the longboat fished him from the sea moments before it claimed him. He had arrived at the fort with nothing but the soaking clothes on his back; a packet containing the ship's log and his letters of marque, which one if his men had rescued from his cabin; and a ball in his chest, which the surgeon had added to his gory collection.

Esteban sat up suddenly. Of course! Why hadn't he thought of it before? He would produce his letters of marque signed by the King and ask the *comandante* for a letter of credit. Thus he would be able to give Rosa a token of his appreciation as well as finance his journey. Perhaps Hernandez could also be cajoled into giving him enough gold pieces to last at least a fortnight or two. After all, the de Larra name certainly had impressed the strutting little martinet, especially when his crew from the *Nancy* had revealed that their capitán traveled under letters of marque from the King himself. He lay back down, relieved that he had found the solution to the knotty problem he had been wrestling with for several days. Perhaps Rosa was right and the Blessed Madonna was looking out for him after all.

But that was impossible. She could not care and still allow his beloved Shona to be so hopelessly lost. On that foggy morning at sea, why had he not heeded his strong conviction that they were heading into a trap? Why had he allowed his men to convince him he was mistaken? Even Fernando had pleaded with him to listen to his own fears. Fernando . . . He had closed his mind to the loss of his friend. He could not bear to dwell on it now. If only he had taken command as he should have, Shona and Fernando would still be at his side.

He stared at the ceiling and, as always, found only images of his golden-haired love in the rough plaster. After a while his eyes grew heavy, and he drifted into an uneasy sleep filled with the dream that haunted him whenever he succumbed to fatigue. Shona lay beside him, her lovely hair burnished red by the candlelight, her breasts bared, their nipples flaring in the warmth of the room. Her sweet breath stirred the hairs on his chest as he leaned over her, staring deeply into her yellow-brown eyes soft with passion, and her sensuous lips were pursed for a kiss. But when he bent to place his mouth upon hers, she vanished, leaving behind only one fragrant, crushed orange blossom where her body had lain. His anguished cry rent the stillness of the room. Then the dream began again.

Rosa plodded slowly about the compound, her dark brown eyes darting this way and that, her heart frozen in her breast at the dreadful thought that somehow she had missed the answer the Blessed Mother of Christ had given, that she would never have another opportunity to receive it, because her faith had wavered. She chewed on her lower lip, her eyes brimming with tears. Surely the compassionate Mother could not refuse to give her another chance. After all, she was just a mortal, and only a weak woman at that. Perhaps if she made just one more circle . . . Her eyes lit upon the frail, thin, dark-haired young woman sitting on a bench beside the outer wall. Was she not the same one who'd been weeping by the *comandante*'s office earlier in the morning? The girl's grief-stricken eyes met hers, and Rosa's heart melted when she noticed tear-stained cheeks and swollen eyelids. Her own problems were whisked away as she made her way to the bench.

"My name is Rosa Gordo, child," she said softly, smiling down at the pathetic figure. "Perhaps I can help you, unless I am intruding?"

The girl smiled tentatively, her lips trembling. "No, please," she said very softly. "It is nice of you to offer, but there is nothing you can do."

Rosa sat beside her and took her cold, shaking hands into her own. "There, there, nothing can be so bad. After all, the good Lord made the sun shine this morning, and I am confident he will bring out the stars tonight. And if He forgets there is always the blessed Mother to remind Him."

The girl stiffened and jerked her hands away. "You are a Catholic," she whispered raggedly.

Rosa chuckled. "Of course. We are all Catholics here."

"I am not!" the girl said fiercely. "I am a Jew, and because I am not a Catholic your comandante will not allow a soldier to accompany me and my betrothed on our journey." Her shoulders shook as fresh tears streamed down her cheeks. "Now Asa and I cannot travel to New Orleans. We have traveled almost a year for nothing. They call this the New World!" She spat. "It is no different here. The world is filled with Jew-haters!"

Rosa stared at the girl, stunned by her vehement revelation. A Jew! But she spoke such flawless Spanish, with the soft lisp of a native! As memory of Spain began to stir, Rosa's cheeks burned fiercely. Of course, there were Spanish Jews, and when she had left her country many years before, they were being persecuted. Many had been condemned to death because they would not renounce their beliefs and be baptized in the one, true Church. She sighed and shook her head.

"Do not judge everyone by what you have experienced, little one," she said softly. "We do not all hate Jews. Hatred is a sin I cannot afford since I have so many others." She smiled broadly. "Such as gossip. Give me a good rumor and I will spread it from wall to wall before the day is out, relishing every single moment though I know it will cost me more penance than I wish to make! Now, tell me, what is your name?"

The girl's lips quivered as she tried not to smile at the picture the older woman had painted. "Rebecca," she said softly. "My betrothed, Asa, and I are from Madrid."

"Madrid!" Rosa exclaimed heartily. "Well, you have journeyed far and long. No wonder you are in tears. Did you just arrive?"

"We have been here two days. We only stopped because the ship's captain told us we should not journey into the interior without a soldier to accompany us."

"But surely your Asa can protect you! Every woman with a strong young man by her side is as safe as a cloistered nun."

Rebecca laughed aloud. "Oh, you have not seen my Asa. He is a young man, but physical strength is not one of his attributes. Instead, he has a strong mind. He is a physician."

"A physician!" Rosa's mouth formed a comical o. "My goodness, how fortunate for you. You must be very proud of him." Though she was speaking to Rebecca, her mind was racing frantically. Perhaps this girl's young man would prove to be the answer to her own problem. Perhaps another physician's opinion would persuade Esteban to postpone his journey until he was completely recovered!

"I am proud of Asa," Rebecca answered quietly, "though he is heartsick right now, for we planned to leave shortly for New Orleans. There is a settlement of Jews there, and Asa is so excited about providing good care for those who are sick."

"Why will the comandante not provide you with a soldier? I understand he does this for travelers all of the time."

"Not if they are Jews," Rebecca said bitterly. "We are free to proceed whenever we wish, but Comandante Hernandez has made it very clear we cannot expect an escort, though our people are expecting us."

"Expecting you? But how? There have been no travelers leaving the fort for New Orleans that I have heard of, and believe me, if anyone would know it is I, for as I said, there is nothing I love better than gossip."

"We have our ways," Rebecca whispered, her eyes downcast. "We Jews learned long ago never to trust the gentiles." She raised her head and looked at Rosa defiantly. "We have an entire web of information. Our people have been scattered over the earth for so long, just get a few of us together and you will soon find every lost shoe and needle and, yes, every lost person too!"

Tears sprang to Rosa's eyes. Thank you, Blessed Mother of God, for providing the answer! If this frail young thing was willing to help, Esteban could gather information about Shona's whereabouts without ever leaving the fort! She leaned forward and grasped Rebecca's hands. "I would like to meet your young man," she said.

"It is out of the question!" Asa whirled about and paced the room, his narrow shoulders shaking from an emotion too great to express. "I do not see how you could have confided in this, this woman!" he declared. "A total stranger and a Catholic! She means nothing to you. She has never even met me! Why would she be willing to help us?" He stared at her, his dark eyes probing, his pale, thin cheeks twitching with emotion. When Rebecca did not respond, he crossed the room and grasped her shoulders, forcing her to meet his gaze. "When are you going to realize that we are alone in this godforsaken wilderness? We have no one now but the two of us. You must trust no one but me! Do you understand?"

She shrugged his hands away and turned her back. "I cannot live like this. All of my life I have been instructed to trust no one but a Jew. Surely there are some kind people on this earth who are not of Abraham's seed!" She whirled about and grabbed his hands. "Look at me, Asa!" she demanded. "I am tired of running, always running, never trusting. Sometime, someplace, we must start to reach out or we are lost. This land was to be a new beginning after all of the misery we suffered in Spain. If we can trust no one here, we are no better off than we were in Madrid. I refuse to live like a hunted animal, forever looking over my shoulder! I like this woman. She has kind eyes. She reminded me of my mother."

"Your mother was burned at the stake by the Inquisition! Have you forgotten that?"

"Of course not! I will never forget. I am only saying that I do not intend to run, ever again. You do not have to trust Rosa

275

Gordo, but at least meet the young man she told me about. Surely he cannot harm us, he is recovering from a near brush with death!"

"But why should we meet him, tell me that? What can he do for us when the comandante has already flatly refused to help. We must leave this place and journey on our own. I will buy a *pistola* and practice until I know how to use it. I will not allow you to be harmed, Rebecca, you know how much I love you, how much I long to make you my wife."

"I also long to call you husband." She put her arms around him and rested her cheek against his chest. "But first we must find a rabbi to perform the traditional ceremony. You are a man of peace, Asa. You know nothing about firearms. Healing power belongs in your hands, not a *pistola*. Please, if you love me, meet this friend of Rosa. She only wants you to examine him as a physician, and perhaps, I say perhaps, tell him our story. He was the *capitán* of a ship and he may be able to help us find someone to accompany us. If you fear him after we talk, I will say no more and we will leave alone tomorrow."

"You promise you will trust my instincts?"

"I promise."

He kissed her cheek with great tenderness. "Then I agree to meet Rosa's friend. There is her knock now. Only pray that she and the man can be trusted. We have very little gold left and *pistolas* are expensive."

Rosa was instantly put on the alert by Rebecca's guarded greeting, but her first impulse when she met Asa was to laugh. No wonder the girl needed an armed escort to protect her! However, the love evident in his eyes when he looked at his betrothed quickly changed her opinion. Bantam roosters were known to be furious defenders of their hens. Perhaps Rebecca would be safe traveling alone with him after all. She shook Asa's hand warmly.

"I am very pleased to meet you, young man," she said sincerely. "Now, we must hurry, for I have told Esteban about you and he is most anxious to meet you."

Asa's high brow was furrowed with worry as they followed the plump figure through the halls. Rebecca's nervous laughter trailed behind them, and he could feel her shoulder tremble against his.

They stopped before a door at the end of the dark corridor. Was this some sort of trap? Asa felt his scalp tingle. Who was waiting in that room? Inquisitors? Had they been followed all this way? He steeled himself as Rosa opened the door.

Esteban rose from the bed. He greeted Rosa warmly and offered his hand to the young man after bowing to the *señorita*. Surely Rosa must have been mistaken. This young couple appeared to be half starved, and were themselves in need of warm food and nursing. How could they help him? And the young man, Asa, was a physician? The old saying "physician heal thyself" popped into his head. He dismissed it and turned his attention to seating his guests on the hard benches which were the only available seats in the room.

"I am sorry I cannot offer you some wine," he said cordially. "I am afraid it is rationed, thanks to my nurse here. She seems afraid I will overimbibe."

Rosa laughed heartily. "Perhaps you will think better of me for this!" She reached into her large apron pocket and pulled a bottle and three cups from its depths. "If you will be so kind, Señor de Larra . . ."

"Why so formal, Señora Gordo?" Esteban teased as he uncorked the bottle and poured the dark red claret. "I seem to recall you calling me many things over the past weeks, but Señor de Larra was never one of them."

Rosa shook her head in mock sadness. "You must forgive my young friend," she said. "I fear the fever has addled his brain."

"I understand you wish me to examine you," Asa said with great formality, the physician in him coming to the fore.

"Examine me?" Esteban stared at Asa. "I do not understand. Rosa said nothing to me about an examination!"

The wine in Asa's cup sloshed over the side, spreading a red

277

stain at his feet. Like blood, he thought to himself. "Then I am afraid we are taking up your valuable time, Señor de Larra," he said as he rose stiffly. "It has been a pleasure to meet you."

Rebecca grabbed his arm. "Please, Asa! You are a physician. How can you refuse?"

"But it is obvious he knows nothing about it!" the young man protested. "She said I was to examine him and then he might help us with our problem. We must go. We have been duped."

Esteban pulled on Rosa's sleeve. "I also have been duped, *señor*," he said gruffly. "You are up to something sneaky, old woman. Out with it."

Rosa smiled placidly and smoothed her skirt to cover the panic she was experiencing. Where were the manners of the old country? Why had Asa been so blunt? "I only thought another opinion could not hurt, Esteban," she said soothingly. "After all, you are going to leave this fort before the army physician has released you. What is the harm in seeking one more opinion?"

"You only want to delay me!" Esteban snorted. "Well, I will not delay my journey, not for you or for anyone else. I am leaving Sunday to look for Shona. God himself could not stop me!"

Rosa gasped, but the two young people were staring intently at Esteban. "You are leaving, *señor?*" Asa asked. "May I ask what is your destination?"

"I do not know," Esteban said. "I am seeking someone . . . someone very close to me. I will very likely travel over the entire Territory until I find her."

"Will your travels perhaps take you to New Orleans?" Rebecca asked in a whisper.

"I do not know, I tell you! I plan to stop at every settlement in the Territory until I find her. I feel Rosa has interfered in something about which she knows nothing. She said that you might be able to help me, but she was obviously mistaken."

"Help *you?*"

Rosa stood and glared down at the three young people. "You said you and Asa had a web of information about lost people," she said to Rebecca. "And you need information about Shona's whereabouts," she directed to Esteban. "So what is the harm in putting the three of you together?"

"But you said nothing about us helping *him!*" Asa sputtered. "You said he might be able to help *us!*"

"And what is your problem," Esteban asked tiredly. He threw back his head and downed his wine in one gulp.

"We are traveling to New Orleans and need an armed escort," Rebecca explained. "Because we are Jews, the comandante refused to help."

"Jews!"

Asa leaped to his feet. "We must go," he said, dragging Rebecca to her feet.

"Wait a moment," Esteban said. "Why are you running off?"

"It is obvious you were not fully informed as to our situation," Asa said stiffly. "I am sorry you were inconvenienced by a pair of Jews."

"*Madre de Dios!* What has your faith got to do with anything? I simply do not understand why Hernandez will not help you because you are Jews. Stop jumping up and down and talk to me. Perhaps we can help one another."

"See, I told you not to worry!" Rebecca told Asa triumphantly. "Now, tell the kind *señor* our story and see if he can help."

Rosa stared at the three of them. "But the examination!" she said. "I thought you came here to examine my patient."

"But we also came for help!" Rebecca wailed.

Esteban, tired to the death of meddling, emotional females, took command. "If both of you women would kindly leave, we will get on with the examination immediately," he said, winking at Asa.

"Yes," the young man agreed. "We must be left alone for

the better part of an hour. There is much involved in such an examination."

"But we will sit here quietly," Rosa protested.

"Go!" Esteban shouted. "Now!"

The two women scurried from the room, and after the door had closed firmly behind them, Esteban and Asa burst into laughter.

"Now we can decide how we can help one another," Esteban said, throwing an arm over Asa's shoulder.

Three days later, soon after the early afternoon siesta, three travelers left the Spanish garrison called Castillo de San Marcos, bound for New Orleans. Rosa watched them leave, tears streaming down her face. Never again would she meddle in the lives of others. She had only wanted to stop Esteban from leaving before he was competely recovered; instead she had insured that he would carry out his plans on schedule. When would she learn to mind her own business? She turned from the gate. Deliberately turning her back on the garden of the Virgin, she headed for the chapel and a very painful confession, sure her penance would somehow involve separating her from most of the gold coins Esteban had slipped into her apron pocket.

Chapter 23

Shona pulled the blanket up over her shoulders and braced her back against the wall as a key grated in the cabin lock. Her muscles ached and her ankle pained her. She did not know how she would escape MacKenzie this time, but she knew she must for she could not tolerate his ungodly invasion of her body! Her mind raced frantically, choosing and discarding thoughts rapidly. In desperation, though she was certain he no longer feared her, she threw out her arm and pointed her finger at the slowly opening door.

"Enter at your own risk," she intoned. "The Strathmore heir awaits you."

Startled brown eyes peeked around the door. It was not MacKenzie! Shona dropped her hand. "Come in, if you must," she said in her normal voice. "I promise not to bite."

A boy with a long thin face and scraggly brown hair stepped around the door, his eyes still wide with fright.

"I said I won't bite," Shona said softly. "What do you want?"

His shoulders jerked and his hands shook as he held out a pair of breeches and a shirt. "The cap'n . . . he said . . . to give you these!" he stammered.

"What's your name? I haven't seen you before."

"No, ma'am." He pressed the clothes into her outstretched

hands and hastily backed away. "I just signed on. Name's Peters, ma'am."

"Thank you for the clothes, Peters."

"You're welcome, ma'am. You don't look like a . . . I mean, nobody'd ever know you was a . . . Aw, hell, I got to git goin'."

"Wait, Peters. I want to thank you for bringing the clothes. Are they yours?"

He looked at the floor and nodded ever so slightly, his cowlick flopping comically. "Yes, ma'am. I hope they fit."

"I'm sure they will." Shona's mind was racing. If she could only convince the boy to leave the door unlocked! "Don't bother to lock the door when you leave. I may want to get some fresh air later."

He tensed, and his face paled. "No! I'm sorry, ma'am, I don't want to make you angry, but I can't do that. The cap'n, he'd have my hide and then some if'n I disobeyed his orders about locking you up tight again!"

"And you're more frightened of him than you are of me?" She raised her hand and pointed a finger at him. "Do you want to bring the Strathmore curse upon your poor unfortunate head?"

He swallowed convulsively and stared at her stabbing finger. "No, ma'am," he croaked. He licked his dry lips. "But your curse might take longer to git me than the cap'n. He's got a temper, he has, and he'll surely flay me alive if'n I don't follow his orders. I'm sorry, ma'am, truly I am!" Before Shona could react, he backed out the door and slammed it. She sighed and shook her head as she heard the key in the lock. "Damn," she groaned. "Now what do I do?"

She pulled herself to the side of the bunk and dangled her legs over the side. Her ankle throbbed painfully and her muscles ached unmercifully, but she felt amazingly strong for having survived that tempestuous ride through the swamps. She would not allow herself to dwell on Fernando's drowning. Though she knew she would have to face his death, she would do it later, when she could do so without breaking down completely. She pulled the breeches and shirt on, wincing as the cloth rubbed her scratched arms and legs. Then she took a few tentative steps. Her ankle was not broken, but it certainly did hurt! She winced as her bare foot encountered something sharp. Stephen's cross lay on the planking, its golden chain glowing warmly. Her heart convulsed. She could not discard something that had lain upon his chest! She scooped it up and fastened it about her neck, her fingers trembling maddeningly. Later. She would think about Stephen later.

She could hear feet pounding on the deck and a hoarse voice screaming orders. What was going on? Where was MacKenzie? She had been so sure he would come the instant the storm ended. What could be keeping him? Could the ship have sustained major damage? She certainly hoped so. Then maybe she would have another chance to plan an escape. If only she could find a map, learn exactly where she was. Shona rummaged through the desk drawers, eying with disgust a moldy piece of bread reposing on a stack of papers in a bottom drawer. She removed it with two fingers, and threw it into the empty slop bucket, then returned to the desk, intent upon finding some sort of map.

She lifted out a sheaf of papers, glancing over them hastily. They appeared to be notes about ship's stores and they were written in English. She looked for a signature. There was none, but she did find a scrawled "JM" at the bottom of the second page. These notes had belonged to Captain Munroe!

She shuffled through the papers. Not admitting to herself that she was seeking some reference to Stephen, she scanned them quickly until she reached the last page. The top half was filled with figures, but there was a short paragraph written in longhand at the bottom.

The first words leaped out at her, taking her breath. "Esteban is exhibiting uncharacteristic good humor," she read. She took the paper to the bunk and sat down, her fingers trembling, her breath frozen in her throat. Should she read on? Should she open wounds she had tried to hard to ignore? No.

283

She could not. Not now. She crumpled the paper into a tight ball and sat staring at it, the words echoing over and over in her mind. "Esteban is exhibiting uncharacteristic good humor."

What had Munroe meant? When had he written this? Curiosity eventually overcame common sense and she unrolled the paper, smoothing it out on her lap. The wrinkles made the writing even more difficult to read. She limped over to the porthole, her heart pounding.

"It is obvious he is smitten with the Scottish girl, and though he denies this, I am sure he plans to take her back to Spain with him."

The words blurred. She closed her eyes and fought against the agony threatening to engulf her. Yes! her mind screamed. He did plan to take me to Spain!

She raised the paper again. "I am certain that is ill advised," she read. "Surely he realizes how poorly she will fit in with his family and friends. The little strumpet is obviously much below his station in life and will undoubtedly become an embarrassment and a burden if he is foolish enough to do as I fear he—"

The sentence was broken off in the middle as though Munroe had been interrupted. She raced to the desk and pawed through the other drawers, wanting to know the rest of Munroe's thoughts. She found nothing. She dragged herself over to the bunk and plopped down, contemplating the floor. But why should she want to know what he thought? Obviously, Munroe knew nothing about her, about her background. Was that how he had seen her—as lowbred? As a strumpet?

She threw herself back on the mattress and covered her face with her hands. Perhaps Munroe was right! Perhaps he knew how Stephen's parents would have reacted to her. She moaned and rocked her head back and forth. No! They would have recognized that she came from good Scottish stock! She would have made them accept her!

She removed her hands and stared up at the ceiling. No! Munroe had written the truth. Stephen's family would never have accepted her. She was much too spirited, too accustomed to doing what no fine Spanish lady ever would. Her smile was twisted as she tortured herself with thoughts of racing about the Valencia countryside bareback, her hair flying in the wind, the de Larras watching her, their faces dark with disapproval— except Tía María. From what Stephen had told her, the sister of his mild and gentle mother was a rebel. She would surely understand.

In her mind's eye, another horse approached her, a white stallion, its muscles bunched and its nostrils flaring with excitement. Its rider sat his plunging mount with such apparent ease, he seemed a part of the beast beneath him. His dark blond curls whipped about his face, obscuring his features, but Shona had no trouble recognizing him. Stephen!

She pulled her rearing horse to a halt, its hooves raising a cloud of dust. Her mare danced and pranced, its skin alive with twitching muscles, as the white stallion pounded closer, closer. Shona's own muscles began to react as her excitement built to a fevered pitch. She slid from the mare's back as the stallion pulled up beside her, rearing and snorting its pleasure, and when Stephen leaped to the ground, he embraced her with an exultant cry. She returned his impassioned kiss, her cheeks burning with the hot fever of their frenzied embrace.

"*Querida!*" he exclaimed at last, holding her away so he could look at her. "Those breeches inflame me with desire!"

She ran her hands down her hips as she laughed up at him. "I thought you found breeches unwomanly," she teased.

His grin was devilish. "I was a fool!" he exclaimed. "Your alluring curves are revealed so completely, I find myself embarrassed by my reaction."

She brushed her hands lightly over the evidence of his arousal. "I am not embarrassed," she said boldly. "Only tantalized."

His right eyebrow rose. "Only tantalized," he repeated. "Not excited?"

She batted her eyelashes. "Of course not," she said.

"Come." He pulled her toward the haven of the orange trees. "My need for you is threatening to stop the breath in my throat."

He tore off his shirt and laid it on the soft earth. Then he undressed her quickly, his fingers expertly managing the lacings at her waist. She pushed his hands away, and seconds later, her breeches lay on the ground, her shirt atop them. He spread his own breeches beside his shirt and pressed her to the ground on top of them.

Their breath came in gasps as he poised himself above her, parting her legs almost roughly.

Her need turned her blood to molten lava, and he took her with one violent thrust. As his velvety, hot shaft penetrated her moist, warm recess, she cried out with rapture, her nails raking his back and shoulders.

"Faster," she murmured. "Don't hold back."

As their hips rose and fell rhythmically, Stephen grasped her breasts and fingered her nipples. His nails bit into her tender skin, and the slight pain only heightened her passion. She groaned frantically as he plunged recklessly in and out of her seething body.

Suddenly, he rolled her over on top. "Ride me," he urged. "Feel my muscle ripple within you!"

"Oh, God, yes!" She rode him with frantic gallops, her hips rising and falling with rapid, violent thrusts. A red haze clouded her vision, and there was a pounding in her temples as her blood raced through her veins. Harder, harder she rode until the red haze burst into a brilliant, crimson cloud before her eyes. Then Stephen's exultant cry blended with hers as the world tipped and toppled, throwing her into the heavens before she landed again on the spinning Earth. . . .

The ship lurched, tossing her to one side of the bunk, and she opened her eyes, staring up at the ceiling, bitter tears of disappointment gushing down her cheeks. It had been so real! She pressed her hand to her mouth, her breast heaving with sobs. Why did she torture herself so? She would never race with Stephen across his land. They would never go to Spain. Stephen was dead. When would that truth become reality for her?

She lay there for a time, willing the tears to subside, and when her breathing had slowed to a normal rate, she forced herself to rise. Self-pity would not sustain her now. She retrieved some of the papers from the desk top and pored over them, willing her mind to concentrate upon them instead of her agony. She memorized the listed items and prices, laboriously adding and readding the long columns until she reached the same answers Munroe had penned at the bottom of each page.

As she was tucking the papers back into the desk drawer footsteps sounded in the companionway outside. She stiffened. Was MacKenzie coming for her? The ship tilted suddenly and began to move. She stood stiffly and faced the doorway. He would not take her without a fight!

The *Loretta* nosed through the cluttered harbor, her sails frosting her ropes and spars with white, her gun crews shouting with excitement as they ran out their cannons. Shona's breath froze in her throat. There, less than half a league away, was the Spanish merchant ship, its red and gold ensign flying proudly. She slumped against the quarter-deck bracing, her mind flooded with pain. Stephen's standard was flying on that ship. She herself had stood proudly beneath those colors as the *Nancy*'s cannons were run out. She had been prepared to swear a lifetime allegiance to that ensign. And, most important of all, Stephen had died beneath it.

But why was the merchant still dead in the water? Why wasn't she fleeing? During the hurricane had she sustained damage that forced her to ride so low in the outer harbor swells? Or, perhaps the *Loretta* was also flying the Spanish colors, and the other captain thought he was being hailed by a sister ship! She looked up. MacKenzie's enormous vanity was waving proudly above her—the Jolly Roger.

She heard MacKenzie's rough bellow and braced herself as the *Loretta* heeled over on one side, then began a wide circle. The crew began screaming and waving their weapons above their heads. Tears stung her eyes. So many lives would be lost this day because of one man's greed.

She saw Evans approaching and tried to lose herself in the shadow of the quarter-deck, but it was too late; he had already seen her. Though the first mate had been most apologetic when he'd dragged her from the cabin and up on deck earlier, she did not like the determined look on his face now. He took her arm and, without a word of explanation, dragged her across the deck toward the accommodation ladder. She screamed and kicked, but she was no match for his strength. He pushed her up the ladder, prodding her with the barrel of his pistol when she hesitated. Atop it, he pulled her toward MacKenzie who stood watching, his hands upon his hips, a scowl darkening his face.

The Scotsman twisted his fingers in her hair and pulled her close. "So you sought to escape me by fleeing the Bastard's Lair, did you? After all I did for you!"

"I owe you no allegiance!" she screamed. He jerked on her hair. "You're hurting me, you bloody bastard!" She twisted, attempting to bite his hand, and when he yanked her head erect, she brought her knee up into his groin. In response, he cuffed her across the side of the face, sending her to her knees.

She spat on his breeches, then clawed at his legs. He hit her again. She fell to her stomach. A stabbing pain burst across her body, ringing it from back to front. Suddenly, as though a bright light had illuminated every hidden crevice of her mind, the truth dawned upon her. She was carrying Stephen's child! The nausea every morning, the tenderness of her breasts. The days had run together while she had been intent only upon escaping, and she hadn't realized until this very moment that she had not had a monthly cycle since shortly after leaving Brunswick! She groaned and clasped her belly as though to plead with the tiny person within not to give up now.

MacKenzie placed his foot on the small of her back. "Bring me the Spaniard!" he screamed. "I'll show you I'm a man what keeps his promises. I'll hae the heathen thirled to the mast and you'll watch him die by inches!"

She knew she could not give in to the monster now, baby or no. "Fernando's dead!" she exclaimed. "You can't threaten me with harming him anymore. He lost his life in the hurricane!"

His foot left her back. He scooped her up by one elbow and pressed his face into hers. "I thought you Strathmores knew everything!" he said exultantly, his sour breath turning her stomach. "We pulled him from the same tree that held you! He's very much alive!" He turned to Evans. "I told you to bring me the Spaniard!"

"But you ordered him put ashore, Cap'n."

"And I also ordered him brought aboard before we pulled anchor!" MacKenzie roared.

Evans' prominent Adam's apple bobbed convulsively. "There weren't time, Cap'n," he gulped.

As the first mate steeled himself for another outburst of rage, a loud shout burst from a man in the rigging. "Another ship! Cap'n, there's another Spanish ship comin' into the harbor. She's closin' fast! My God, there's two!"

MacKenzie dropped Shona's arm and raced to the railing, followed by Evans. Shona slumped to the deck and lay gasping for breath, her mind filled with one glorious thought: Fernando was alive! Somewhere on that horrible little island, her dearest friend awaited rescue. The pains in her back and belly had subsided to a dull ache. There was still hope that the child could survive. She cupped her smarting cheek in her hand, her heart racing with joy. Then she laughed aloud when MacKenzie bellowed with rage. So the approaching ships were Spanish—the merchant ship was only a decoy!

MacKenzie stomped back and stood over her. "This is all your doing, you and that damned Spaniard! I dinna know how

289

you done it, but I know you're behind it!" He jerked her to her feet and bent her arms behind her back. "Well, it willna work! We'll stand and fight! We'll beat the heathen bastards at their own game!"

"We can't," Evans protested. "There's three of them, Cap'n. They'll blast us out of the water!"

MacKenzie dropped Shona's arms and cuffed Evans back against the railing. "Quiet, coward!" he screamed. Shona watched with fascination as he grabbed the first mate's shirt front and shook him as he would a recalcitrant puppy. The cords of MacKenzie's neck stood out and his eyes bulged with rage. "There are only two of them what can fight, you fool!" he ranted. "That's a merchant ship, unarmed, and her hold's filled with siller and goud!"

He released Evans' shirt and made a grab for Shona. "Take this bizzem and tie her to the mast! She'll watch us cut those Spaniards to tiny pieces, then I'll strip her and have my fun right on deck before the whole crew. She'll see who her master is!"

Evans did not argue again. He took Shona's arm and led her across to the ladder, his body trembling, his face pale with humiliation. She stumbled on the rungs and drew back when his arm rose above her. But instead of striking her, he steadied her and braced his body against hers as they descended.

Her mind raced with thoughts of how to escape. She could not allow him to tie her to the mast. Once secured in the open, she would be an easy target for both sides. She and the tiny life she held within her would never survive.

She allowed Evans to drag her to the main mast. But when he loosened his hold and reached for a rope, she whirled and slashed at his face with her fingernails. He shrieked and grabbed her into a bear hug. She wrestled and strained against him, but her strength was not sufficient to gain release.

Her energy spent, she leaned against him, gasping for breath. When he pressed his cheek against hers, she steeled herself, sure he was going to punish her in retaliation for the bright ribbons of blood streaming down his face.

"Don't struggle!" he hissed. "I won't leave you tied for long. Don't put your curse on me!"

Her curse! My God, he still feared her! "And why shouldn't I?" she panted. "You're no better than that bloody beast!"

"Keep your voice down!" he whispered hoarsely. He whirled her around and bound her hands together. "Please hear me out. I don't want you to come to any harm. I'll put Peters on guard. As soon as the fighting starts, he'll cut you loose."

Her hopes soared. "You can't leave me unarmed, get me a weapon!"

He shook his head as he pressed her against the mast. "You ask too much." He wrapped the rope around her body, pinning her to the mast. "I'll tell Peters to pass you a knife, but you'll have to wait. This is the best I can do. The cap'n's gone mad. None of us will survive this day." He walked away quickly, not staying for her words of gratitude.

She slumped against her bonds, the rope biting into her flesh. "None of us will survive this day." She laughed bitterly. He was probably right. And she and Stephen's child would be the first to die.

She bowed her head, trying desperately to find within herself even one tiny spark of hope. Peters would cut her free, and surely he would at least give her a knife! But what good would that do when the Spanish balls were falling upon the deck? She laughed aloud at the irony of her situation. Stephen, a Spaniard, had renewed her life. And today, another Spaniard would take it away.

She heard cannon fire and raised her head. Her eyes widened. MacKenzie, that deranged monster, had ordered his crew to fire upon the helpless merchant ship! Another cannon boomed. She peered through the smoke. The second shot, like the first, fell short, sending a second geyser of water into the air.

She twisted against the ropes. Another loud explosion rent

the air. This time, the *Loretta*'s cannonball found its mark. She cringed at the sound of splintering wood and the screams of pain carried across the water. Evans was right, MacKenzie had gone mad!

Suddenly, the gun crews on the opposite side of the deck erupted into bedlam. She turned her head and her breath froze. A Spanish ship, its white sails full in the wind, was tacking into position. And what a ship! She was larger even than the *Loretta*, and her deck teemed with men. White puffs of smoke erupted from her railing and the boom of her cannons filled the air. The *Loretta*'s cannons spoke in unison.

Fountains of water leaped high, and an earsplitting crash wiped out all other sounds. As the deck heaved beneath Shona's feet, she was thrown against the ropes binding her. A dismembered arm, the hand still clutching a burning punk, ricocheted off her legs. Her scream of horror was drowned out by the agonized shrieks of the wounded.

She retched and strained against her bonds. Then another grinding crash jarred the ship, this time from the other side. Acrid fumes burned her nostrils and tears streamed down her cheeks. The other Spanish ship had moved into position. The *Loretta* was being bombarded from both sides!

A ball screamed across the deck, tearing into bodies, severing limbs. She closed her eyes, unable to bear the carnage. When a hand gripped her arm, she looked up to find Peters sawing at her bonds with his knife. Streams of blood ran down the lad's cheeks from a head wound and his face was white with terror.

Suddenly, the forward mast exploded, showering her with splinters and scorched pieces of sail. The knife fell from Peter's hand and he grabbed for her, his eyes opened wide in surprise, a bright gush of blood spewing from his mouth. His fingers slid slowly from her as he collapsed at her feet, a piece of splintered wood protruding from his back.

Panic overcame her then. She lost all sense of reason. She screamed and writhed against her bonds, her body numbed to the burning pain of the ropes, her mind impervious to everything but her need to escape. Her breath labored for release. Her screams became animal-like grunts, and flecks of saliva exploded from her mouth. She pulled and twisted, but her bonds held firmly.

Her grunts turned into disjointed sobs, then moans of despair, inaudible in the uproar surrounding her. She slumped helplessly, her exhausted muscles twitching spasmodically. She knew her eyes were open, yet she could no longer see through the darkness closing in around her. She felt as though a warm liquid were being poured over her head. The noises of the battle slowly faded into silence. She closed her eyes as a black shroud covered her face.

Lights flickered off and on behind Shona's closed lids. She blinked, willing the lights to go away, to leave her alone in the peaceful darkness. The lights persisted. A noise roared in her ears. She moved her head from side to side, mentally cursing the intrusion. Then the noise became a voice, rising and falling with a persistent cadence. Slowly, the noise assembled itself into words.

Her own moan startled her and she opened her eyes. A strange shape hovered over her. She blinked and the shape congealed into a man's face.

A spout of rapid words spewed from his mouth. She moved her hands and was surprised to feel rough wood beneath her fingers. She tried to lift her head, but it was much too heavy. She closed her eyes again, willing the voice, the entire horror-filled world, to go away and leave her alone.

"Señorita!"

The word seared itself into her mind, wiping away her tranquility. "Go away," she said hoarsely. "Leave me alone."

Another spate of rapid words followed, and even in her fatigue she recognized that the speaker was proclaiming her deliverance from death—and he was speaking in fluent Spanish!

She opened her eyes and struggled to rise. A firm hand

pressed her back. "Let me up," she moaned.

The face loomed before her. "You must lie still, *señorita*," a heavily accented voice said softly. "You have endured much."

A firm hand gripped hers and her surroundings became clear in a rush of painful sensations. Her temples pounded with each beat of her heart. Her breath burned in her breast and every muscle in her body screamed in protest. She knew instantly that she could not be dead—not unless she was suffering the fires of hell! Her hands kneaded her belly. The pain had disappeared.

"You must not try to rise, *señorita*. When you have sufficiently recovered, I will carry you below to a bed. Do not fear me, I am Diego Izquierdo."

She studied the Spaniard kneeling at her side. His face was lined with age and silver peppered his black hair. His mouth was wide under his prominent nose, and his hazel-brown eyes were soft with concern. "Where am I?" she croaked through cracked lips. "What happened to . . . to . . ."

He smiled. "You have been rescued from your captors. You are still aboard their ship, but you have nothing to fear now. My *capitán* has ordered that you be treated with great kindness. As soon as our surgeon has finished with the grievously wounded, he will tend to you."

"But you sank our ship," she whispered. "I remember the smoke and the blood."

"No, *señorita*. There was a mighty battle, but our forces were too strong. The ones holding you captive were overcome, and those who still live were transferred to our ship, the *Inez*. Even now, they strain against their chains, awaiting the judgment of our *capitán*."

His words sank into her weary brain, charging her body with renewed energy. She struggled to a sitting position, ignoring the pain.

"MacKenzie! Did you kill MacKenzie?"

The Spaniard sat back on his heels. "You must not upset yourself. I do not know this Señor MacKenzie."

"He was the captain! The beast who had me tied to the mast!" She clutched at the Spaniard's hands. "Please tell me he's dead! Tell me his soul is rotting in hell!"

He recoiled from her words and hastily crossed himself. "You must not talk like that, *señorita*. Whoever this man is, whatever he did to you, his fate is in God's hands!"

"But you don't understand! He's a beast! A demon from hell! He killed my . . . Oh, God, he's an animal!"

His face flushed red and he dropped his eyes. She was suddenly flooded with memories. She clutched at his hands again.

"I must see your captain! You must rescue Fernando!"

His brow wrinkled. "Fernando?"

She nodded quickly. "He's Spanish, too. He was captured with me when MacKenzie took our ship." She knew she was babbling, but she could not stop herself. "He's an old man, and he has been through so much! He's on the island! You must take me to your captain!"

The Spaniard patted her hand. "There will be time for that later. I am sure my *capitán* will not desert a countryman. He has already ordered us ashore as soon as we have taken care of the dead and wounded. You must be patient."

She collapsed against him. "But Fernando's old, and alone, and he doesn't know what has happened to me!" she sobbed. "He's all I have left in the world!" The Spaniard appeared extremely distressed by her tears. He patted her back awkwardly, murmuring soothing words she did not want to understand.

Her body was too exhausted to sustain her grief for long, and her tears were quickly spent. She knew she should preserve her energy for the growing child. She sniffed and wiped her nose on her sleeve.

"If you are sufficiently recovered, I will help you below."

"And you'll bring your captain to me?"

The Spaniard sighed and nodded his head. "The moment he is available."

295

He pulled her slowly to her feet, and she leaned against him, burying her face in his coat, until her head stopped reeling. His uniform smelled of smoke and death. She shuddered.

"Are you sure you are strong enough to walk?" he questioned.

"Yes, if you'll just hold on to me."

He pulled her arm over his shoulder and walked her slowly to the hatch. "The ladder will be difficult," he said.

She clenched her teeth. "But not impossible."

He went first, and she crawled slowly down the ladder, her mind concentrating upon reaching the next rung, and the next. At last, she stood at the bottom, her hands tightly clutching the railing.

"You may let go now." The Spaniard pulled her arm over his shoulder again and led her toward the end of the companion-way.

She stopped suddenly, tugging at his coat. "No, not that cabin. Please. Take me to that one." She pointed in the opposite direction.

He stared at her for a moment, obviously perplexed by her vehemence. Then he nodded slightly and turned around.

Shona trembled as they neared the first mate's quarters. Where was Evans? Had he been killed? Though he had tied her to the mast, she knew that he had done so reluctantly. She hoped he had survived. A picture of Peters' young, bloody face swam before her eyes. She blinked rapidly.

The Spaniard opened the door and led her into the cabin. The floor was littered with clothing and the bunk was tilted in one corner, knocked from its straps by the violent concussions the ship had suffered.

"Can you stand while I prepare the bed?"

"Yes, if you hurry."

She leaned against the wall and watched him work. Like Fernando, his age did not seem to be a handicap. Within moments, he had the bunk firmly lashed again, and the blankets thrown back.

She sank onto the mattress with a grateful moan.

The Spaniard hovered over her. "Are you in pain? Can I bring you anything?"

"Some water, if you don't mind."

He pulled the covers over her and tucked them in. "Of course. I will also bring something to bind the sores on your wrists. I will be back in a moment."

She grabbed his hand. "And your captain. See if he will come with you. Please!"

"I will see, *señorita*. But I promise nothing." He quit the room, closing the door softly behind him.

Shona pressed her head back against the pillow and moaned. Now that she was lying still, her entire body throbbed with pain. She closed her eyes, determined to ignore the discomfort, but horrible, nightmarish pictures immediately leaped into her mind.

She opened her eyes and kneaded her temples. Would she ever be able to erase the memory of what she had just seen? Or would this day, like the gory battle of Culloden, forever haunt her nights with screams of death and the cloying odor of spilled blood? And worst of all, would it mark her unborn child?

She smiled softly as she caressed her belly. So many things had happened. She carried Stephen's unborn child within her body, and she must do everything within her power to see that it grew strong within its safe nest. The mattress dug into her sore back, and she struggled onto her side where she could watch the door. Fernando's white-stubbled face swam before her eyes. Had he stood upon the shore watching the black smoke fill the western sky? Had the roar of the cannons filled his heart with dread? She blinked back her tears. Somehow, she would convince the Spanish captain to rescue her beloved companion. Surely he would be eager to save the life of another Spaniard. And if he wasn't? She pushed the nagging thought from her mind. She would make him return!

And what would Fernando say when she told him the news of her pregnancy? She could picture his merry face writhed with a broad smile, his lips parted in astonishment. It would be a boy, it had to be a boy! Another Esteban to carry on the de Larra name. She closed her eyes and moved her head from side to side, tears spilling down her cheeks. "Oh, Stephen, Stephen," she whispered. "You would have been so proud to have a son, why did you have to leave me?" She imagined how Stephen would react, if she could tell him. His dark blue eyes would widen, and she was sure his right eyebrow would rise in surprise. Then, he would smile and take her into his arms and whisper endearments. She wiped angrily at the tears. It was not fair! Stephen's son deserved a father!

Her musings were interrupted when the door opened and a stranger strode quickly into the cabin. He was very tall, and his dark blue uniform hung loosely over his painfully thin frame. His long jet-black hair was scooped into a black net at the nape of his neck, and his face was pale and gaunt with high cheekbones. His black eyes, hooded by prominent lids, were so sunken that Shona was reminded of a cadaver.

He stopped at the bed and stared down his hawkish nose at her, his thin lips set in a firm line. "You wished to see me, *señorita?*"

His voice was low and husky, and almost toneless. She shivered and licked her lips nervously. "You are the captain?"

He bowed stiffly. "I am Capitán Francisco Muñoz of His Majesty Ferdinand the Sixth's Royal Spanish Navy. I am at your service."

She stared at him wordlessly. This was the same Francisco Muñoz that Stephen had told her about, it had to be! The one he had called his enemy. Her heart leaped into her throat. Dear God, what would become of her now?

Chapter 24

"You look at me open-mouthed. Tell me, *señora*, have I inadvertently committed what the French call a social faux pas?" His thin lips twitched at the corners.

Shona blinked rapidly. "*Señorita*, not *señora*. No! You have been a perfect gentleman."

"I apologize, *señorita*, for assuming you married. I but noticed the ring upon your finger."

She raised her hand and stared at Stephen's ring. "It . . . it is not a wedding band."

His cold fingers clasped her hand and carried it closer to his face. He studied the ring, his nostrils flaring. "I know this crest!" he gasped. "Where did you get this ring?"

She winced as his nails dug into her rope-burned wrist. "You're hurting me!"

He dropped her hand and stared down at her, his face blanched of all color, his eyes glittering like two chips of black onyx. "Once again I owe you an apology," he purred softly. "But I must repeat, *señorita*, where did you get that ring?"

She tore her gaze from his and twisted the gold ring with trembling fingers. "It was given to me by a very dear friend."

"Esteban de Larra?"

The question, though put to her in the softest of tones, sounded to her ears like a shot from a pistol. She threw back the blanket and glanced frantically about, seeking an avenue of escape. But when she tried to rise, those cold fingers once again encircled her wrist and she fell back upon the mattress.

His face loomed only inches from hers. "You must not fear me," he crooned. "But you must answer what I have asked. Did Esteban de Larra give you that ring? Where is he?"

Her blood pounded in her throat. She tried to remember all that Stephen had told her about Francisco Muñoz, but could only remember him calling him an enemy—and of course there was his sister, Inez. Would Muñoz have her put to death for having associated with Stephen? No! She could not endanger the baby. His fingers dug deeper into her tender flesh. She would have to answer him, to placate him somehow. And above all, she would have to keep the knowledge of her pregnancy a secret. She could not allow Captain Muñoz to know that she carried the son of his enemy deep within her belly. "Yes," she whispered. "It was Esteban de Larra. But you don't have to worry about him anymore. He is dead."

She heard the quick intake of his breath. He dropped her wrist. She glared up at him, her lips clenched over her teeth. His eyes were almost lost behind their hooded lids. She could see the blood pounding through a vein in his temple. Suddenly, his eyes opened wide, and he took a quick step backward. "I do not believe you!" he barked shrilly. "You lie!"

She shook her head slowly. "I do not lie. The pirates killed him."

"When?"

"Several weeks ago."

"You were with him?"

"Yes. We were on our way to Louisiana."

"Just the two of you?"

"No. We were on a ship Stephen captured at Brunswick. The pirate leader, Kenneth MacKenzie, set a trap and our ship was overcome."

"You were the only one taken prisoner?"

"There was one other. And now, you must go back and

300

rescue him. Fernando must not be allowed to remain on that island. He could be killed."

"Fernando? Ah, Fernando Mendoza. Of course, de Larra would have his servant with him."

"Then you know Fernando! Please make haste! He is all alone and has no idea what has happened to me. After all, he is a fellow countryman."

The answering smile involved only his lips. "Of course, *señorita*. We have been patrolling this coast for weeks now, waiting for the pirates to return to their island and become relaxed and complacent. And when that happened we were ready for them. You must allow my crew time to savor their victory for I have only your word that Señor Mendoza is on that island. For all I know, he may even be a spy for the pirates, or even the French!"

She struggled to her feet and stood swaying before him. "Now it is you who lie!" she spat. "I have never heard such nonsense. If you know Fernando at all, you know that he is a loyal son of Spain. He's there, I tell you, and if any of the pirates were left on shore with him, he's in danger of losing his life!"

His lips trembled, and Shona wondered if she had gone too far; but she could not allow him to abandon Fernando on that despicable island.

"You have spirit," he said suddenly. "Perhaps I could send a longboat ashore later, but there is much to be accomplished before I take such action. After all, Fernando is a very old man. Perhaps he is already dead."

Suddenly realizing that he was baiting her, Shona steadied the backs of her quivering legs against the bunk.

"You know that isn't true. But he might be killed if you don't rescue him."

He leaned back against the doorjamb and studied her. "And what is Fernando to you? Why are you so interested in his rescue? He is an old man. Surely you and he are not—"

She launched herself at him, but his hands quickly

301

imprisoned hers. As he held her tightly against him, she could feel his body shaking in silent laughter. "You're despicable!" she cried. "Fernando is a friend, the only friend I have left in the world. Surely, as a Spaniard, as a Christian, you'll not allow him to die, alone and forgotten."

He stiffened and pushed her away. She stumbled against the bunk and huddled against the side of the mattress, overcome with rage and indignation which were intensified by an almost overwhelming fatigue.

She winced as his fingers brushed her shoulder. "Do not be so dismayed," he said softly. "I have already ordered one of my most trusted crews to your friend's rescue. As the *capitán* of this venture, it was imperative that I learn where your loyalties lie. You have convinced me that they lie with Spain."

She grabbed at his coat. "You'll bring him here? So I can see him?"

He shook his head. "No. I am having you transferred to my flag ship. Once aboard the *Inez*, I will have our surgeon attend to your wounds. By that time, Fernando Mendoza will have joined you."

She stared up at him. "Why did you make me believe you would abandon him? How could you be so cruel?"

"I have already told you. I needed to be sure you were not a very clever spy planted by the pirates." He opened the door and stood looking down his nose at her. "I am told you asked to see the pirate leader hang. I regret to inform you that the articles we signed with him will deny you that pleasure. He and his men will be set ashore in their longboat."

"But he's a murderer!"

"I assure you, the information we have received from him in exchange for his miserable life is well worth the exchange. His island base will be wiped from the face of the earth and another pirate's nest will have been eradicated forever."

"You'll live to regret this. He'll just find another ship and begin all over again."

"I think not. He will carry with him a constant reminder

that the Spanish are not an easy prey. The loss of his right hand will convince him once and for all of the error of his past ways." Ignoring her gasp, he straightened his shoulders and his stern gaze softened. "Now, rest. I will send my man for you shortly. You will accompany us to New Orleans, where I personally will see that you are settled and made comfortable. Along with your friend, Fernando, of course." He bowed and closed the door softly, leaving her alone.

Bile rose in Shona's throat as his footfalls faded away. She swallowed convulsively. His right hand! Such a punishment was nothing less than that horrible brute MacKenzie deserved. He had caused Stephen's death. He had tried to rape her. But there was something so horrible about disfigurement. It was almost worse than seeing someone hang.

She pulled the blanket about her shoulders and huddled beneath it. What about her? Muñoz had said he intended to take her and Fernando to New Orleans. What would they find there? How would they make a living? She could not allow Fernando to carry the burden of supporting her and the child. She would have to find some sort of work, something she could do until the baby came, something not too strenuous. She chewed on her lower lip thoughtfully. There was only one occupation for which she was trained—but she would not allow herself to think about going into servitude again. Surely she could find something else to do. She would rather die than kowtow to the gentry while she eked out a bare living in some hovel. Her baby deserved far more than doing that would provide. She fingered the cross lying on her breast. There had to be more to life than serving others—and she would find it, or die trying.

Francisco Muñoz climbed the companionway ladder slowly, his mind occupied with what the girl had told him. De Larra dead? No, he could not believe that! She was mistaken, he was sure of it. He could not imagine any pirate, no matter how clever, taking the life of Esteban de Larra. And what of Perez? Though he had tried with veiled questions, he had been unable to find out from the girl the fate of the faithful lieutenant he had sneaked into de Larra's service. Perhaps Perez had escaped and awaited him even now in New Orleans. He would not believe that de Larra was dead until he heard it from Perez's own lips.

And the girl. What had she meant to Esteban? She wore his ring, and Muñoz had not missed the cross nestling between her full breasts. Had his worries for Inez's future been in vain? Had Esteban fallen in love with some Colonial *puta*? Had he been on his way to Spain with her?

He hailed one of his men and waited impatiently while the boat was prepared to take him back to his ship. The girl had been correct about one thing. He was a Christian. And even more important, he was a Jesuit! He knew where his duty lay. He would take her to New Orleans and see that she was given shelter and instruction by the Holy Ursuline Sisters. It was unfortunate that the order was run by such a lenient abbess, but that was the way of the French, soft and ineffectual and given to dramatics. He would have to assert his considerable influence to ensure that the girl was given the discipline she so badly needed. Perhaps in time, she would do enough penance for her whoring way of life to realize she herself had a calling. And if not, well, he would think about that if and when the occasion arose. Though he had been celibate for years, he was still a man, and he had been unable to ignore the voluptuous curves of her body and her huge, pleading yellow eyes.

He fingered his prayer beads. He would have to spend much time with the governor, Marquis de Vaudreuil, oiling those corrupt hands in order to wheedle more time in New Orleans. The French had a natural aversion to the Spanish—a fear really—and he dreaded the time he would have to spend courting the governor at the decadent Place d'Armes with its fountains and opulent furnishings. He shivered with dread, fearing in his very soul that some of the licentiousness might rub off on him. Then he determined that he would spend many hours mortifying his own flesh with the whip and hair shirt. That would give him the moral strength to face the situation the girl had forced upon him. Yes he, Francisco Muñoz, would make sure he was in New Orleans often enough to see that she had no further opportunity to endanger her very soul.

Chapter 25

Wispy feathers of Spanish moss waved like dejected gray-green ensigns from the boughs of leafless oak trees while pig frogs and crickets shrilled insistent choruses from the waist-high weeds lining the muddy levees. From afar, carried on the rain-laden wind blowing out of the wild cypress jungle called Bayou Laforche, came the coughing bark of an alligator. Shona shivered and pulled her heavy cloak closer about her shoulders. Beside her, Fleurette, the *fille de cassette* assigned to accompany her, grinned impishly and tossed her saucy curls with a quick movement of her small head. "We get wet, *non?*" she giggled.

"We get wet, yes," Shona grumbled. Fleurette ignored the cross reply and skipped gaily ahead, sloshing muddy water high into the air. Shona shook her head and bit the inside flesh of her lower lip. When, oh when, would the Mother Abbess trust her enough to send her out alone? This young girl's constant inane chatter gave her a headache, her cloak was splattered with gooey red mud, and her new boots looked as though they were years old. She transferred the heavy market basket to her left hand and blew on her cold fingers. To make things even worse, she had been unable to find a single speck of the precious white flour that the convent cook had requested. She could imagine that overworked sister's reaction when she pulled the heavy sack of corn meal from the basket and deposited it on the table in the scullery. She humphed to herself. More than likely it was wet through from the insistent drizzle.

A sudden flash of lightning, followed by an ear-splitting roll of thunder, momentarily lit the darkened sky. Shona quickened her pace, cursing under her breath at the cold, the rain, the mud, the entire bloody world! As she did so, the deluge began in earnest, the sheets of water soaking through her heavy woolen cloak and gown in seconds. Fleurette grasped her free hand and huddled close, her eyes wide with fear. "I don't . . . like . . . this!" she gasped, her teeth chattering. "It is like a . . . a sign from God . . . of his displeasure!"

Instantly, Shona's anger melted at the terror evident on the girl's upturned face. She pulled Fleurette close and grinned wickedly. "Then we'd best hightail it!" she shouted. She quickened her stride until she was running, pulling the reluctant Fleurette along with her.

The cleansing downpour quickly erased the last vestige of Shona's vexation. This was fun! She raised her booted feet high and brought them down hard, giggling with delight, reminded of the brashes she had run through on the moors of Scotland in hot pursuit of her brothers. Though the thunder and lightning continued to roll around them, Fleurette soon forgot her fear and joined in the hilarity. Together, they splashed and cavorted and giggled their way through the pools of lantern light spilling from the doorways and windows of the businesses on Chartres Street—the Austrian butcher's shop, the Catalan's tavern, the dry goods store. The few other pedestrians turned in their direction, and linen window squares were quickly twitched aside by curious stay-at-homes. More than a few faces were wreathed with smiles at the unexpected sight they beheld on that long, rainy February afternoon.

Shona did not care that they were creating a spectacle. For this one brief moment, she was a child again. She forgot the hours of catechism, the throb of knees pressed to unrelenting stone, the gut-numbing fear of Francisco Muñoz with his beads and his gloomy demeanor. She even forgot to worry about Fernando and how he was faring in his cramped cottage on Canal Street; forgot the lonely, grieving, bittersweet nights filled with dreams of Stephen; and, most of all, forgot the responsibility of the baby growing deep within her.

She raised a hand in a jaunty salute to the *gen de couleur* militia man, posted at the foot of Jackson Square, laughing aloud at the surprise registering on his broad black face. Then she pulled Fleurette across the square toward the convent, forcing herself to slow their headlong flight, lest they slip and fall on the grassy verge. The square was deserted, filled with dark shadows and an aura of winter gloom. By the time they reached the heavy wooden gates, the mantle of respectability had once again settled upon her shoulders and she rang the bell with one sedate tug.

They were hustled in through a passageway to the back door by a nun with a glowering countenance and a sharp tongue. "You two!" she scolded. "You look like swamp rats! What's the good Mother to think! How do you expect us to find you decent, God-fearing husbands when you act like girls of the street!"

Shona pinched Fleurette's hand to keep the girl from giving a saucy answer. This was no time to bring Mother's displeasure upon their heads. No doubt all the items in the market basket were ruined, and the wrath of the stern sister in charge of the cooking would be quite sufficient for one day!

But the cooking chores had once again rotated and Shona's favorite, gentle, soft-spoken, shy Sister Claire, was the one to greet them when they stepped meekly into the kitchen. She sent a novice to fetch dry clothing while she pressed giant mugs of hot tea into the girls' blue hands, and clucked and murmured until she had them settled before the roaring fire.

"I'm afraid the marketing is ruined," Shona said. "The rain came down so hard!"

"Not to worry," Sister Claire said in her gentle voice. "A

shop owner brought us three lovely, fat chickens and I have a hearty *potage à la reine* simmering on the back of the stove for our evening repast."

"But I couldn't find the white flour either. I had to buy cornmeal."

"Then cornmeal it will be." Sister Claire smiled sweetly. "There is a little of the white flour left. I'll mix the two so cleverly, the sisters will never know their morning bread has been adulterated by Colonial corn."

Shona sighed deeply, too exhausted to even think of spending the long evening hours upon her knees. "Can I help, Sister?" She ignored Fleurette's horrified gasp. "I know how to bake."

Sister Claire's serene gaze was altered only by the twinkle in her blue eyes. "I appreciate your offer, but I'm afraid you cannot be allowed to miss the evening devotionals. Mother seems to think you are improving."

"You mean she doesn't sigh out loud anymore," Fleurette put in quickly. "Even I noticed that!"

"Surely you should be attending to your own prayers," Sister Claire chided softly. "None of us is so good we can allow our minds to wander to how others are behaving."

"But I'm not here to become a nun!" Fleurette protested shrilly. "I'm only here until Mother can find me a husband! I'm not like Shona! She doesn't want a husband! She's not natural! She's—"

Sister Claire placed her hand over the girl's mouth to quench her vindictive words. "That is quite enough, Fleurette. Here is your dry clothing. You must go to your room and change or you will be late for Evening Vespers."

Fleurette made a face and minced from the room, carelessly trailing her clean gown across the floor behind her. Sister Claire held out Shona's dry clothing. "Are you warm enough, child?" she asked. "Would you like more tea? You look a little peaked."

Shona basked in the warmth of the sister's smile. "No thank

310

you," she replied. "I'd better get out of these wet clothes."

"You can change here before the fire if you desire. I'll stand watch at the door."

Shona shook her head quickly. "No! No thank you. I'm . . . I'm a little shy about . . . about . . ."

Sister Claire nodded and turned back to the table where she busied herself unpacking the market basket. "I understand."

Shona walked as quickly as allowed through the halls toward her room in the correction wing of the convent. Two bright spots of color burned high on her cheekbones. It was hard to mislead poor Sister Claire, but she could not disrobe in front of others now, not with her thickening waist, her swollen breasts, and the telltale bulge swelling the base of her belly.

She entered her cell. Closing the door, she removed her ruined boots and threw them into the corner, then quickly undressed, her teeth chattering anew in the frightful cold of the tiny room. God, when would this all end! There had to be some way to escape this confining, unnatural life!

She rubbed herself dry with a strip of harsh sacking. It was that Francisco Muñoz's fault. He was a religious fanatic and he was getting even with her for loving Stephen, punishing her for what he surely considered a "loose" life. She pulled the fresh gown over her head and unbraided her hair. Then she sat on the hard cot and ran the brush through her wet hair, digging the bristles into her scalp until it tingled.

Shona knew she must soon get away from this place. It was long past the Christmas season, and she was sure she could not keep her growing pregnancy concealed much longer. Tonight, after evening devotions, she would ask for an audience with Mother, and she would firmly put forth her plans for her own future. She smiled as she remembered how the thought of opening a mercantile establishment had gradually intruded into her mind. It had originated from her frequent shopping trips to restock the convent pantry. She had quickly discovered that the stores in town were ill stocked and that the available items were poorly displayed. She spent hours rummaging through stacks of merchandise to find what she needed. Various types of cloth were jumbled together, and packages of pungent-smelling soaps were stacked alongside bags of tea, a situation which left much to be desired unless the shopper liked a drink with a bitter, acrid taste. Barrels were not labeled, which meant you had to lift each lid until you found what you were seeking, thus wasting valuable time. She recalled the list of ship's stores she had found in Munroe's cabin, and the idea of opening her own establishment was born.

She dreaded having to talk to Mother, for the abbess reminded her of velvet over granite, soft and pleasant at first contact, but unbending beneath it all. And so much depended upon the outcome of her audience!

She rebraided her hair, railing at the convent rule that banned mirrors. How did they expect her to look decent when she could not check her own appearance?

Her hand flew to her mouth. Mirrors! She would have to stock mirrors! Her heart began to race. She retrieved her sodden cape and removed a sheet of paper from the lining, smoothing it out and studying it closely. She had found an empty shop fifty-eight feet by one hundred and twenty, in a brick building located on Chartres Street, only a few blocks from the convent. The price requested was too high, but she knew she could bring it down with some skillful Scottish trading. She had seen it during a shopping expedition just the past week, and today, she had maneuvered Fleurette past it without arousing the girl's curiosity. The structure was new and sturdy, and best of all, it had a second story with a nice sleeping room and a great room complete with a large cooking fireplace. The upper story would suffice for living quarters for herself and Fernando—and the baby when he came.

She would start with a few items; then, as her nest egg grew, she would expand until she had a fine mercantile establishment. Fernando could help with the stocking and selling, but she would be responsible for the buying. She would carry the usual candles and try to find a reliable source for the scarce white flour which was brought down the Mississippi from the midwest. But unlike the other establishments in town, she would concentrate upon quality cloth and household furnishings. And, of course, she would stock toad flax for the negroes and calico for the planters' wives. She would never be too uppity to sell what people wanted!

She folded the paper and returned it to its hiding place. Then she lifted the thin mattress and removed her small bag of coins. She spilled them out onto the cot and ran her fingers through them, enjoying the silken, slippery feel of the gold. Bless Fernando and his hard labor. This was her future—and her baby's! She would not allow anyone to stand in her way. Not Mother, not Francisco Muñoz, arrogant bastard that he was. She chided herself inwardly for her language and, for the hundredth time, reminded herself that she was a lady now. She was carrying Stephen's child, and she would have to conduct herself with decorum if she was to be a proper mother.

Shona was promised an audience with the Mother Abbess, but not until the following afternoon. She spent a restless night, tossing and turning on the hard cot, her mind going over and over what she would say. She wondered when Francisco Muñoz would show up in New Orleans again. She had been in the community only a little over three months and already he had paid four surprise visits to the convent. How and why he came were a mystery to her. It was obvious the Spanish were looked upon with distrust by the local citizens. No Spanish ships, other than the *Inez*, ever tied up at the levee on Decatur Street. Even the much larger Algiers levee was used by British and French trading ships only. Why was the *Inez* allowed moorage in New Orleans? What power did Francisco Muñoz wield over the local governor? Was de Vaudreuil afraid of him?

She could not completely understand her own fear of the man. He was outwardly polite, and always proper. He had given money to Mother for the purchase of a new wardrobe for

Shona, and he had never looked upon her with lust. He had said time and time again that he had only her best interest at heart. Yet, she sensed an inward streak of cruelty beneath the smooth, judicious exterior he presented to the world. His hooded black eyes reminded her of bottomless pits where nameless scenes of terror were enacted to wreak vengeance upon what he considered to be sin.

Yet, Stephen had not feared him, only disliked him. How she wished she knew more about the man, for surely even he had a chink in that pious armor he wore wrapped so tightly about his entire being. She knew one of his weaknesses but was reluctant to bring it to bear; his sister, Inez. No, better to let sleeping dogs lie. Surely any mention of the betrothed Inez would provoke bitter words of recrimination and, perhaps, far worse.

She attended her catechism class in the morning and mouthed the memorized responses with the others, all much younger girls. When she was first told she would be required to attend the classes, she had refused, stating that she was a Protestant and therefore uninterested. But Mother had been adamant. While she enjoyed the protection of the convent, she would have to attend. Besides, Señor Muñoz had insisted. So Shona acquiesced, not to assure herself a place in the convent, nor to please the Spaniard, but to learn more about the religion Stephen had embraced. She was a model student, and soon the responses came automatically, though she did not espouse every doctrine of the Roman Church deep within her heart. She understood and liked the Father Fernando worshiped, but she was fearful of the wrathful, judgmental, unbending God forced upon her every day in the Jesuit-supported convent classroom.

Today, her responses were automatic, without thought. She was still rehearsing her talk with Mother.

At last, long after the noon meal which she could barely choke down, she was summoned for her audience. She raced to her room and quickly changed her gown. After rewinding her braids with trembling fingers, she pinched some color into

314

cheeks she knew, even without the use of a mirror, were pale. Then she followed the novice down the brick-lined passageway, and though her head was held high and her back was straight, her knees were shaking and there was a lump in her throat. She shuddered at the thought of having to confront the head of the convent. Her only audiences with Mother had been cordial and she had always been treated with kindness, yet she found herself in awe of the tiny, wrinkled, black-clad figure. In many ways, Mother reminded Shona of the grandmother she barely remembered from her childhood, and her grandmother's sharp tongue and keen insight had always intimidated her as a little girl.

She shook herself and put thoughts of the past from her mind. This was now, and she was no longer a child. She would show Mother the gold coins Fernando had given her from his earnings at the brickyard, and she would tell her in no uncertain terms that it was time to get on with her own life. She was not a *fille de cassette,* one of the girls brought over from France with modest dowries to bolster the Territory's meager female population. She had no intention of being married off, let alone to a man of the Church's choosing. She would be polite, but she would be very firm. This was not France or England. She was in the Colonies, and she was free to make her own life.

When the heavy oaken doorway at the end of the passage was thrown open, Shona entered a long, high-ceilinged room, her eyes properly downcast. She heard the door close with a soft thump behind her. She stopped in the center of the room and stood waiting.

"Come closer, child." The voice was, as always, soft and gentle.

Shona stepped slowly toward the figure standing in the shadows beneath the long window at the far end of the room.

"You can look at me. I don't bite, you know."

The dry humor in the voice startled her. She sank to her knees and bowed her head. A tiny wrinkled hand was presented, and she kissed the gold ring with trembling lips.

"Rise." Not a request. A command.

Shona pushed herself to her feet, her eyes going to the large black beads of the rosary spilling down the skirt of the black habit.

"You wished to see me? Are you unhappy here? Do you feel you have been mistreated?"

She looked up, startled by the questions. "No," she answered quickly, then lowered her eyes again. "Everyone has been very kind."

A soft hand cradled her chin, forcing her gaze to rest upon the lined, kindly face before her. "Then why are you here, child?"

As Shona stared at the Mother Abbess, her tongue cleaved to the roof of her mouth. Mother's gray eyes, sunken and faded with age, were filled with infinite patience. Her cheeks, crossed and crisscrossed with deep lines, still bore faint pink traces of a robust girlhood, and the corners of her mouth were turned up slightly, as though to give encouragement. Shona swallowed and wet her lips.

"I . . . I wish to speak to you."

Mother nodded and patted her shoulder. "Then, come. Let us sit before the fire. This room is much too large and drafty."

She led Shona to a stiff, high-backed chair and gently pushed her into it, then seated herself opposite.

"I must apologize for the uncomfortable furniture," she said with a chuckle. "It seems our sponsors, the Jesuit Fathers, feel that to mortify the flesh is a necessary virtue."

Shona blinked rapidly, startled by the veiled criticism.

Mother sighed and bent forward, turning her hands to the warmth of the fire. "Of course, they have a point, though they do take it a bit too far, or don't you agree?"

"Yes, no . . . oh, I don't really know."

"You don't have to be afraid to speak your mind here, child," Mother continued. "Contrary to what the girls say, these walls do not have ears." She settled back in her chair and fingered her beads. "Now what were we talking about? Oh, yes, the uncomfortable furniture. Now, when I was a girl, growing up on the outskirts of Paris, we had marvelously soft sofas, with bright, silken covers, and there were always heavy draperies at the windows to keep out the chill. But even though we were very well off, for my father was in the King's service, he always insisted that our bedroom be unheated. He felt that rising to an icy cold world would be good discipline for his many children."

She stared into the fire and Shona waited impatiently, unwilling to interrupt.

"Of course, Père was right. He was always right. He was a wonderful father, filled with laughter and surprises—and love. What about you, child, did you have a happy childhood?"

"Yes," Shona answered rapidly. "Though my mother died when I was a bairn—a child—my father was much like yours. He was everything to me. And my grandfather lived with us, so it was like having two fathers."

"And your mother, while she lived? Was she a good mother?"

"I don't remember much about her—only that she smelled sweet, like lavender, and her lap was always soft and her voice was filled with music. She was always singing."

"That is a gift, you know. My mother also sang a great deal. Though her songs were lullabies, for she almost always had a new child at her breast."

Shona suppressed a smile. It seemed so unreal, the Mother Abbess of the Ursuline Convent talking so casually about suckling a child!

"Will you be a good mother, Shona Cameron?"

The question startled her, and she stared at Mother with her mouth wide open.

"Don't look so surprised. And answer my question, please."

Shona twisted her hands in her lap. Surely, Mother was only talking about the far future. Surely, she could not know! "I will do the best I can when the time comes," she whispered.

"Do you love the father of the child you carry?"

"Yes—no! Oh, what are you talking about? I'm not with child!"

Mother rose and stood, staring down at Shona, her eyes dark, her fingers twitching her beads impatiently. "Don't lie to me, child. I come from a large family, and the signs are unmistakable. You are pregnant, about four or five months, I should think. Now, answer my question. Do you love the father?"

Tears welled in Shona's eyes and spilled down her cheeks. She clasped the cross about her neck until her knuckles turned white.

"Yes." She almost choked on the word. "I love him with all my heart. But he's . . . he's dead!"

Warm arms enveloped her and pulled her to her feet. Her cheek rested against the starched wimple as tears of relief rolled down her face. How good it felt to share her secret at last! She had not even told Fernando about the baby yet, lest he refuse to help her with her new business. But what would happen now? Would Mother also refuse? She sniffed, took the kerchief pressed into her hand, and blew her nose.

Mother pressed her once again into the chair. "Now, I want you to start at the beginning." She leaned forward and grasped Shona's hands. "Tell me all about it. Everything."

The story came forth haltingly at first, for much of it was painful and not easily shared. But as her capture at Culloden, her misuse by Cumberland, and her life with the Currys unfolded, she began to find the telling easier. Words poured out of her like water from a fountain. It was only when she talked about Stephen that she stammered, and then only because she found it so difficult to put into words what he meant to her, what they had shared. Shona wept again when she told of Stephen's death, and even Mother's eyes grew misty. She skipped over some details of the horrible stay with MacKenzie, unwilling to give voice to what an animal he had been, and at last, she was finished. She slumped deeper into the chair, exhausted, but feeling more at peace within herself than she had in a long, long time.

The shadows in the room had lengthened, and only the flickering fire lit Mother's face. She sat quietly, her head bowed, her lips moving slightly, as though in prayer. Suddenly, she looked up, pain darkening her eyes and creasing her wrinkled cheeks. "You have been sorely mistreated," she said. Without another word she rose and, taking a punk from the mantel, proceeded to light the oil lamps scattered about the room. She moved slowly, her shoulders bent as though she shared the burden of all that Shona had suffered. When soft light bathed even the darkest corners, she returned to stand before the fire.

"You will be a good mother," she said, her voice firm. "But now, we must make plans for your future. I assume that is why you requested to see me."

The dread Shona had felt before the audience was gone. She squared her shoulders and answered steadily, "Yes. I have some money my friend Fernando has given me. You remember Fernando, he came with me that first night?"

Mother nodded for her to continue.

"I have found a shop to be let. I want to start a mercantile store. Nothing grand to start with, but in time I want to have the best shop in New Orleans. There is a second story to the building. I can live there, with Fernando—and with my son when he is born."

"And if the child is a girl?"

The question startled her. She wrinkled her brow and studied the flickering flames. "It won't be, but if it is, I'll love it just as much."

"You are aware that people will talk?"

"About what?"

"About your living there with a man, even though he is old enough to be your grandfather. About you having a child, when you are without a husband."

Shona stood up. "I don't care what people say—or think.

319

There are always those who criticize. They don't mean anything to me. I just want to raise my child."

"And Señor Muñoz? What about what he thinks?"

Shona's heart raced. Why was there always an obstacle? She wrung her hands. "Muñoz doesn't own me. I'm very grateful that he saved me, but he does not own my life!"

"He feels responsible for you. For your soul."

"He has no right to do so. My soul belongs to me. And to God."

"He left you here with the stipulation that you become a good Catholic. Are you prepared to meet that wish?"

"You don't understand. Whether or not I become a Catholic is not important. He will kill me when he finds out about my child! There's something evil about that man. Something terribly frightening!"

Mother sighed and nodded her head. "I quite agree with you—don't interrupt, hear me out. I don't know Señor Muñoz well, but I do know he is very friendly with our sponsors. There has even been talk that he was once a priest. It has been said that he is hostile to those of the Jewish faith and that he supports the Code Noir our French government has so foolishly imposed upon both Jews and blacks. But, be that as it may, I feel you have been abused quite enough for one lifetime. It is time you found encouragement and help. The question of your becoming a Catholic is something that will be answered in time. For now, it is the duty of this convent, of its sisters, and of myself, to see that you are given every opportunity to make something of your life."

Shona began to tremble from head to foot. "Then . . . then that means you'll help me?" she gasped.

Mother smiled sweetly, her eyes sparkling with a new light. "I thought I made that very clear, dear child," she answered with a chuckle. She took Shona's hand and walked her slowly to the door. "Now, I fear our time has run away. We must both prepare for the evening devotionals. But you are to come to me afterward. There is much to discuss."

Shona went to her knees. "I can never thank you enough, Mother," she said. She showered the hand held out to her with kisses.

Mother pulled Shona to her feet. "Enough of that! Save your thanks for God, it is He who deserves the credit. Now, out with you!"

Shona raced down the passageway toward her room, her feet barely touching the rough bricks. From now on, her life would belong to her. She would live with Fernando in their cozy little apartment, she would run her store, and she would have her baby! To hell with what Francisco Muñoz thought. To hell with what anybody thought. No more strictly enforced behavior! No more people to tell her what to do with her life! No more servitude! At last she was truly free.

Chapter 26

Asa's forehead was creased with worry, his eyes were bloodshot from lack of sleep. "I tell you, Esteban, you cannot go further. Your fever has broken, but your body cannot tolerate another journey, no matter how short. Rosa Gordo was right, these past few weeks of travel have proven too hard for your weakened state. You must stay in this settlement. There are many good German women willing to take care of your needs."

"But we are so close. *Madre de Dios!* New Orleans is only a short barge trip down the river. I tell you I am going even if I have to crawl to that barge!"

"You do, and I will be returning with a dead man. Is that what you want? Is it what your Shona would want?"

Esteban turned his face to the wall as Asa pulled the blanket up around his shoulders. "I cannot bear to delay another moment, I tell you," he groaned. "Shona may be in New Orleans. I must look for her."

"I have told you repeatedly that Rebecca and I will look for you. We have contacts in New Orleans, people who should know if a girl of her description has come to town. You must rest here while we do your seeking for you. I will send Rebecca back the moment we have word."

"But you cannot recognize her if you see her on the streets.

Only I can do that."

"You have told us what she looks like. Surely there are not many young women with the golden hair and yellow eyes you have described. Also, we understand that she prefers to wear breeches and shirts, and we will look for her in the guise of a young man as you have warned." He pulled Esteban up on the bolster and lifted a cup to his lips. "Drink this tisane I have prepared. It will bring strength to your blood."

Esteban gulped the bitter liquid and wiped a hand impatiently across his lips. "Ugh." He shuddered. "Much more of that and I will surely be a dead man."

"Did anyone ever tell you that you make a very uncooperative patient?" Asa asked with a grin. "The woman I find to care for you must have the patience of one of your saints and the strength of a mule."

"Just as long as she does not have the tongue of a viper," Esteban mumbled.

"Then I will try to find someone so old she cannot do ought but utter a few croaks between her toothless gums."

"You are laughing at me again."

"But with love, friend, and with much concern."

Esteban raised up on an elbow and grasped Asa's hand. Then he shook his head. "I have been nothing but trouble to you and Rebecca."

"You have been our friend and our protector," Asa replied, squeezing the Spaniard's fingers tightly. "Without your *pistola* we would be lying dead beside the road, or have you forgotten those robbers you put to flight?"

"It was not my *pistola*"—Esteban snorted—"but my Spanish which frightened them away. They were convinced we were only the vanguard for a large army."

Asa shrugged. "Perhaps. But the poisonous snake you killed before it could strike Rebecca could not understand any language. Your ball tore it in half."

Esteban threw himself back on the cot. "Why are we wasting time talking like this? Go! Find Rebecca and take the next barge to New Orleans, or so help me, I will crawl out of this bed and go in your place even if I have to make my way on my hands and knees!"

"Patience! Rebecca is at the landing now and our belongings are all packed and waiting at the wharf. As I have told you, we will find a small dwelling to live in while we make our inquiries. You must be patient. We will do our very best."

"I know you will. Would it be inappropriate for me to bid you go with God?"

"Of course not. I would be pleased." Asa turned away from the cot, pausing in the open doorway. "Do not forget what I have told you. Rest and patience, these are the keys to a speedy recovery. I will send a woman to look after you."

"*Vaya con Dios.*"

Esteban watched until Asa was out of sight. Then he turned his face to the wall and fought to control his rising anger. To be so close yet unable to seek Shona himself was almost more than he could bear. He raised his hand to his face and studied his trembling fingers. Asa was right, Rosa had known the trip would prove too hard. Yet he did not regret even one painful mile he had traveled. Perhaps it was only a desperate dream, but he felt he was traveling closer to Shona.

He turned so he would watch the doorway, not wanting any meddling woman to sneak up on him, but the tisane soon took effect and he found it impossible to stay alert. At least the rigors of the journey had broken the pattern of dreams he had suffered at the fort. Now, he often found joy and peace in sleep. He closed his eyes and surrendered to exhaustion.

. . . Shona stood on the deck of the *Nancy*, the wind whipping tendrils of pure gold about her face, her britches plastered to her enticing thighs and calves. He walked slowly toward her, devouring with his eyes the sensuous curve of her hips, the soft swell of her breasts beneath her dark green shirt. Why had he insisted she wear gowns? Her outfit today was enticing enough to cause a tightening in his groin. She pursed her full lips and blew a kiss toward him, then held out her arms in welcome. He walked slowly forward, his breath laboring in his throat, his heart beating wildly.

Her amber eyes were filled with dancing dark brown flecks as she playfully stepped backward, out of his reach, beckoning him with a toss of her head and an impish laugh. As he walked slowly forward, she stepped ever backward, staying an arm's length away, her full, pouting lips tilting at the corners as she teased him with her mischievous laughter.

But he was too quick for her. He caught her about the waist, pulling her into his arms. She wrestled with him, raising his senses to a flaming, fevered pitch. Then she melted against him, her full, ripe breasts rubbing his chest, her mouth tasting of honey to his hungry lips. Their tongues entwined and he scooped her up in his arms and strode across the empty deck which dissolved slowly into a green meadow filled with wildflowers.

He laid her on her back amidst the fragrant blossoms and knelt beside her, devouring her with his eyes and his hands. She suddenly flipped over on her stomach, burying her head coquettishly in her mass of copper curls. He sat back on his heels, smiling broadly. "Two can play at that game, *querida*," he said with a laugh. He got to his feet and walked several feet away, pretending great interest in the small white flowers carpeting the meadow.

He watched her out of the corner of his eye as she turned her head, sweeping away the curls covering her eyes. At the flicker of bewilderment that crossed her face, his insides twisted, and he almost gave in.

Shona rose to her knees in one languid motion. She closed her eyes, raising her face to the soft, warming breeze. Then she untied the laces of her shirt, her fingers moving over the strands of riband with maddening slowness. His thudding heart roared in his ears as she pulled the shirt up, inch by inch, gradually revealing the soft fullness of her breasts, their nipples flaring in soft, pink petals in the warmth. She rose to her feet, dropping the shirt beside her.

He gasped as she raised her arms over her head, then stretched her long, slim fingers toward the sun, her face lit by a soft smile. He could see the tiny pulse beating in the hollow of her golden throat. He turned to study her openly, appraisingly, appreciatively.

She brought her arms down in a wide arc, her fingers nimbly loosening the ties at her waist. Once again, with maddening slowness, she eased her breeches down over her hips, stopped just below the golden wedge, then stepped out of them with one fluid motion, her delicate feet barely brushing the carpet of flowers.

Passion flared in his eyes, but she only smiled softly, turning her back. The sun cast shadows in the dimples of her buttocks, and played flickering games over the mass of reddish-gold curls cascading down her back.

He covered the ground between them in three long strides, catching her about the waist, his hands moving slowly over her tawny flesh as he turned her roughly around in the circle of his arms.

Her nimble fingers worked on the fastenings at his waist. He stepped out of his breeches, then removed his shirt, throwing it to one side impatiently. He lowered her to the grass and lay down beside her, his mouth circling the tightening bud of one breast while his fingers lightly massaged the secret, moist recess he knew so well.

While she stroked his throbbing manhood with hard, rapid thrusts, he buried his face in the fragrant hollow of her throat, his tongue flicking softly upward against her honeyed flesh until his mouth covered hers. Her lips parted eagerly, her tongue seeking his, her breasts heaving against his chest. He drank from the well of her sweetness until his passion built to such a frenzied pitch, he could no longer contain himself.

Her hips arched and she whispered words of love as he mounted her and plunged his hard shaft into her hot, welcoming body. Her nails raked his buttocks and he thrust harder and harder until she cried out and he slowed their

327

coupling to a slow, luxurious rhythm as he stared down into her eyes.

"I love you, Stephen de Larra," she whispered. She closed her eyes, her long, dark golden lashes forming half-moons on her cheeks. He gently kissed each eyelid, his own heart bursting with wonder. "And I love you," he whispered.

A sudden breeze chilled his body. He heard a loud bang and closed his eyes against the wind bringing tears against his eyelids. . . .

When he opened them, Shona, the meadow, the flowers were gone. He lay on his cot, his arms frantically clutching at the bolster. Only his tears remained, wetting his cheeks as the bittersweet memory of his love washed over him.

He lay staring at the door the morning breeze had blown shut, knowing he should be grateful that he had been allowed to spend a few glorious moments with Shona in a dream, yet feeling cheated that their time together had been cut short by a mere gust of wind.

A knock sounded, and he sighed as he turned over on his back.

"Come in," he snapped.

He recognized the pretty young woman who tiptoed into the room. She was the wife of the self-appointed leader of the settlement, Dieter Warner. What was her name? . . .

"I hope I have not disturbed your slumber," she said as her gaze swept the meager contents of the one-room dwelling. "I am Joanna Warner and Asa asked me to look in on you."

Though her smile was warm, her dimpled good looks only irritated Esteban and he grunted a rude greeting. She appeared to take his ill humor in stride, straightening the bedcovers without chatter, fetching him a fresh cup of water from the well outside, giving him time to gather his thoughts and remember his manners.

By the time she had set a pot of aromatic soup boiling over the firepit and sliced the fresh loaf of rye bread she had brought in her basket, Esteban had control again.

"Thank you for your help," he said. "I apologize for not rising, but my legs are still a little shaky."

She said nothing, yet she smiled warmly, and he could not help but admire the efficient, quick way she worked. Her busy hands soon had a steaming bowl of soup and a mug of foamy cows' milk at his elbow.

"I would help you sit, but I am sure you would like some privacy while you eat. After you have had your fill, I will remove the dishes and you can wash your face so you will be presentable for your gentleman caller."

"Caller? What caller? I know no one here."

Her soft brown eyes sparkled as she made a rueful face. "I am sorry, I thought I told you." She ran a hand across her forehead. "Perhaps Dieter is right and I am a little addled. Anyway, a Herr Cabrillo has asked to see you. Do you not know him?"

"Cabrillo . . . no. The only Cabrillo I know is a seventy-year-old scholar in Madrid. Nothing could lure him from his book-lined study. Surely he has not traveled all this way—"

"I do not know. At any rate, a Herr Cabrillo is sitting in our parlor making a hearty meal of schnitzel and noodles. But do not worry. You will have more than enough time to meet him after you have eaten. You look much too thin, so clean up all of the soup. I will show him the way here later."

"You are going?"

"Of course. I have left a guest without a hostess. Besides, Dieter gave our son, Johann, a new puppy yesterday. I am sure he is feeding the animal from the table."

He watched her gather up her basket and let herself out the door with a breezy *"Auf Wiedersehen."* Then he attacked the delicious chicken soup with more gusto than he had shown in weeks. He even drank every drop of the milk, the first he had tasted since childhood. Dieter might call his wife addled but to Esteban's mind she was wonderful. Leave it to Asa to find the perfect woman, one who was not a chatterer, and one who could cook every bit as well as old Bonita back home.

He wiped his hands and face on the sacking she had thoughtfully provided and leaned back on the bolster, realizing he felt stronger already. Well, if he was going to have a visitor, and a strange visitor at that, he would just rise and greet this Don Herr Cabrillo—what a strange name—sitting in a chair.

Moments later, he was sitting at the tiny table, his face pale from the effort. He eyed the bottle of wine in the middle of the table, but decided to wait until his visitor arrived. After all, he had little enough to offer a caller.

His wait was not long. Joanna soon knocked, then stuck her head in the open doorway.

"You are up!" she exclaimed happily. "I told Dieter the chicken soup would work a miracle. See, here is your visitor as I promised." She pulled a large, balding, dark-skinned man into the room by the sleeve of his well-tailored, black wool waistcoat. "Herr Edmundo Cabrillo, this is Herr Esteban de Larra, whom you wished to meet. I will leave you to your talk." She quickly placed two pottery cups on the table and made her departure, smiling happily.

Esteban eyed the stranger warily. Cabrillo was of middle age, a large man with a well-muscled chest which was slipping inexorably toward his protruding belly. His well-groomed mustaches drooped sadly at the corners of his full lips and his enormous nose filled much of his broad, high-cheekboned face. His mild brown eyes were gently appraising. "I apologize for this intrusion, Don de Larra," he said softly. "But Dieter Warner said you were the only one of Spanish blood in the entire village."

Esteban struggled to his feet and offered his hand. "Please sit and make yourself comfortable, Don Cabrillo," he said. "And pour the wine, if you please. My hands are still too shaky."

Cabrillo's grasp was warm and firm. "I understand perfectly," he said. "Be seated, Don de Larra. I will not be responsible for causing a relapse in the very man I have come to woo with an offer."

Esteban sat heavily. "Offer? I am afraid I do not understand. Do I know you?"

Cabrillo's hearty laugh filled the room. "Indeed not, but we shall soon rectify that." He offered Esteban a glass of wine and sipped his own appreciatively. "Not a bad vintage, must be Spanish," he said absent-mindedly. Then he squared his shoulders and placed his blunt, square-nailed hands flat on the table. "I do not believe in mincing words, so I will get squarely to my proposal. First, let me tell you that I own a very large hacienda in the Tejas Territory, far west of here. The land is vast, almost uninhabited and thirsting for new settlers to till the soil and run the vast herds of cattle which only the Tejas plains can support."

"Surely you do not think that I—"

Again Cabrillo's booming laughter. "Oh, of course not! I realize you are not a farmer, de Larra, nor even a rancher. No, I have found the settlers I wish, right here in this settlement. I want Germans to come to Tejas!" He leaned forward, his eyes sparkling with excitement. "There are no better farmers in the entire world than the Germans. Hard, industrious workers, with a vast knowledge of farming techniques, especially these Rhenish settlers here. And they know hardship and how to overcome obstacles. It is only the government which is shortsighted."

"Government? Which government?"

"Why, the Spanish government, of course! You see, our King has allowed the church to launch a massive effort to civilize the Indians in our territory. The good *padres* have built several missions, all in an effort to lure Spanish settlers into the land, but they have failed miserably."

"Why? Have the missions been unsuccessful?"

"To a certain extent, yet. Oh, they bring in the Indians to do the labor of erecting buildings and tilling fields. They even baptize a few of them, but as soon as the mission appears to be thriving, the Indians simply pull up stakes and return to their nomadic ways. These tribes seem particularly obstinate about

331

maintaining their culture and are even quite warlike when provoked. It goes against their tradition to settle in one place."

"So the *padres* do not like your idea of German settlers?" Esteban finished his wine and sat back, his interest peaked.

"Exactly. They feel it threatens their own plans. After all, if I succeed where they have failed . . ." Cabrillo tapped his fingers on the table, staring out into space.

"Then why are you here?"

Seemingly startled by the soft question, Cabrillo hunched forward, his face grim. "I will not allow a few pious, albeit hard-working dreamers to thwart my plans. I am willing to risk everything I own to bring my scheme to fruition."

"And how do I figure into your plans?"

"Do not get ahead of me, please, Don de Larra. I have only told you part of my problem—of our problem—actually. You see, the French have had a sudden awakening of interest in the Tejas Territory. I do not know what has whetted their appetite for new conquest, but nonetheless, they are pushing ahead with a plan to settle the land with their own people. Now, I know they have been having problems finding Frenchies willing to come to such a vast, unknown place. I also know that the French cannot hold a candle to the Germans when it comes to farming and ranching. You only have to compare New Orleans to this settlement, for instance, to see that."

"I have not yet visited New Orleans."

"I know. Dieter has told me of your unfortunate injury. He has also told me that you have been seeking the whereabouts of a Señorita Shona Cameron. Have you found her?"

Startled, Esteban shook his head. "No. I have only been here a short time."

"And when you do find her? Are you going back to Spain?"

"I do not know."

"Then I wish to make you an offer, something you can spend much time thinking about after I take my leave."

"I am in no position to take any offer now. I am under commission to the King. I would have to be released from my

332

duties before I could take on any others."

"Of course, of course. But what I am going to offer could be both a most difficult and a most rewarding position. Don de Larra, I know your father. Oh, do not look so startled. I met him many years ago when he was arguing the case of the hacienda owners for water at a hearing in Valencia. He is a man of honorable reputation, and I am sure his only son is likewise. I would like to offer you the position of emissary for my endeavors. I am no longer young. I need a strong, intelligent young man to act as intermediary between our people and the Germans. I need you, and your lady friend when you find her—if you wish her to accompany you—to journey to Tejas with the first settlers, to see that they are not harassed by the *padres* and their people, to see that they are protected from the Indians on the long, arduous journey."

Esteban leaned back in his chair, his brow furrowed. "You flatter me, Don Cabrillo. We have never met, yet you offer me the cornerstone position in your endeavor. But, of course, I must refuse. I am in a state of flux right now. I do not know when I will find Shona, nor do I know where. She may be in New Orleans or I may spend the rest of my life seeking her whereabouts." His last words were spoken in a ragged whisper.

"But I do not seek your reply immediately!" Cabrillo exclaimed with a wide smile. "You see, I am here on what you could call an exploratory expedition. I am only feeling out the settlers and now I have also presented my proposition to you, which is more than I could have dreamed of doing when I left my hacienda many months ago." He rose and grasped Esteban's shoulder. "I only ask that you think about what I have said, that is all. I have business to attend to up the river. I will return in several months' time. Perhaps you will have an answer for me then. No, do not rise. I have sorely taxed your strength already. I will let myself out."

Esteban insisted upon seeing his visitor to the door, however, and they shook hands warmly, the young man strangely drawn to the older one. "Think on my offer, de Larra, for it may be the beginning of a whole new life for you. *Adios.*"

"*Vaya con Dios,*" Esteban called as Cabrillo strode quickly out of the yard. Then he closed the door and shuffled to the bed where he collapsed with a grateful sigh. Too much, too soon. *Dios*, this wound had turned him into a milksop! He settled against the bolster and clasped his hands behind his head. Don Cabrillo was right about one thing. He certainly did have a lot to think about.

Of course, interesting as it appeared, the entire proposition was completely out of the question. He had not yet found Shona, and doing so could take a long, long time. He sighed raggedly. When he made her his bride, he had promised to take her back to Spain with him. What kind of a life could he offer her on the trail to this dangerous, Indian-infested Tejas Territory?

A sudden picture of his mother's disapproving stare brought him up short. On the other hand, what kind of life could he offer Shona in Spain? He knew his countrymen only too well. She would always be an outsider, a foreigner with outlandish manners and unacceptable views on womanhood. Oh, Tía María would understand Shona, would love her even, but the rest of his family would make her life a living hell. How soon would she tire of her role as interloper? How soon would she be ready to leave, to run away even, just to escape her miserable state?

He sighed and closed his eyes, seeing in the blackness behind his lids a picture of Shona riding astride across a vast plain, her golden curls trailing in the wind behind her, her face lit by joy. His eyes popped open. No. It was a ridiculous thought. It would never work.

Chapter 27

Shona quickly discovered that freedom demanded far more from her than she had envisioned. For the first time in her life, she was totally responsible for her own well-being, as well as the well-being of her unborn child, and though Fernando continued to offer moral as well as monetary support, she felt responsible for him as well. True, he was physically strong for a man of his age, but since his rescue from the beach and his tearful reunion with Shona, his emotions appeared to be more and more out of his control. He had shouted with joy when Mother had brought her influence to bear upon the owner of the building, who just happened to be a parishioner, and the rental contract had been signed at a much lower price than first stipulated, and he had worked like a whirlwind preparing their living quarters, his lips pursed thoughtfully as he carefully placed each piece of furniture the good sisters had donated. But when he had fetched Shona from the convent and they had settled in, he had wept copious tears and had spent the entire evening alternating between weeping and laughter.

He had gone completely to pieces when Shona had finally told him about the child she carried. She'd watched in distress as his face crumpled and he collapsed onto the kitchen chair. As tears coursed down his cheeks and great sobs shook his body, she kneeled beside him, grasping his hands in hers.

"What's the matter?" she asked. "I thought you would be pleased."

He shook his head and pulled her head into his lap, running his trembling hands through her hair.

"I am," he gasped. "I am."

She pulled away. "Then what's the matter? Why are you crying?"

He sniffed and wiped his sleeve across his face. "Oh, my precious little Madonna," he moaned. "You do not understand what this means to me. You do not know how I prayed those first few weeks for a sign, even though I knew I was sinning when I pleaded for you to be with child. You and my Esteban were never married!"

"Is that all!" She leaped to her feet and stood over him. "That means nothing to me, Fernando. You and others like you may think I have sinned, but I don't care. Look at me! I am carrying Stephen's child! That's all that matters."

He looked at the hand she had cupped protectively over her belly, and his face crumpled again as he patted her hand. "And that is all I find important, Madonna." He sobbed. "It is a miracle. A gift from a very loving God."

She stroked his hair and rubbed his shoulders as he wept.

At last, he raised his head and blinked rapidly. "We must make plans," he said. "We must hide this from Muñoz, or all will be lost."

Shona pulled away and began to pace the room. "What do you mean? I know he'll be furious with me, but what can he do now? It's too late!"

Fernando shook his head. "No. It is never too late for people like him. If he learns that you are carrying Esteban's child, he will do something terrible!"

She stopped and stared at him, her heart constricting with fear. "Stop talking like that. You're frightening me."

He rose and put his arms around her shoulder. "I did not mean to frighten you, Madonna, just to make you realize the gravity of the situation. Francisco Muñoz is a devil hiding

336

within the protection of the church. He will stop at nothing to remove anyone connected with the de Larras from this world."

"But he hasn't harmed me."

"He does not think you are a threat to him. After all, he does not know that you and Esteban were in love. I am certain he thinks only that you had a few romps in bed, nothing for him to worry about. But even though he has not harmed you, he has intruded into your life by placing you in the convent, you must not forget that."

"And my child will be a threat?"

"Yes. A child with the de Larra name, especially if it is a boy, will be an enemy the moment it is born."

Shona sat down slowly, her hand still cupped protectively over her belly. "Then we'll have to hide it from him. Tell him I was carrying MacKenzie's bastard. He'll believe that."

Fernando stared at her, his forehead wrinkled. "Perhaps that is what we must do since he will undoubtedly be very angry with you for leaving the convent. Perhaps you can use your impending motherhood to soften his feelings, especially if you cleverly call upon his Christian leanings. You must weep and wail before him, allowing him to believe you are distraught at the thought of being the unwilling victim of that animal's rape."

"But when the child is born? What then?"

He shook his head slowly. "I do not know. If the child looks like Esteban . . ." He pursed his lips. Suddenly, he slapped his knee. "I have it! You will tell him the child is puny, sickly. And then we will do everything we can to keep him away."

"I am sure Mother will help. She told me she thinks Muñoz is evil."

"You must not trust her completely. She is the head of an Ursuline convent founded by and completely financially dependent on the Jesuits, of which Muñoz is an avid member. Perhaps we should leave New Orleans quickly. Perhaps tonight."

Shona gasped. "No! We have this building, and soon I'll

have a business which will support us. I'll not have my child on the run! From now on, I am going to live a normal life. Stephen's child will not know fear or oppression or need." Suddenly exhausted, she lowered her head to her hands.

Fernando pulled a chair close and sat next to her. "I did not mean to cause you pain, Madonna," he said soothingly. "I want only what is best for you and for Esteban's child. Are you in pain? Can I get you anything?"

"No. I'm just a little tired."

He patted her head awkwardly. "Then you should go to bed. I have erected a screen which will have to do until I can build a permanent wall to separate my bedroom. I will give notice at the brickyard tomorrow and then I will start on the shelves in the storeroom. You are not to worry. We will face whatever problems Muñoz might pose when they come. Who knows, perhaps he will think nothing of the child. He is a strange man."

She stood and stretched, kneading the small of her back. "You're right. I think I will go to bed. But I'm going to spend the next few hours thinking about what I will tell Muñoz when he comes. He has a way of showing up at the oddest times."

Shona spent many hours that night, and many in the nights to come worrying about Muñoz and his reaction to her pregnancy. Still, weeks passed and the Spaniard did not visit New Orleans. Fernando finished the shelves in the storeroom and in the store itself; then he installed a long counter for measuring cloth and stacking small items. He found a hungry young cooper who would work for a pittance, and soon sturdy oaken barrels with neatly lettered labels were stacked along the walls.

Shona walked the docks, dickering with ship chandlers over the goods they carried in their holds. She delighted in the bargaining, and always came away satisfied that she had gotten the best price for whatever it was she bought. She sent Fernando to the convent for a list of parishioners who made candles and other household goods, and then she walked through the streets, contacting every person whose name appeared on the list, arguing, pleading, bargaining. She bartered with the local Houma Indians for sassafras and bay leaves, giving them beads and trinkets in trade.

Unable to find quality fresh produce anywhere in New Orleans, she inquired about the docks and was told of a German settlement up the river and only a few hours away by barge. Though Fernando was against her traveling alone in her state, she would not brook his arguments and departed one morning with the rising sun. The trip was leisurely and she used the time to relax, finding peace in the mist rising over the tree-lined banks and in the soft gurgle of the river. The men manning the poles chanted in unison, filling the air with their boisterous harmonies which brought a smile of contentment to her lips. If only Stephen were here to share this experience . . . She sighed deeply and smoothed her skirt over her protruding stomach.

The barge nosed into the wharf long before she had expected, and she gazed with wonder at the fields of freshly planted cabbages and budding potatoes. After asking directions from the barge master, she soon found herself dickering with the local farmers for their wares. Though there was no fresh produce to buy at this time of year, she quickly purchased sauerkraut, pickles, sturdy beeswax candles, and hand-woven woolens dyed in the soft pastel colors obtained from wild berries and herbs. The workmanship was so exquisite that she could not believe her good fortune. She also exacted several promises that she would be sold some of the vegetables these industrious Germans could produce later in the spring. Exhausted, but extremely pleased with the results of her trip, she retired to the dock to wait for the returning barge.

She sat on a pickle barrel, watching a small tow-headed boy play with a large, clumsy puppy. The two were having such a glorious time, she felt tears rise to her eyes. She would have to make sure her son had such a puppy to play with when he was a few years old. The boy threw a stick into the water and she held her breath, fearing the pup would respond and be swept away by the fast-moving water. Instead, he raced to his young master and knocked him to the ground, slathering his face with a dripping tongue. When the boy screamed in protest, Shona found herself laughing aloud for the first time in ages. She watched as a pretty, young brown-haired woman appeared at the boy's side, scolding him with a laughing voice and dusting off his breeches, which elicited further howls of protest.

The tooting of the barge whistle startled Shona, and her attention turned to the clumsy vessel being tied to the wharf. After overseeing the loading of her purchases, thoroughly relaxed by the warm sun, she plopped down on a bale of woolens and gazed lazily back toward the boy and his mother. They were walking hand in hand toward a neat little cottage set back from the road. Suddenly, the boy started to run, the frisky puppy at his heels. A man appeared in the doorway of the cottage, and as he stepped out of the shadows, Shona felt her heart turn over in her breast. Dear God, *he looked just like Stephen!* She leaped up and raced to the railing, realizing for the first time that the barge had been cast off and was several yards from the wharf. She screamed his name over and over, but if he heard her, he paid no attention. He ruffled the boy's hair, patted the dog and exchanged a few words with the young woman. Shona strained against the railing as he ushered the woman and boy into the cottage and closed the door.

She screamed at the barge master to stop, but he shook his head and grinned broadly, pointing to the moving current which had already drawn them far out into the broad river. She slumped down on the bale, shading her eyes with her hand as she scanned the now-vacant cottage stoop. It *was* Stephen! It *had* to be! Oh, if only she had been closer. His hair was curly and dark blond, and he had the same lithe, muscular build. But she had been much too far away to see the color of his eyes, or to search his cheekbone for the small crescent scar. Yet, if that man was Stephen, why had he not responded to his name, and what was he doing in this little settlement, hundreds of miles from where they had been forced to part? She sobbed aloud, covering her face with her hands and rocking back and forth, knowing in her heart that it could not have been Stephen she had seen, that he was dead and she was only grasping at straws.

She spent the remainder of the journey downriver huddled on the bale in a dejected heap, the glorious, adventuresome day ruined by the black clouds of grief hovering over her. As the barge docked in New Orleans, she silently vowed to return to the settlement at the first opportunity and set to rest, once and for all, her doubts.

But her multitudinous duties interfered with her plans and she gradually came to believe that she had been mistaken, that she had only seen a German farmer, who bore a startling resemblance to Stephen, greeting his wife and child. Unable to bring herself to share the experience with Fernando lest she falsely raise his hopes, she kept her secret to herself, locked away in one corner of her leaden heart.

By the middle of March, her shelves were stocked with cones of sugar, packages of soap, tobacco, indigo, stacks of thread stockings, hats, linen handkerchiefs, ells of cottonade and flannel and linen, boxes of tea, thread, needles, herbs for cooking and for doctoring, and pewter forks. The barrels lining the walls bulged with kraut, West Indian rum, butter, and salted meat. Baskets and kitchen utensils hung from the walls alongside cascading ribands, cloth flowers, and braids for hats and coats. And everything in the store was displayed attractively and labeled when necessary. None of her customers would waste endless hours pawing through stock for what they needed!

She poured over her ledgers far into the night before the opening, adding and readding each column until her eyes smarted and her mind swam with figures. Fernando, exhausted from his labors, snored gently behind his screen. Finally, she closed the last ledger and pushed it aside, kneading the small of her back as she often did of late. She knew she should go to bed, but she was much too excited to sleep. So much depended upon the morrow!

Would people come? She had laboriously penned a sign which Fernando had hung in the front window—Cameron's Mercantile—but would it bring any buyers into her store? She closed her eyes and mentally went over every display, every item. There should be a larger selection, but that would come in time. First, she must make sales—many sales—to replenish her empty gold sack. She fretted over the shortage of coins in New Orleans and the overuse of bills of exchange which often had wildly inflated values. She would have to be firm in refusing paper. Only cash would be accepted until she became established enough to offer credit to her most valued customers.

She entered her bedroom and closed the door softly. Undressing quickly, she climbed into bed with a sigh of relief. It would do no good to worry about how her business would fare. Tomorrow would come soon enough.

By the time Shona unlocked the front door the following morning, customers were lining the board sidewalks, eager to be the first to enter the new establishment. Plantation owners from downriver jostled housewives and slaves to get first pick of the merchandise, and she and Fernando found themselves running to keep up with their customers' demands. By noontime, Shona was beginning to panic. At this rate, her stores would be depleted within the week!

Fleurette flounced into the store at midafternoon, towing a reluctant, red-faced, and obviously very uncomfortable young husband. "I do so admire you, *chérie*," she crooned to Shona. "Who would have ever thought—" She broke off suddenly to pull her husband over to the display of ribands. "I do so need one of each color," she said sweetly, her lips pursed in a pretty pout. "Do be a dear and pay the . . . the lady."

Shona ignored Fleurette's sarcastic tone as she had ignored the slight of not being introduced to her new husband. She wrapped the ribands in a paper and handed them to Fleurette with a smile.

"I hope you will be very happy," she said softly.

Fleurette's nose rose in the air and she frowned slightly. "Thank you," she said primly.

She left quickly, once again towing her husband who had the grace to smile apologetically as he disappeared through the door. Shona was sure she had seen the last of her one-time companion. The girl had only wanted to satisfy her curiosity and to show off her handsome young husband.

Soon after Fleurette's departure Shona was astounded to see Mother and Sister Claire making their way into the crowded room. She quickly completed the sale she was making and made her way to them.

"It appears your establishment is meeting with success," Mother said with a smile. "I am sure everyone in town has been dying to meet the young woman who so boldly walks the streets and docks in search of wares to sell."

Shona's cheeks burned. Had she been so obvious? "I have you to thank for all of this," she answered. "Without your help, I—"

"Nonsense," Mother snapped. Then her gray eyes twinkled and she jabbed Sister Claire with her elbow. "Do tell Shona what we have come for, Sister. This crowd is threatening to crush me."

Sister Claire smiled sweetly and leaned close. "Do you, perhaps, have any of that lovely white flour? Our meager store is quite depleted, and the sisters are beginning to grumble over bread made with corn."

Shona smiled and nodded. "I've saved several sacks for you. I'll have Fernando fetch some from the storeroom."

Mother placed a restraining hand on Shona's arm. "Sister is quite capable of fetching the flour herself. Aren't you sister!"

"Of course. Just tell me where."

Shona pointed to the door at the back of the room. "In there, on the middle shelf to the right."

Mother did not release Shona's arm, even when Sister Claire disappeared into the storeroom. "I have something you must know," she whispered. "Is there a place where we can talk?"

Shona looked around quickly. "We can go upstairs," she answered.

Mother shook her head. "No, that is not necessary." She pulled Shona into the corner and removed a barrel lid, busily examining the salted beef inside. "Señor Muñoz has returned," she said. "He was most upset not to find you at the convent."

Shona gasped. "What did you tell him?"

Mother held up a piece of beef and examined it critically. "The truth, of course. He will undoubtedly be here before the day is spent."

"He is very angry?"

Mother replaced the beef and dusted the salt from her hands. "Very. I trust you are prepared to meet his protests with vigor? And I suggest that you have your friend Fernando with you when Señor Muñoz arrives. He can be most persuasive."

She fastened the lid on the barrel and took Shona's hand, pressing it between her dry palms. "You must not allow him to intimidate you, Shona," she said softly. "You must stand firm on this."

"You didn't tell him about—?" Shona gestured toward her belly.

Mother shook her head. "No. Nor must you until it is absolutely necessary. The gown you are wearing is very concealing. No one would guess that you are with child."

"I have the flour, Mother." Sister Claire labored toward them, burdened with two large sacks. "This should last us for at least a month!"

Mother shook her head, then sighed and gave a small laugh. "Well, pay Shona and let us depart. I have been cloistered too long. I find these crowds overwhelming."

"There's no charge," Shona said quickly. When Mother began to protest, Shona shook her head firmly. "I owe this all

344

to you. It is the least I can do."

"Thank you, child. And please let us know how you are faring. We will see you at your catechism class early Saturday morning, and remember all that I have told you."

"I will. Good-by, and thank you again."

Shona watched Mother and Sister Claire until they disappeared down the street. Though her hands were soon busy filling another order, her mind was consumed with one thought only. Muñoz had returned! She stumbled through the remainder of the day, laboring over change, making mistakes, apologizing to antagonized customers.

When the dinner hour at last approached, she hurried the last customer out the door and then locked it firmly behind him. Fernando was sitting on the counter, sighing, shaking his head from side to side.

"*Madre de Dios*," he groaned. "I have never worked so hard in my entire life! You must be exhausted, Madonna; you have not even stopped for a sip of tea!"

Shona leaned against the counter and massaged her aching calves. "We're going to have to have help," she said. "I must buy more stock, and you can't handle so many customers all alone."

"But they come to see you, Madonna," Fernando protested. "You must be here to satisfy their curiosity."

"What on earth are you talking about?"

"It is true! I overheard many admiring conversations. These people think highly of a young woman with such courage and foresight."

"That's hogwash and you know it, Fernando! If they are curious, it's to see what we have stocked, and that means I've got to start buying tomorrow!" She picked up one lamp and blew out all of the others. "Bring the cashbox and the receipts. I'll have to stay up half the night preparing lists of what we need."

He groaned as he got to his feet. "You are a glutton for punishment," he chided. "And my stomach tells me it has not been filled for over twelve hours."

"I'm sorry. I'm not hungry myself, but I'll fix you some of that soup on the back of the stove."

"You must eat, Madonna. You are feeding two."

Shona made a face as she mounted the stairs to the apartment. "I haven't told you the news. Mother was in and she said that Muñoz is in town. I'm sure he'll be pounding on the door at any moment."

Fernando coaxed and cajoled Shona until she had eaten one large bowl of soup. Then he prepared a pot of highly spiced tea liberally laced with sugar. "You must keep up your strength," he chided when she wrinkled her nose at the sweetness of the concoction. "And you must promise me that you will eat a hearty breakfast in the morning." He blew on his tea and rolled his eyes. "There will be no time for a noon meal if tomorrow is like today."

Shona sighed deeply. "It looks as though I miscalculated the potential sales. And I don't know how I can get out to do more buying when there are so many customers. One person can't handle them."

"You must find someone to help. Now, before the baby comes. That way, they will be well trained when you are . . . are . . . indisposed."

She startled him by planting a moist kiss upon his cheek. "This must be very hard for you, Fernando. You've served the de Larras all of your adult life, and now here you are, working in a mercantile store and playing maid to a pregnant, unmarried, runaway indentured slave."

He gasped and tears rose in his accusing eyes. "You must never, never call yourself such things. You are like a daughter to me. I am not so special that I cannot work with my hands. After all, I have spent my entire life serving others, and though they were titled, they did not have any more courage than you."

She shook her head and stirred her tea aimlessly. "I'm not so sure I have courage, Fernando. Right now, I'm scared silly at the prospect of facing Muñoz."

"And well you should be. But you must do as the good Mother instructed. Stand up to him. He has no legal bond upon you, and there is no reason you must spend the remainder of your life repaying him for saving it. After all, he was performing his duty; you just happened to be rescued in the process. You must be strong."

"Well, I—" A loud pounding on the door downstairs interrupted her thought. She stiffened and clutched her abdomen with both hands. "He's here!" she hissed.

"Shall we ignore his knock?"

"No. He's seen the lights and knows we're still up. I'd rather face him now, before I lose courage completely. Let him in."

Shona ran a comb through her hair and straightened the folds of her full gown, hoping frantically that Mother was right, that she did not appear to be with child. She wrung her hands as she heard footsteps and voices on the stairs, then bit her lip as the door was thrown open. She stared incredulously at the huge figure standing in the doorway.

"Jephtha!" she gasped as she sank to the floor in a faint.

Chapter 28

"I thought you were dead! Oh, Jephtha, they said you died in that explosion! I thought I'd killed you!"

Jephtha pressed her back against the mattress and tenderly wiped her forehead with the damp cloth Fernando pressed into his hand. "They were wrong, Shona girl," he said gruffly, his voice hoarse with emotion. "I've looked fer you for months, knowing the good Lord wouldn't let you be killed when that ship blew up."

She grasped his hands, devouring his familiar features: his low hairline covering with the shock of dark hair above it, his broad face, high cheekbones, his soft brown eyes which radiated love and friendship. "But how did you find me? How did you know I'd be in New Orleans?"

He chuckled deeply and kissed the backs of her hands. "I didn't, not fer sure. But when them bastard Spanish released me, I looked up Curry. He said he'd heard the sailors talk about raiding New Orleans when they finished with New Brunswick. I knew it wasn't going to be easy, but I vowed I'd never give up looking till I found you. I've been to every settlement from Brunswick south, and I have to admit, I didn't know where I would go if I didn't find you in New Orleans. I just arrived here, came down the Mississippi by river boat, and I was walking around, trying to find a place to spend the night when I seen the sign with your name on it in the window. God, I never though you'd be here, but when I knocked on the door, this here fellow answered and said you was upstairs."

When Shona sobbed and threw herself into his arms, Fernando, who had been pacing the floor of her tiny bedroom, his brow wrinkled in distress, admonished Jephtha. "You must not upset her so. You have said you are a friend, and obviously you care for her. She must not lose the child."

Jephtha stiffened and gently pushed Shona away. She could see the shock in his eyes.

Shona turned her head to the wall, unable to face his accusing gaze.

Jephtha rose stiffly. "I see," he said. "You found that man you was lookin' fer, the one what would take care of you and give you lots of money and security—like this store—the things a smithy could never provide. And now look what he's done to you."

"No! It wasn't like that!" Shona gasped as the baby kicked and rolled within her belly.

Fernando kneeled at her side and patted her hand awkwardly. "You must not allow yourself to become so upset, Madonna," he soothed.

"But he must understand what happened. I must tell him."

Fernando rose and stared up at Jephtha. "No. I will tell him. You must get some rest. You are distraught; you are in danger of losing the child."

He pulled the blanket up over her and blew out the lamp. "I will tell him everything that has happened. It will be fine, you will see."

"You'll come back when you have talked?"

"Of course. Now you go to sleep. You have had a very trying day."

Shona watched as Fernando pushed Jephtha out into the kitchen. She closed her eyes and moaned as the door closed softly behind them.

The low hum of their voices went on for what seemed like

hours. When they were talking, Shona could relax, and at times doze, but when there were long silences, her muscles tensed and her eyes remained open. What was taking them so long? Would Jephtha understand? Would he remain the rock of strength he had always been to her, or would he stalk out of her life, his heart cold and unrelenting?

At long last, when the door opened a crack, she sat up, her heart beating wildly. Jephtha walked softly into the room and kneeled beside her bed, his brown eyes soft. He took her hands into his own huge paws, then bent to kiss her cheek.

"I'm sorry, Shona," he whispered. "That Spanish fellow told me everything. I figure you've been through more than anyone deserves."

"Then you forgive me?"

"There's nothing to forgive. It's me what needs your forgiveness. I was thinking a lot of rot about you. I should have known better."

She rested her cheek against his massive chest. "I can't bear the thought of losing you again," she said.

"You aren't going to." He caressed her hair awkwardly. "I'm goin' to stay on here in New Orleans. You need a real strong, stubborn man fer a friend. One old Spaniard ain't enough to look after my favorite girl."

Jephtha spent the night at a lodging house, and when he returned to the small apartment early the following morning, he found Shona and Fernando up and dressed.

"You have to eat breakfast," Shona scolded when he asked for hot tea only. "You look like you've lost at least a stone. Your clothes hang like a vagabond's and your face is gaunt."

He laughed and accepted the plate of fried salt pork and eggs she held out before him. "I'll never be gant and you know it. It's just all the walking I've been doin'."

Shona found that her own appetite had returned, and all three did justice to the meal. She was pleased to see Fernando

351

and Jephtha getting along so well. She could not know that the only things they had in common were their gentle natures and their love for her.

She sipped her tea and smiled lovingly at both men. "We'll just have to find some way to enlarge this place," she said suddenly. "When the baby comes, we're going to be tripping over one another."

Jephtha mopped the last of the yolk with his bread. "I'm not staying here," he said through a mouthful of food. "I'll find me a little place to bunk. Don't want any talk going on about you havin' so many men folk sharing your place."

"But that's silly! You're my friend!"

Fernando shook his head solemnly. "He's right, Madonna. I am old enough to be your grandfather, but this young man, well, you cannot do anything to jeopardize your position in town, what with the business getting such a good start."

"But you'll work with me? We'll go into partnership!"

Jephtha's rumbling laugh filled the room. "Oh, can't you just see me handin' some lady customer a frilly froufrou? Why, I'd be so tongue-tied I'd most likely pass out right in the middle of your store. No, I aim to go into the smithing business, where I belong. I've been toting my tools all around the countryside, and I've still got some money from selling my forge and the land my shed stood on in Brunswick." He swigged his tea noisily. "I kept my eyes open as I traveled. I've picked up some right fine new ways of making pots."

"Then I'll buy them from you to sell in the store! The only smithy I could find who did decent work was upriver. Just make sure your smith is nearby. You're going to be taking your meals here with us. We'll be one big happy family!"

"I think that is an excellent idea," Fernando said. "With the two of us seeing to it, she'll eat the way she is supposed to. For two!"

"I'll be close, all right. I want to be here when that Muñoz fellow shows up. He'll find out right fast that nobody tells my Shona what to do!"

"Please be careful with him, Jephtha," Shona said. "He seems to have a lot of influence in New Orleans. He could ruin my business, and besides, he did save my life."

Jephtha got up and clumped heavily around the room, his brow wrinkled with concentration. "That don't mean he can *run* your life!" he said finally. "I'll be politelike, but I just want you to know that with me around, you don't have to fear the man."

When Shona was taking a quick inventory before opening the store, she was surprised to find that the luxury items (fragrant soaps, expensive cloth, specialty teas) were in the shortest supply. Luckily, there was an English frigate tied up at the Algiers levee. She would have to visit the ship's chandler in the afternoon. She made a quick list of what she needed, then unlocked the front door for customers were already milling about on the boardwalk.

Shona and Fernando bustled about, helping buyers make selections and counting out change while Jephtha stood in front of the storeroom door, shuffling uncomfortably from one foot to the other. "Go find a place for your smithy," Shona whispered to him at midmorning. But he shook his head and remained where he was, his black eyes darting toward the door each time a new customer entered.

At noon, when Shona approached the storeroom for a fresh supply of tea, she was startled to see Jephtha glaring toward the front door, his lips drawn back in a snarl. She spun around and her heart leaped into her throat. Francisco Muñoz stood in the doorway, his hooded eyes insolently raking the room.

"Is that the bastard?" Jephtha muttered.

She dug her fingers into his arm. "Please don't start anything!" she whispered urgently. Then, squaring her shoulders, she walked forward to greet Muñoz.

His face was impassive as he bowed over her hand, but she did not miss the sparks of light leaping in the depths of his

353

black eyes. "*Señorita*," he purred.

She withdrew her hand and smiled politely. "How do you like my establishment? It's already a tremendous success." She motioned toward the customers lining up at the desk. "I'm already running out of some provisions." She gave a rueful laugh, hoping it sounded casual enough to mask the terror she was feeling.

Muñoz ignored her attempt at conversation. "We must talk!" he rasped. "Somewhere private!"

She tossed her head. "Oh, that's quite impossible now, Señor Muñoz. I'm much too busy."

She gasped as his hand snaked out and grasped her forearm. "Now!" he hissed.

Jephtha appeared out of nowhere. He yanked Muñoz's hand from her. "Is there a problem, Shona girl?" he asked, placing one arm across her shoulders.

"No!" Shona said quickly. Dear God, there was going to be trouble, she knew it! "Señor Muñoz just wanted to have a word with me, and I told him I was too busy now."

Jephtha squeezed her shoulder. "Then you'd best let the lady be about her business, *señor*," he drawled.

Shona had a hard time suppressing a hysterical giggle at the look of pent-up rage on Muñoz's face. Though he was nearly as tall as Jephtha, it was obvious he was very aware that the smithy outweighed him by half. His lips drew back in a ghost of a smile.

"Perhaps we could talk another time," he said.

"I reckon Shona's going to be busy for a long time to come."

"And who are you, might I ask, to be interfering in our business?"

"He's a friend from home," Shona interjected quickly. "He just got into town and he's going to be helping me. It's so good to see him again." She squeezed Jephtha's arm.

Muñoz frowned and looked down his nose at the customers milling about. "I must say, your establishment appears to be a tremendous success. May I congratulate you?"

354

Shona's smile was filled with relief. "Of course. Thank you."

"And may I add that I am in a position to be of some aid. I know a great many of the genteel people in New Orleans. I am a personal friend of Governor de Vaudreuil."

His words startled Shona, and she wondered what he was up to. She could not believe that he had her best interest at heart. After all, he had lost control of her life.

"Thank you," she said, "but I don't believe that will be necessary. If your 'genteel' friends wish to trade with me, they will have to find my establishment on their own."

Muñoz's lips twitched and a vein in his temple throbbed. But his eyes, when he lowered them to Shona, were hooded once again behind their prominent lids and she could not read his expression.

"The customers are waitin', *señor*," Jephtha said very softly.

Muñoz straightened, and his lips turned up in a sneering smile. "Of course. But may I make one suggestion? It appears that you have much business, yet you are pale and appear somewhat ill. Please promise me that you will find suitable help. You must not endanger your health."

Shona's breath froze in her throat. Did he know? Had he seen the telltale bulge beneath her voluminous skirts?

Jephtha answered for her. "Fernando and me, we've already talked that over. It's as good as done."

Muñoz bowed and backed away. "Then I will take my leave." He turned toward the door, but halfway there he whirled about and stabbed a forefinger at Shona. "You will not forget your classes at the convent, I trust?"

Shona placed a restraining hand on Jephtha's arm. "Of course, Señor Muñoz," she said sweetly. "Mother has become a very dear friend."

"Yes, I know," he said. He whirled about and walked stiffly out the door, his aquiline nose held high in the air.

Shona's knees trembled, and she clung to Jephtha for

support. "Oh, dear God, he was angry!" she muttered under her breath.

"I don't like him," Jephtha said. "A mean streak runs through him."

Fernando pressed close. "What happened?" he asked under his breath. "I have been helping customers and I could not hear anything."

"He left in a huff," Shona answered. "But he'll be back when he thinks he can get me alone."

"He won't do that," Jephtha declared, pulling Shona from the doorway. "I've been thinking all morning, and I've got a plan. You know that room at the back of this place? Well, with it havin' a back door and all, I've been wondering about renting it from you. It's small, but it's plenty big enough, and on clear days I can pull my forge outside."

"Oh, Jephtha, I'd love to have you use it, and for free! That'll mean you'll be close all the time!"

Jephtha winked at Fernando. "I know it. Just let that Spanish bastard—excuse me, Fernando, I forgot you're Spanish—just let him come back here tryin' to bull you around. I'll show him a thing or two!"

Shona spent three hours at the docks in the late afternoon replenishing her supplies while Fernando and a very reluctant Jephtha ran the store. During that time a barge left for the German settlement and she looked longingly at its wake, wondering when she would ever find the time to see that German settler who so strongly resembled Stephen. She wanted to put to rest the small niggling of hope she could not help but feel. When she returned to the shop at dusk, exhausted and out of sorts because of a backache and badly swollen ankles, she was greeted by a very irate Fernando, and an equally angry Jephtha.

"This bear of a man conducts himself as though he were the king of a mighty empire!" Fernando exclaimed. "He has insulted no less than three people today!"

"Now just a minute!" Jephtha protested. "I did the best I could. How was I to know you don't use linen sacking fer women's petticoats! At least I didn't cough all over the customers like he did!"

Fernando snorted. "That was the least of his mistakes. He actually had the temerity to suggest to Señorita Mevins that she get up off of her 'duff' and make her own soap if she could not find what she wanted here!"

Shona groaned. "Not Mrs. Mevins! Why, she spent a fortune in here yesterday!"

"And, he told an old woman, a very old woman, that she would not need a remedy among the herbs for her staggers if she would just stay away from the rum barrel!"

Shona stared up at Jephtha, her foot tapping.

He bowed his head. "Well, it was true," he muttered. "Her nose was all red and she smelled like a brew pot."

"She smelled of vinegar!" Fernando interjected heatedly. "I heard her tell you she was wearing a poultice on her chest to ward off the spring ague!"

"It was likker! I've smelled likker and I—"

"Enough!" Shona shouted. "Both of you! I've heard enough!"

She removed her cape and slumped into a chair. "You're both behaving like bairns and I won't stand for it another minute!"

"But Jephtha—"

"Not another word, I said!"

"But that old man—"

Shona whirled around and pointed a finger at Jephtha. "If you so much as squeak, I'm going to knock you flying!" she hissed.

He blinked rapidly. "Don't hit me, Shona. I'm sorry. I was dead wrong."

"And I, too, am sorry I have caused you so much distress," Fernando said.

She drummed her fingers on the table top. "This is a fine fankle," she said, lapsing momentarily into the Gaelic of her childhood. "Here you are, fechtin' when you should be workin' cheek for chow." She leaped up suddenly and began to pace the floor. "We'll have to find some help. I'll fix something for you to eat, then I'll go see Mother."

"I'll go!" Jephtha said quickly. "If you but tell me the way."

"There you go again"—Fernando sneered—"trying to take charge, and you do not even know the good Mother. *I'll* go!"

Shona stopped pacing and glared at them. "You both act like biddy hens fighting over the same nest." She stared until they both lowered their heads to avoid her stern gaze. "Or like two banty roosters with their combs raised and their feathers flying." She began to chuckle. Within seconds, she was doubled over with laughter.

The two men watched her suspiciously. Then her laughter infected them and they, too, began to chuckle. Before long, all three were laughing hilariously.

Fernando made a trip to the convent that evening and returned with assurances that Mother would send the only *fille de cassette* presently in her charge early the following morning.

Shona slept well and sang as she dressed, her only concern Fernando's cough, which seemed to be worsening by the hour. After a brief training period, the new girl would free her to do the buying. She greeted Fernando with a smile and baked pan bread for their breakfast, fretting only over Jephtha's absence.

"He said he would be looking for a forge today," Fernando said. "He will return in time for the evening meal. You know how he enjoys eating," he added in an innocent voice.

"No more of that!" Shona exclaimed. "I don't know what's gotten into you two, but you'll break my heart with your bickering."

Fernando leaped up and clutched her hands. "Oh, Madonna, I am truly sorry. I would not cause you pain for anything."

"Then you'll try to get along with him?"

"Yes. I will do my best."

"Good. Let's go downstairs. It's time for the girl Mother promised me to come knocking at the door."

Shona was horrified when Mignon showed up at the door an hour late, dressed in a bouffant silken gown crisscrossed with layers of lace. She eyed the girl's tiny porcelain features and delicate white hands with trepidation. Whatever could Mother have been thinking of, sending such a girl to work in a mercantile shop?

"I am ready to learn, madame," Mignon said in a breathless little voice. "Mother said I am to do everything you say."

"Then we'll start by orienting you to what we have to sell. Have you ever worked in a place like this before?"

The girl's pale blue eyes widened. "Oh, no, madame!" she exclaimed. "I come from Paree, where my Pere was a professor of music. He would never have allowed me to work."

Shona sighed. "Well, there's a first time for everything," she muttered under her breath.

She spent an hour instructing Mignon in the placement of the wares, all the while quivering inwardly at the burden this was placing on Fernando. His short legs ran untiringly from customer to customer, and he soothed and calmed the impatient ones with his suave Spanish manners. Only his persistent cough caused him to stop occasionally for breath.

Fortunately, Mignon had a quick mind. By midmorning, the young woman was helping the customers with the aplomb of a seasoned clerk, and Shona regretted her hasty first impression. Mignon was a good worker, after all.

Shona got the first hint that all was not well during an afternoon lull in business. When a handsome young man came into the store, Mignon quickly stepped in front of Shona.

"May I help you, monsieur?" she questioned, wrinkling her nose hungrily like a child before a platter of sweets. "I am Mignon, and I am from Paree, and I have never before had to work, but the convent sent me here, because they have not yet found me a husband." She batted her long brown lashes and flipped one blond curl over her shoulder.

The young man's mouth opened in surprise. He glanced about, as though seeking an avenue of escape from this husband-hunting adventuress from France. Shona stepped forward quickly. "That will be all, Mignon. Please restock the ribands; we have sold most of the blue."

The girl tossed her head and, without another word, turned to do as she was bid. But as Shona helped the gentleman find the tobacco he was seeking, she knew Mignon was glaring daggers at her from behind the counter. Then she forgot the incident because of the before-dinner rush.

Finally, having just ushered the last customer out the door, Shona was turning the key in the lock when the door was pushed open. Jephtha grinned at her and kissed her wetly on the cheek.

"I've got my forge!" he crowed.

She pulled him inside. "That's wonderful! But how on earth did you get so dirty?"

His grin widened. "Got a beautiful set of bellows, too. Had to help the man move it to my shop. Didn't you hear all that banging and hollering going on back there?"

"No, we've been too busy. Oh, Mignon, I would like you to meet a friend, Jephtha Clemmons. He's opening a smithy at the back of our shop. Mignon is the girl Mother sent over."

Jephtha stared wordlessly down at the tiny white hand thrust into his own.

"I am most pleased to meet you, Monsieur Clemmons," Mignon trilled.

He blushed beet red. "Uh, yes," he mumbled.

Mignon turned to Shona. "But you did not tell me you had such a handsome friend," she said breathlessly. She ran her fingers over his forearm. "And such a strong one." Suddenly, she removed her hand and gasped. "Oh, I fear I have smeared ink on your shirt. You must allow me to wash it, monsieur, unless you have an *épouse*—a wife—to do that most pleasant chore for you."

Shona's cheeks burned. The sight of Jephtha's smitten face and Mignon's batting lashes was too much.

"That will be all, Mignon," she said firmly. "I will pay you for the day's work and you can tell Mother that I will not be needing your services any longer." She reached for the cashbox and pressed a handful of coins into the girl's hand.

Mignon's eyes filled with tears and her lower lip jutted out. "But, mademoiselle, just this afternoon you said I was quick to learn."

"But . . . but this little girl is just what you need!" Jephtha sputtered.

Shona ignored his pleading eyes. "I'm afraid I need someone who is much stronger. This child would hurt herself lifting the heavy sacks, and you know I can't do that now." She turned her back and busied herself at the counter.

"I will see her home, then," Jephtha said.

Shona gritted her teeth and straightened her shoulders. "As you wish," she answered shortly.

Only Fernando commiserated with Shona that evening. Jephtha returned from the convent very late, wolfed down his food, and retired with only a gruff good night.

"I fear the giant is smitten," Fernando said as the door slammed behind Jephtha. "But, of course, you are right. That girl flirted with every man who came in the door."

Shona would not admit that she was feeling a bit jealous. After all, Jephtha was her own special friend, newly restored to her. She didn't want to share him with that French minx. She stomped her foot in frustration. "But she was a good worker! Oh, damn! Why did Mother have to send someone so young— and pretty!"

Fernando chose to ignore Shona's curse. "You are just tired, Madonna. You also are young and pretty, and you have forgotten that Mother told me she had only the one girl to send.

I am sure she did not know how unsuitable she would prove."

"But what am I going to do now? We need help!"

Fernando smiled brightly. "This morning, while you were busy with the girl, a woman came in asking if you could use a clerk. I told her no, but I did have the foresight to ask her name and where she lived. I will go to her home this evening. Unlike the child Mother sent, she is not very attractive, and she looks strong as an ox."

"But you shouldn't go out in the night air. You have been coughing for hours."

"Nonsense. It is only a little cough, nothing more. I will be back shortly."

She threw her arms around him. "Oh, Fernando, what would I do without you."

Shona's gratitude was short-lived. Mrs. Pearson arrived the following morning wearing her gray hair in a braid wrapped about her large head, a starched white apron over her ample bosom, a grim smile upon her face.

"I've had a lot of experience, you know," she said in a loud voice. "And I can tell you right now that you're going about this all wrong."

Shona's heart turned over. "Oh?" she asked. "And how would you do it, Mrs. Pearson?"

The woman picked up some ribands in her huge hand. "Look at these. Tomfoolery, that's what they are. You need to get rid of such things and concentrate on what people need." She stalked along the counter, her cheeks flushed. "And this-here sweet-smelling soap. Why, only a flibbertigibbet would buy this! And these herbs! Why, there's a surgeon in this town, you know, and he's got all of that in his house. And you've got things too orderly. People like to work their way through stacks of things. Reminds them of what they need and can't remember." She picked up a pile of neatly packaged herbal tea. "I'll just start by getting rid of this."

Shona grabbed the tea from Mrs. Pearson's hands. "Oh, no you don't," she said through gritted teeth. "This is my shop and we do things my way, or we don't do them at all!"

Fernando sidled over and took the tea from Shona's hand. "We have customers," he hissed.

Shona blushed and glanced hastily about. Several women were staring at her with open mouths. She swallowed and pulled an astonished Mrs. Pearson toward the storeroom.

Moments later, they both emerged and Mrs. Pearson stomped out the front door, her head high, her eyes blazing. Shona walked quickly to a customer, her heart beating wildly, her breath coming in gasps. The nerve of that woman! Trying to tell her how to run her own shop! Well, she had set things right immediately. To hell with Mrs. Pearson!

She wrapped salt pork for the customer with shaking fingers, but by the time she had made change, she had herself under control. As she listened to Fernando's persistent, hacking cough, regret set in. She would have to send him upstairs to bed, but who could help her? They were right back where they started.

She motioned to Fernando whose shoulders were shaking with another fit of coughing. "You are to go up to bed this instant," she said.

"But Madonna," he gasped. "I cannot!" He coughed again, his face beading with sweat.

"I insist. I will close early and fetch a surgeon." When he started to protest again, she realized there was only one way to get him to rest. "You must do as I say. If you stay here you will only worsen and then you will be a terrible burden. How could I possibly nurse you back to health and run the shop at the same time?"

He bowed his head, then shuffled toward the stairs, casting one last pleading glance in her direction. When she met his gaze with a stern nod of her head, he walked slowly up the steps, trying desperately to control another paroxysm of coughing.

Shona worked like a madwoman that afternoon, trying desperately not to offend any of her customers by making them wait overly long. She rushed from customer to counter to customer until she felt as though her feet would surely fall off.

At last, Shona closed the shop, an hour early. Then she gave a young boy a sweet sop and instructed the lad to fetch the surgeon. That done, she climbed slowly up the stairs, massaging the small of her back.

She was grateful that the boy returned with the surgeon so quickly, for Fernando could scarcely breathe, so great were his fits of coughing. The young doctor administered a tisane, covered Fernando's chest with a poultice, and then stared at Shona until she felt her cheeks burn. What was the matter with the man? she wondered. Why was he studying her like that?

He pulled the covers firmly over the poultice and stood, still staring rudely. "You must not allow him to remove the blankets. He will sweat out the fever, but you will have to administer the tisane several times a day for at least three days."

Shona could not suppress her gasp of dismay. She chewed on her lip as she motioned the surgeon away from Fernando's bedside. "Could I find some woman to nurse him?" she whispered. "I have my shop to run, and with Fernando ill, I am all alone. Not that I will endanger his life, of course, he is a very dear friend."

The surgeon nodded his head slightly, his brown eyes soft with understanding. "I see. Perhaps I can help. My betrothed is without employment at the present. I am sure she would be more than willing to help you in your shop."

"But I couldn't impose upon you like that! I will just have to close the shop until Fernando is better."

"Nonsense. You will not be imposing, *señorita*. I see you are with child. You should not work too hard in your condition."

Her cheeks flushed as he continued to stare at her. Then he gathered up his satchel and grasped her hand.

"You will like Rebecca. She is a hard worker. I will fetch her, so you can meet her."

He left the apartment before Shona could react, and she followed him quickly down the stairs, unlocking the shop door with trembling fingers and then securing it after he had gone. What a strange man! she thought. Why on earth had he stared at her so intently? And why had she allowed him to talk her into meeting his betrothed.

Shona was so exhausted, she could scarcely move. She turned away from the door and mounted the stairs slowly, shaking her head in wonder.

Asa trotted down the street, his heart singing with joy. He had found her, Esteban's Shona. He couldn't wait to tell Rebecca the good news! He quickly made his way home, laying his plans as he went. He would take Rebecca to the apartment. Then, when she had confirmed what he knew was true, he would send her upriver to Esteban. What a joyous reunion awaited the two lovers!

Chapter 29

Shona squirmed, uncomfortable beneath Rebecca's steady, unrelenting gaze. What was wrong with these people? Why were they staring at her? She turned to the stove and removed the steaming teapot.

"You shouldn't have bothered to come tonight," she said. "Tomorrow morning would have been soon enough."

"It was no bother," Rebecca replied quickly. "I need employment. It was most kind of you to agree to meet me."

Most kind, my eye, Shona thought to herself. I was forced into it by that pale, emaciated man you call Asa. She forced a smile as she studied the girl's long black hair, silken and shiny, spilling over her shoulders. Rebecca's skin was a creamy olive, and her large gray eyes were framed by the longest black lashes Shona had ever seen. Her dark green gown, patched though scrupulously clean, was much too large for her thin body; and her hands, clasped together, were large-knuckled and chapped. It was obvious she knew the meaning of hard work.

Shona poured three cups of tea and offered her guests cream which they refused. Perhaps if she confronted them, they would stop staring at her. But before she could speak, Fernando muttered in his sleep and Asa went to his side, pulling the screen into place behind him. She turned back to the girl. "So . . ." she said aimlessly. "Why are you seeking employment? Your betrothed obviously has a very good profession."

She regretted her harsh tone when tears appeared in Rebecca's eyes. "You do not understand, *señorita*," she whispered. "Asa works hard, but he receives no pay for what he does."

"No pay! What on earth are you talking about? Everyone gets paid for . . ." She stopped in midsentence, her mind racing. Everyone except indentured servants, as she herself knew so well. "Is he indentured?"

"Oh, no, *señorita*, he is not a servant. He is a physician, and he helps the surgeon with his work." Rebecca's gray eyes glowed proudly. "He will have his own patients someday."

"But surely the surgeon pays him for his labor. If not, why doesn't he find work elsewhere?"

Rebecca stirred her tea. "There is no other work for people like us. I have found some washing to do, for the poor people; but they cannot pay me. I have begged Asa to leave New Orleans, but he says this is his chance to learn from a man who knows much and . . ."—she stopped as though swallowing some further revelation, then continued—"besides, no matter where we go, it is the same."

"People like you? I don't understand. What makes you different from the rest of us?"

Rebecca grasped Shona's hand. "Oh, *señorita*, if I tell you, you must vow not to reveal this to anyone. If you do, we will be whipped and cast from the town, and we will never be able to marry!"

Shona squeezed Rebecca's hand. "I don't understand, but I promise to keep silent," she said.

When Rebecca threw back her head, Shona was amazed by the transformation in her. Her face was twisted by a look of pain so acute, so deep-seated, that Shona almost gasped aloud.

"We are Jews, *señorita*," Rebecca said softly.

"Jews?" Shona said. "What's so different about being a Jew? Why would you be forced to leave New Orleans?"

368

Rebecca laughed harshly. "You do not know about the Code Noir? We were here only two days when that dreadful paper was nailed to the tree on the common. You should have heard the people shout and hoot with laughter as the only rabbi living here was kicked and shoved and forced to flee for his life, along with his wife and three daughters. All of the Jews, our new friends, were made to go."

"I'm sorry. I've only been in New Orleans a short while and most of that time I've spent at the convent."

"You are a . . . a Catholic?" Rebecca asked breathlessly.

"No. I was brought here by a man who placed me in the convent so I would have a place to stay. I've never known any Jews, but my grandfather told me many stories about your people. I have only the greatest admiration for them."

"I am grateful to hear you say that."

"There's one thing I don't understand, Rebecca. If, being a Jew, you are not supposed to live here, how are you allowed to stay on?"

"Because they have no proof. We have hidden most of our belongings in a hole we dug in the floor of our cottage. We buried all of those things which would reveal our heritage."

"Then, if no one knows you are Jews, why have you had such a hard time finding work?"

"First, because we are Spanish, then because they suspect we might be Jews. I do not know how it is so, but it is usually easy for a Gentile to pick us out."

Shona sighed and shook her head, unwilling to add to the girl's misery by acknowledging that Fernando, very obviously a Spaniard, had not had any trouble finding work in New Orleans. "Then why did you come here in the first place?"

"We came to this great wilderness from Spain. There, we were persecuted by the Jesuits and their bloody Inquisition. We thought—we dared hope—that here, in this new land, we would be permitted to live our lives with dignity. But we find that things are no different here. We must still hide our beliefs and pretend to be Catholic."

"You won't have to pretend around me. I desperately need someone to help in my shop, and I think you'll do."

"Oh, *señorita*, I do not know how to thank you. I have a very important, short journey to make tomorrow, but I will begin the day after, if that is all right."

Asa came out from behind the screen. "Then you have decided that Rebecca will make a good salesperson for your shop?" He took his tea and swigged it thirstily, his eyes dancing with laughter.

"Yes," Shona replied, intrigued by the conspiratorial glances passing between the two. "I'm sure she will do nicely. Without Fernando, I'll be completely alone." She was astounded when they both burst into laughter. "What are you laughing about?" she demanded. "What is so funny?"

Rebecca wiped her eyes and looked questioningly at Asa. He nodded his head, then chuckled.

"Are you sure, Asa? After all, she is great with child. Such a shock might cause her great harm."

"I am sure. It will be less of a shock this way."

Shona leaped to her feet. "What are you two talking about? What will be less of a shock? Are you sharing some sort of jest?"

"I am so sorry, Señorita Shona," Rebecca soothed. "We do not make fun of you." She grasped Shona's hand. "I have some very important news for you, but I do not know exactly how you will receive it. Perhaps you should sit down."

"What is all of that noise?" Fernando rasped from behind his screen. "Someone help me remove these blankets before I suffocate!"

"No, you must not take the covers off!" Asa hurried to the screen and removed it, allowing Fernando to look out into the room.

"What are you arguing about? I . . ." Fernando coughed raggedly and gasped for breath.

Shona hurried to his side. "Don't let them bother you," she said. "They are leaving."

"Not until you hear our news, *señorita*."

Asa's softly spoken, calm pronouncement made goose flesh rise on Shona's body.

"Then speak your piece before I throw you out!" she shouted, as she forced Fernando's plucking hands away from the blankets.

"We wish to tell you that there is someone waiting very impatiently to see you."

"Me? What are you talking about? I know no one here."

"But he is not here, *señorita!*" Asa exclaimed.

Rebecca pushed him aside. "Oh, Asa, we must simply tell her and be done with it. Señorita Shona, Señor Esteban de Larra is staying in the German settlement upriver. He was too weak to travel, and he sent us to seek your whereabouts."

"*Stephen?* My God, Stephen's alive?" Bright pinpoints of light burst across Shona's vision, and she clutched at the bed to keep from falling.

Fernando was struggling to rise. "Do not bring false hope to the *señorita*," he rasped, "or I will personally cut out your hearts and feed them to the dogs."

"But it is true!" Rebecca exclaimed. "He only agreed to allow us to come in his stead because we promised the moment we heard anything we would return to the settlement for him."

"Esteban is dead!" Fernando said harshly. "He was shot and thrown into the sea months ago!"

Shona whirled about, grasping for Rebecca's hand. "Wait! I saw him! They speak the truth! Only I thought I was imagining things. I saw him when I went to the settlement to buy produce!"

"Mother of God and all the Saints be praised!" Fernando fell back upon the bolster, tears rushing down his stubbled cheeks.

"Tell me about him, is he all right? You said he was too weak to travel, is he terribly ill?" Shona knew she was talking too fast, but she could not stop herself. A giant bubble had burst within her, releasing months of grief and suffering.

"He is going to be fine," Asa answered. "He is only a little

371

weak from a fever brought about by his haste to reach New Orleans. We met him at a fort in the Florida Territory, and he agreed to act as our armed escort if we would accompany him to New Orleans and seek information of your whereabouts."

Shona leaped to her feet, ignoring her unwieldy belly. "I must go to him!" she exclaimed. "Oh, please help me, I must go to Stephen!"

"But we will bring him here, *señorita,*" Asa said. "You must get your rest and tomorrow morning, Rebecca will take the glorious news to the settlement."

"Never!" Shona paced frantically, wringing her hands. "I am going tonight. Do you think I would allow someone else to reunite us? Do you think I will spend another miserable night in my lonely bed without the man I love more than life itself?" She raced to the cupboard and grabbed her cloak, throwing it over her shoulders. "I must find a boat to take me upriver."

"But you cannot go alone!" Fernando wailed, fighting to remove the restrictive bedding. "Please, *señor,* make her wait for me."

Asa pushed Fernando down onto the bed. "You are going nowhere, is that understood? If you go out into the night air, you will undo all of the good the tisane and poultice have already produced. You will succumb to lung fever in only a matter of days." He motioned to Rebecca. "Come here and hold him down! Sit on him if you must. I will talk to Señorita Shona."

"You're not going to talk me out of going," Shona declared, tying the hood of her cape with a determined jerk.

"But I only wish to offer my services to walk you to the dock. Once there, I will find a boat and commission the barge master to deliver you safely to the settlement."

Shona, overwhelmed by emotion, fell into Asa's arms, sobbing. He held her firmly, patting her back and clucking like a mother hen until she had cried herself out. Then he pushed her away and offered her a large bandana for her runny nose.

"I fear this has all been too much for you," he said softly.

"Please finish your tea before we leave."

Shona gulped her tea down in three swallows. Then she wiped angrily at her teary eyes and clutched her belly.

"I'm ready," she said firmly. "Please, let's go. It's been so long. . . ."

Bright, golden rays of sunlight broke over the horizon and flashed across the surface of the Mississippi, pressing invading fingers beneath the soft blanket of mist covering the water. Shona moved her cramped feet restlessly as she scanned the shore. Only a little way to go now, for there was that lovely field of cabbages she had admired on her last visit. She rose clumsily to her feet and walked slowly toward the rail, her hands clenched at her sides. Why must the polers move so slowly? Did they not know her heart was fairly bursting with joy? Could they not sense her impatience to reach the settlement?

She held her breath as the wharf came into view. Push! Push, she urged the polers silently. Hurry! Take me to Stephen! She looked at the wharf as she drew closer and closer to it, imagining how it would feel to have Stephen's arms around her, to feel his beating heart next to hers, to taste him, to smell him, to know—really know—that he was truly alive.

She gripped the rail tightly as the barge slipped into its berth and bumped against the pilings. Not waiting for the gangplank to be lowered, she climbed awkwardly over the rail and jumped to the wharf before the ropes were made fast. She could hear the barge master muttering obscenities, but she ignored him. Nothing mattered now but finding Stephen.

She walked quickly up the road toward the little white cottage she had seen on her last trip, wanting to run, but unable to do so because of the burden of the baby. She swallowed convulsively as she mounted the steps. It was so quiet. Was he still abed? Should she simply walk in and throw herself onto his cot? Dear God, she had not thought about how

373

to approach him in her haste to see him again.

She raised her hand to knock, but could not make herself touch the wood. Instead, she opened the door quietly and stepped inside, glancing around hastily. Bitter disappointment flooded her. The room was empty, covers neatly folded at the foot of the cot, an empty mug in the middle of the table. Embers still glowed in the fireplace so he could not be far away. She saw a shirt hanging on a peg beside the bed and could not resist burying her face deep within its folds to inhale the manly fragrance she knew so well, knowing now that it was really true. *Stephen was alive!*

Shona walked outside and circled the yard, shading her eyes from the glaring morning sun. She heard a cow lowing and spied a small shed tucked into a copse of trees nearby. She walked quickly toward the building, her senses acute, her heart thudding in her breast.

"Hold still, cow, or I will make buttermilk out of your yield." The familiar voice stopped her in her tracks. She could not take one more step. Her entire body shook as though with the ague and she swayed and gasped for breath.

Stephen patted the cow's rump affectionately, then picked up the milk pail, feeling more than a little proud as he eyed its frothy white contents. Imagine, Esteban de Larra milking a cow! Oh well, he had to earn his keep somehow. And no one could say he had not done a good job, for the proof was in the bucket. He shoved a pile of hay into the manger as he contemplated the conversation he had had with Dieter the previous night. The German had asked—no, begged—him to stay on and act as a guide for the many Jews coming through the area. When questioned as to his motives for wishing to help strangers, Dieter had explained that he, too, knew the meaning of persecution. As a Rhenish German, he had been the subject of ridicule his entire life and had finally left his homeland rather than subject his wife and son to that shame. Esteban sympathized with the Jews, and he knew they needed all the help they could get. Indeed, he felt he could never do enough to repay Rebecca and Asa for their assistance. However, he had spent hours explaining to Dieter why he must first find Shona. After all, time was of the essence. The longer she remained lost to him, the more faint her trail would become.

He sighed now and shrugged his shoulders. This afternoon, he would take the barge to New Orleans to begin his search in person. He breathed a silent prayer for guidance as he opened the shed door. Catching a glimpse of a woman standing a few feet away, he shielded his eyes from the sun. "You did not have to check up on me, Joanna," he grumbled as he turned to fasten the hasp. "I have succeeded in milking the cow completely dry. She would not give one more drop." He turned, stopped—stared. The milk bucket flew through the air as he bounded forward with a strangled cry.

Shona sobbed Stephen's name over and over as he showered kisses upon her face and neck. He rocked her back and forth, his hands caressing her shoulders, her arms, her hair. I will not faint! she told herself resolutely, pushing back the black veil threatening to engulf her.

"*Mi tesora!*" Stephen said raggedly, his voice throaty with tears. "Oh, Shona, my Shona, I was so afraid I had lost you forever!"

"Hold me! Just hold me and never let me go!" Shona cried, her trembling fingers digging into his back, her senses reeling from a joy so overwhelming she did not believe she would survive. Then his lips sought hers, and she felt herself drowning in sweetness as their tongues twined in desperate union. His hands trailed over her breasts, down her belly.

He gasped and pulled away, his eyes raking over her swollen body, shocked disbelief twisting his features.

She laughed and grabbed his hands, placing them upon her belly. "Meet your son, Stephen," she cried.

Her heart stopped beating as he stared at her, his eyes blank as though her words held no meaning. Then, suddenly, he dropped to his knees, his trembling fingers stroking her belly. "A child!" he choked out. "You carry my child!"

He buried his face in her gown and she sobbed aloud at the wonder and joy in his voice. "Your son," she whispered.

She felt her knees buckle. Only his strong hands kept her from falling prostrate before him. When he rose and pulled her into his arms, she pressed her face against his chest and reveled in his familiar manly scent, in the warmth of his embrace.

A laugh rumbled deep in his chest and burst forth in a shout of joy. "A son! I sought only the one I could not live without, and now I find two!"

He cupped her face between his palms and stared deeply into her eyes. "You have made me the happiest man alive," he declared solemnly. "I dedicate the rest of my life to caring for you both. I swear I will not fail you ever again."

"Oh, my dear, you have never failed me!" Shona exclaimed. "You could not have known about the pirates—about Perez! Don't punish yourself, Stephen. We're both alive and I cannot stand another moment of talking. Hold me and kiss me and make me yours with the love only you can give."

"But is it safe? I mean, for the child . . ."

"Of course it's safe!" she laughed. "I am well."

He helped her to her feet and lifted her up into his arms, glancing briefly at the house, then striding quickly toward the shed.

"The barn! But there's a perfectly good bed in the house!" she protested weakly.

"It's not large enough for what I have in mind." He laughed as he kicked the shed door aside. "There is a soft, fragrant pile of hay over in that corner, and I promise you that the cow is firmly penned. "You have never lived until you have had a romp in the hay, my love!" He pressed her down onto the hay and lay beside her.

"I had much more in mind than a mere romp," she teased, a pout on her face, but he caught her lower lip between his teeth and nibbled delicately on the tender flesh until she pushed him away, her fingers frantically working the lacings on his shirt.

He caught her hands, however, and pressed them to his lips,

kissing each delicate nail with slow deliberation. "We have waited far too long to hurry now," he said huskily.

She took a deep breath, then exhaled slowly. "You are right, we must take our time."

He rose upon one elbow and reached for a straw, first trailing the tip lightly over her cheeks and forehead, then tracing the outline of her full lips. She caught the straw with her teeth and sighed deeply. "Not this slowly," she moaned.

He pulled her to him, breathing in the fragrance of her hair, of her honeyed skin. "I have lived for this moment," he said. "We must savor each look, each touch, each taste. There is no yesterday, no tomorrow. Only this moment."

She nestled against him, nodding her head in silent agreement as he brushed her earlobes with gentle fingers. Then, eyes closed, he moved his fingers lightly over her face, memory bringing each precious feature vividly before him.

She fingered his hair, his neck, his shoulders, her gentle touch sending the blood coursing through his body in hot, molten streams. As she ran her hands down his arms, he grasped one of them and entwined her fingers with his. She could feel the pulse of his wrist against hers.

"I am drowning in your touch," she whispered.

He pulled her even closer, until her thudding heart beat in rhythm with his and her fragrance enveloped him. His hands moved over her shoulders, then tangled in her hair as he pulled her face to his, his mouth closing over her parting lips. He fingered each nipple through the thin material of her gown while his tongue explored the sweet recesses of her mouth.

Shona suddenly pulled away and looked up at him. His blue eyes were dark with passion and his nostrils flared as he stared down at her, his lips parted, his breathing ragged. "I love you more than I can ever say," she said softly, her gaze drinking in the beauty of his rugged, high cheekbones, his manly, straight nose, dimpled chin, and the arched brows set above those azure blue eyes.

He sat up quickly. Pulling her up beside him, he lifted her

gown over her head, then pulled her shift off, tearing one sleeve in his eagerness. Shona quickly slipped his shirt off, but her shaking fingers, betraying her impatience, broke a lace on his breeches.

She frowned briefly at the pallor of his muscular body, the small, puckered scar on his chest. Then he was gathering her into his arms and in the warm, familiar circle of his embrace all was forgotten.

He cupped her breasts in his hands, and ran his tongue around the nipples until they stood up in tight little buds of desire. Then, as his hands trailed down over her swollen belly, his eyes danced with delight.

She caught his hands and, bringing them to her mouth, kissed each finger, then buried her face in his palms. He lay down beside her, his leg imprisoning hers, his tongue trailing over her cheeks, her lips, her throat. She moaned and pulled his hands down to the aching, throbbing mound between her thighs, gasping aloud as his fingers gently brushed and probed.

Her entire body trembled convulsively when he gently turned her over on her side. He ran his fingers lightly across her shoulders, then trailed them down her back to her buttocks. Her cheeks flamed and burned hotly as his finger delicately probed and rubbed.

"It's not fair!" she exclaimed, "I can't reach you!"

He pressed her down, laughing with delight. "Your turn will come," he said. "Allow me to experience my dreams in this moment's reality."

As his fingers continued to work their magic on her helpless, tingling body, a languid heat built inside her, until she felt as though flames were dancing inside her defenseless flesh, threatening to consume her completely.

Unable to bear it any longer, she turned over with a loud cry, and slid down on the hay, her lips closing over his hot manhood. She lapped at its velvety softness, her tongue circling the swollen head in slow, languid circles, reveling in the man-taste of him.

Then he drew her away and pressed her down on her back, placing his knees between her parted thighs. She thrust her hips forward, impaling his manhood within her, crying out as he entered her. His first gentle thrusts quickened until their union became a frantic, wild ride toward the edge of heaven itself, Shona grasping his back and pulling him deeper, deeper into her until she felt her body was merely an extension of his vibrant, demanding flesh. Her breath caught and her heart pounded in her throat as a deliciously warm sensation began in her groin, spreading upward until she was sure it must surely drive the breath from her straining lungs. She heard Stephen cry out in ecstasy, and her own body responded, sending wave upon wave of sensation crashing over her.

He lay on his side, his hands kneading the small of her back. "Was it too much, *querida?*" he asked huskily.

She shook her head as she succumbed to the warm lassitude. "It is never too much, my darling."

"But the baby?"

"Your child is moving within my belly like a veteran sailor on the deck of a tossing ship. Nothing could unseat him now."

He buried his face in the hollow of her throat and breathed deeply. "It was the memory of you, and you alone, which kept me from giving up long ago."

"I was so sure you had died in the sea that day!" She buried herself deep in his arms. "Oh, Stephen, you don't know how many times I wanted to join you in death."

"We are together now and no one can separate us ever again."

"It must be God who reunited us," she murmured. "Only God could have saved me when Muñoz's ships attacked the *Loretta.*"

"Muñoz!" Stephen jerked away. "Not Francisco Muñoz?"

She stared up at him, appalled by his expression of horror, yet knowing that she must tell him about his enemy, and the sooner the better. "Yes. Francisco Muñoz rescued me from that devil MacKenzie—don't look like that, Stephen, he did

379

not touch me."

"*Dios!* You dare to defend that *bastardo!*" He pushed her away and knelt beside her, his eyes dark with hatred."

"But you don't understand!" she exclaimed. Tears stung her eyes. "He took me to New Orleans and put me into a convent, to save my soul, I'm sure. But I cannot stand the man, Stephen! He makes my skin crawl, though he has always behaved like a gentleman."

"He is incapable of a kind act!" Stephen spat. "He is an evil canker sore spreading illness and death over all he touches."

"I know he's evil," she said. "I tried to get away, but he wouldn't let me out of his sight until I was at the convent, and even there, he checked on me. I could not have survived if Mother Superior had not helped me start my mercantile with the money Fernando made at the brick—"

"Fernando!" he exclaimed. "Fernando is alive? But I saw him shot! I saw him fall to the deck!"

"He's very much alive and waiting impatiently in New Orleans for your arrival." She ducked her head, suddenly embarrassed. "I didn't want to share this moment with anyone."

"Oh, *mi tesora*. First you! And now Fernando, my dear old friend. Not even the mention of Muñoz's name can dampen my joy."

She nestled in his arms and savored the taste of his lips. "We cannot allow him to know you are alive," she said suddenly. "He hates you, Stephen. He saw your ring on my finger, and I know he didn't believe me when I told him you were dead. If you could have seen the look upon his face!"

"He hates me almost as much as I detest and abhor him," Stephen said. "He is so filled with blackness, nothing delights him more than seeing suffering. Even as a child, he took great delight in that ghastly Inquisition. He would spend hours telling anyone who would listen all about the torture the Jews were forced to endure."

"I think he's still involved in their torture. There is a Code

Noir in New Orleans now, and it is very strange that it came into being so soon after he arrived."

"And I sent Asa and Rebecca there! This Code Noir, what does it mean?"

"That Jews are not welcome in New Orleans. Rebecca and Asa are safe at the moment, but they won't be for long if Muñoz is behind all of this. I'm sure he is furious that I have left the convent. He's sure to seek me out at my shop and then—"

"Shop? Don't tell me I am going to marry a business-woman!"

"Marry?"

"Of course. As soon as possible. You do not object, do you?"

"Only that it cannot be right now, at this very moment."

"Come here, my little shopkeeper."

He pulled her close and once again, his fingers and lips worked their magic, soothing away her fears of Muñoz, and her concerns about the baby and their future. All that mattered was the moment as he drank from her body and slowly and tenderly completed their union into one flesh—one soul. She teetered on the brink of fulfillment far longer than she thought possible, and this time it was she who cried out as she plunged over into a place of quivering ecstasy.

Chapter 30

A dazzling arc of lightning blazed across the black night sky; then deep thunder rolled over the countryside, rattling glass-paned windows and sending whimpering dogs and idle Indians racing for the nearest cover. Within seconds, the black clouds burst and cascades of driving rain pounded New Orleans, shredding palmetto leaves, turning the dust-laden streets into muddy quagmires, and flooding the drainage ditches with swift-running torrents of dirty water.

Shona slid out from under the light blanket, grimacing as she lumbered ungracefully to her feet, fearful lest she awaken Stephen. She wiped beads of sweat from her forehead as she padded barefoot over to the window. Pushing aside the linen sacking, she peered out, but the lightning was to the north and she could not see beyond the deluge. She sighed and stretched. The baby had become so large, Shona now stood sway-backed, her belly protruding in front of her like a huge melon.

She glanced back at the bed. Stephen lay on his side, his arm cradling the pillow, his blond hair curling boyishly about his face. Her eyes misted suddenly with tears of gratitude as she realized he was completely recovered from his bout with fever. She recalled that she had insisted he stay in bed for several days and that he had babied *her* for the three weeks they had been together, and she smiled through her tears.

Her smile broadened as she thought back upon Fernando's reaction when Stephen had come rushing into the apartment. The old man had thrown up his arms, and his face had glowed with happiness. After an emotional greeting, he'd forced Stephen to sit beside him for hours, relating in detail his miraculous rescue from the sea and his long journey to New Orleans. Fernando had not spoken, but tears had come to his eyes and he'd stared with deep devotion at the dear face he'd not dared hope to see again.

Finally, his tears spent, Fernando had insisted that Stephen and Shona be allowed complete privacy. He had declared his intention to move in with Jephtha for his cough was almost gone and his fever had broken that morning. But Shona had not allowed such a sacrifice lest Fernando weaken and fall ill again. Instead, grateful that the shop was closed for the Lord's day, she had sent him back to bed with a hot mulled wine. Then she had spent the remainder of the day in bed with Stephen, reaffirming their love with whispered words and long, lovely stretches of silence broken only by passionate gasps and satisfied sighs. The pearly gray dusk of evening was upon them when Stephen had pulled her into his arms and spoken the words which made her happier than she had ever thought possible.

"We must be married as soon as possible, *querida*," he'd whispered. "I have dreamed about making you my wife for so long, I do not want to wait another moment."

She had melted further into his embrace, unable to reply through her tears.

In the following days, her hours in the shop had flown, for she'd looked forward to the hours of privacy Fernando allowed them by taking long walks about the docks every evening—to exercise his weak legs, he had said with a sly wink. But Shona's joy was short-lived. She feared that Muñoz would somehow find out that Stephen lived, and that he would stop their marriage from taking place. Though Stephen had remained hidden in the apartment for the past three weeks she knew he was becoming more restless with each passing day. She would be unable to restrain him much longer, for he was already filled with plans for helping the Jews coming into the area find homes in the German settlement.

Now, she sighed and made her way silently back to bed, lying cautiously on her side of the Spanish-moss mattress, trying to lose herself in the sound of the rain drumming on the tin roof overhead. But her mind was racing, and she could draw no comfort from the monotonous patter.

The baby's birth was only four weeks away, and though Muñoz had been absent for over a month, she knew he would make an appearance any day now. She stifled a moan and wriggled closer to Stephen. He reached for her in his sleep, drawing her into the safe circle of his arms. She knew he would do everything he could to protect her, yet she was still fearful. It was no longer possible to hide her pregnancy from Muñoz. Even her customers had begun to look askance as she plodded awkwardly between the aisles. She was grateful that Rebecca had circulated the tidbit that Shona's husband was in the Spanish navy. At least she had not been branded a loose woman!

Rebecca. Shona smiled into the darkness. What would she have done without the wiry, plucky young Jewish girl these past few weeks? Her assumption that Rebecca was no stranger to hard work proved correct, for she caught onto the business very quickly and was soon ready to step into Fernando's shoes. Besides being a hard worker, she was fast becoming a dear friend. To Shona, who had never had a close relationship with a young woman of her own age, the growing friendship was a miraculous tonic for her tired body and for the burden of responsibility.

And Asa, Rebecca's betrothed, serious, thin to the point of emaciation, but possessing a fervent glow behind his large brown eyes, and a heart filled with compassion, had insisted that he be present when her birthing time came; for according to him, she was much too valuable to entrust to the ignorant

385

hands of a New Orleans midwife!

The baby kicked and rolled inside Shona, and she placed a hand over her belly to feel the movement. Stephen's child! She felt sure it would be a boy. But Muñoz... Her heart constricted. She could no longer ignore Francisco's warning. Francisco Muñoz would be furious if he learned that she was carrying Stephen's child. She knew Stephen would never approve, but the moment Muñoz arrived in New Orleans, she planned to confront him with a tale of being raped at the hands of MacKenzie. She prayed fervently that she could convince him it was true. Though such a sham would infuriate Stephen, she could not allow him to confront Muñoz now. So far, he had acquiesced to soothe her, for he was unwilling to upset her in her state of advanced pregnancy. Also, she knew his plan to help the Jews kept him in hiding. But this situation could not last much longer. After all, Stephen was a proud man and living like a rabbit gone to hole went completely against his nature.

She shivered and pulled up the covers. Muñoz presented a threat on more than one front. He was obviously furious about Jephtha's friendship, and, of course, it was possible he would find out that she had hired a Jewess. She bit her lip in frustration. If only there was no Muñoz! She wished he had simply dropped her in New Orleans and sailed out of her life forever! But he had not. For some reason known only to himself, he continued to act as though he were responsible for her. Shona moaned aloud, and Stephen awakened instantly.

"What is it?" he whispered, his hands going to her swollen belly. "Is it the child? It is too soon!"

"No, there's nothing wrong, I just can't get comfortable."

"Here, let me rub your back. That always helps you sleep."

She turned on her side, her face flaming. Why had she lied? Why hadn't she simply told him she was concerned about Muñoz? She knew that they had to talk seriously and she herself would have to broach the subject for Stephen was always trying to protect her from unpleasantness. She relaxed as his fingers kneaded away the tightness in her muscles. It was only when his hands strayed to her breasts that she turned over and faced him, straining to see in the darkness. "We have to talk," she said.

"I do not want to talk," he answered, his voice already husky with passion. "I want to make love."

She batted him away. "Not now!" Catching one of his hands, she brought it to her lips, easing her harsh words with soft kisses on each knuckle. "I want to go to Mother Superior and ask her help in finding a priest to marry us," she said. "And I want to tell her about Rebecca and Asa."

He tensed. "I thought you agreed we would tell no one about my being alive."

"But that was Jephtha! And I want to tell him tomorrow, too. You know he won't tell anyone. After all, he's my friend."

Her heart beat madly as the seconds ticked by. When he finally spoke, his voice was flat and hard. "He is not *my* friend. I have promised Dieter Warner to help the Jewish immigrants. The fewer who know about me the better."

"Then you were only fooling me when you talked about marriage." She pulled away and sat doubled over on the side of the bed, her heart a frozen stone in her breast.

He pulled himself up beside her, but she turned away, unwilling to let him witness her agony. "You know that is not true, *querida,*" he said softly. "I want more than anything to make you my wife."

She could not speak. She began to tremble and even after he had drawn her into his arms, she could not reply.

"Listen to me," he said. "I would marry you tomorrow, if that were possible. Perhaps you are right. Perhaps you should tell Mother Superior. She helped you with your shop, she might help you find the right priest."

She buried her head against his chest. "Are you sure?"

"I am sure. And you can also tell her about Rebecca. If she knows what I am going to do she may be able to help. But first, you must find out how she herself feels about the Jews. You must be sure she will not report me to Muñoz."

387

"She fears him as much as we do," she exclaimed. "I know she will help, but I promise to find out how she feels first."

He caressed her cheek. "Then I can leave you for a few days without fearing for your safety?"

"Leave me?" She jerked away. "But why? Where are you going?"

"First to the settlement, then to the trail through the bayous. Asa brought word that there is a group of Jews on their way to New Orleans. I want to intercept them and take them to the settlement instead."

"You'll be in danger."

"We have already discussed this. You said I was right in wanting to help."

She laughed harshly. "That was when it was only talk!" She threw herself against him. "I cannot bear the thought of losing you again."

He kissed her. "You must not fear for me. Dieter has devised a clever disguise. I will be garbed as a simple Spanish priest guiding his people to a safe haven. You must have faith that nothing—no one—can ever part us again. My darling, you know I don't want to leave you. I am only complete when we are together. But I owe Rebecca and Asa a great deal. Without them, I might never have found you. I must do all I can to help their people. I promise to return in two or three days at most. In the meantime, you talk to Mother Superior. I also agree that you may tell your friend Jephtha about me. It is time for Fernando to move in with him so we can have complete privacy."

"Two or three days!" Shona raised her lips to his. As their kiss sparked the flames of their passion, he lowered her onto the bed and lay beside her, his fingers lightly brushing her breasts.

"I dreamed about this when we were apart," he whispered.

"So did I." She pulled his hand down and moaned with delight as his fingers began to probe her secret place. Her negative thoughts, her fears, were pushed away by her

388

mounting desire as his lips and fingers worked their magic on her flushed body. Their coupling was slow and tender, as though both longed to delay their parting. They cried out softly together as he gave and she accepted; then they lay side by side, their bodies still joined, their lips touching.

"I love you more than life itself," he said softly into the darkness.

"You *are* my life," she replied.

He pulled on his breeches just as the false dawn streaked the horizon. The sky had been swept clear by the rain and hundreds of stars twinkled far away in the dusky-gray distance. Shona handed him his shirt. "I'll make you a basket of food."

He laughed softly. "You will get back into that bed and stop trying to make me into a fat man." He pulled the shirt over his head and tucked it into his waistband. "I do not want you to awaken Fernando," he added. "And please insist he move his things as soon as possible. I want us to be alone when I return. I will come when it is dark, after you have closed your shop. I am no longer willing to share you with anyone."

"You resent the time I spend downstairs?"

She thought she detected a slight frown in the soft lamplight, but her fears were dispelled when he smiled. "Of course not." He kissed the tip of her nose. "At first, I was so overwhelmed at finding you, your being a shop owner meant nothing. I admit I resented the time you spent away from me that first week I was here. Remember, in Spain, women are never allowed to conduct business. But now I have almost become accustomed to the idea. For the time being, it is a good diversion. It keeps you out of trouble."

"Trouble!" She pushed him back onto the bed. "And just what kind of trouble are you talking about?"

"This kind." He pulled her down beside him and nibbled delicately on her earlobe. "You must get rid of Fernando," he whispered huskily.

"You sound cold and heartless," she teased.

He hugged her tightly. "If I had time I would show you how cold I am," he replied with a chuckle.

"Show me!"

"You are a vixen," he groaned as he pushed her back on the bed and stooped to pick up his stockings. "But I must be off before daybreak."

Later that morning, Shona, dressed in her most becoming gown, walked quickly to the convent, forcing herself to count the horse-drawn carts already stirring up the mud in the road in order to distract her mind from her fears for Stephen's safety.

Mother received her in her office. "You look well, child," she said softly. "Motherhood becomes you, for your face is radiant."

Shona smiled. "I have good reason." Mother's face and the familiar, peaceful surroundings erased her fears as though they had never existed. Completely forgetting Stephen's warning, she threw caution to the winds and hugged Mother impulsively. "My Stephen is alive! We have been together for three weeks!"

Mother stared at her. "But I thought you said he was dead!" she declared after a shocked silence.

"I thought he was. But some of his crew saved him from drowning. He's spent the past few months looking for me." Tears pricked Shona's lids as she relived the joy of discovery. "Oh, Mother, I've never been so happy!"

"My dear child, I share your happiness. Now, your child will have the father it so richly deserves and you will have the husband you have desired."

"That's one of the reasons I'm here. We need your help, Mother. We want to be married at once."

The older woman turned and paced to the window. She parted the drapes and stood silently for a moment, staring out at the garden. When she turned, she was frowning. "I am afraid that presents a problem," she said. "First you must be confirmed in our Faith, then the marriage banns must be read from the pulpit three times before your marriage can take place in our chapel. I don't think I need remind you that Monsieur Muñoz attends the services faithfully when he is in town. You have told me there is no love lost between your Stephen and Muñoz. Dare you take such a chance?"

Shona's face blanched. "Three times! Oh, Mother, can't we make other arrangements? Can't you help? I must not allow Muñoz to find out that Stephen is alive right now. He would surely try to kill him!"

"There is nothing I can do about the banns." Mother squeezed Shona's cold hands. "You see, it is a law of the Church. Perhaps it is time for your Stephen to face Muñoz. He cannot remain in hiding forever."

"I know that. But there is a very good reason why he must not reveal himself now." Shona squeezed the older woman's hands until she winced. "That's the other reason why I came to see you." She chewed on her lip as she looked down at the floor.

"Yes, child?"

Shona studied the simple wooden crucifix on the far wall. Her courage had fled, leaving her weak and lacking the resoluteness she possessed earlier. Mother gripped her arms. "If you have a problem, you must tell me," she said. "I have told you many times that I am your friend. Have you no faith in me?"

Shona raised her eyes quickly. "Oh, yes," she gasped. "It's just that . . . oh, Mother, I am in a real stew this time."

Mother's brow wrinkled. "Stew? I take you to mean you have a problem you cannot handle alone?"

"Yes. I hired a girl several weeks ago—to help in the shop."

"And . . ."

Shona swallowed. "She's Jewish," she whispered.

Mother stared at her for a moment. "There are no Jews in

391

New Orleans," she said firmly. "They all left when the Code Noir was posted in Jackson Square."

Dear God, Mother did not believe her! Shona felt tears prick her eyelids. "But they didn't all go," she said brokenly. "Rebecca and Asa remained, for Asa, who is studying with the surgeon, was unwilling to leave. They have been pretending to be Catholic."

"Catholic!" Mother's eyes narrowed. "And just how have they managed to keep up this pretense?" she asked stiffly.

Shona's breath froze. She had foolishly failed to ascertain Mother's position on Jews as Stephen had insisted. Now she had endangered them all. She turned toward the door.

"I must have been mistaken," she said. "I really must go."

Fingers of iron grasped her arm. "Stay!" Mother commanded. "You have not answered my question."

"Oh, Mother, please forget I said anything. I have to get back to the shop."

Mother's unrelenting fingers dug into her arm. "Have you lost all faith in me, child?" she asked. "Your face is pale and you're trembling. Do you think me a Jew hater, too?"

Shona could not answer. Mother patted her arm and guided her over to the same large, uncomfortable chair she had sat in before. Had it really been only weeks since she had poured out her plans for opening a shop? It seemed like years!

"Now," Mother said firmly, "it is time for us to talk. You say you have hired a Jewess, and obviously this upsets you or you would not be here."

"It doesn't upset me that Rebecca's a Jew! I'm just afraid that someone will find out and tell that nosy Muñoz."

"Oh. Now the pieces are beginning to fall into place." Mother's eyes clouded. "You have reason to fear Muñoz if the girl is really Jewish. Remember, he is a Jesuit, and they are the fathers of the Inquisition."

"But what can I do?" Shona wailed. "Rebecca couldn't find work because people suspected, only suspected, that she might be a Jew. And Asa, who is her betrothed, gets paid nothing for his work with the surgeon. They were hungry! I couldn't just turn my back on their need!"

"Of course you could not," Mother clucked. "I fully understand why you gave the girl a job, but that does not lessen the danger you have placed yourself in." She whirled away and began to pace the floor, her fingers busy with her beads. "You said they pretend to be Catholic. What did you mean?"

"I guess I stated that poorly. I only meant that they're pretending they are not Jews. Rebecca said they buried all of their belongings that might be suspect in a hole and they're going about their business as if they were no different from anyone here in New Orleans."

"You say Asa is her betrothed. How do they plan to marry? The only rabbi in New Orleans was forced to flee for his life."

"I don't know. I suppose they are hoping another rabbi will come here to settle. But, Mother, you would love Asa! He's intelligent, they both are, and you can tell he's a hard worker. And he has a wonderful sense of humor." She ducked her head. "You wouldn't believe how ignorant I am. Just yesterday, I offered him a breakfast of fried pork!"

Mother clucked dryly. "I take it he wasn't offended?"

"Oh, no! He laughed and tried to make me feel better by making fun of himself, but I was so embarrassed!"

"That's just one of the many customs you will have to become accustomed to if you are going to associate with them. Is he going to allow Rebecca to work on Saturday, which, I understand, is their Sabbath?"

Shona made a face. "No. That was the first thing he told me. Though he did say he would see her work rather than rouse undue suspicions."

"This Asa sounds like a very wise young man. Now, tell me, how can I help you?"

Shona leaped up and threw her arms around Mother. "I haven't told you everything. Stephen is planning to help the Jews coming to New Orleans. He wants to round them all up and sneak them into the German settlement upriver. The Rhenish Germans there have emigrated from the upper Palatinate of Germany to escape religious persecution. There were violent conflicts there between Catholics and Protestants. These German settlers have offered to provide the Jews with land and to help them build their homes. That's why we don't dare let Muñoz know Stephen is alive. It will be hard enough for him to help the Jews without fearing Muñoz's intervention."

"Then you must warn your Jewish friends not to do anything to arouse suspicion." Mother patted Shona's back. "And you must tell them that if they are thinking of marriage, I would suggest they do what several young Jewish couples have done in order to remain here in New Orleans—become baptized Catholics!"

"There are others?"

"Yes, several. But they used the Church as a refuge long before the Code Noir came into being. Perhaps they are not as firmly entrenched in their own religion as many, but I am sorry to say, I believe they did the right thing. It is not an easy life, being a Jew. They are persecuted wherever they go."

"What would Muñoz do if he found out the truth?"

Mother shook her head and her eyes were filled with sadness. "I do not know. It is said that he has much influence upon Governor Vaudreuil who is a very weak, corrupt man. He only received the governorship because his mother persistently petitioned Versailles in his behalf, and any man who would hide behind his mother's skirts is not to be trusted." She fingered her beads. "I am certain Muñoz would make their lives most miserable, and he would wreak his own brand of terrible vengeance upon anyone who had befriended them."

"Then I must try to keep him from finding out the truth. And I must find a priest who is willing to bend the rules."

Shona, who expected a vehement outburst from Mother, was astounded when the woman merely nodded and smiled.

"Exactly. And if you need encouragement you must come to

me. In the meantime, I will see what I can do to help. Quietly, of course."

"I can never thank you enough."

"Nonsense. Our dear Lord chose a very weak vessel when he selected me. Monsieur Muñoz has let it be known that he considers me ineffectual and emotional and perhaps he is right. But God does not always choose the strong and single-minded to accomplish his ends."

"And I thank Him for that."

"Yes, I do also. Now, stand still, child, and receive your blessing. I am weary and there is much work awaiting me at my desk."

As Shona walked slowly back to her shop, Mother's words of warning ran over and over in her mind like relentless tides ravaging a beach. *"You must warn them not to do anything which would arouse suspicion."* She clutched at the amulet nestled, along with Stephen's cross, between her swollen breasts. She should never have allowed Rebecca to hang it about her neck, but the girl had been adamant, insisting that the ruby Kemiah, called the Stone of Preservation, would ward off miscarriage.

She smiled ruefully. These Jews had many strange customs, especially the ones determining what they could and could not eat. She could understand the rule pertaining to pork, for she knew that many people found the fat meat revolting, especially after watching pigs wallowing about in filth, eating anything thrown into their pens. But she had stared open-mouthed as Rebecca had recited a long list of other meats that were forbidden. Then, there was the time she had invited Asa and Rebecca to dinner. The entire evening had turned into a horrible fiasco. First, Jephtha had unexpectedly come pounding up the stairs, proclaiming that his cupboard was bare and he was starving. His spontaneous visit had forced Stephen into the bedroom to hide, for though he'd said he believed her when she assured him that Jephtha could be trusted, he had made it very clear to Shona that he did not want anyone to know he was alive. Indeed, he had hidden all evening in the cramped little bedroom while she had served that horrible meal. She thought she had followed all of Rebecca's instructions properly, but her large platter of pale gray beef liver was greeted with gales of laughter.

"There is no need to soak liver in water and drain it as you do other meats," Asa chuckled. "A liberal salting, and a good hot fire will cleanse it of all blood."

Jephtha had refused to eat any of the meal, and Shona had told him the following morning that he had acted like a boor. This had done nothing to ease the growing tension between them. It was obvious that he was very uncomfortable about something, but she could not make him give voice to it. She imagined he was seeing Mignon whenever he could, and perhaps feeling guilty about it. Of course, he could not know she had Stephen now and that she hoped Jephtha could find such happiness. Mignon was very pretty, obviously intelligent, and from a good background. And even more important, she was ready for marriage. Jephtha needed a good wife. Shona decided she would simply have to seek him out in his shop and forced him to talk it out.

But when she eyed the horde of customers milling about on the walk outside her shop she knew she would have to postpone visiting Jephtha until later. She unlocked the door and prepared to serve the first shopper, her heart heavy with concern.

Chapter 31

Fernando spent a comfortable night tucked into his little corner cot, totally oblivious to Shona's distress, whereas she tossed and turned on her mattress, experiencing wretched pangs of guilt for not obeying Stephen's order to tell Fernando it was time for him to move in with Jephtha. She knew she should have made the arrangements, yet she had delayed for one simple reason: she was terrified of spending the night alone in the apartment! Without Stephen's presence to distract her, her mind was filled with dark and shadowy fears. She feared Muñoz's return. She feared that something dreadful would happen to Stephen. She feared she would be unable to break down the barrier Jephtha had erected.

She sighed noisily and thumped the bolster. Where were the simple days when she had enjoyed life without a care greater than wondering how to best her brothers in a game? She would even welcome back some of the trying times when she had faced each day with courage and the knowledge that she would do her best to overcome every adversity. The baby rolled about in her belly, reminding her that she was no longer a child depending upon others to smooth her way. Nor could she merely take her life into her own hands. She was an adult now, almost a mother, with a mother's responsibilities.

But that still did not explain her constant fear. She cupped her hand protectively over her belly. Could it be that her pregnancy was causing her to lose all perspective? She could never remember a time when she had felt so unable to cope with life. Well, she was a Cameron, and Cameron women did not use their unborn children as excuses for cowardice! She turned on her side and pulled her damp hair away from the nape of her neck, prepared to do battle with her fears, many of which, she suddenly realized, were completely out of her control.

First, she would face Muñoz when he returned and carry out her plan of deception. Second, though her heart railed at the thought, she realized there was absolutely nothing she could do to protect Stephen. She would have to trust him to take care of himself. Jephtha, however, was another story. She would go to him the very first thing in the morning and do everything she could to effect a reconciliation. She sighed and stared into the darkness. To think she had spent hours fretting over such simple decisions! She closed her eyes, her new-found peace bringing sleep almost immediately.

The morning dawned sunny and humid. Shona choked down a piece of bread and a cup of tea, her stomach rebelling as she watched Fernando attack the hearty breakfast he had prepared. When he sopped up his egg yolk with a slab of buttered bread, she pushed herself away from the table with a groan. How could he tolerate heavy food on such a sweltering day?

Making her bed brought a moment of unexpected pleasure. She found herself humming under her breath as she smoothed the blankets, anticipating Stephen's return and the glorious lovemaking which would follow. Fernando went down to stock the shelves for the first customers, but Shona puttered about the apartment, musing over her impending visit to Jephtha. Her heart lurched at the thought of trying to break through the wall he had erected between them. Somehow, she would have to find out how she had offended him and make immediate amends.

She twisted her hair into a heavy coil and pinned it firmly into place atop her head. She was tying on her large white apron when she was interrupted by a knock at the door.

Her hand flew to her mouth. Dear God, was it Muñoz? Surely Fernando would not have allowed him upstairs! Perhaps it was Stephen! She dashed across the room and threw open the door.

A brown-haired young woman with twinkling eyes and plump, rosy cheeks smiled a greeting. "You are Shona, yes?"

"Yes!"

"I am Joanna Warner. I bring a message from Herr de Larra."

"From Stephen?" Shona, her heart constricting, pulled the woman into the room. "Is he all right? Nothing's happened to him!"

Joanna laughed merrily. "Oh, no, he is fine." She held out a crumpled piece of paper. "He sent this. I am only a messenger."

Shona grabbed the paper and read hastily. She groaned. "Oh, no, he's been delayed. He won't be home for five more days!"

"I am sorry. I know what it is like to be alone. Though I have Johann, my son, my Dieter is also gone. Dieter is my husband," she added. "He has accompanied your . . . Stephen, I believe you call him."

"Yes. Stephen."

"Could I perhaps have a cup of water? The water on the barge was warm and tasted very bad."

"I'm sorry. Of course."

Shona filled a gourd with fresh, cool water from the crock, and Joanna drank thirstily, then wiped her mouth with the back of her hand.

"I must return to the settlement now," she said. "Johann can be very naughty when I am away. I do not want to impose upon my neighbors longer than necessary."

"Oh, please don't rush off." Shona pressed her into a chair

and sat across the table. "Tell me about your son. How old is he?"

"Almost three." Joanna made a face. "And he is almost more than I can handle, especially now that he has his puppy. Those two get into more trouble than you can imagine."

"Of course! I knew I had seen you. He has blond hair, and the puppy's yellow! I saw you on the riverbank when I was at the settlement buying supplies."

"That must have been the morning he ran away." Joanna sighed and wiped the damp hair away from her sticky forehead. "He has been told repeatedly to stay away from the river, but he is fascinated by water. He frightens me more times than I am willing to admit."

Shona patted her belly and chuckled. "I imagine I have quite a few scares in store for me."

"I do not want to imply that I do not enjoy my son," Joanna said hastily. "He is a joy most of the time." She laughed heartily. "Especially when he is asleep."

"Was he born at the settlement?"

"Yes. I was heavy with child when we landed at New Orleans and began our trek up the river seeking land to farm. Luckily for me, his birth was easy and quick. We have no physician at the settlement, only an old midwife with frightening stories about dreadful birthings."

Shona's heart leaped. She would have to tell Asa immediately about the need for a physician in the settlement. Perhaps he and Rebecca could find a permanent home there. She leaned forward.

"Tell me, what is it like living there? I only visited two times, and I really don't even know how many people you have."

"I don't know either!" Joanna said. "We are adding to our numbers every day. I suppose there must be at least thirty homes now, but it changes so quickly that is only a guess."

"Stephen has told me about your husband. It is wonderful that he is so willing to help the . . ."

"Jews?"

400

"Yes. I wasn't sure I should speak about that."

"Oh, I know all about what Dieter and Herr de . . . Stephen are doing." Joanna sighed. "After the persecution we were forced to endure in our homeland, I suppose it is only natural that Dieter should want to help. After all, we are more fortunate than most. We have found acceptance here. Though I must admit there are times I resent him being away so much of the time. I had hoped we could have a normal family life, but he has always been one to take on the problems of others less fortunate."

Shona bit her lip, not sure she should question further, but unable to help herself. "Is it dangerous?" she blurted. "I mean, what they do? Are they in danger?"

Joanna considered the question for a moment. "I suppose it is," she said finally, "though they take every precaution not to be discovered. So far the militia has ignored our little settlement, but Dieter fears this cannot last long. Someone, perhaps a barge master, is sure to report to the governor that a number of Jews are settling there."

"And when he finds out—the governor, I mean?"

"I do not know what he will do. He is so weak, he may not wish to do anything at all. After all, we are not a part of New Orleans itself, and he seems concerned only with his town. We can only hope and pray that he leaves us alone." She smiled. "Do not fret. Your Stephen is very careful. He can take care of himself."

"I only wish I could believe that."

"But you must," Joanna said fervently. "If not, you will only harm yourself and possibly the child you carry. You must trust God to look after your man. I do. That is the only way I can survive when I spend day after day without Dieter. Prayers and hard work. You cannot know how hard it is to run a farm without your husband. I only make out because I have two hired men to help and a delightful friend, Trista Becher, though she, too, has accompanied Dieter and Stephen on their journey."

"A woman went with them?" Shona's cheeks began to burn fiercely.

"Not just a *woman!*" Joanna exclaimed. "Trista is the most unusual person I have ever met. To look at her, you would never imagine that such a delicate, tiny person could possess such strength, such purpose. Her father, a brilliant student of languages, was martyred in our homeland. Though Trista was only a child, she has never forgotten how he died. Just show her a person suffering persecution and she turns into a—how do you say it—tigress! She will be a great asset to our men."

"Is she pretty?" Shona almost choked on the question.

"She is more than pretty, she is beautiful, both inside and out. She usually watches Johann when I must be away. She is one of the few people he obeys without question. She has a way with children."

"Of course. She would!"

Shona's ironic tone brought a soft, understanding smile to Joanna's lips. "You must not fear Trista," she said quickly. "She only went on the mission to act as a diversion. She is always saying she will never find a man she can love. That there is no one in the whole world as smart, as handsome, as brave as her father was. I often tell her she will never marry if she does not lower her expectations." She patted Shona's arm. "You must not forget why Dieter and Stephen have made this journey. They think only of saving the Jews from further persecution at the hands of the militia. Besides, it appears that our men are not attracted to raven-haired beauties."

Her words only added to Shona's discomfort. Inez had been a tiny, dark-haired beauty, hadn't she? She found herself blushing beneath Joanna's scrutiny. Dear Lord, what sort of person was she becoming? Was she looking for yet another reason to fear Stephen's work?

"Of course," she said. "I am sure she will be a great asset, though it must be hard on you, having her gone."

"Yes. I have left Johann in the care of a woman with a brood of five children of her own." She rose. "I really must be getting back. I am so afraid he has been dreadfully naughty."

Shona saw her to the door. "Thank you for bringing the message," she said. "I'm sorry to have inconvenienced you."

"It was no trouble!" Joanna laughed. "You cannot know how wonderful it has been to have a little time to myself."

"I'll see you again, I'm sure."

"Of course. Perhaps you can come to the settlement with Stephen. I'll fix some strudel and we'll gossip over coffee and cake."

Shona watched Joanna bounce down the stairs, her mind filled with regret at the young woman's hasty departure. She knew instinctively that Joanna Warner was someone she coveted as a friend, and she refused to dwell on thoughts of Stephen being drawn to the raven-haired Trista Becher. If she could not trust him out of her sight, she was unworthy of his love. She smoothed her apron and closed the door. Right now, she must visit another friend before he became hopelessly lost to her.

She told Fernando that she was going to see Jephtha, then hastily elbowed her way through the door and out onto the walk. Though the streets were twelve inches deep with mud, the town was crowded with locals and planters who had journeyed to New Orleans for the company's plantation slave sale. The saloons and eating establishments were already doing a booming business. Shona ignored the customers congregating on the sidewalk outside her shop and made her way to the back of the building where Jephtha's smithy was located.

He was bending over his forge, and she stood and watched him silently for a moment. His thews bulged as he pumped the bellows, and his unruly black hair stuck to the sweat pouring down his forehead. She realized once again how much he meant to her. In many ways, he replaced the brothers she had loved so desperately and lost. Somehow, she must overcome whatever it was that had alienated him. She greeted him brightly.

He dropped the bellows with a grunt and looked up. "What

are you doing here so early?" he grumbled. "I suppose you want me to do something for you. Well, I can't. I've got a big order to fill."

"That's not fair, Jephtha. I haven't asked you to help me. You've always volunteered."

He grabbed a large iron bar with a pair of tongs and held it over the fire. "Well, things are going to change. I've my own business to think about now." He removed the white-hot bar and, placing it on the anvil, began to pound it into shape with a heavy mallet.

"It's time we had a talk. We can't go on like this, acting like strangers."

"No time now," he grunted.

Shona shook his arm. "We'll make time. I value your friendship too much to have it end like this. Please!"

He jerked away and plunged the bar into a pail of cold water, mumbling something, but the hissing steam covered his words. Shona grabbed his arm again.

"I'm not leaving until we talk!" she shouted.

He wiped his hands on his leather apron. "Then talk."

She sat heavily on an upturned crate. "I have some news, but I don't know how you'll receive it. You've been so surly lately! Not at all like the friend I have come to rely upon. But before I tell you my news, I want to know what's been bothering you. You act as though I've committed some horrible sin against you. What have I done?"

His face turned red. "Nothing to me!"

They were getting nowhere. Shona squared her shoulders. "It's Mignon, isn't it? You've fallen in love with her and you're ashamed to face me."

He recoiled. "No! What have I got to be ashamed of? She's a right pretty little thing."

Shona was astounded by the look of guilt on his face. "Exactly," she said. "But somewhere in that thick-skulled head of yours, you've got the idea that I'm jealous." She rose and grabbed the corner of his apron, pulling him to her. "I have to admit I didn't understand at first. I wasn't used to having to share you with anyone." She sighed heavily. "I guess it's time for me to tell you my news. Stephen's alive. Asa and Rebecca brought us together."

His mouth fell open. "But you told me he was dead!" he exclaimed.

He looked so perplexed, she couldn't help laughing. But she sobered at once when she saw the hurt in his brown eyes. She reached for his hand.

"Oh, Jephtha, my Stephen is alive, I tell you! He's been hiding in my apartment!"

"How long have you been hiding him? Did you think I would kill him? Is that why you didn't tell me? How could you think I would do anything to hurt you!"

"It's not that, Jephtha." She had always known he was not overly bright, but he had an animal's cunning and she realized there was no way she could tell him the truth, that it was Stephen who had not trusted him to keep quiet. She searched her mind frantically. "I didn't tell you because . . . because we needed time to be alone. Surely you can understand that." The lie fell so easily from her lips.

His frown deepened into a scowl as he digested her words. "That's all?"

She nodded.

Slowly, the scowl turned to a lopsided grin. "I guess I can understand that." He pulled her close and kissed her sloppily on the cheek. "I'm real happy for you, Shona, though if I didn't have Mignon, I reckon I'd be downright jealous. But now, I want to meet him. I think I'm going to like him."

"Just as I like Mignon. I think it's wonderful that you two are falling in love."

His eyes widened and he exhaled loudly. "You do? But you let her go and hired Rebecca! I thought you didn't like her!"

"I let her go because she is too pretty and too much of a distraction to have in the shop. Rebecca is plainer. She doesn't take attention away from the merchandise."

"But you're pretty!"

Shona laughed and patted her huge belly. "You can say that at a time like this? I've got a mountain out in front of me and my ankles are so swollen I waddle! Oh, Jephtha, you're blind!"

He ducked his head and studied the ground. "I've always thought you were the prettiest girl in the world," he said softly.

"Until Mignon."

"But that's different! She's . . . well, she's tiny and helpless. She needs someone to look after her. She doesn't have your strength—your fire!"

"My pigheadedness."

He grinned hugely. "Your pigheadedness."

She held out her hands. "Then we are friends again?"

He pushed her hands aside and grabbed her up into his arms. "We sure as hell are!" he exclaimed happily.

Shona kissed him on the cheek. "Then if that's settled, I'd better get to work. This town is almost as crowded as it was at Mardi Gras."

She returned to a shop thronged with eager customers. Fernando had worked much too hard and was pale and trembling. Shona sent him upstairs with a firm order to take it easy for the rest of the day. Bereft of Fernando's help, Shona and Rebecca were kept at a dead run filling orders and making change.

Shona was tired and out of sorts by early afternoon when a planter from Attakapas insisted upon giving her a bill of exchange for his purchases. She politely explained her policy, and pointed to the sign she had penned stating that payment would be accepted in cash only, but the man was adamant. His angry shouts quickly drew a crowd of rough-looking men in from the streets. Petrified lest there be a riot, Shona told Rebecca to fetch Jephtha, but the crowd would not allow the trembling girl to pass. Someone pushed a stack of calico onto the floor. A pile of cottonade followed. A barrel of rum was pushed over onto its side, filling the shop with a pungent, heady aroma. Shona screamed at them to stop, but her voice

406

could not be heard. Furious, she squeezed behind the counter and pulled a wicked-looking cheese knife from the shelf. Wielding it overhead, she moved forward through the crowd who quickly stepped back, tripping and cursing at one another.

"You get out of here!" she shouted, slicing the blade through the air above her. "Or I'm going to cut the bunch of you to pieces!"

The planter who had started the riot grabbed at Shona and threw his body against hers. The knife slipped from her hand, and she was pinned against the counter. The crowd surged forward.

Suddenly, a shot rang out and a mighty bellow erupted from the front door. Fernando stood on the stairs, holding a smoking pistol pointed at the ceiling. Jephtha bulled his way in from the front walk, throwing grown men from his path as if they were children. "Get out of here!" he roared. He grabbed the recalcitrant planter by the shirt front and threw him to the floor. "I'll kill you for touching her!" he shouted. Women customers, who had pressed themselves against the walls in an attempt to remain unharmed, screamed as the crowd rushed for the door. Within seconds, the store was empty.

Jephtha grabbed for Shona. "Are you all right?" he asked. "Did he hurt you?"

She shook her head and threw her arms around him. "Oh, God, Jephtha," she gasped. "I tried to send Rebecca for you, but they wouldn't let her through."

"I heard the ruckus and come," he said. "But it looks like that little old Spaniard had things well in hand."

Shona went quickly to where Fernando was comforting Rebecca. "Thank you, friend," she said, embracing him warmly. "Why don't you go back upstairs and rest. Everything's under control now."

Fernando squeezed Rebecca's arm. "Oh, Madonna, I heard the shouting and was afraid Muñoz had returned and started something over—"

"Did I hear my name spoken?"

Shona gasped and looked up. Francisco Muñoz was leaning insolently against the doorjamb. He eyed the disheveled room, his gaze lingering upon the cluttered floor. "It appears you have had some sort of trouble," he said with the ghost of a smile. "I have arrived just in time."

Shona froze as Jephtha growled deep in his throat. She cast him an imploring look and stepped from the circle of his arms. "It was just a misunderstanding," she said as she made her way toward Muñoz.

She stopped in midstride, aware that his hooded eyes were raking her body from head to toe. She felt a blush begin at her neck and flush up over her cheeks. Of course, he had noticed. She looked down at the bulge the folds of her gown could no longer conceal.

"Come in, señor," she said. "You undoubtedly have some questions. The others will clean up here. We will talk upstairs."

She glared at Fernando and gestured violently at Jephtha when he started to follow her. "Your help is needed down here," she hissed. She preceded Muñoz up the staircase, her knees shaking and her heart pounding a wild tattoo in her breast. She had known this moment would come, but despite having rehearsed what she would say, she feared her panic would tie her tongue into a thousand knots, rendering her speechless.

She ushered him into the great room and offered to take his coat. He shrugged her hand away and motioned her to a chair.

"Would you . . . would you care for a cup of tea? The water over the fire is hot."

He ignored her attempt at hospitality, standing wide-legged before her, his hands clenched behind his back, and her skin began to prickle from his cold gaze. She opened her mouth to speak, but the words froze in her throat.

"I am waiting," he breathed softly.

She nodded. "I . . . I know you must have questions. . . ." she said hesitantly.

408

When his eyes did not leave the bulge of her belly, recriminations raced through her mind. Coward! Stupid coward! she thought. Tears rose in her eyes. This man—this deadly enemy—could harm Stephen's child. She could not fail now. Somehow, she must convince him so Stephen and his child would not be in danger.

Tears spilled down her cheeks, and her breast heaved as the dam of pent-up fear burst, releasing her tongue. "Oh, Señor Muñoz!" she sobbed. "I have been sorely used! I tried to tell you about that beast MacKenzie, but I could not reveal all he did to me!" She twisted her hands until her knuckles throbbed. "He forced himself upon me time after time! He hurt me! And now I am forced to bear his . . . his child!" She lowered her head and the tears she wept were genuine, for just talking about MacKenzie and his treatment of her brought back all she had suffered with a painful rush.

She felt his hand upon her shoulder and forced herself not to wince. Her child's future depended upon her ability to bring out every shred of pity this man possessed. If, indeed, he possessed any.

He patted her shoulder awkwardly. "Do not cry, *señorita*," he said. "Your tears distress me."

She raised her tear-stained face as a sudden idea struck her. "You cannot know what it is like," she moaned. "You are not a woman, but if you have ever loved a young girl, if you have ever cared about her future, you will take pity upon me!"

His pale face blanched even whiter, and she knew he was instantly reminded of his sister, Inez. Good, that was her intention.

"You must not become so upset!" he declared. "You might harm yourself or your unborn child!" He grasped her hands in his icy fingers.

Shona forced herself to grip his palms as she stared up into his face. "Please say you understand, Señor Muñoz! And that you forgive me, for I would have killed myself rather than submit to that animal, but he kept me locked in his cabin, and there were no weapons available."

He recoiled, jerking his hands away. "Suicide is an unpardonable sin," he said sternly as he began to pace the floor before her. "Though I can understand why the thought would enter your mind." He paused before the fireplace and stirred the embers with the poker.

She watched him silently, a feeling of peace spreading throughout her body. He was thinking about what she had said. He believed her!

He turned and fastidiously wiped the soot from his hands on a clean white kerchief. "What will you do with the child?" he asked suddenly.

"I'm not sure," Shona exclaimed. "Though keeping it and nurturing it would be the Christian thing to do, I suppose."

His face flushed and his hands went instinctively to the beads hanging from his waistband. "You are to be commended," he said very softly. "If you are sure the bastard is MacKenzie's child."

She recoiled. *"Señor!"* she cried. "You do me a grave injustice!" She placed her hands over her face and rocked back and forth. "Oh, why did this have to happen to me?" She grasped her belly and moaned.

He rushed to her side. "I apologize," he said quickly. "You must not harm yourself or the child. After all, the Holy Father, in His infinite wisdom, can turn this curse of all curses into a blessing. You can give the child to the sisters at the convent to raise. Perhaps you yourself can take the veil!"

She groaned loudly. "Oh, you don't know what you are saying, *señor*," she gasped. "I lived at the convent for a long time and I know how unworthy I am to become one of them. I will think about giving them the child, but in the meantime, I will—"

A loud rapping on the door interrupted her. Muñoz leaped to his feet and threw open the door.

Jephtha stood outside, his broad face grim. "You're needed downstairs," he said to Shona. His dark eyes narrowed with concern. "They're short-handed."

Muñoz blocked the doorway. "You must tell them they will have to do without Señorita Cameron's help this afternoon," he said sternly. "She needs to rest."

Shona scrambled awkwardly to her feet. "Yes!" she exclaimed. "Please tell them I'm feeling tired. I'm going to lie down for a while." She turned to Muñoz. "I want to thank you, *señor*," she said. "I feel much better knowing you understand."

He bowed. "I only wish you had told me sooner. If there is anything I can do, please feel free to call upon me." He studied Jephtha intently. "Perhaps this friend of yours is the answer to your dilemma," he said suddenly. "Tell me, young man, are you wed?"

Jephtha's face flushed beet red. "I don't see where that's any of your—"

"No, he's not!" Shona interrupted, her heart once again beating wildly. "But he's betrothed to a *fille de cassette* staying at the convent. Besides, Jephtha is only a very dear friend."

Muñoz gave a slight nod. "Too bad," he mused. Then he brightened and Shona saw the closest thing to a smile she had ever seen on his face. "I have not yet told you my news. I am resigning my commission and building a home here in New Orleans. We can attend mass together after your confirmation."

Her heart plummeted. Dear God, now the nosy Spaniard would be harassing her constantly. How could she keep Stephen's presence a secret with Muñoz living so close? She forced a smile. "How nice. I will enjoy that, *señor*."

Chapter 32

The wet, early spring gave way to a suffocatingly hot, humid June. Clothing mildewed in the presses, black mold sprouted on salted meats, and the sour, fetid odor of decaying vegetation hung over New Orleans in a cloying pall. The last few weeks of Shona's confinement were made even more difficult by several nasty incidents in her store, all instigated by loud, abusive men claiming that her merchandise was faulty or priced much too high. Stephen was convinced Muñoz was behind the unpleasantness, and it took her and Fernando hours of pleading to persuade him not to confront his enemy, not when his expeditions into the bayous to guide the Jewish settlers were proving so successful. Already, over fifteen families had been comfortably housed in newly erected homes in the German settlement; adding a tanner, an apothecary, a note collector, and several other much-needed merchantmen to the growing community.

Though Shona's fears for Stephen's safety did not completely disappear, she was able to put them aside and enjoy the little time they spent together. She even conquered her jealousy of the phantomlike heroine Trista who always accompanied him on his expeditions.

All appeared to be going well until one particularly sweltering, muggy night. A pesky, buzzing mosquito had somehow invaded the privacy of their bedroom, and Shona tumbled restlessly on top of the damp sheets, swatting frantically at the damnable insect which had landed on her forehead, then buzzed off into the darkness, leaving a burning welt in its wake. She rubbed the spot, sighing loudly. If only she could turn onto her stomach and hide her face in her hands! But her cumbersome belly made that impossible. She struggled up until she was sitting on the side of the bed. Holding her heavy hair off of her perspiring neck helped for a moment, but soon her entire body was dripping from the slight exertion.

She stared over at Stephen, willing him to awaken and rescue her from her discomfort. Instead, he turned over on his side, and the sound of his even breathing soon drove her to madness. How dare he sleep so soundly when she was so miserable! She shook his shoulder.

"Stephen!" she said. "Wake up!"

He groaned and mumbled. She shook him again. "Wake up, you miserable Spaniard!" she hissed. "I need you!"

He sat up beside her. "What is it? What is happening?"

"I am being eaten alive by mosquitoes, and it is so hot and humid my gown is wringing wet!" she exclaimed crossly. "Do something! Please!"

He struck the flint and lit the lamp beside him. Her ill humor was instantly fed by his chuckle. "You look like a rumpled, lumpy hopsack of wet potatoes."

Shona stared at him, her lower lip trembling with indignation. Then she swiped helplessly at the tears stinging her eyes. "You are a callous, hard-hearted boor," she declared. "Being a man, you know nothing about the discomfort involved in the making of a child—your child!" Tears slid down her cheeks.

He was beside her in an instant. "I am so sorry," he crooned as he gathered her into his arms. "I did not mean to hurt you. I was only trying to make you laugh."

She hugged his neck, burying her face against his shoulder.

414

"But you are right—I *feel* like a lumpy, wet hopsack of potatoes!" She sobbed.

He patted her back until she quieted. Then he held her at arm's length. "I will first get rid of the mosquitoes, then I will fetch some cool water to ease your misery."

She shook her head balefully. "It won't work." She sighed. "It's so hot and sticky, I'll only be hot again in moments."

"Then I will just have to find a way to distract you." He chuckled.

She shook her head as he left the bedroom. He still did not understand! She heard him rummaging quietly about in the great room and breathed a silent prayer that he would not awaken Fernando. Moments later, he appeared beside her, his arms laden with a large jug of water, fresh clothes and a small jar of ointment.

She watched him leaping nimbly about as he chased the buzzing mosquito. When he had succeeded in killing it, he pressed her down on the bed, pulling the insect netting firmly into place. Then he stripped her gown over her head and threw it on the floor.

"You must learn to sleep naked," he said as he dipped a cloth into the jug and dabbed at her perspiring face.

Her cheeks burned and she turned away. "I can't," she said stiffly. "I'm too ugly!"

"On the contrary. Your body has never been more beautiful."

"You're crazy," she moaned. "My belly sticks out like an overripe melon and my breasts look like those huge grapefruits they sell at the market!"

"Your belly should stick out!" he protested. "After all, you carry my child!" He pressed his finger beneath her chin and forced her to meet his gaze. "Our child, Shona," he repeated. "And your breasts have never been more enticing."

"I don't believe you!" she exclaimed, her amber eyes dark with misery. "I know you find me clumsy and ugly! You haven't made love to me in weeks!"

"Dios," he breathed out. "Surely you know how hard I have worked to keep my passion under control. I do not want to hurt you—to hurt our unborn child."

"But I need you," she said. "I need to feel your love. I cannot bear to have you stay over on your side of the bed, your back turned to me as though you find me so unattractive you can no longer even look my way."

Stephen pulled her against his chest, and his hands tangled in her golden hair. "I have tried to protect you from my own unbridled passion, and instead, I have hurt you."

He laid her back on the mattress. "But now I will bathe your body and rub some of this fragrant, cooling salve on your stings."

She sighed deeply as he patted her face and neck with a cloth dipped in water. Then he wiped the perspiration from her shoulders and breasts. His hands lingered lovingly over her belly before moving refreshingly down her thighs and calves to her feet. Though the water was tepid, it was far cooler than her burning body, and by the time he had turned her onto her side and lovingly patted her back and buttocks with the dampened cloth, she felt much cooler, much more in control of her errant emotions.

As he smoothed salve over the welts on her forehead and cheek, his touch light and adoring, she sighed and peeked out from beneath lowered lashes. There was no mistaking the kindling passion in his blue eyes. She dropped her gaze to the tangle of hair at the base of his belly. His aroused manhood belied the control he would keep over his desires. She smiled.

He rose and wiped his own sweaty body with another cloth. Then he lay down beside her and she nestled deeply into the circle of his waiting arms.

They lay quietly for a moment, their gazes locked, their chests rising and falling to the same primitive beat. He brushed her chin with his lips, then nuzzled the hollow of her throat, the tip of his tongue moving in ever-widening, tantalizing circles. She caught her breath as he delicately nipped at one earlobe, then the other, breathing ever so softly into each ear. Then his lips moved over her forehead, her brows, the bridge of her nose, her cheeks. They traced the outline of her full lips ever so slightly, and he planted a playful kiss on the tip of her nose before his soft lips closed over hers, moving tenderly, yet persistently until her lips parted eagerly.

She tasted his sweetness as their tongues touched. The tiny flame flickering deep within her sparked hotly into flames which spread over her entire body as his tongue gently probed her mouth. She sighed deeply, knowing she could never have enough of him, that she would never tire of his taste, of the salty, manly scent of his flesh.

She stifled a moan when his lips left hers. He kissed each corner of her mouth, his lips moving sensuously down, down, until he was lipping her throat, her shoulders, the beginnings of her full breasts. Her nipples tingled and tightened with desire—with need. She gasped when he circled one nipple, then the other, with light strokes of his tongue. He teased each tingling bud of desire tenderly with his mouth as his fingers moved down her swollen belly, each light touch bringing shivers of delight in its wake.

Shona's throat moved convulsively as he explored her secret place nesting beneath its mound of golden hair. She arched her back, thrusting her hips forward against his cupped hand. As he met her growing need with a firmer touch, a sweet, fiery glow permeated her entire body. Then he titillated her throbbing flesh with long, lingering strokes.

She suddenly needed to express the feeling of enormous love washing over her. "You," she whispered. "I want to love you."

He moved slightly so her fingers could close over his swollen desire. Then he groaned and pressed his lips to her throbbing flesh. His mouth moved over her lightly, then firmly until she was panting with a passion so overwhelming, she doubted she could bear it much longer. Tiny sparks of light flickered and flamed behind her closed lids; her body was on fire. She was being consumed by the raging flames fanned by his lips, his

417

probing tongue.

Suddenly, Stephen cried out. Her answering flesh exploded into a million, shimmering pieces. Stars flashed across the blazing skies and the sun itself fractured into tiny, quivering slivers of ecstasy. The entire world was afire and she exulted in the conflagration.

He gathered her close, his arms gentle and protective. "Did I hurt you? Is the baby all right?"

She took his hand and placed it on her swollen belly. The babe deep within her womb moved, sending wide ripples across her taut flesh. "See? We have only awakened him. He is fine."

For a long time afterwards she watched his chest rise and fall softly as sleep claimed him. At last, she reached over and snuffed the lamp, then nestled close, her heart and body at peace.

Stephen spent many fruitless hours, traveling up and down the river, seeking a renegade priest who would be willing to perform their marriage ceremony without the required three-week posting of the banns, but he never gave up and would not allow Shona to succumb to her fears that his search was hopeless.

Shona spent several days at the docks early in the month, then gave in to Stephen's demands and Fernando's pleading and allowed Jephtha to take over the buying. He did so happily—for her sake only, he stated emphatically—for it was obvious from their first meeting that he and Stephen would never become friends. Instead, whenever they were together, they circled one another warily like two male dogs, their hackles raised for imminent battle. Shona was convinced that only her own cheerful acceptance of Jephtha's growing love for Mignon kept the two men from each other's throats. Though their enmity distressed her, she realized that their jealousy was something she would have to ignore, for they were both too pigheaded to ever change.

Though she fretted about Muñoz's presence in town, she did not see him until the first week in June, when he began to drop into the shop on Saturdays, presumably to check up on her progress with her catechism classes. The first Saturday, he remarked upon Rebecca's absence and accepted with good grace the story Shona told him: the girl was not feeling well. But the second Saturday, his eyes narrowed dangerously and it was obvious he was not ready to believe Rebecca had taken the day off to move into a new, larger cottage.

"She belongs here, and you belong in bed," he stated firmly.

"But she works very hard. I couldn't have gotten along without her help."

Muñoz sniffed. "I do not care how hard she works. Saturday is your busiest day. You were remiss in giving her this time off. I expect to see her working here next Saturday, or I myself will take her to task."

"But she can't!" Shona cried.

His black eyes flashed. "I am beginning to believe that you have inadvertently hired a Jew!" he spat. "They never work on Saturdays, you know."

"She's not Jewish," Shona said quickly. "It's just that she's going to be out of town next Saturday. I've . . . I've asked her to go upriver to the German settlement, to bring back some vegetables for the shop. All of my customers are begging for fresh greens and with the baby due soon, I can't make the trip myself."

"Then you must send that big, burly friend of yours. I understand he is doing your buying now."

Shona was astounded! Exactly how much of her business did he know? "It's just that Jephtha's so busy with his own work," she said in exasperation. "I really can't ask him to take more time off from his smithy."

"Then I will! I will not have you endangering your life and the life of your unborn child, no matter if it is a bastard!"

"*Señor!* Please lower your voice! You distress me with such harsh words!"

419

He looked around hastily, his narrow chin raised high. "No one has heard me, *señorita*," he said. "But I am sorry if I have caused you pain. I am only concerned for your welfare."

"Then I must ask you to leave. You are keeping me from my customers."

He bowed low. "Your wish is my command. But I will come back next week, if not sooner."

Stephen returned from a trip to the settlement late that night to find a very distraught Shona pacing the floor, wringing her hands, and moaning about Jews and Catholics and the insoluable problems separating them.

He drew her into his arms. "You must not carry on so, *querida*," he soothed. "I believe it is time for me to face Muñoz. He cannot be allowed to jeopardize innocent lives any longer."

"No!" She hugged him close. "You must not endanger your missions!" she exclaimed raggedly. "There is too much at stake."

"But I won't have you suffering so."

"Oh, Stephen, what are we going to do? He will be back. If he doesn't find Rebecca working next Saturday, he will do something dreadful."

"Then there is only one answer to this dilemma. Rebecca must work on Saturdays."

"But how can I ask her to go against what she believes?"

"You won't have to," he said firmly. "I will ask her myself. I will go right now and fetch her and Asa."

"But it's the middle of the night!"

His face twisted into a grin. "Have you forgotten that you are betrothed to a fugitive? What better time to make my way through the streets?" He rose and leaned over to kiss her cheek tenderly. "Make some tea, Shona. I will return shortly."

The lamps burned in the little apartment far into the night as the four discussed Muñoz and his threat. Asa and Rebecca took the news that she would have to compromise her faith with serious faces, but they agreed that Muñoz's suspicions must not be aroused.

"I cannot allow Rebecca to fear for her life," Asa said solemnly. "After all, the Shabbat is meant to enable one to rest from the daily toils and to regain human dignity through serenity. There is no serenity in anticipating persecution."

Shona leaped to her feet. "But why not do what other Jews have done—become baptized Catholics so you can live as freely as anyone!"

Asa shook his head vehemently. "I know there are a few Jews who have become *conversos,* but we cannot do that. We will continue to live as brother and sister until Elohim himself provides us with a rabbi!"

"Brother and sister! But that's unnatural. Don't you love one another? Aren't you living as husband and wife now? After all, you share the same house!"

Rebecca grasped Shona's hand. "Please, Señorita Shona," she exclaimed, "though I do not pass judgment on you or Señor Stephen, please do not believe we would live in sin. I will work on Saturdays, but do not talk anymore about us converting. We were born Jews and we will die Jews." She squeezed Shona's fingers. "We will find a rabbi someday, and then we will marry. You do not realize, but in Spain we could not even have broken bread with you Gentiles, lest we then drink wine with you, and ultimately intermarry outside of our faith. But here, in you, we have found true friends we can trust. We must break some of our laws in order to stay alive, but we cannot break them all."

"I applaud your integrity," Stephen said. "Now, I must see you back to your cottage. It will soon be dawn."

"That is not necessary," Asa said. "It will be safer if we stay here until it is time for Rebecca to go to the shop. I, for one, could use another cup of tea, but you, Señorita Shona, must rest, for your face is pale and your limbs tremble with fatigue."

"If you're sure you'll be all right alone . . ."

"Go to your bed," Rebecca urged. "We must spend a few moments with Señor Stephen; then he will join you."

Shona was too exhausted to protest. She allowed Stephen to tuck her into bed, and said nothing about being excluded from their conversation. Within moments, she was sound asleep.

The moment Stephen returned, Asa handed him a piece of paper. "We received this late this evening," he said.

Stephen read quickly. "But that's on Saturday!" he exclaimed. "I do not want to leave Shona alone when Muñoz is sure to appear to check on Rebecca."

"I know," Asa said. "But Dieter says there are over ten in the party and there are several small children. This will be your most dangerous journey of all, for children are hard to quiet when frightened. You must go, señor. God will protect Señorita Shona and my Rebecca from danger."

Stephen sighed. "Your faith shames me," he said softly. "I will go, but unlike you, I will worry the entire time."

Muñoz, true to his word, appeared the following Saturday. Shona was sure she detected a look of disappointment on his pale face when he found Rebecca working. Shona's back ached unmercifully, and she lost patience when she saw his eyes following Rebecca everywhere she went.

"Please stop staring at the poor girl!" she snapped. "She's here and that's what you wanted!"

"I did not see her at mass last Sunday," Muñoz drawled. "Surely as a Catholic she must have hated missing Mass."

"It's none of your business!" Shona exclaimed, "just as it's none of mine." The baby thumped about in Shona's belly, causing her to gasp. "Please go, *señor*," she said. "I don't feel well. I think I'll go upstairs and rest."

"Is it your time? Do you want the girl to go for the midwife?"

"No. I'm just tired."

"But we have not discussed your classes, and how you are progressing."

Shona lost all patience. "I didn't go to class this morning,"

422

she snapped. "I can't walk that far now. Please, just go."

"But I am going, *señorita*. I have a very important errand to attend to, very important indeed. The governor has chosen me to lead the militia into the bayous in search of a party of Jews reportedly approaching New Orleans. It is said there is a renegade Catholic who has agreed to accept their filthy money in return for guiding them to safety. Well, we will see how he manages to spend his Judas silver when he is hanging from a cypress branch. Perhaps I will tell you about it next week."

His mocking words brought goose flesh coursing over her body. Dear God, he was talking about Stephen! She swayed and clutched at the counter for support.

"*Señorita*," he said softly. "Surely my words have not distressed you. If I didn't know better I might suspect you of being a Jewish sympathizer."

Shona stared at him, heart pounding, mind racing. "Of course not," she said, keeping her voice calm with an enormous effort. "You can do whatever you want. I am just tired."

"Then you must go to bed. I will help you up the stairs."

"Thank you, but no." She pressed against the counter. "I can manage on my own."

He inclined his head in a curt nod and, without another word, turned on his heel and shouldered his way out the door. Shona gasped aloud as a series of sharp pains stabbed across her back.

Ignoring the pain, she drew Rebecca away from a startled customer and called to Fernando to follow. She led them into the storeroom and closed the door, tears streaming down her face. "The militia is setting a trap for Stephen!" she sobbed. "We have to warn him."

"How do you know, Madonna? Did Muñoz tell you?"

She nodded wordlessly.

"Tell us exactly what he said! Here, take my kerchief and wipe your face. Take some deep breaths."

Shona gulped for air and fought down her rising panic. "He

423

said he's leading the militia into the swamps after the Jews. And he knows Stephen is leading them."

Rebecca clutched at Shona's sleeve. "But how could he know when he believes Señor Stephen dead!"

"Oh, he doesn't know who it is, he just knows they have a local man—a renegade Catholic, he called him—leading them to safety. You must go to the settlement and warn them before it's too late!"

"But it is already too late, Madonna!" Fernando exclaimed. "Esteban left long before daylight. He is surely deep into the bayous by now. There is no way Rebecca could find them."

"Señor Fernando is right. By the time I reach the settlement, they will be many miles away, and I do not know what trail they have taken."

"But Joanna will know! Her husband Dieter is with Stephen. She surely knows where you can find them!"

Fernando sighed raggedly. "Then you must go, Señorita Rebecca. Hire the fastest barge you can find. I would go myself but your young legs are much faster than mine."

Rebecca nodded. "I will go at once. Only, who will help in the shop with me gone?"

"I'll close the damn shop if I have to!" Shona gasped. "Just go!"

"Be very careful Muñoz does not see you at the dock," Fernando warned. "Take money from the box beneath the counter. You may need much to convince a barge master to interrupt his schedule."

Rebecca embraced them quickly and slipped out the door.

Shona sat heavily on a keg. "She cannot be too late," she breathed raggedly. "They must be warned!"

Fernando patted her shoulder. "She will do her very best, you know that. But you must get upstairs to bed. All of this has been too trying with your confinement so advanced. I will get Jephtha to help me in the shop. We could have trouble if we try to close it on a Saturday, especially with so many people in town."

"But you know what happened last time!"

"I may be much smaller than that giant, but I promise to stomp that oaf into the ground if he offends a customer. Now, please, Madonna, up to bed. We dare not leave the shop unattended much longer or there will be no merchandise left to sell."

Shona waited on as many disgruntled customers as she could until Fernando returned with Jephtha. Then she climbed the stairs to the apartment, her heart so heavy with concern for Stephen she was scarcely aware of the pains spreading across her back.

Her labor started in earnest shortly after she set the breakfast dishes to soak. Unable to believe her time had really come, she reluctantly took the baby's clothing the sisters had given her from her chest and laid it on a chair in her bedroom. She cleaned the great room, stopping when her belly drew up, and moving again when the contraction eased. She was so distracted by her concern for Stephen's safety that she paced the floor for over an hour, alternately sobbing and praying for his safety.

Finally, the contractions too close together for her to walk, she lay upon her bed, massaging her hard belly. There was no reason to bother Fernando and Jephtha until the shop closed, though the pains were coming very close together now. She lay back and closed her eyes. An image of Stephen's face filled her mind and tears pricked her lashes.

"Oh, Stephen, Stephen," she moaned. "God protect you, my love! Oh, why aren't you here now? I need you!"

She groaned as another pain gripped her belly, tightening it into a hard ball. Then she felt a tiny wrench, and something hot and sticky flooded the mattress between her legs. She had been present at a birthing in Brunswick and knew that her water had broken. It was time to summon Asa, but how was she to get out of bed? She tried to roll over onto her side, but another pain, hard and racking, immobilized her. She fell back and moaned. Why had she allowed Stephen to go? Why did no one come

425

to help?

She looked toward the window. Oh, God, it was still daylight! It might be hours before the shop closed! She panicked and tried to rise, but the pains were coming one on top of another now and she could not move. She clamped her teeth down hard upon her lip until the salty taste of blood filled her mouth. She strained and pushed, her loud grunts filling the room, her mind reeling with self-recrimination. Why hadn't she told Fernando about the pains in her back? Why had she foolishly waited so long?

Then her laboring body consumed every portion of her body and mind as the birthing progressed. Stephen's dangerous journey was forgotten. The need for help was forgotten. There was only the grinding, wrenching pain and the need to bear down. Time lost all meaning. Moments blurred into hours as she gave herself over to her labor, her neck strained and her back arched. She knew she was uttering animal-like grunts, but she did not care. Push! her body commanded. Push! Her hands raked the sheet.

Shona strained until she felt she would surely die. Then, suddenly, a bright, burning pain seared through her.

"Stephen!" she screamed.

Chapter 33

The cool, early morning mists gave way to the scorching rays
of the noonday sun, leaving the bayou sweltering beneath a
heavy blanket of suffocating, humid vapor, redolent with the
cloying stench of decaying vegetation and rancid water. Night-
hunting animals whimpered as they burrowed deeper into their
nesting holes, seeking relief in the damp earth, but the long,
straggling line of humans stumbling in single file along the ill-
defined path winding between pools of shallow, slimy water
were forced to endure the stupefying heat in silence. Mothers
cradled their listless children in their arms and fathers peered
anxiously through the fetid undergrowth, their eyes burning
with sweat and fatigue.

Stephen pushed aside tendrils of Spanish moss and glanced
back over his shoulder at the straggling line, his forehead
creased with worry. Why had Dieter not told him this group
was in such poor physical condition! He wiped impatiently at
the sweat stinging his eyes, knowing such a warning would
have made little or no difference. He was committed to seeing
these people safely to the settlement, despite the fact that
many of them were suffering from fever and malnutrition. But
they had to make better time! At the rate they were traveling,
they would not make the settlement before darkness fell, and
traveling through the snake and crocodile-infested bayous at

night was both foolhardy and dangerous. Many times the path all but disappeared into the green weeds that clogged the water between the trees and cypress roots. Trying to find their way in the dark would be impossible. He held up his hand, silently bringing the line to a halt.

Trista and Dieter shouldered their way past the stoic travelers to his side. "What is it?" Dieter whispered. "Have you lost the trail?"

"No. But I am concerned about the time. We must branch off at the next crossing and travel on the easier trail or we will not reach the settlement before nightfall."

"But that is too dangerous!" Trista said. "That is the major road leading to New Orleans. There is no telling who we might encounter!"

"I know that!" Stephen exclaimed. "But we must take the easier road. Many of the women are ready to collapse. We must make better time."

Dieter nodded. "I have been thinking the same thing." He patted Trista's shoulder. "He is right. We will take the next branch onto the main road. These people are so terrified, even an innocent turtle could cause them to panic. In the meantime, perhaps each of us should carry a child belonging to one of the more exhausted mothers. And I will tell the fathers they must share in the burden of carrying their own children."

Stephen eyed Trista anxiously. So much depended upon her cooperation, for without her encouragement and uncomplaining aid, they would never have made it this far. She looked up at him, her dark eyes wide with concern. Then her full lips trembled and turned up in the ghost of a smile. "All right," she whispered. "But please pray the militia is practicing their marksmanship back in New Orleans. This group, with their beards and ear locks, could never pass for anything but Jews."

The children were quickly settled into fresher arms and the group continued silently toward the fork leading to the main road into New Orleans. Stephen cradled the little boy he was

428

now carrying tenderly, pressing the nodding head onto his shoulder, his mind filled with prayers for their safety. When a grackle raucously performed his acrobatics over the water and the child whimpered in fear, Stephen patted his back, whispering words of encouragement in English and Spanish. Though he knew the German-speaking boy did not understand, he hoped the child would be comforted by the gentle tone. His thoughts turned to Shona and the child she would soon bear. God grant that his son would never be forced to make such a dangerous journey!

He thought back upon their conversation early that morning, and his heart filled with love and longing. If only they could live peaceably, without the constant separations forced upon them by his own intense sense of duty. He smiled when he recalled her concern about his reaction to her owning a shop. He had handled that rather well, hadn't he! There was no way he would be truthful with her until their child was safely born and she had recovered her strength. He had little doubt that there were rough waters ahead for them when he revealed how he truly felt about her profession, for the moment he could safely reveal the truth, he would insist that she sell the shop and devote her time to being a wife and mother. After all, she was a woman, wasn't she? And women did not own shops. They cared for their husbands and children.

His heart constricted when he reached the fork and chose the wider, more traveled road. He stood still for a moment, straining to catch any unusual noise through the subdued murmur of crickets and whisper of the wind in the Spanish moss and the scraping of the spiked palmetto leaves.

As the vanguard, he would have to be very wary for Trista was right. These people with their heavy black clothing would never pass for Gentiles.

He breathed a grateful prayer for the uncomplaining, discerning help Trista Becher had provided time after time. She was a strange little thing, so small of stature, so fragile, yet so strong and resolute about helping others less fortunate than herself. And her bravery and quick thinking had saved them all more than once. What a shame she held herself so aloof from the men in the settlement; she would make some fortunate man a remarkable wife, he thought. In some ways she reminded him of Shona, though they did not resemble one another physically. Whereas Shona was like a tall, slender spike of golden wheat, Trista reminded him of a small, helpless black kitten—though from the bravery she had exhibited recently, he admitted it was a wild kitten. Trista had the same bravery and fortitude he so admired in his beloved Shona, but Shona desired the freedom to live any way she chose, while Trista seemed content to fulfill her role as a woman. She only railed against the restrictions society put on a woman's education. Yes, she would make some man very happy, but she did not seem at all interested in doing so. He smiled broadly. Though she was a Protestant, perhaps he should enlist the aid of the Jewish *Shadchan*, the marriage broker, to overcome the hurt she had obviously suffered in the past.

He forced his mind back to the present and straightened his shoulders resolutely. This group must get through, for there was a rabbi traveling with them! He grinned widely when he pictured Asa's and Rebecca's reactions to that news. Soon, they could become man and wife. If only he could find a priest so he and Shona could also be joined by the church.

And then what? He shifted the sleeping boy to his other shoulder. Should he ignore his many doubts about her happiness and take Shona back to Spain? Or should he consider Don Cabrillo's generous offer? He could not ignore the fact that every time he pictured Shona in the Tejas Territory, he felt great peace. There were so many decisions to be made! At times, he felt as though the weight of the entire world rested upon his shoulders. And when his son was born, he would have an even heavier burden of responsibility. His steps quickened. All morning, he had fought his fear that

Shona's confinement was drawing to an end. He must guide this group safely to the settlement so he could take a barge downriver to New Orleans before the morning light.

Trista plodded slowly down the road, her legs moving automatically. She held the little girl tightly, refusing to admit her own growing fatigue, but she almost staggered when she thought of the responsibility she and Dieter and Stephen faced this day. Almost twenty lives depended upon their strength and courage! She glanced back at Dieter who brought up the rear. He was carrying a fever-ridden boy upon his back, and his brow was creased with concentration for he did not want to step in a wagon rut and unseat the ailing child. Ahead, almost out of sight, Stephen strode warily along, his burden cradled tenderly, his head moving from right to left as he eyed the road ahead. Trista suddenly found herself envying Joanna and Shona the men they had married. She tutted to herself. Though the two men were brave and clear minded, as her father had been, they still fell far short of the mark. Her father had possessed all of their qualities and far more. She frowned and sighed heavily. Perhaps she would never find a man like him. Perhaps she would spend her entire life in spinsterhood, looking at every man she met with a jaundiced eye.

The little girl she was carrying whimpered and Trista sang a German lullaby under her breath until the child closed her eyes and slept. Such a poor little thing, so thin, so poorly clad. She almost felt guilty over how happy she had been in her own childhood, dogging her father's footsteps through the streets, her tiny fingers cradled tightly in his protective hand. He had had such patience. He'd spent hours explaining why the sun always rose in the east and where the birds got their songs, and he had guided her through her Latin and Greek studies, filling potentially tedious hours with excitement and joy. He'd seemed sad only when she'd asked about her mother. But, even then, he would patiently tell her of her own difficult birth and of the long days and months during which his beloved Ingrid

431

sank lower and lower into ill health. Tears had sparkled on his eyelashes as he'd recounted her final hour. But he'd always ended his sad remembrances with the amusing story about how his lovely wife had insisted he choose a name for his daughter, and how he had chosen a Greek name, which Ingrid had been unable to pronounce. Consequently, Trista's mother had refused for the few months she had lived to refer to her daughter as anything other than *"Liebling."*

Then had come that dreadful day when the Catholics had taken her father away for daring to teach the heresy that all men should be free to choose their own faith. He had kissed her tenderly and had walked away bravely, his shoulders straight, his chin held high. Tears filled Trista's eyes at that memory. She concentrated upon the woman ahead, not willing to allow herself to dwell upon such painful thoughts.

Suddenly, she was startled out of her reverie by the low murmur that passed through the line of travelers. She froze in her tracks, her eyes instantly seeking Stephen. He stood stark still, one hand raised, his head turned to the lazy curve in the road ahead. A faint, metallic click filled the silence, then another, click, then several more. She was sure she could hear the sound of tramping feet. Her heart leaped; her breath froze in her throat. Stephen gestured violently, and the weary travelers melted into the underbrush at the side of the road.

Trista took cover behind a large tree. The little girl she was carrying awakened and began to cry softly, so Trista rocked her back and forth, praying the child would quiet down. But the youngster's cry strengthened, becoming a thin, reedy wail of protest. Trista rocked her harder, cursing herself soundly for having chosen the only orphan in the group; this child had no mother to soothe her.

The little girl threw herself from side to side and her protests became loud screams. Even as Trista frenziedly sought to quiet the child, she knew it was much too late. A bird, startled by the screams, added its cries to the clamor. Trista knew there was only one avenue of escape for them all.

She stepped boldly into the road and began walking quickly, counting her steps as she passed the line of refugees hiding in the bushes. She glimpsed Stephen crouching behind a tree, his hand over a little boy's mouth. He nodded his head encouragingly as she passed.

Trista gasped aloud as she rounded the curve. The road was filled with brightly uniformed men marching, four abreast, toward her, swords clanking at their sides, hats pushed jauntily back from sweating brows. The French militia!

Her mind worked frantically as she eyed the underbrush, but she knew it was much too late to change her mind now. She slowed her steps as she studied the tall, black-clad man leading the militia. Though he was not wearing a uniform, she knew from his haughty carriage that he was in control of the troops. She forced a relieved smile and stumbled down the road toward him.

"Thank God!" she cried loudly. "You've brought help!"

Muñoz recoiled as the tiny woman with her screaming burden collapsed at his feet. *Madre de Dios*, what was this? He stepped backward, avoiding the woman's clutching hands as he sought to understand her guttural sobs. German. The filthy wretch was speaking in German! He shook his head repeatedly as she poured out her unintelligible gibberish, crying all the while.

"Silence!" he shouted at last. "I cannot understand you!" Though it was obvious from her perplexed stare that she had not understood the command he had impulsively spoken in Spanish, at least she stopped prattling and sat looking up at him. "I do not understand you," he said slowly in Spanish. She shook her head. He tried French. Again, she shook her head. He felt his face growing hot. "I do not speak German!" he screeched in English.

Her face lit up with a smile. "But I speak the English!" she said with a heavy accent. "Oh, *mein Herr*, you appear out of

433

the wilderness as a savior for me and my poor, sick child."

He stepped back from her and motioned to one of his men, indicating that the militiaman should help her to her feet. The child had stopped crying and now stared at him with round eyes. His stomach turned at the sight of the little girl's wet and trembling chin. *Dios*, how revolting! He handed the woman a clean white handkerchief and averted his gaze as she wiped the child's face.

"Thank you, *mein Herr*," she said softly.

He turned back to her. "What are you doing here?" he asked coldly. "Why is that filthy urchin crying?"

The woman's face crumpled, and he stiffened himself against another onslaught of tears. But instead of weeping, the woman only sniffled loudly. "Oh, I was sure we would never be rescued!" she said. "I have run so far, and my strength is almost gone." She swayed and he automatically steadied her, his nostrils flaring with distaste as he touched her dirt-encrusted arm.

"Please explain," he demanded. "I am in a hurry. I cannot delay my mission."

Her eyes clouded. "Your mission? But did you not come to rescue me? And my child?"

"Rescue you from what? Talk sense or I will leave you here!"

"But you cannot," she wailed. "They will take us again and we will never be free!"

He felt his face flush. "Take you? Who will take you?"

Her large dark eyes widened. "The Gypsies!" she gasped, throwing a quick look over her shoulder. "They took us from our home last night. I only managed to escape by pretending to be ill."

"*Gypsies!*" He felt as though he had been dealt a blow in the stomach. "But there are no Gypsies here!"

"That is what we thought, my husband and I, but we were mistaken. They came to our farm yesterday, begging, and when he refused them food, they hit him over the head and ran off with our child. I followed them all night through the swamps, fearing they would kill her. Then, at daybreak, they captured me."

Muñoz stared down at her, his chest heaving. "I cannot believe this!" he exclaimed. "I have heard of no Gypsies around here! Surely you are mistaken!"

She shook her head as she patted the child's back. "No, I am not mistaken. In Germany, I saw many Gypsies and I know what they look like, how they speak. I am not mistaken. There were about twenty of them and they were Gypsies," she said firmly.

"And they are coming after you?"

She nodded. "I am sure they are. I am certain I heard them only a short while ago. That is why I was running."

Muñoz was filled with elation. Gypsies! Next to Jews, there was nothing he liked better than putting a group of filthy Gypsies to the lash. "You must show me!" he said. "Where did you see them last?"

She gasped, her hand flying to her mouth. "Oh, do not ask me to take you to them!" she moaned. "They will kill me!"

"Nonsense. We will protect you." He watched in dismay as she sank to the ground, the child cradled in her arms. "You must tell me!" he exclaimed. "Was it on this road?"

"No," she said quickly. "About a mile back, there is a small fork to the right. They were on that path. I got a good head start, so they are probably still far short of the main road," she added.

He barked an order in French, and one of the militiamen stepped forward. "This man will escort you and your child back to New Orleans," he said. "We will take care of those Gypsies, never fear!"

Trista stared up at him in dismay. She could not allow a militiaman to remain behind. "Please," she cried softly. "I must rest. Let me stay beside the road and wait for you. I am

435

too weary to travel any further."

She watched anxiously as the arrogant Spaniard gazed up the road, his nostrils flaring. Suddenly, he whipped around and shouted an order. "Very well," he said to her. "You must wait beneath that tree over there, where you can be afforded shade. We will return shortly—with those Gypsies in bonds!"

Trista allowed one of the Frenchmen to help her to the side of the road; then she watched, her heart in her throat, as the militia disappeared around the bend. God grant Stephen and Dieter still had everyone safely hidden and the children quiet!

Without the brightly uniformed militia to distract her, the little girl began to cry again, but Trista rocked her, singing softly in German, and the child soon fell into a fitful sleep. Then Trista concentrated upon the road. After many long, anxious moments, when Stephen came around the bend, Dieter fast upon his heels, Trista leaped to her feet and raced into their arms.

"We must hurry!" she whispered raggedly. "I sent them off after a band of imaginary Gypsy kidnappers. It will not take them long to know they have been duped."

Stephen laughed softly. "You are amazing," he said. "Gypsies! You do not know it, but that was Francisco Muñoz leading the militia. You could not have chosen a better story!"

"I knew she had a cool head," Dieter said to Stephen, "but I could never have allowed her to pass me without trying to stop her. How did you know what she was going to do?"

Stephen shrugged. "I did not know, but I trusted her to use her head. She has never failed us yet."

"That is why I chose you to lead us," Dieter said softly. "You never panic."

Trista's heart was filled with joy as Stephen picked up the child and motioned her to follow, but he stopped suddenly and motioned her to his side.

"You know that you must not allow Muñoz to see you ever again. He will never forgive you when he spies our tracks and follows them back to the main road."

She nodded. "I realize that. I only wanted to buy us some time."

"And you did—but now we must hurry," he whispered. "Dieter, tell the others to come along. The trail to the settlement is not far ahead. We can make it easily before nightfall."

Chapter 34

Shona's excruciating pain ceased miraculously when something wet slipped out between her legs. She gasped and lay panting on the sheets, sweat rolling off her face and body. Gathering her last ounce of strength, she half-rose. Her child lay between her knees, its tiny arms flailing helplessly. She tried to sit up, but her strength failed and she lay back on the bed, gasping for breath. Dear God, she had to do something for the child, yet she was too exhausted to move!

Suddenly, the apartment door slammed. She turned her head toward it. "Fernando!" she cried weakly. "Help me, please help me!" She fell back as Fernando's face swam in undulating waves before her. "Help me," she whispered.

"Asa and Rebecca are in the shop!" Fernando cried. "I will call them!"

Within seconds, Asa was in the room. She heard a baby's thin cry.

"You have a lovely little girl," Asa said, his voice sounding very distant to Shona.

Disbelief washed over her. "No," she whispered. "It's a boy. It's Stephen's son." She drifted off into a black pit of exhaustion.

Fernando watched Asa clean the infant. Then he took the little bundle Asa had wrapped in sheeting and looked through blurring tears at the tiny red face. *"Dios,"* he breathed. He lifted a shining face to Asa and Rebecca. "God is good," he said brokenly.

He placed the baby on the mattress at Shona's side. "Madonna," he whispered. "Here is your child. She is the image of our Esteban. She has his dark golden curls."

Golden curls? Shona opened her eyes. "Is it over?" she asked through parched lips. Fernando nodded, his face wreathed in a gigantic smile. "All over. Your daughter is here." He picked up her hand and placed it upon the infant's head.

Shona recoiled and turned her face to the wall. "It should have been a son."

When Fernando looked helplessly at Asa, the young man pulled on his beard and nodded his head slightly. He pushed Fernando aside and leaned over the bed. "You should look at your daughter before it is time to pass the afterbirth," he said. "Your work is not yet over." He looked up at Fernando and winked. "Besides, how do you know she does not have two heads or twelve fingers?"

Shona gasped and turned to the baby. Her tiny mouth was pursed. One little hand, with five perfect fingers, moved toward her lips, and the silence was broken by a very loud smack as the infant began to suck upon its own fist. Fernando, Asa, and Rebecca smiled at one another.

Shona did not see their smiles. She saw only the dark golden ringlets framing her daughter's perfect head, the dusky blue eyes turned dreamily up at her. The thin lines of the baby's dark eyebrows had just a hint of an arrogant arch. She picked up the tiny hand and pressed it to her lips, tears spilling down her cheeks.

"She's beautiful," she said. "Oh, Stephen, you have a beautiful little daughter." She stiffened suddenly. "Did you reach him in time?" she asked Rebecca. "Is he all right?"

The girl smiled and nodded. "He is fine. I got there much too late to warn them, but they arrived safely at the settlement just before sundown."

Shona sighed and closed her eyes. "Then my prayers were answered," she said softly.

The child was an avid nurser. She worked her mouth eagerly when first placed at Shona's breast, and she kneaded the mound with her tiny fingers, while her toes curled in pleasure. When she dropped the nipple, she groped frantically, her rosebud mouth sucking noisily.

Asa insisted that Rebecca stay the night to help with the infant, and in turn, Rebecca convinced Asa that his place was with his betrothed; so Fernando made pallets for them on the floor before the great fireplace, piling them high with blankets from the storeroom, more to pad the hard wood than to give warmth, for the evening was still hot and sticky.

While Shona dozed in the bedroom with the child cradled in the crook of her arm, Rebecca set about cooking a belated evening meal. Asa and Fernando sat before the open window, taking advantage of the faint breeze as Rebecca quietly related the close call Stephen and the others had experienced.

Fernando shook his head, sighing loudly. "It is much too dangerous, this work Esteban has undertaken. I shudder to think what might have happened if that girl Trista had not been so clever."

Asa murmured an agreement. "We must set up some sort of system for warning them while they are on the trail," he said. "Rebecca did not stay to talk to the group, but Señor Stephen told her he was sure they were finished when he saw Muñoz leading the militia."

Rebecca set the trenchers on the table with a loud thump. "Can we not do something about that man? He is a threat to so many!"

Fernando grunted. "He is a blight on the Spanish people!" he exclaimed. "But I fear he is much too close to the governor now. We will have to caution Esteban when he returns. He is taking far too many chances."

Jephtha appeared at the door just as Rebecca was putting the

441

food on the table. "What's going on?" he asked with a grin. "The cashbox is sitting on the counter and the curtains are still wide open!"

Fernando eyed him with mock gravity. "Something has happened in your absence. You have missed a great deal of excitement."

Jephtha's face flushed. "It's that bastard Muñoz, isn't it! I knew he would cause trouble. I should never have gone downriver with that order." He looked around. "Where's Shona? I've got good news for her! I brought back several boxes of candles. Got them for a good price, too!"

Fernando placed his finger to his lips. "Lower your voice, you roaring bear." He took Jephtha's arm and led him toward Shona's bedroom. "If you promise to be quiet, you can see what happened while you floated, unconcerned, upon the great Mississippi." He opened the door quietly and pulled Jephtha inside. "See?" he whispered.

Jephtha's eyes widened. He stepped to the side of the bed and looked down, his mouth opened wide. "The baby . . ." he breathed softly. He brushed the tiny cheek with his fingertip, then recoiled in horror when the sleeping child stirred and instinctively groped with her mouth.

Fernando chuckled as he pulled the sheet higher about Shona's shoulders. "Come," he whispered. "The new mother is exhausted."

Jephtha tripped over his own feet in his haste to escape the bedroom. Rebecca and Asa laughed, and Fernando chuckled inwardly. The great bear became a cowardly house cat when confronted with a mere infant!

"Do you not want to know what it is?" Rebecca asked.

"I don't have to ask. Of course it's a boy."

Fernando scowled. "Do not ever call my goddaughter a boy! She is an angel from heaven."

All eyes turned to Jephtha. He blushed and stared down at his feet. "Oh, that's all right," he mumbled. "I should have known, what with all that yellow hair."

"Do not tell me you, too, are disappointed!" Asa exclaimed. "What is the matter with you people? My people treasure their girl children. They are the most precious gift a loving Father can bestow upon a home."

"I ain't disappointed!" Jephtha protested. "I'm just surprised, that's all. Shona was so sure it was going to be a boy, she had me believing . . ." His voice faded. "What do you mean, me too? Was Shona disappointed that it is a girl?"

Rebecca poured tea into the cups and gestured toward the table. "Please sit before the food is cold. We will tell you all about it as we eat."

The three sat at the table far into the night, talking. Asa finally got to his feet, his shoulders slumping, his eyes bloodshot with fatigue.

"I am going to brew an herbal tisane for Shona. It will help her recover her strength. Then, we must all get some sleep. Señor Stephen will surely return soon, and he must have time alone with his new little family."

A lusty bawl sounded from the bedroom and Rebecca smiled broadly. "I think the new member of the family is asking for more food. I'll go help Shona."

Jephtha picked up his flat-brimmed hat. "I'd better be going, then. Time to get them candles into the storeroom and lock up proper."

Stephen crept into the darkened apartment an hour later, his eyes bloodshot and his shoulders slumped with fatigue. He groped through the dark and stumbled over Asa's sleeping body, cursing beneath his breath. Fernando quickly rose from his cot and lit a lamp, motioning him to be quiet. "You will awaken Shona," he remonstrated softly.

Stephen looked down at Rebecca and Asa, now sitting on their pallets. "What is going on here?" he gasped. "What happened today? Did that bastard Muñoz harm Shona?"

As Asa struggled to his feet, he ran his hands through his rumpled hair. "No, Señor Stephen. Muñoz did come, but he left as soon as he saw Rebecca at work."

"Then what—"

A thin wail interrupted him. He turned toward the bedroom, his eyes wide. "The baby! My son has arrived!" He leaped for the bedroom door before any of them could react.

The soft lamplight streaming through the door illuminated the bed where Shona lay, cradling their child. He kneeled beside it, drawing them into his arms. "My precious *tesora*," he crooned. "You have given me a son."

Shona pulled away, her hand automatically covering her child.

Asa shouldered Fernando aside and gripped Stephen's shoulder. "God has blessed you with a beautiful daughter," he said. He stared at Stephen, as though daring him to react poorly.

"A daughter." Stephen stared back at Asa, his eyes mirroring disbelief.

Shona sat up suddenly. "I am sorry if you are disappointed, Stephen," she said, "but she is everything I have ever wanted! I do not care one whit that she is not the son I promised," she added vehemently.

He looked at her wild, flashing eyes, her flushed cheeks. Then he leaped to his feet and leaned over, grabbing her close. "Oh, my love, I am only surprised. But disappointed? Never!" He showered her face with kisses until she wriggled free.

"Then look at your daughter," she said.

He watched, wide-eyed, as she pulled back the sheeting. Then he touched his daughter's tiny cheek lightly, marveling at its softness. As he fingered the infant's golden curls, his eyes filled with wonder.

"My daughter," he whispered, "my beautiful, precious little daughter."

Asa and Fernando tiptoed from the room, their eyes bright with tears.

Stephen remained in the apartment for several days. The

444

only problem that presented was his insistence that he hold the child whenever she was awake. It soon became evident that the bond between father and daughter was very strong, for the moment the baby was placed in his arms she stopped fussing and slept peacefully.

Joanna appeared at the door the fourth morning, out of breath and very distraught. "Dieter went on a mission without you, and he has not come back!" she cried. "I fear something dreadful has befallen him!"

Stephen cursed. "I have told him repeatedly not to go alone. How long has he been gone?"

"He left the day before yesterday. It was a long journey, but he should have returned by last night at the latest." She wrung her hands.

Shona pressed the baby into Stephen's arms. "I'll get Fernando," she said. "We'll ask him if he has heard anything."

Fernando could not recall talk in the shop about the capture of any Jews. The only thing he could state for certain, was that he had seen Muñoz walking by every morning and peering in the window, his lips pursed and his eyes hooded.

"There," Stephen said. "That means he has not been out with the militia. Dieter has probably had some sort of problem. Perhaps there was illness in the group."

"But he went after a husband and wife only!" Joanna said. "Surely two people would not take so long to bring to safety!"

Shona took the child from Stephen's arms. "You must go," she said softly. "We will be safe until you return."

Stephen pulled her into the bedroom and closed the door. "I do not want to leave you!" he murmured, pulling her close.

"I know you don't. But you must! Joanna is sick with worry, and I know just how she feels. But make your way through the streets with great care lest you run into Muñoz." She looked down at their daughter sleeping peacefully in her arms. "Return safely. We both need you."

*   *   *

445

Shona sat in a chair cradling her child, her fears for Stephen's safety settling like a dead weight in her breast. Surely he had made it safely through the streets or she would have heard something.

A soft rap on the door sent her to her feet, her heart pounding wildly. She laid the child on Fernando's cot and raced to the entrance, dreading what she would find. When she opened the door a crack, she almost collapsed with relief. Mother and Sister Claire stood on the stoop, their faces wreathed with smiles.

"We have heard the good news," Mother said. "May we see the child?"

"Of course. Come in!"

Shona proudly picked up her daughter.

"She looks like an angel," Sister Claire said, brushing tears from her eyes.

Shona laughed as she shifted the baby into the crook of her arm and sat on the kitchen chair Mother held ready. "She might look like an angel, but she's got her father's temper. You should hear her when she's hungry."

Mother tucked the blanket over the baby's feet. "What are you going to name her, child, or is it too soon to ask?"

"Not at all." Shona looked down at her child, her face shining with love. "Though I have to admit, I was planning on another Stephen, it was easy to decide once I saw her. We've named her Juana María. Juana after Stephen's sister, and my father whose name was John, and María after my mother Mary and Stephen's beloved Tía María."

Mother pulled a package from her skirts. "Then we have a gift for Juana María." She tore the paper away. "All the sisters helped with the sewing."

She held up a finely woven, long white gown edged with delicate lace and embroidered with tiny white flowers. Shona fingered the soft material.

"It's lovely!" she exclaimed. "Please give my thanks to everyone who helped. It must have taken weeks!"

446

"It's a baptismal gown," Sister Claire announced proudly. "We knew you would want the child baptized as soon as possible."

"That is quite enough, Sister," Mother scolded. "When Shona is strong enough, she will finish her own lessons and be confirmed. Then she will have the child baptized."

Shona looked up anxiously. "I've been meaning to ask you about that, Mother. Can she be baptized in Stephen's faith? I mean—"

"You don't have to explain, I know what you mean. I have already talked to Father Jerome. He will be most happy to perform the ceremony, once you have been received into the church. After all, you only have one more lesson; then you will be ready for your confirmation."

Shona smiled, but her heart was constricting with fear. "After you are confirmed, we will attend mass together," Muñoz had said.

Mother's sharp eyes caught the flicker of fear on the girl's face. "Is something the matter? You do not seem pleased."

"Oh, of course I'm pleased! I was just recalling a remark Señor Muñoz made the other day."

Mother straightened. "Sister Claire, I do believe Rebecca could use some help in the shop. Perhaps you would be so kind as to offer your services while I chat with Shona."

"Of course, Mother. I will come back as many times as I may, Shona, to see you and your precious little girl."

Mother waited until the door closed softly behind Sister Claire. "Now, we must talk," she said.

Shona began to tremble. "I told him about the baby, not that I had any choice, being as big as a horse."

Mother nodded. "Señor Muñoz came to see me after mass last Sunday. I must say, he seemed in good spirits. Of course, he was full of talk about his new home, and his plans for settling in New Orleans. He did say he felt you were misused in a most horrible way, but he felt that you had the moral stamina to overcome your past."

"Overcome my past! Why that . . . that . . ."

The baby began to cry and Mother took her from Shona's arms. "I will do everything I can to help you handle Señor Muñoz." She laid little Juana across her lap and gently patted the infant's back. "But I feel you may have erred in telling him the pirate was the father. You have told me how he hates your Étienne. Surely he will know the truth the moment he sees the child, and he told me he intends to visit you this Saturday."

Shona leaped up and began to pace. "He must never know!" she cried. "He hated Stephen, and he'll do anything he can to erase his line from the earth!"

"Surely you do not believe he would harm an innocent child!"

Shona stopped in front of her. "I believe it with all my heart. That's why he must not come near her! I have decided to tell him that she's sickly."

"That will not keep him away once he makes up his mind to see her."

"It must!" Shona collapsed into the chair, her hands over her face.

Mother patted her hand. "There, there," she crooned, "you are overwrought with fatigue. Fernando told me you are talking about returning to work in the shop. You cannot take care of this infant and resume your work. I am sending you Mignon. She can watch the child and keep your household running smoothly. We will think of some way to handle Señor Muñoz, but in the meantime you must accept Mignon's help."

"Oh, I can't!" Shona cried. "She has a life of her own. I can't ask her to help me after the way I treated her!"

"Her life is very much wrapped up with that giant friend of yours. I found her a very respectable husband, and she turned him down most ungraciously. I realize she did not work well in your shop, and I think I know your reasons for dismissing her. In the past, she has been somewhat of a flirt. But now she is sick with love for your Jephtha. She will leap at the chance to work so near him."

Shona nodded gratefully. "Then I'll accept her with open arms. I know it sounds crazy, but I miss the shop. There's something so fulfilling in providing what people need."

Mother nodded. "Have you found a priest?" she asked suddenly. "Though I have inquired discreetly, I have not been able to locate a single one I would trust."

"No," Shona said. "Stephen has sought one up and down the river. Sometimes I think it's hopeless."

"I would like very much to meet your Étienne."

Shona's face fell. "He's not here," she said. "He had to go off into the bayous and I'm sick with worry. There is a couple missing and . . ."

Mother held up her hand. "Say no more," she remonstrated. "The less I know, the better."

"But you will pray for them?"

"You know I will. Many times a day."

Shona was much calmer after Mother took her leave. After all, with the prayers of that holy woman added to her own, how could God not answer by guilding Stephen home safely by midnight, at least?

But her fears returned with a vengeance with the dawning of Saturday morning when there was still no word from Stephen.

Chapter 35

Shona moved about the shop in a trance, her mind a jumble of agonizing thoughts. Dear God, what had happened to Stephen? Though she had sent Jephtha to the settlement the evening before, he had not yet returned. How could she possibly endure the long, busy day ahead without some assurance that her beloved was safe? And to add to her misery, this was the day Muñoz had promised to visit!

She talked to customers, took their money, wrapped their purchases, yet all the time she felt she was operating much like the intricate French enameled clock in Mother's office, ticking away the time without a thought to the past or the future.

Her only distraction was the hasty trip she made upstairs to nurse Juana. Mignon had brushed aside Shona's apology and gone to work with a vengeance. Having been the oldest child in a house full of children, she was completely at ease caring for Juana and the apartment. Thus, Shona was grateful to find a contented (though hungry) child, and a spotlessly clean apartment.

By midafternoon, the oppressive heat had sapped the little strength she had nurtured so carefully. She asked Fernando to pull the sacking over the windows to keep out the beating sun; then she moved about in the shadows, wiping listlessly at the sweat pouring off her forehead.

She could see Rebecca eying her anxiously. "It's just the heat," she whispered. "I don't think I'll ever get used to it." The girl brought her a cup of cool water, and she drank it down in hasty gulps. The cold liquid hit her stomach with a rush, shocking her out of her torpor.

"Perhaps you should go upstairs and lie down. Fernando and I can manage alone now. It will soon be closing time."

Startled, Shona looked up quickly. "It's that late already?"

"You must not worry so. Señor Stephen is safe or you would have heard otherwise by now. I am sure Señor Jephtha will return at any moment with good news. And it does not appear that Señor Muñoz will come today, so please go up and rest."

She could not leave Rebecca and Fernando alone for she did not doubt that Muñoz intended to make a late arrival, after making her worry all day. "No, I'm better now. Here comes Mrs. Mevins. She hasn't set foot in here since Jephtha insulted her. I'd better see if I can smooth her ruffled feathers."

Shona took a great deal of time and care with Mrs. Mevins, but her mind was not on this difficult customer. She kept glancing at the open doorway, alternately praying that Jephtha would appear and dreading Muñoz's arrival.

Business slowed. Fernando waited on the last customer, then set about covering the counter with its dust cloth. While Rebecca was taking a hasty inventory in order to replace merchandise they had sold from the stock in the storeroom, Shona took the key from its hook and walked to the front door.

"I see I was almost too late."

The hated head with the arrogant face and prying eyes peered around the closing door. "I must see you. The Mother Superior told me you had had your child."

Shona quelled a rash impulse to slam the door and crush Muñoz's head like a ripe melon. Instead, she stepped aside and opened the door wide.

"Come in, *señor*."

Muñoz stepped inside. His eyes raked her body, sending goose flesh coursing over her arms and legs. "You are looking well," he said.

"I'm feeling fine." She could not bear his oily stare. She turned her back. "Please leave the door open," she said as she paced restlessly toward the counter. "It's stifling in here."

His footsteps rang on the planking. "I trust you have completely regained your health?"

She smoothed the sacking on the counter and cast a warning glance at Fernando, who looked as though he were about to speak. "I have told you, *señor*, I am feeling fine."

Rebecca came out of the storeroom laden with stacks of Rouen linen, and Shona humphed to herself when Muñoz made no move to help the burdened girl. Fernando quickly took the cloth and placed it on a shelf.

"You must not strain your back, Rebecca." Shona's voice sounded more cross than she'd intended. "You've worked far too long today, why don't you go home now?"

Rebecca glanced nervously at Muñoz who was examining her openly. "Asa is coming by for me," she whispered. Then her face brightened. "Here he is now."

Muñoz whirled like a snake about to strike. His thin neck rose from his shoulders as he eyed the bearded young man coming in the door. His aquiline nose rose high into the air, the nostrils flaring. "So . . ." he breathed out.

Asa's smile of greeting faded beneath Muñoz's scrutiny, and he did not make his usual good-natured small talk. He did not ask about the baby or Shona's strength, nor did he comment upon the sweltering weather or his own hectic day. Ignoring the heat pulsating in the shop, he grabbed Rebecca's shawl from her fingers and placed it firmly upon her shoulders.

"I've come to walk you home," he said in a low voice.

"I do not believe we have been introduced," Muñoz drawled insolently.

Shona patted Asa's shoulder and pushed Rebecca toward the door. "I'm sure you two have plans for the evening," she said, completely ignoring Muñoz's look of surprise. "Have a nice day off. I'll see you Monday morning."

She sighed with relief as the two made their hasty exit.

"Once again, you have exhibited rudeness," Muñoz snapped.

Fernando stiffened and dropped the stack of material he was arranging. "It is very hot, *señor*," he said belligerently, "and we are all tired. Perhaps you could make this visit a short one."

The two men stared at one another, hostility sparking between them.

"Fernando, why don't you go on upstairs?" Shona said quickly. "I'm dying for a bath. You can heat the water for me."

When she narrowed her eyes, silently commanding him to obey, he sighed. "Very well, Madonna," he growled. "But I hasten to remind you that you have been on your feet too long. Please come upstairs as soon as possible."

"I'll be up shortly."

Muñoz and Shona stood in silence until the door on the upstairs landing closed. Then Muñoz snarled deep in his throat, startling her. "I do not understand how you can surround yourself with such people! That old man is up to no good, hanging onto your skirts for support, and I'm convinced more than ever that those two are Jews! Just listen to their names, Rebecca and Asa!"

Shona's pent-up fear was instantly transformed into a bright bubble of anger. "I've heard enough from you on that subject!" she exclaimed. "Just exactly what do you have against the Jewish people?"

His face flushed, and he brushed aside her question with a violent toss of his head, which threatened to unseat the black net from his long dark hair. "I am certain those people are Jews," he declared vehemently. "They are making a fool of you!"

Realizing that no good would come from arguing with such a fanatic, Shona replaced the tea bags he had knocked from the counter. "I must go upstairs now," she said in a calmer voice. "It's late and Fernando is right, it has been a long day."

"What in hell's going on?"

Shona almost collapsed with relief as Jephtha stepped into the shop.

"Nothing, the *señor* was just leaving," she said hastily, her heart pounding. "Have you any news about . . . about that shipment from the settlement?"

Jephtha glared at Muñoz, then nodded his head briskly. "Yep, I sure do. That shipment is in perfect order. It should arrive any time."

She bit her lip to keep from exploding with joy. "That's good," she said quietly. "Mignon's upstairs. She'd love a visit."

"I'd better see the *señor* out and lock the door for you."

"That's all right. He is leaving. I'll be right up."

She watched Jephtha reluctantly climb the stairs, then she turned to Muñoz. He had unclenched his fists and was massaging his long, aesthetic-looking fingers. "I will go with you. I will see your child."

Shona's anger almost choked her. The very nerve! "No. You will not!" she exclaimed coldly. "I am not proud of the child. She is sickly and ugly. You will spare me the embarrassment of a visit."

His smile was twisted as though he derived pleasure from such news. "Then take my suggestion and place her in the convent. The sisters will treat her well."

Shona's gaze was unrelenting. "Perhaps I will, but in my own good time. Good evening, *señor*."

He stared at her wordlessly for a long moment, then stalked stiff-legged to the doorway. When he turned, she could not repress the gasp provoked by the look of hatred upon his face.

"Watch your child carefully, *señorita!*" he barked. "She is in danger of becoming a Jewish sacrifice! I will work day and night to prove to you that they are Jews!" He spun on his heel and threw himself out the door.

Muñoz paced angrily down Chartres Street. The little tramp was incredibly naive and rude. Why did he continue to involve himself in her affairs? He flicked his kerchief from his cuff and

455

mopped his forehead, then eyed the soiled cloth with distaste before dropping it into the dirt. The pervasive dust ever present in the air would filter through his clothing and cover every inch of his body, forcing him to bathe again tonight and further irritating his sensitive skin which already itched unmercifully from the harsh lye soap he insisted upon using. His mother's pious words echoed through his mind, "Cleanliness is next to godliness." He would bathe tonight.

He pushed a Negro slave roughly from his path and did not even look back as she sprawled onto the dusty street. Damned negroes. Damned Jews. They were the curse of the world! His brow creased and he clenched his hands behind his back as he walked swiftly toward his unfinished house. He usually took pleasure in the knowledge that his new home was situated in the elite part of town, directly across from the governor's Place d'Armes. This evening, he was too irritated to draw solace from anything.

Shona Cameron was a constant thorn in his flesh. She was so beautiful, so filled with life! He recalled the first time he had seen her, lying on the bunk on the *Loretta*, her huge yellow eyes wide and pleading. For only the second time in his life, he had felt drawn to a woman. He had agonized over his feelings of lust, praying upon his knees until the simple act of standing was torture. Yet, the God he served so zealously had refused to answer his prayers, as he had refused on that other horrible occasion when he'd been dismissed from the seminary. Why did his flesh torture him so? Why did he still dream of that young girl who worked in the seminary kitchen? Why could he not control the burning desire to feel Shona's soft, silken flesh beneath his fingers? His moribund manhood stirred at the thought of stroking her body. He slapped his fist into his palm and shouted, "No!", thereby startling a prowling dog into a violent fit of barking.

He kicked the mutt out of his way and strode on, ashamed before God that he would have to put the lash to good use again this night, for obviously the hair shirt he wore beneath his

456

black waistcoat was not uncomfortable enough to keep his mortal flesh from betraying him.

He fingered his beads, but his first Ave was interrupted by yet another horrible thought. What if Shona already knew her help was a Jewess? What if she was deliberately flaunting the girl just to anger him, just to show her own independence? He choked and broke into a violent fit of coughing. Surely this could not be true, not after he had sent that letter to Inez.

He had made such plans. Unable to locate Perez, and still unconvinced that Esteban de Larra was dead, he had, nevertheless, written Inez that her betrothed had fallen in a battle with pirates. He had then insisted that she join him in New Orleans, for he had no desire to assume the responsibility of maintaining the huge family estate now. His new home was large, and would provide ample room to house the three of them. Once she'd been properly instructed in the doctrines of the Church, Shona Cameron would make an admirable companion for his sister. Inez was delicate and prone to faintheartedness; the fiery young Scottish girl was just what she needed. And, if his inner feelings proved correct, and de Larra was not dead, what a sweet revenge his control over Shona would prove!

He laughed aloud. With his sister cared for by a suitable companion, he could bring to fruition his intricate plans for his own future. He was convinced that Spain would soon take over the Louisiana Territory from France. And he, Francisco Muñoz, would be in an admirable position to be chosen as its next governor!

The soft tinkle of the fountain situated in the courtyard of the Place d'Armes intruded on his thoughts. He walked quickly by, ignoring the bright candlelight flooding the lovely formal gardens situated in the center of the circular drive, his jealousy of the Marquis de Vaudreuil softened by the surety that he himself would one day live in that palace! He was spiritually strong. He would not allow himself to slip into decadent living, even when surrounded by such splendor.

As he crossed the road, his mind returned to Shona. He was certain she would soon welcome his offer of a new home, for the men he had hired to create a disturbance in her shop were planning a final, destructive incident in the near future. And the problem of the Jews? He pushed his way past the construction litter in his own courtyard, certain now that he had made the right decision. He would order his servant Diego to do the dirty work, thus freeing himself to plot his future course carefully. This very night, he would instruct Diego to hire as many men as he needed and to wait until Rebecca and Asa were away from their cottage before searching diligently for anything which would prove once and for all their miserable Jewish heritage. Once Diego had performed his mission, he would confront Shona with the proof in hand. Then let her tell him he was mistaken!

Chapter 36

Shona raced up the stairs to join Jephtha, Fernando, and Mignon. "Tell me about Stephen!" she said to Jephtha. "What has kept him away so long, didn't he know I'd be miserable with no word? How could he be so cold-hearted?"

He smiled and patted her shoulder awkwardly. "He couldn't help it, Shona. You know we don't get on so well, but this time you're dead wrong about him and I ain't afraid to tell you so!"

She turned her back so he could not see the tears filling her eyes. "Then tell me," she said brokenly. "I'm waiting."

"Well, they got held up in the bayou, that's for certain. That woman Dieter went to fetch turned out to be only a girl—younger than you, Mignon—and she was as fat as a melon ready for picking." He flushed again. "I mean, she was going to have a baby," he added hastily.

"A baby!" Shona exclaimed. "Dear God, what happened?"

"Well, she had the baby all right, only not one—two! And she almost died in the birthing. Dieter couldn't leave them to go for help because her husband was only a boy himself. So he waited, sure Joanna would send someone. And then Stephen got there."

Shona groaned. "First our child, then two more!"

Jephtha nodded. "It was a mess, all right. Here was this girl, holding two puny little babies wrapped in her husband's coat, and she was almost dead. Stephen and Dieter had to make a fire and boil water so's she could have something to drink. It was lucky for them that your man had the sense to take along some food, otherwise she would have died for sure."

Shona stared at him, her heart aching with concern. "But she's all right? They got back safely?"

"The babies lived?" Fernando asked, his forehead creased with worry.

Jephtha nodded. "They packed the girl full of moss to stop the bleeding, then they made a kind of bed from cypress branches and moss and drug it along behind them. It took them three days to travel only seven leagues. They reached the settlement yesterday about midday."

"And the babies? They're all right?"

"They sure are! Once Joanna give that girl several mugs of fresh cow's milk, she fed them babies so full they slept all afternoon!" He sat back, exhausted from his long recital, eying Mignon anxiously.

She smiled sweetly. "That was wonderful. Now, you both must eat. I have prepared a hearty stew."

Shona picked at her food while the others quietly discussed the day's happenings. With her fears for Stephen laid to rest, her mind had returned quickly to Muñoz and his visit. His parting words still rang in her ears. *"I will work day and night to prove to you they are Jews!"* She pushed her trencher away and sat staring at the dying embers in the fireplace.

"You must eat," Mignon chided, "or your milk will dry up."

"I can't. It sticks in my throat."

Jephtha reached across the table and grasped her hand. "You're fretting over Muñoz, aren't you! What did he threaten you with today?"

Shona squeezed his palm and cast him a warning glance. "Nothing special," she said. "Just his usual tirade."

"You don't have to worry about Mignon," he said. "I've told her everything. She doesn't have any bad notions about Jews."

When Shona jerked her hand away and turned to Fernando,

her eyes wide with fear, Mignon leaned forward.

"What Jephtha says is correct," she said earnestly. "My *père*, he had many professor friends who were Jewish. Though I have never met the man, I think that Monsieur Muñoz is horrible!"

The tight coil of terror slowly unwound from Shona's heart. "You must tell no one about Rebecca and Asa," she told Mignon sternly. "Muñoz has ways of finding out the most well-kept secrets and he said today that he intends to find proof of their faith."

The girl smiled sweetly. "It shall be our secret."

Jephtha slurped his tea noisily. "Why don't they just go to live in the German settlement. There's a new rabbi living there."

Shona's mouth flew open. "A rabbi? Are you sure? Why didn't Stephen tell me?"

"He had the birth of his child to distract him," Fernando said.

She stabbed a finger at Jephtha. "Then, why didn't you tell me?"

He pushed a piece of bread into his mouth. "Just did," he mumbled.

"How does this rabbi live among the Germans?" Fernando asked. "Do they accept him as one of them, or is he living there secretly?"

"It all looks pretty open to me," Jephtha said around another mouthful of bread. "There's a whole bunch of Jews living there now. The rabbi, he has a small cottage. One of the farmers showed me his place. Of course, none of those Germans are Catholics, so maybe that makes a difference."

Mignon tossed her head. "I am Catholic," she said with a sniff, "and I have nothing against them."

"He didn't mean anything, Mignon," Shona said soothingly. She leaped to her feet. "This is the news Rebecca and Asa have been waiting for! I've got to go tell them."

Fernando intercepted her at the door. "Not tonight,

461

Madonna. You cannot go walking the streets alone."

"Then come with me!"

He shook his head. "I am weary and you are reeling on your feet with fatigue. We will tell them the first thing Monday morning. Nothing can happen to them in one day. Besides, Esteban will be returning shortly. You surely want to be here to greet him."

"I'll greet him, all right." She exclaimed, "and then I'll give him a piece of my mind for not telling me about the rabbi!"

Fernando smiled. Though her words were harsh, he did not miss the bright spark of excitement flashing in her eyes.

Stephen crawled into their bed shortly after Shona had dropped off into a restless sleep. She awakened instantly and threw herself into the warm circle of his arms. He stroked her hair, murmuring soft words of love.

"Oh, I was so afraid something dreadful had happened to you," she mumbled against his chest. "Please hold me tighter."

"Did Jephtha explain? I told him to tell you why I was detained for so long."

She nodded and burrowed even closer. "Yes. Are the girl and her babies all right?"

"They are fine, though they could have used Asa's help. If only we could convince him to settle there. They need a physician desperately."

She suddenly pulled away. "You didn't tell me about the rabbi!" she exclaimed.

"I forgot. I had a few things on my mind. By the way, how is our daughter?"

"She's sleeping, so keep your voice down. She's a little pig and I'm not about to feed her again so soon. I—"

His lips claimed hers, and she fell against him, savoring the salty sweetness of his mouth upon hers. As his hands caressed her shoulders, her back, her thighs, she moaned.

"Love me, please love me," she gasped.

"It is too soon, my *tesora*, you know that."

"But I need you!"

"And I need you. Here, turn over and I will hold you. We will have to be satisfied with that for a while longer."

She nestled into his embrace, her heart heavy with rebellion. Too soon! Dear God, how long would she have to wait to feel him within her? His hands moved over her back, tenderly easing her knotted muscles. Then she began to smile. As Stephen had shown her, there was more than one way to skin a cat!

She caressed his chest, her fingers tangling provocatively in the mat of dark blond hair. Her smile broadened as his breath quickened, and she pressed her lips against his, her tongue probing.

When he pulled away with a loud groan, she smiled temptingly at him, her eyes provocative and alluring. Then she ran her tongue over her reddened lips.

"Witch!" he exclaimed. In one lithe movement he rolled over on top of her, his hands pinning hers above her head, his mouth claiming hers fiercely. She twined her tongue around his, revelling in his sweetness.

Then he released her hands, her mouth moved down his chest, her lips pulling at the matted hairs with teasing tweaks. He moaned as her caresses trailed down his firm belly, then he gasped aloud as she took his swollen manhood in her mouth. She rolled her tongue provocatively up and down his helpless flesh, her hands kneading his buttocks.

He waited until he felt ready to explode, then he pulled away and rose to his knees, his fingers and lips alternating between her two delicious breasts. She acquiesced willingly, moaning softly as his caressing fingers and probing tongue turned her blood to molten lava.

For an endless time, they kissed and fondled and stroked, their hands and mouths giving silent expression to their raging passion. Higher, higher they soared, their bodies writhing, their hearts pounding, their blood pulsing.

Then they were crying out together as the heavens exploded

463

with blazing, splintered light, showering their bodies with particles of splendor.

Satiated at last, in one another's arms, they caressed each other languidly until their ragged breathing slowed and sleep claimed them.

Shona spent a miserable Sunday. Though she was filled with gratitude for Stephen's safe return and for the night they had spent making sweet, delightful love, she was terribly worried about Asa's and Rebecca's safety. Even Stephen could not convince her that Monday would be time enough to warn them about Muñoz's threat. His angry words rang out over and over again in her mind until she thought she would go mad with worry.

She tossed and turned in bed on Sunday night, and was finally forced to rise lest she awaken or, even worse, roll over on the baby. She paced the floor in the darkness, fanning her face and sighing deeply. When she began to stumble with weariness, she returned to bed, but nightmares plagued her exhausted sleep. Time after time she dreamed of Stephen falling to the deck of the *Loretta*, a startled look upon his face, the front of his shirt splotched with a bright patch of blood. She huddled against him, trembling with fear.

When morning dawned, she rose reluctantly, feeling as though she had not slept a wink. Stephen was busy mapping out a plan for setting up some sort of warning system, and Juana, who was cross, cried loudly even after she left Shona's breast. Shona walked the floor with the infant, irritated that this morning, of all times, Juana had to be naughty.

It was well past ten before Juana dropped off to sleep. Shona laid her on the bed and tiptoed from the bedroom. She raised a finger to her lips and motioned Mignon and Stephen to be very quiet. They nodded. Then Stephen went back to his plans.

"Little Juana will sleep for a long time," Mignon whispered. "Would you like a cup of tea?"

Shona shook her head. "I've got to go downstairs and tell Rebecca the news."

But because it was Monday morning and the shop was crowded with customers, it was late in the afternoon before Shona could share Jephtha's account of the rabbi with Rebecca, and when she did she was glad she had waited until the store was empty.

"A rabbi!" Rebecca exclaimed. She danced about the shop, her large gray eyes brimming with joy. "I cannot wait to tell Asa! He will be so excited!"

Fernando caught the whirling girl. "You'll fall and break your neck," he cautioned. "Do calm down before you hurt yourself."

Rebecca hugged him, then threw herself into Shona's arms. "Do you know what this means?" she exclaimed. "We can be married!"

"And you can live in the German settlement, for Stephen and Dieter have brought in over thirty Jews and they have been well received by the Germans."

Rebecca's smile faded, and she dropped her hands at her side. "I fear Asa will never change his mind about leaving New Orleans," she said sadly. "He is planning to have his own patients."

"But they need a physician in the settlement," Shona said. "And Asa has said that only the most poor will call upon him here. In the settlement he can help everyone. You must try to change his mind. Just think, Rebecca, you could live without fear there!"

The girl made a face. "I have heard that before," she said. "But I will try to talk to Asa about moving. Oh, he is here now!"

Asa remained adamant—he would not leave New Orleans—but he was eager to discuss the plans for their wedding. The four retired to the upper story, where, joined by Stephen and Mignon, they talked about when and how they would accomplish that long-awaited event.

465

"I will stay with Juana, if you are not gone too long," Mignon offered.

Shona shook her head. "That won't work. The trip upriver is much too long. I'll take her with me, and that way, you can have a whole day to yourself."

Mignon pouted. "But I've never seen a Jewish wedding."

Shona grabbed her and whirled her around. "Then you'll go with us! We'll all go. Sometime this week!"

Stephen cleared his throat loudly. "I fear you are being presumptuous," he said. "Asa should travel with Jephtha to the settlement and discuss the arrangements with the rabbi. Perhaps that gentleman has other duties this week."

Jephtha was dragged from his forge by a bubbly Mignon, and forced up the stairs to join in the plans. After much discussion, it was agreed that time was of the essence, so Jephtha and Asa made plans to meet at the dock on the following morning.

They returned late Tuesday night, dusty and tired, but exuberant. The rabbi, a young man of Asa's age, had agreed to marry them on the sixth day, Friday, so the young couple could have the Sabbath alone at home. The two had remained silent about Rebecca being forced to work, lest they antagonize the rabbi. Asa admitted the rabbi had been reluctant to perform the marriage at first. He'd had to be assured that the couple had followed the custom of a full year's betrothal, but he'd finally taken Asa's word that they had. Jephtha had agreed to act in Rebecca's father's place, and a simple marriage agreement had been drawn up.

Rebecca, however, was strangely quiet after Asa and Jephtha had shared their day's experiences, and it took Shona several minutes to draw the truth from her.

"But that's silly!" Shona exclaimed. "I'll just close the shop! We've made so much profit this month, one day won't kill us."

She was much too preoccupied to notice the smile of satisfaction upon Stephen's face.

After the others had gone, he led her firmly to a chair.

"There has been too much excitement," he said after he had her comfortably seated. "Your face is drawn and you are getting much too thin."

"It's all that milk our little monster is drinking," she laughed. "You have fathered a little pig!"

"You seem so sad when you talk about the wedding. Is something bothering you?"

She dropped her eyes. "I guess I'm a little jealous," she whispered.

He drew her up into his arms. "Our time will come," he said. "If I do not find a priest soon, we will be married by anyone willing to perform the rite."

"But we can't marry outside of your Church. You have said yourself that such a marriage would be a farce."

He cupped her chin and stared down into her face. "That was before I realized how very much I want to make you mine completely." He kissed the tip of her nose. "We will discuss this later. I do not like your paleness. It will do you good to get away for a day. But are you sure little Juana is old enough to make the journey on the river?"

"Of course. The fresh air will do her good."

"Perhaps Rebecca and Asa should have waited a few weeks. Both you and Juana will be much stronger then."

"They can't wait! Have you forgotten Muñoz? He is always causing trouble. He won't rest until he has found his proof!"

Stephen groaned. "I will be so happy when I can put an end to his troublemaking. I did not tell you, but Fernando told me yesterday that Muñoz left New Orleans heading a large detachment of militia. I must find out what he is up to."

"You're not leaving again so soon!"

"I must. I will meet you at the settlement on Friday. Come to bed. I want to hold you until it is time for me to take my leave."

She placed a finger to her lips and nodded toward Fernando's bedroom. Then they tiptoed with exaggerated care into their own bedroom and Stephen closed the door softly. Shona checked Juana, who was fast asleep in her new cradle in the far corner, before they fell onto the bed, giggling like children about to venture forth on a forbidden bit of mischief.

Stephen undressed her slowly, fumbling deliberately at her laces, grimacing and uttering childish oaths under his breath, causing her to double over with laughter. She pretended wide-eyed innocence when he knelt beside her on the mattress, devouring her with his deep blue eyes. In response, he tweaked one breast, then the other.

"And what, pray tell, are you doing, sir?" she asked primly.

"I am playing with my beloved," he answered with a wide grin.

Then he dove on top of her, pinning her hands with his own and nuzzling her face. Shona writhed delightedly and bit at his ear lobes, thrusting her hips forward to meet his heated thrusts.

As he moved lower and pressed her thighs apart to thrust his tongue against her quivering mound, she tangled her fingers in his hair, pulling his face even closer, her body burning with frantic desire. He lapped, he kissed, he fondled, until she was writhing beneath him. Then he rose up, took her in his arms, and cradled her close, his lips claiming hers.

They played for hours, expressing their love with throaty whispers, sporadic bursts of plying fingers, and long, lingering kisses—his imminent departure forgotten in their fevered, joyous coupling.

Then they made love again, this time with great tenderness. He whispered words of endearment, and her love-filled eyes spoke eloquently of her adoration as he brought her slowly, gently to fulfillment. Together, they felt the earth tilt beneath them. Together, they breathed their soft cries of completion. Then they slept, their bodies close, their faces barely apart.

When Juana's lusty, hungry cries awakened them sometime in the early morning hours, Shona leaped up, her breasts dripping as she made her way hastily to the cradle. Stephen dressed while she fed their daughter, and only the babe's satisfied gulps and gurgles broke the silence. There was no need for small talk, nor for any expression of fear at his leave-taking. They had placed a final seal on their love. It would endure any separation.

The remaining days before the wedding passed slowly. Shona buried herself in her work, grateful that business was brisk. By Thursday afternoon, her excitement was at fever pitch, but Rebecca was trembling so that she constantly dropped things and even Fernando's usually calm façade was shattered. He approached Shona several hours before closing time with the suggestion that they lock up early so they might prepare for the coming day.

She eyed the few customers milling about. "Perhaps we should," she admitted finally. "I'll put the closed sign in the window and draw the curtains."

But when she approached the window, she gasped, her hand going to her throat. Several burly men were crossing the street to the shop, their faces dark and glowering. She whirled about.

"Quick!" she shouted to Fernando. "Get Jephtha. There's going to be trouble!"

She pushed the door closed and pressed the key into the lock. But she was too late. She heard a woman customer scream as the door splintered beneath a heavily booted foot, and she found herself staring up into a bearded, scowling face as a man shoved his way into the shop. He was quickly followed by three others. The leader pushed her aside roughly.

"We've come to put you out of business!" he roared.

He grinned broadly as he pushed a pile of thread stockings onto the floor, then an entire shelf of English shoes. A violent flash of anger burst through Shona. She dashed to the wall and pulled down a piece of heavily ironed harness. Twirling it over her head, she lashed this way and that, scattering the men as they attempted to overturn barrels and trample on the contents. One of the intruders screamed and clutched his bleeding cheek.

Instantly, the harness was yanked from her grasp, and she

469

was gripped from behind. Strong hands sought her throat. Though she twisted and turned, she could not escape the iron grip. She fought for breath, panic flooding over her. Through the haze that clouded her vision, she saw Fernando. He was trying to make it to her. She knew he would never reach her in time.

But the hands suddenly loosened as a loud roar almost burst her eardrums. Rebecca stood beside her, triumphantly eying the long, bloody hatpin she clenched in her fist. Shona staggered backward and collided with a man clutching a bleeding wrist.

She glanced over her shoulder as another roar filled the room. She could not believe her eyes. Mrs. Mevins, wielding a large iron spider like a club, was battering one of the intruders across the head and shoulders, a satisfied smile pursing her prim lips! Another customer—a small black woman from a downriver plantation—was brandishing a pitchfork, her black eyes sparkling with glee!

Fernando thrust the harness back into Shona's hands and waded into the fracas, his own weapon the heavy lid of a barrel. She laughed exultantly as the four men were driven across the shop. "Take that you bastard!" she screamed as the heavy iron ring at the end of the harness banged against one of their heads with a satisfying thud.

"I'll kill you for that!" the man bellowed.

"Oh, no you won't," another customer, Mrs. Collins, a tiny, delicate woman who had six equally delicate daughters, declared just before bringing a heavy iron spade down upon that man's head. She watched him crumple to the ground; then she triumphantly rubbed her small gloved hands together.

Jephtha then bulled his way through the splintered door of the shop, his eyes wild. He grasped the man lying at Shona's feet by the seat of his pants and tossed him onto the sidewalk, disposing of his three cohorts in a similar fashion.

Shona eyed the overturned stock, the utter shambles her

shop had become. She could not decide whether to laugh or cry. Fernando was trying to take the spider from Mrs. Mevins who was protesting loudly. Rebecca and Mrs. Collins were looking at their soiled gowns, and their shoulders were shaking with laughter. The little black woman was hugging herself, her rich laughter rolling out in waves. Shona joined in; she laughed until she could scarcely get her breath.

"We showed them no-gooders!" the slave hooted. "They won't be back afore a month of Sundays!"

"They'll never come back, but if they do, we'll give it to them again!" Mrs. Collins shouted.

Mrs. Mevins banged the spider on the counter. "There'd better not be a next time; we'll beat them into a pulp!" she cried out.

Jephtha grabbed Shona. "Are you all right? Did they hurt you?"

She gently pushed away, and laughed. "I'm fine! With friends like these I could face the entire French militia!"

Mrs. Mevins laid down her spider and looked around, her hands on her hips. "Well, if we're going to fight the militia, we'd better straighten up this place before they arrive."

"Oh, you can't!" Shona protested. "I can never thank you enough for your help. You go on home. I'll have Jephtha repair the door, then we'll clean up."

The unlikely trio of customers shook their heads in unison. "Not on your life, we're going to help," Mrs. Collins said. "This shop is the only one in town with decent merchandise at prices we can afford."

The other two nodded.

"I'd pay you to help after the way this took my mind off my rheumatism miseries!" the black woman laughed.

Shona embraced them and stood back, shaking her head. "Rebecca, break out the aprons. We've a big job ahead of us."

At Stephen's side, Shona wept softly all through Asa and

471

Rebecca's short wedding ceremony. Though she had been warned that many of the customary rites had been set aside due to lack of time, she found the simple ceremony strangely moving. Rebecca looked lovely in the pale blue gown Shona had given her, and her gray eyes shone softly through the delicate lace veil she had retrieved from its hiding place for this glorious occasion. Asa stood proudly at her side, wearing his best shirt and breeches. He had trimmed his beard and pulled curls of hair to the front of his ears, as the rabbi did, and his prayer shawl gave him a serious and mature air. The two stood beneath the traditional wedding canopy. First, they stated that they had both fasted, as an atonement for their past sins. The rabbi then intoned the Psalm of Thanksgiving, and offered the bride and groom a sip of wine from the cup he held. When the rabbi nodded his head, his wife and two young sons, holding lighted candles aloft, marched solemnly around the couple seven times. Asa then slipped a thin gold band upon Rebecca's trembling finger, reciting his words in a clear voice.

Shona glanced at Mignon. The girl was watching the ceremony with tears in her eyes, her hand tightly clutched in Jephtha's huge paw.

The rabbi uttered the Seven Nuptial Blessings, and passed a new cup of wine for the couple to share. Rebecca sipped from one side, Asa from the other. Shona was astounded when Asa then threw the cup to the ground and stomped on it.

The rabbi's wife and sons shouted *"Mazel tov!"* so loudly that Juana, who had been lying asleep in Shona's arms, awakened and began to scream.

Stephen immediately took his daughter, and Shona joined the others congratulating the couple. The rabbi's wife approached her with a smile.

"Perhaps you would like to use our home to feed your infant," she said in a heavily accented voice. "We have prepared a simple wedding feast with the gold coin that tall young man gave us," she added, nodding toward Stephen.

"I would like that," Shona said. "She slept all the way

upriver and she's ravenous."

"Then, come. Our home is small and we have not been here long enough to be completely settled, but we are grateful to Elohim every moment for our good fortune."

Shona retrieved Juana and fell into step beside the rabbi's wife. "Are you happy here? It's not at all like New Orleans."

The woman trilled a laugh. "Oh, my dear, we are never accepted completely. But the people here are Germans, like us. They are good people, and hard workers. They do not bother us, and we do not bother them. They made only one stipulation when we came here—that we not try to convert any of their people." She laughed again. "So we tend our farm and wait for other Jews to join us." She leaned closer. "Of course, it is hard for my husband, not having any official duties to perform. This wedding has brought a sparkle to his eyes."

"I'm sure you're disappointed that Asa is adamant about not moving away from New Orleans."

The woman sighed. "Of course. It would be very encouraging to have that lovely young couple beside us—but we will survive. Our people have lived through the most cruel persecutions. Here, it is like a paradise!"

Shona paused at the doorway of the tiny wooden house. "Are you sure you want all of us to come in? I understand it isn't customary for Jews to break bread with Gentiles."

The woman clucked her tongue and shook her head sadly. "Alas, that is the way of some of our people. But we are from Germany, and our customs are different. Come in! Come in!"

The meal was spread on a wooden plank set in the middle of the great room. Brightly burning candles gave the occasion a festive air and soon everyone was eating and talking loudly. Shona greeted Joanna who introduced her to Dieter and to little Johann. She had one bad moment when Stephen brought Trista Becher to meet her, but it passed quickly for the beautiful young girl excused herself from the festivities, pleading a headache.

Stephen sat at the table beside the Warners while Shona sat

in the corner, a piece of sacking hiding her suckling infant. She looked longingly at Asa and Rebecca who sat with their heads together, their hands entwined. It was not fair. She and Stephen should have a wedding feast such as this. They should be looking, with love, at one another across a marriage cup.

She placed Juana across her shoulder and patted her until the infant burped loudly. Then she sat rocking her child quietly while the festivities continued. She regretted that Stephen would be forced to wait until nightfall to return to New Orleans. How she would have enjoyed his presence on the barge! When he looked longingly in her direction, her hurt was eased by the knowledge that he shared her thoughts.

The gay group sang songs and told jokes much of the journey downriver, and Shona joined in, her pensiveness swept away by the joyous mood of the others. As they neared the dock in New Orleans, the veil and prayer shawl were quickly hidden, and the songs and jests died in throats suddenly constricted by the fear that pervaded their lives.

The little party accompanied Asa and Rebecca to their cottage and then left them sighing and looking shyly at one another. As they proceeded homeward Jephtha momentarily forgot how frightened he was of infants, and lifted Juana up into his arms.

"You look done in," he said to Shona. "I'll carry her home for you."

They walked quietly, Mignon beside Jephtha. She moved as though in a dream, a soft smile lighting her pretty face. Shona motioned to Fernando to drop back with her.

"I feel there will be another wedding soon," she whispered.

He nodded, and gave a tired smile. "I hope they wait for a while," he said softly. "I am too old to go through such festivities often."

Shona tucked the sleeping Juana into bed, then returned to the kitchen to share a cup of tea with the others. They were subdued now and their conversation was limited, for it had been a long, exhausting day. Still, there was a camaraderie in the air, and each basked in the friendship shared with the others. Their talk had now turned to the riot at the shop the day before, and they discussed the unexpected help they had received.

Their peaceful exchange was suddenly interrupted by a loud banging on the shop door. Shona leaped to her feet, upsetting her teacup in her haste, and one hand flew to her throat.

"Who on earth can that be?" Mignon shrilled.

Jephtha caught Shona's arm. "Don't answer. No good news comes so late at night."

"But I must! Someone may be in trouble!"

Fernando pushed Shona back into her chair. "I will go. You stay here, and lock the door behind me."

"I'm going too," Jephtha growled.

Shona and Mignon waited breathlessly as the moments ticked by. Shona was sure it was Muñoz, but why did she hear no raised voices? At last, footsteps rang on the stairs. She rose and clasped her hands tightly together.

The door opened, and she breathed a sigh of relief as Fernando and Jephtha stepped inside. But her breath froze in her throat when she recognized the man following them— Diego Izquierdo, Muñoz's servant!

Izquierdo bowed, but she did not acknowledge his show of manners. "What are you doing here?" she asked harshly.

He gestured to Fernando. "Perhaps you should tell her, *amigo*," he said, his voice quavering. "I am too old, and afraid."

He swayed and would have fallen, but for Jephtha's steadying arms.

It was only then that Shona noticed the pallor of Fernando's face and the angry set of Jephtha's mouth.

"Seat him over here." Shona gestured toward a chair, then went to stand stiffly before the man. "Now tell me why you have come."

He looked helplessly up at Fernando. "Please . . ." he whispered.

Shona whirled about. "Will one of you tell me what is going on? You're frightening me to death, and look at poor Mignon. Her face is stark white."

Fernando took her arm, but she wrenched it away from him. "I'm not going to stand for this! What is going on?"

"It is Muñoz," Fernando said at last. "He has found the proof he was seeking. He has gone to the governor's house to convince him to call out the militia to arrest Asa and Rebecca."

Chapter 37

Shona stared at Fernando in horror. Then she collapsed into a chair. "But how? What could he possibly find?"

Izquierdo bowed his head. "He ordered me to search their home. The men who were helping me found a loose floorboard. It took very little digging to unearth several things, including a candle holder and a ruby amulet."

Shona groaned inwardly. Why had she returned the amulet to Rebecca after Juana's birth? "But that doesn't prove they're Jews!" she exclaimed.

"The amulet does," Izquierdo said. "As does a prayer shawl. Señor Muñoz is an expert on what to look for. He was well trained by the Inquisition."

Shona leaped to her feet and began to pace. "You're despicable," she said to Izquierdo. "You should be horse-whipped for what you've done!"

Fernando intercepted her. "Please, Madonna, you should be grateful that Diego was willing to come here to tell you. He knows what Señor Muñoz is doing is wrong, and he has placed his own life in grave danger."

She pushed Fernando aside. "Jephtha, come with me. We've got to get Rebecca and Asa out of New Orleans."

"We must wait for Esteban to return!" Fernando cried. "He will know what to do!"

"There isn't time," Shona said firmly.

"Then let Jephtha go alone," Fernando cried. "You must not place your own life in danger."

Shona whirled about. "I will not let Muñoz ruin any more lives! I know he won't harm me!"

"And your child?" Fernando asked quietly. "You think he will not harm her?"

Shona stared at him, her breast heaving with emotion.

"He's right, Shona," Jephtha said. "I'll go warn them. You stay here with the others."

She pushed him aside. "No! I'll go with you. Fernando and Mignon can take Juana to the convent, and warn Mother about what is happening. Mother will find a wet nurse in case I am delayed."

"I do not want my Jephtha to be in danger," Mignon said in a small voice.

Shona wanted to scream out her scorn, but a sudden picture of Stephen falling to the deck flashed before her eyes. She put her arms around the girl and hugged her. "Nothing's going to happen to him," she said. "If we hurry, we'll get them out long before the governor can muster his troops."

"I must get back to the house before Señor Muñoz returns," Izquierdo said. "But I wish you all Godspeed."

Shona and Jephtha hurried through the back streets, avoiding the pools of light spilling out of the windows. She did not know what Jephtha was thinking, but she now regretted her brave words. The closer she got to Rebecca and Asa's cottage, the harder her heart pounded, for she had lied when she'd said she knew Muñoz would not harm her. She was sure he would stop at nothing to be rid of the Jews.

They skirted a clump of patio banana trees and crept around the last house separating them from their destination. The back of Asa's cottage was dark, and Shona prayed that the newlyweds had not retired for the night. She breathed a sigh of relief when she saw that a single candle shone from a front window.

She tiptoed up onto the porch and rapped lightly on the door. Jephtha smiled grimly at her when the squeaking of a bed frame sounded in the stillness. She rapped again. "Asa!" she hissed. "Hurry, it's Shona!"

Moments later, the door was opened a few inches and Asa's face appeared in the crack. Then he threw the door wide. "What is the matter?" he asked. "Why have you come?"

Shona and Jephtha pushed their way into the house. Rebecca sat on the side of the bed, her hands smoothing her wrinkled bed gown. "You haven't any time to lose," Shona said urgently. "Muñoz dug up your treasures while we were at the wedding. He's gone to the governor for the militia."

Asa rushed to a small rug in the corner and threw it back. He pried a board from the floor and gave a small cry. "It's gone!" he exclaimed. "All of it!"

He ran to Rebecca. "Hurry!" he urged with a shaking voice. "Get dressed! We have been found out."

Shona helped Rebecca into her clothes while Jephtha and Asa collected a few of their belongings and wrapped them in a blanket. When Rebecca was dressed, she looked about frantically. "But how did he find out? What are we to do? Where are we to go?"

Shona threw a blanket over the girl's quivering shoulders. "Jephtha will explain everything later. He'll take you upriver to the rabbi. You can hide there until we send word that everything's all right."

"But Asa's practice!" Rebecca wailed. "He has made such plans."

Asa pulled her into his arms. "We will stay at the settlement as long as we must," he said softly. He smoothed the hair back from her forehead. "As long as we have each other, we have everything."

"Better hurry," Jephtha grunted. "I'll carry your bundle."

The four crept down the porch stairs and around to the back

of the cottage. There, Shona embraced Rebecca and gave Asa a hasty kiss on the cheek. "Go with God," she whispered.

She stood in the shadows, watching the three scurrying figures until they were out of sight. Then, she sighed deeply and began her lonely journey home, her mind filled with prayers for the safety of her friends. The barking coughs of the alligators in the bayou on the outskirts of town made her flesh crawl with dread. Perhaps it was just the dark night, and her solitude, that made her edgy, but as she neared the business district, even the hilarious laughter from the numerous taverns did nothing to lessen her growing certainty that something dreadful was about to happen.

At last she reached her shop, gasping for breath and bathed in sweat. She checked the curtains to make sure they were completely closed, then she locked the front door firmly behind her. Upstairs, she groped for her bedroom door, unwilling to light a candle lest Muñoz walk by and wonder what was keeping her up so late.

She undressed quickly and donned her lightest bed gown, for sweat was rolling down her body. Then she threw herself onto bed and clutched the bolster to her breast. Why did something always happen to upset her happiness? She smoothed the sheet beside her, longing to reach out and touch the form of her sleeping child. It was not fair! Asa and Rebecca were such decent people! They only wanted to live their lives in peace.

She threw herself onto her stomach. What was keeping Fernando? He should have made it back to the apartment before her! And where was Stephen? It had been dark for several hours! Unable to quiet her pounding heart, she leaped out of bed and groped her way into the great room. Though she was still sweating, chills coursed over her body, and she could not rid herself of the fear that something awful was about to happen.

She paced the floor in the dark, clutching her gown about her shoulders. Perhaps Mother had sent Fernando to fetch a wet nurse. Or perhaps the sisters had all been abed and Fernando had been forced to stand at the gate for a long time, waiting for the bell to rouse them. Her shoulders slumped. Mignon, who still lived at the convent, had a key to the back gate. Shona stumbled over a chair and cursed the darkness. This was ridiculous, hiding in her own home!

She sat in the chair and rocked back and forth, her body suddenly filled with a frantic longing for Stephen's strong arms. Why couldn't he be here—now—with her? Why must she sit alone in the dark without his comforting presence? She dropped her head into her arms and moaned as bright pictures of Stephen's face appeared before her eyes. His azure eyes sparkled with laughter, and that damnable right eyebrow rose in mock disdain. He was so real, she could smell the fragrance of his body, and the pulse in her throat leaped. She reached out her hands, but he faded into the darkness.

She sobbed and jumped up. To hell with Muñoz! She was going to have light, or go mad! She crept carefully toward the fireplace. If there was even one little ember glowing beneath the bed of coals, she could stir it into enough light to chase away the mind pictures haunting her. She reached for the poker, but her hand froze in midair. What was that sound? She strained, but only the thudding of her own heart sounded in her ears. She humphed to herself and groped for the poker. Again her hand froze. Someone was rattling the front door of the shop!

She crouched before the fireplace, her hand at her throat. Had Fernando lost his key? No, surely he hadn't. And even if he had, he would knock on the door, not rattle it impatiently. Perhaps Stephen had forgotten his key, and was letting her know he had arrived. The tinkle of breaking glass drove her to her feet.

She backed into the table and stood immobile, staring in the direction of the door. Was that footsteps on the stairs? Her breath came in gasps as though it was being choked from her lungs. She pressed her way around the table and, dropping to her hands and knees, crept toward her bedroom door. Why hadn't she locked the apartment door? Why had she been so stupid?

The footsteps grew louder, and she huddled against the wall, her arms and legs refusing to obey her frantic signals. She heard the doorknob turn, the hinges squeak softly. Then a bright light suddenly flooded the room. Her breath left her body. Francisco Muñoz stood in the doorway, a lantern held high above his head!

She shrank lower as he swept the light in a slow arc from right to left. God, don't let him see me, she prayed.

His short barking laugh dried the last bit of saliva in her mouth.

"So, Señorita Cameron! Do you always crawl about on the floor in the dark?"

His sneering, arrogant tone sparked the fire of hatred within her breast. She pushed herself to her feet. "No. Do you always break into people's homes?" she croaked. "I thought you were a thief!"

He placed the lantern on the table and bounded across the room. "Don't lie!" he spat out. "You knew it was me! What have you done with them?" He grasped her arm and twisted it cruelly. "Tell me where you have hidden them!"

Pain fueled Shona's anger. "Let me go you pious, lying bastard!" she screamed.

He bent her arm behind her back. "You are a slut!" he shouted, "but I know how to deal with sluts!" He forced her head back against the wall. "Now, you will tell me where you have hidden those pagan Jews, and I will help you rid your soul of its sin!"

The pain in her arm was excruciating, but not as horrible as his hot breath on her cheek. When she tried to pull away, he slammed her against the wall.

"Where is the girl and her lover?" he purred softly. "You will tell me."

"I don't know what you're talking about!" she gasped. "Let

go, you're hurting me!"

"Would you rather feel the fires of hell? That is where you will spend eternity if you do not cleanse your soul of your sin! Where is the one you call Rebecca? I have found the proof I was seeking."

Shona stared into his eyes, sure she could see the fires of hell flickering in their black depths. "Rebecca's not a Jew!" she gasped. "You couldn't have found proof."

He dropped her arm and reached into his waistband. "And what do you call this?" He dangled the ruby amulet before her face. "I have seen many like this. Do you see the way the setting is shaped? It is the Star of David!"

Shona stared at the sparkling stone, ruby red like the blood she was about to shed. "I'll never tell you!" she whispered.

He tucked the amulet back into his waistband as he stepped back. "So, you did know they were Jews!"

Shona rubbed her throbbing arm. "You'll never find them. They've gone far away!"

He shook his head slowly. "Perhaps," he said so softly she could barely hear. "But you have lied to me about two very important things. You must be punished."

"What are you talking about? I've not lied to you about anything else!"

He grasped both of her wrists and pulled her close. "Oh, yes you have," he breathed. "You led me to believe that you had a meaningless romp with de Larra. Instead, you were consorting with him regularly, while he was betrothed to Inez!" He pressed his face close to hers. "And, less than an hour ago, my men intercepted a certain Fernando Mendoza on the verge of Jackson Square. He was hurrying toward the convent, and in his arms was a very important burden."

A red haze appeared before Shona's eyes. "My baby! What have you done to my baby?"

He stared down his nose at her. "Esteban de Larra's infant and his mewling servant have been taken to my home. They will remain there until you have been cleansed of your sins."

"No!" Shona wrenched away, but he caught her firmly in his arms. She kicked at his shins and sank her teeth into his hand. In return, he pushed her against the wall and brought back his arm. The last thing she remembered was the blur of his fist before her eyes.

Fernando rocked the sleeping infant back and forth in his arms as he paced the dirt floor of the small shed confining them. He had to find a way out, for little Juana would surely awaken and begin to cry for food soon! He pressed his face to a crack in the door, but he could see only darkness. He turned to the small lantern resting on the floor in the corner. No. It would be too dangerous to start a fire. If only he was alone . . .

He knelt in the dirt and clasped the baby close, wondering what had happened to Shona and the others. He was grateful that he had been able to warn Mignon away when he'd seen the strangers beginning to surround them, but she was the only one he could be sure was safe. He groaned and closed his eyes tightly. "Oh, God," he prayed, "please keep Shona safe. And deliver her child from this terrible place." He transferred the child to the crook of his left arm and crossed himself reverently.

Then his hand stopped in midair. He heard footsteps approaching. He cradled the baby close to his chest and got stiffly to his feet, prepared to defend the life of Esteban's child. As a key rasped in the lock, he backed into a corner. When the door swung open, he released his breath in a loud hiss.

"Diego!"

Izquierdo stepped inside and closed the door quickly. "Quiet!" he warned. "There may be some of the men around."

"You must get us out of here!" Fernando whispered. "The infant needs changing and feeding!"

"That is why I have come. But we must go quickly. I do not know when the Señor will return."

"You were always a good man, Diego. I prayed to God for his

help, and he sent you!"

Diego shook his head. "Don't thank God, Fernando," he said with a grimace. "I am not sure I believe anymore after serving the Señor for so long. Thank instead the fact that we are distant cousins by marriage. Here, put this dark blanket over you and the child. We must not be seen."

Fernando smiled broadly. "We will go to the convent. The child will be safe there."

Diego nodded. "Come, let us hurry!" He left the lantern burning where it was and opened the door. "I am locking the door," he muttered. "With the light shining from the cracks and the door locked, we may buy a little time. I will lead the way. Follow as closely and as quietly as you can."

The men hurried into the trees at the side of the house, making their way quickly toward the back of the undergrowth where the darkness was deepest. Then Fernando tripped.

"Slow down!" he whispered. "I might drop the baby!"

He followed Diego's dark outline through the weeds at the edge of the levee. When a mosquito buzzed about him, he pulled the blanket over the baby's head. Frogs croaked, and in the distance, a dog barked. Sweat rolled down his cheeks. When Juana stirred and whimpered, he held her over his shoulder and patted her back as he walked. Poor little girl. She was much too young to be in so much danger!

They made their way carefully past cottages with darkened windows, until they were one block from the foot of Jackson Square. Then Diego went ahead to find the exact location of the *gen de couleur* militia man on duty. He returned shortly, his thin face grim. "He has positioned himself where he cannot miss seeing us cross the verge," he whispered. "All is lost."

Fernando raised his hand. "Do not give up so soon, old friend. We will go to the back gate. I know the way. Follow me."

They backtracked a block and then turned off onto a side street. As they turned a corner, Diego stopped dead in his tracks, signaling Fernando to do the same. They shrank into the shadows at the base of a large building. Footsteps sounded on the planking in front of them, and Fernando's eyes widened as a group of the governor's personal militia men marched by, their shoulders thrown back proudly, their eyes straight ahead. Juana kicked her legs and whimpered, so Fernando pressed her face into his chest, his heart beating wildly. She struggled to free herself, but he watched the last of the militia pass before he began to rock the child from side to side.

Diego grabbed his arm. "Come!" he whispered. "If she cries, all is lost."

Fernando led the way once again. The pounding of his heart did not ease until Juana stopped struggling and slumbered again. At last, they ran into the high brick wall enclosing the convent grounds. "This way," Fernando whispered. As he skirted the last bush beside the back gate, his foot caught on a root and he stumbled. He clutched the baby close, but it was too late. Her strident wail filled the night air.

"Pull the bell!" he urged Diego. "And don't stop pulling until they answer." He cringed against the gate as the bell pealed and Juana screamed. "Hurry, answer the bell!" he urged.

He heard a man shout in the distance. The *gen de couleur!* He mentally prepared a story to explain his presence at the convent so late in the night. The bell pealed on and on, and Diego shook his head wildly from side to side.

"It is useless," he exclaimed. "The good sisters sleep like the dead! We are finished!"

Another shout, this time much closer. Again Juana screamed loudly. Just then, a light appeared behind the iron gate and bobbed slowly closer.

"Let us in!" Diego shouted. "We need refuge!"

A heavy key grated and the gate was opened a crack. Diego pushed his way through and pulled Fernando inside the courtyard. "Lock the gate!" he instructed the sister. "Quickly!" When her hands fumbled with the key, he grabbed it from her. Only after the gate had been firmly locked did he press the key into the bewildered sister's hands with an apology. "I am sorry if I frightened you, Sister," he said. "Please, can we take the infant inside?"

As she swung the lamp upward, Sister Claire's frightened eyes shone in the light. "Señor Fernando!" she gasped. "And little Juana! What on earth are you . . ."

Fernando grasped her arm and pulled her toward the building. "I will explain everything as soon as possible. Right now, the child needs some food. Do you have any milk?"

Sister Claire trotted to keep up. "Yes." She panted. "But why doesn't Shona feed her? Surely her mother's milk—"

"She can't!" Fernando exclaimed, suddenly out of patience. Juana's screams and the events of the evening had given him a blinding headache. "Just take us to the kitchen. I will tell you everything once we have quieted this bundle of noise."

Sister Claire nodded toward Diego. "Who is this strange gentleman?" she asked as she ushered them through the kitchen door. "I have never seen him before."

"Later!" Fernando snapped. Then, seeing the tears glittering on her pale lashes, he thrust the baby into her arms. "First the milk, Sister! Please!"

Sister Claire rocked Juana from side to side. "We have a young mother staying with us right now. She has an infant. I am sure she would be willing to—"

"Then take Juana to her! Hurry, before that child wakes the entire convent! And after that, we must see Mother!"

The gentle sister cast Fernando a withering look as she pulled the blanket from the baby's face. "You have almost smothered her! Do not worry, these walls are thick, and it is not the first time the other sisters have heard a hungry child!"

Fernando collapsed into a chair. "I am sorry. I am most anxious to see Mother as soon as you have the child taken care of."

Sister Claire smiled sweetly. "But Mother is with a very important visitor," she said. "He has come a long way, and has much to tell her. I am afraid you will have a long wait."

Fernando threw up his hands. "I will wait all night, if necessary, Sister, but I will see Mother if I have to wait for an eternity."

"That will hardly be necessary. I am here, now."

The droll voice shocked Fernando out of his rage and onto his feet. Mother stood in the doorway, her hand on her hips, her lips pursed.

"I am most sor . . . ry, Mother," he stuttered. "Please forgive my rudeness. Señor Muñoz has—"

Mother raised her finger to her lips. "Shh. Sister Claire, please take Juana to that young mother in the nursery." She watched as the sister disappeared through a side door, then turned back to Fernando. "You must lower your voice. Come with me into my office. I will offer Don Cabrillo a room for the night and then we can talk."

"There is no time for that," Fernando said. "I must tell you now." He lowered his voice to a whisper. "Señor Muñoz has found proof that Asa and Rebecca are Jews. Shona has gone to warn them."

Mother clasped her beads, her knuckles white. "You must protect Shona from that dreadful man," she said. "I am sure he means her great harm."

Chapter 38

The full moon, looking like a ripe cheese, hung suspended on the horizon as the first gray smudges of dawn softened the eastern sky. Thick rancid air hung over the slimy water of the cypress swamp, but the first breath of a morning breeze ruffled the Spanish moss and sent spiked palmetto leaves rasping against one another with irritated sighs.

Muñoz poled the pirogue with one hand, using the other to bat at the no-see-um's swarming before his face. He heard a soft plop close to the bow and hesitated before plunging the pole deep into the muddy bottom. It was only a curious turtle out for his early morning meal. He pushed the pirogue past the outreaching arms of a cypress tree and poled toward the center of the bayou. Once safely away from the knobby cypress knees which could knock a careless poler from his craft, he glanced down at the bound figure lying at his feet.

"We will be there soon," he said. He eyed the yellow hair fanned out over the demure white bed gown. "You are fortunate it is so warm. You would not want to catch the ague."

Shona thrashed about despite the ropes binding her wrists and ankles as he turned away with a grim smile. "You won't get away with this!" she exclaimed. "Someone will raise a cry when I don't open my shop this morning. They'll come looking for me."

His laugh was as dry as the sound of old parchment being torn. "No one will ever look here," he said. "Only my own men and I know where I am taking you. It will not do as well as a dungeon in Madrid, but it will be much better than the governor's palace, where I first considered taking you. You know what cowards the French are when it comes to witnessing pain. It was timely that Diego found this place for me to be alone to meditate and pray."

"Pray! What kind of a God would hear your prayers? You're an animal!"

He laughed again. "I serve a righteous God! One who will bless me richly for driving the sinful thoughts from your mind and the lusts from your body."

Chills ran through Shona. Muñoz was not only a religious fanatic, he was mad! She struggled against the ropes until tears of pain and frustration poured down her cheeks. It was no use. They were all doomed: she, Fernando, and her child!

The pirogue slowed, bumped softly, and stopped.

"We have arrived," Muñoz said.

She watched fearfully as he stepped out and pulled the pirogue up onto a strip of muddy bank. Suddenly, she stiffened. *Dungeon in Madrid!* Dear God, what sort of purging torture did he have in mind?

He reached down and hauled her up. "I am going to carry you now, and if you make that difficult for me, it will go much harder on you later."

He struggled as he pulled her over his shoulder, and she found enough humor in his contortions to smile. Obviously, his gaunt frame was unaccustomed to labor. But her smile quickly disappeared as he mounted rickety wooden stairs and entered a dark, evil-smelling hut.

He dropped her onto the dirt floor with a loud grunt. "I will hide the pirogue now," he said. "Do not think you can escape. Only water, poisonous snakes, and alligators surround this small island of mud."

She shuddered as he left her lying on her back in the dirt.

Then the cloying odor of urine and the fetid smell of something rotten permeated her nostrils. She raised her head. Piles of rags cluttered the floor, and huge dusty spider webs hung in intricate tatters from the rafters.

When a sudden movement caught her eye, she turned her head. Hazy light from the doorless entrance reflected upon red, beady eyes staring at her from a pile of rags in the corner. Rats! She struggled to sit up, but her legs and arms were numb from the biting ropes. She moaned and stared at the dark brown, hairy forms creepily slowly toward her. Something soft bumped her leg, and she screamed and tore at her bonds. One rat ran across her body, then another. She shrieked as she shrank from their hideous yellow fangs and tearing claws.

Stephen took one look at the broken shop window before sprinting up the stairs while calling Shona's name. He searched the apartment frantically, knocking chairs out of his way in his frenzy. Then he ran into the bedroom again, calling Shona's name in a wild voice. But there was no answer. He stopped in the middle of the great room and stood with his head bowed, his lungs straining for air. She was gone. His Shona was gone! His shoulders shook and he groaned aloud. *Madre de Dios*, what had happened? His own fears had materialized. Muñoz! It had to be Muñoz!

He raced down the stairs and around the back to Jephtha's smithy. The door was firmly locked and no light shone in the window. He pounded on the door for several moments, then leaned his head against the rough wood, his breath coming in sobs. Something dreadful had happened, he knew it! Why had he remained at the settlement until dark? If only he had accompanied Shona and little Juana home. He pushed himself away from the door and dashed out into the street, his mind in a frenzy; then he turned his racing feet toward the convent, his last hope for information.

He met Fernando and Izquierdo crossing the verge.

Fernando quickly told him how he and the baby had been kidnapped, and he outlined their subsequent escape with Diego's assistance. Stephen shook his head, agony darkening his eyes to midnight blue. "Then Muñoz has taken Shona."

"We do not know that, Esteban!" Fernando exclaimed. "Perhaps there is another explanation. Perhaps she did not go back to the apartment after warning Asa and Rebecca. Maybe she became frightened and ran away!"

"The window was broken and the lock forced," Stephen replied. He turned suddenly to Diego. "Think man!" he shouted. "Where could he have taken her? Could she be at his new house?"

Diego shook his head. "That would not be private enough, what with all of the workmen about." His forehead crinkled as he pushed a graying lock of hair from his wet forehead. "There is one place. . . ."

Stephen spun about. "Where? Tell me!"

"If he wanted to be truly alone, there is only one place I can think of that he would take her. Deep into the bayou."

Muñoz untied Shona's ankles, then pulled her to her feet. "Surely you are not frightened of a few rats! Why, I thought nothing brought fear to your breast! See how easily I drove them away with a stick? That should make you grateful to me."

Shona wrenched away. "You're more of an animal than they are! They're just following their instincts, but you . . . you . . . bastard! You're evil to the very core!"

He pushed her roughly to her knees and stood leering down at her. His satanic grin reminded her of a death mask, and she averted her eyes, fearful that his wicked glare might somehow rot her very soul. "Do what you want with me, only spare my child if you are the Christian you call yourself."

His taunting laughter filled the tiny hut. "Oh, my dear Shona, you are being dramatic! Do you think I would kill an innocent child?" He walked away, shaking his head. Suddenly, he whirled about. "I have plans for the child of Esteban de Larra!" he taunted. He walked closer, his finger stabbing the air before him. "First, I will carry through with my plan for my sister, Inez. When she arrives and hears what I have to tell her about her beloved Esteban, I can assure you she will raise the child. And she will have only two missions in life—to serve the Church faithfully as a Jesuit Sister, and to hate with all of her heart the name of de Larra!"

Shona stared at him open-mouthed. "You're so confused, you don't even realize what you just said. A sister cannot serve God and harbor such hatred!"

He threw back his head. "Oh, my dear Shona, you are very ignorant if you believe that." He looked down his nose at her, his haughty gaze stark as though the consciousness those black eyes revealed was filled with dark memories. "The God I serve demands justice! It is His will that we hate those who do not fulfill His will! It is with His righteousness that we hate!"

He jerked her to her feet. His bony fingers dug deeply into her upper arms, but she clamped her lips together tightly over a groan. She would not allow him to see how much he hurt her! Never! She threw back her head and stared unflinchingly up at him.

"You are much, much too proud," he said. "Perhaps instead of having her take the veil, I shall instill in your child a hatred so great that she goes to Spain and knifes to death every last de Larra!"

"No!" Shona launched her body at him, her bound hands seeking his eyes. But he grabbed for her and his hand clutched one breast, bringing a scream of horror to her lips. He tore the cross from her neck and ground it into the dirt with his foot. Then he began to rip her gown, his breath coming in rapid grunts, flecks of saliva flying from his lips. She shrank away, trying to loose herself, her mind screaming in horror at the look of lust in his eyes. Surely he would not rape her! Not a man who had studied for the priesthood, one who had so roundly professed his love for the Church!

He tripped her to the ground and stood panting over her, his hands tearing at his own clothing. When she attempted to roll to one side, his foot pinned her to the dirt. "You'll not escape God's judgment!" he screamed. "Not this time!"

Shona pounded at his leg with her bound arms until he applied so much weight to his foot that the breath was driven from her body. She gagged and gasped for air as he yanked off his breeches and threw them onto the floor. When he strode stiffly to a corner and busied himself with something he'd removed from a tow sack, she stared with fascination at the scars crisscrossing his back and shoulders. She heard the rasp of a flint, and watched, wide-eyed, as he turned and crept toward her, a burning candle held out before him.

He stood over her, his swollen manhood twitching. Then he kneeled at her side. He grabbed one breast. When she jerked away, he grabbed it again, his nails digging into her tender flesh.

"Fire will drive the demons of hell from your body!" he hissed. "Then the seed of my body will purify you!"

As he brought the burning candle closer and closer to her breast, she shrank away from the heat, her hips twisting, her head thrashing from side to side. A blob of melted tallow dropped onto her breast and she screamed in agony. The flame was only an inch from her flesh. She spat fully in his face and rolled violently to one side.

He dropped the candle and threw himself over her, his fingers tearing at the tender flesh of her thighs. Saliva drooled from his lips, and his eyes had rolled back in his head. She screamed as he reared back and drove his engorged flesh toward her body.

Stephen drove the pole deep into the mud and pushed with all his strength. Sweat streamed down his face, half-blinding him. He pulled the pole out and drove it down again, ignoring the dull pain from the freshly healed wound in his chest. He was driven by his fears. God grant that he had followed Diego's direction—bear left at every branch! And, God grant that he was in time!

His stomach knotted with fear. No one knew better than he what Muñoz was capable of doing to Shona. Hadn't he been aware of the man's growing insanity as they'd come to manhood together? Hadn't he watched a keen mind disintegrate under self-inflicted pressure to serve what it perceived to be a relentless, demanding God?

He swiped at the sweat blinding him. Seven left turns, Diego had said, and the one up ahead would be the seventh. He whipped a drooping cypress branch from his path and pushed ahead, driven by the same burning love which had fueled his months-long search for Shona, and by a gut-twisting guilt that he himself was responsible for her capture by Muñoz.

He poled the pirogue to the left for the final time and strained to see off into the distance. There it was—the hut. He poled the boat faster, his muscles bulging beneath his shirt, his breath coming in grunts. Though it took only moments, it seemed an eternity before he grounded the pirogue on the muddy bank. He threw the pole to the ground and raced for the stairs leading up to the hut.

Suddenly, a shrill scream split the air. The hair stood up on the back of his neck, and he took the stairs in two leaps. His eyes, blinded by the sunlight, barely took in the two struggling figures on the ground before a roar erupted from his throat as he launched himself through the air.

He hit Muñoz from behind, driving him to the ground, but the grinding pain in his chest took his breath, allowing Muñoz to come to his knees. When Stephen butted him in the chest with his head, Muñoz fell to the ground, and Stephen was raising one foot to stomp on him, when the other leg was pulled out from under him.

He fell with a loud grunt, and Muñoz grabbed his hair and jerked his head back. Stephen then jabbed his elbow at Muñoz's chin, but the man moved aside and the elbow just grazed his cheek.

As the two men rolled over and over in the dirt, grunting and cursing loudly, Stephen regretted his clothing, for Muñoz's naked sweaty body was too slippery to grasp. Muñoz staggered to his feet and kicked out, catching Stephen full in the chest. Bright pinpoints of light flooded Stephen's eyes as violent pain pierced him, threatening to deprive him of consciousness. He shook his head, and, ignoring his growing weakness, launched himself at Muñoz who was quickly retreating through the doorway.

Stephen dived after him just as he was clearing the last step, and they rolled across the bank and into the water. As tepid, slimy wetness closed over Stephen's head, he gritted his teeth and flailed out. His hand glanced off flesh, and he grabbed it, digging in with his fingernails. Then he lurched upward, his face clearing the water. A violent thrashing roiled the water beside him, and Muñoz's head rose to the surface. Stephen grabbed the long black braid now freed from its confining net, jerking it backward, then pushing down with all his might. The rage he had feared all his life was now completely out of control. His mind was blank. He felt only one burning desire. *Kill! Kill!*

Bubbles rose from the water, but he pushed and pushed, his breathing explosive grunts, as Muñoz fought to free himself from his watery grave. A sudden shriek from the hut brought Stephen back to sanity. He pushed Muñoz under one last time and then stumbled toward the shore shouting Shona's name.

Shona lay with her face in the dirt as the sounds outside gradually subsided. Her right breast throbbed, and her sobs threatened to choke her. At last she raised her head. No, it was not her sobs! The candle Muñoz had dropped had set the rags on fire! The hut was burning! She pushed herself onto her knees, then fell back, the acrid smoke from burning rags and wood sending her into a paroxysm of coughing. She had to find

496

the door! She struggled to her knees again, but she could see nothing through the curtain of thick, oily smoke. She threw her bound hands over her head and dropped to her stomach, then clawed along over the dirt, moving forward inch by inch. When the heat intensified, she wriggled around until she was facing in the opposite direction, and began to crawl again. Tears streamed down her face, and she felt as though she would die if she could not draw a clean breath. Where was the man who had driven Muñoz away? A spark fell on her bare back. She screamed and reared up. Smoke filled her lungs. She coughed until she gagged as her body tried to expel the deadly fumes. Then she lay gasping, her face pressed into the dirt.

Somewhere, through the sound of crackling timbers and popping fire, she thought she heard her name being called. She tried to raise her head, but she could not. Then something wet was thrown over her, and someone grasped her arm. She felt herself being dragged across the floor. Dirt filled her nostrils. She was sure that the last breath of life was being driven from her lungs.

Rough boards tore into her tender flesh, then she moaned as someone picked her up. Seconds later, she was dropped onto the muddy bank. Her lungs felt as though they were on fire. She coughed and retched, straining for a full breath of fresh air. Her wrists were released from their bonds, and something warm and wet was poured over her face. She struggled to sit up, then collapsed, her mind filled with pictures of bodies lying dead and bloated, of carnage and blood, of Stephen falling, falling, falling into the sea.

"Shona!"

Shona, Shona, Shona, her own name echoed and rechoed in her ears. As she opened her eyes, a face undulated before her. She blinked and coughed weakly.

"Shona! *Madre de Dios*, tell me you are all right!"

All right, all right, all right.

She struggled as her head was raised. "No!" she moaned. "Leave me . . . alone."

497

"Shona! Open your eyes!"

A familiar voice was barking commands. She looked up. The face that had filled her dreams loomed into view.

"Oh, Stephen, don't torment me with anymore nightmares," she groaned. "I can't bear to see you die over and over!"

Soft lips brushed her cheeks and forehead. "I'm not dead, *querida*. You know that I am not dead, we have spent months together. See how I adore you."

More tender kisses soothed her hot skin. Then, lips covered hers, nibbling, caressing; and the familiar, warm man-smell filled her nostrils. She stared into azure blue eyes just inches above hers. Then she jerked her head away and struggled to sit up.

"Stephen!" she gasped. "Oh, God, it's really you!"

He pulled her into his arms and rocked her back and forth. "Oh, my darling little *niña*," he whispered. "You are all right now."

Tears of relief and joy poured down her cheeks. She clasped his bare shoulders and buried her face in his chest. Then she gasped with laughter as his chest hairs prickled her cheek.

He nuzzled her hair and pulled her face up to his, and her lips parted to receive his kiss. She knew she would never again feel such joy. Her Stephen had arrived in time!

Chapter 39

The crimson sun thrust its flaming body above the horizon, sending newly awakened birds into a frenzy of activity. Night-prowling animals nestled deep into their burrows as the great blue herons winged their way silently above the treetops. Windows and doors of the gambling halls and taverns were thrown wide to rid the interiors of the odor of sweat and smoke, and at the convent, Father Jerome prepared to bless the sacramental wine for the Lord's Day Mass.

Shona nestled her face against Stephen's throat as he pulled the shop door closed behind them and then mounted the stairs.

"I can walk," she protested weakly. "What will people think?"

He chuckled. "At least we are alone here. We generated enough gossip when I carried you up the street from the bayou, with only my wet shirt wrapped around your tantalizing body."

She blushed and buried her face in his neck. She had been much too caught up in her rescue from Muñoz to notice that the streets were peopled at this early hour!

He pulled her closer as he threw open the door. "Besides, I will carry you forever if I desire," he whispered in her ear.

He walked quickly to their bedroom and laid her gently upon her bed.

"Hurry!" she urged as he slipped out of his shirt.

He hesitated. "Are you sure it is not too soon after birthing Juana?"

She raised her arms. "I feel wonderful! Juana and Fernando are safe—and I can't believe I'm really alive. Come, prove it to me."

When he'd torn off his breeches and lay beside her, she nestled into his arms, reveling in his smell and the touch of his fingers as he stroked her breasts. Suddenly, she stiffened and her hand went to her throat.

"Your cross!" she moaned. "He tore it off in the hut."

"I will buy you another."

"But it was special. I wore it constantly. It brought me a great deal of comfort when I thought you were lost forever, and now it's gone."

He stroked around the small red burn on her breast. "The cross can be replaced, but your flesh cannot."

"That's nothing. I don't even feel it anymore," she replied, then pressed closer. When he took a nipple into his mouth and sucked lightly, shivers coursed over her flesh. He moaned and showered kisses over her belly while his fingers lightly stroked both of her breasts. His caresses kindled an aching fire in her groin, and she buried her fingers in his tangled hair, then pulled his face up to hers.

"I need you," she whispered.

"We have waited too long to hurry," he murmured. "I've dreamed of this moment for weeks!" He took her hand and nibbled gently on her fingers. "I want to taste every inch of your beautiful body," he said.

He slid lower on the mattress and kissed the backs of her knees. Then his lips moved lightly down to her rope-burned ankles, and to her toes. She moaned and her head thrashed as the flush of desire consumed her body.

He turned her over and his lips traveled up the backs of her legs, over her buttocks. She gasped as his tongue caressed the nape of her neck, evoking a shiver. Then he pulled her into the curve of his body, and she felt his hard, throbbing manhood pressed against her.

"Please, Stephen, hurry," she whispered.

He turned her onto her back and lowered himself gently on top of her, his trembling hands pressing her thighs apart. She gasped as she received him, for her joy was too great to be contained.

Her hips moved in unison with his as he kissed her and their tongues intertwined, love melding their bodies and souls into one. The flame in her groin grew brighter and brighter until it threatened to consume her. When he raised his head and stared down at her, she was engulfed by the molten blue fire of his eyes and her cry joined his as the flames of their passion exploded into fragments of burning light which showered their bodies from head to toe.

After a moment he rolled to her side and pulled her into the circle of his arms. "You are truly my *tesora*," he breathed.

She smiled and fingered the puckered scar on his chest. "I still can't believe you survived that wound." She sighed deeply. "I wish I'd been able to show the surgeon who saved you my gratitude."

He tickled her breast with his fingertip. "Show me instead," he whispered.

She moved closer, sure that she would never taste his body enough if they lived for a hundred years!

Much later, Shona smiled over at Stephen. "You have an insatiable appetite!" She laughed.

He grinned and his right eyebrow rose. "Your hunger is not a small thing," he teased.

She threw herself into his arms. "Don't ever leave me again, Stephen, or I'll die."

He rubbed her back. "You will never be more than a step from my side," he promised. "I thought I would go crazy when I realized that *bastardo* Muñoz had captured you."

"Are you sure he's dead?"

"Unless he can breathe underwater like a fish."

She lay quietly in his arms, her eyes closed. "If Fernando

doesn't bring Juana for a feeding soon, I'm going to explode," she said sleepily.

When he did not answer, she looked up. His lashes lay upon his cheeks, and his chest rose and fell steadily as he slept. The discomfort of her engorged breasts and her parched lips wiped all thought of sleep from her mind. She realized she was so thirsty, she could think of little else. She moved gently out of his embrace.

Pulling on a light gown, she quietly closed the bedroom door behind her and made her way quickly to the water jug. She gulped down several cups of water, forgetting in her thirst how much she disliked drinking the water pulled from the river. She eyed the two inches of sediment in the jug and shuddered. Then she roamed around the great room for a long time, her lips curving softly every time she glanced at the bedroom door. She knew she had never been more contented in her life.

She had just set some beans to soak when she heard footsteps on the landing. She rushed to the door and threw it open.

"Fernando!" she cried. "And Jephtha! Oh, you've brought my little Juana home! Is she all right?" She took the baby in her arms and showered her tiny face with kisses. Then she pulled back the blanket to inspect her child. Only after she had satisfied herself that Juana was unharmed did she step out of the way and allow Jephtha and Fernando to express their delight at her rescue.

"But what of Muñoz?" Fernando asked. "Has he been arrested?"

"He's dead!" Shona exclaimed.

"Dead!"

Jephtha grinned widely. "I didn't think anything could ever kill that piece of cow dung!"

Fernando clutched at her sleeve. "But Esteban? Where is Esteban?"

"He's sleeping," Shona said softly. "He and Muñoz were fighting. When they fell into the water, Stephen held him under until he drowned."

Fernando crossed himself solemnly. "May his tortured soul rest in peace," he said softly.

Juana squirmed and whimpered, so Shona pulled a chair into the corner and threw a piece of sacking over her shoulder. "Turn your backs while I get her settled. She's starving." She unlaced her bodice and settled the baby at her breast.

"That is why we brought her with us," Fernando said. "From what the wet nurse says, she cannot get enough so Mother suggested we see if you had returned."

"And you were chompin' at the bit anyway, wantin' to come!" Jephtha crowed. "Them short legs of yours almost outpaced me all the way here."

"I am not ashamed to admit my concern," Fernando replied stiffly. "And I did not see you refusing to accompany me."

Shona shook her head and laughed. "Oh, do be quiet you two. Your bickering is going to awaken Stephen. He told me about meeting you on the verge. What did Mother think when you showed up at the convent so late at night?"

"She was surprised, but you know Mother, nothing seems to upset her. However, a few moments after I returned from leaving Esteban with Diego at the bayou, the governor's militia came to the gates and threatened to arrest Mother if she did not tell them where you had hidden the Jews!"

Shona gasped. "What did she do? What happened?"

Fernando smiled broadly. "She did not have to do anything. Mother had a visitor staying with her, a Don Cabrillo, who said if the troops did not disperse immediately, he would challenge the *capitán* to a duel. The commotion roused the sisters and they all stood around Mother, claiming that if she was arrested, the militia would have to take them all in! So they left to report back to the governor, who just happens to be a personal friend of our good Mother. I am sure the leader of the militia was acting on his own."

"Under Muñoz's orders!"

At these words, they all turned. Stephen stood in the

bedroom doorway, clad in his wrinkled shirt and breeches, running his hands through his tousled hair.

Fernando and Stephen exchanged embraces as Shona transferred Juana to her other breast.

Jephtha, obviously feeling left out, cleared his throat loudly. "It seems somebody around here ought to wonder how my night fared."

Shona raised her head quickly. "I'm sorry, Jephtha. So much has happened! Did you get Rebecca and Asa settled safely?"

"They're with the rabbi, if you care to know," he growled. "And they received such a warm welcome and were told about so many people needing his help, Asa is beginning to consider settling there."

"That's wonderful! Now maybe they can have the happiness they so richly deserve."

She pulled the baby from her breast, put her over her shoulder, and walked quickly to Jephtha. "We all thank you from the bottom of our hearts," she said softly. "We owe you more than we can ever repay, for I know your journey was fraught with danger."

Jephtha scuffed the toe of his boot across the floor. "Well, I did have a mite of trouble finding a barge so late at night."

Fernando began to chuckle. "Do you realize, Madonna, that with Muñoz out of the way, you and Esteban can also be married?"

She stared at him for a moment, then smiled radiantly. "Of course!" she exclaimed.

Stephen laughed aloud and bent to kiss her cheek. "I will ask that our banns be read from the convent sanctuary starting this morning!"

Shona felt as though her heart would burst with joy. "Then you must go to the convent immediately and talk to Mother." She patted Juana's back. "And while you're gone, I'm going to try to think of someone who can replace Rebecca in the shop."

Stephen pulled her into his arms. "Do not waste your time,

beloved. I will soon have to make a decision about our future. In the meantime you will sell the shop and take your rightful place as wife and mother."

Shona jerked away, two bright spots of color brightening her cheeks. "Sell the shop! What on earth are you talking about?"

His right eyebrow rose dangerously. "Just what I said. It is time you became the wife and mother God intends for you to be."

Aroused by their loud voices, Juana began to scream. Shona thrust her into Fernando's arms and stood staring up at Stephen, her eyes blazing. "Like hell I will!" she exclaimed. "It took me months to build that business! And what do you mean, you will have to decide our future? I have as much stake in what happens to us as you do!"

"Lower your voice, woman! We will discuss this later when we are alone!"

"Don't use that condescending tone of voice on me! We will settle this once and for all, right now!"

Stephen's face paled, and his nostrils flared. "I command you to be quiet!" he shouted.

She stomped her foot. "I will say what I want, when I want. You will not issue commands to me! *Ever!*"

Stephen whirled and stalked, straight-backed, across the room. When he reached the door, he turned and stabbed a finger at her. "You are an impossible woman!" he shouted. "I do not know why I ever though we could be happy as man and wife!" He jerked the door open and rushed out, slamming it loudly behind him.

Shona took several steps toward the door, her mouth opening and closing. Then she turned to Fernando, brushing wildly at the tears burning her eyes. "I've got to stop him!" she exclaimed brokenly.

Jephtha grabbed her arm. "I'll go!" he said. "I'm bigger than you. Maybe he'll listen to reason with my fist crammed down his throat!"

"Don't you dare!" she screeched. "I'll beat you bloody if

you so much as lay a hand on the man I love!"

Fernando stepped between them, shoving Juana back into Shona's arms. "That is enough talk about violence. Jephtha, you go after Esteban. Explain how much the shop means to Shona. Try to get him to listen to reason." He patted Shona's arm awkwardly. "Let Jephtha go. You stay with me. You have been through too much for one day."

Shona paced the floor wringing her hands. "They've been gone for hours! What's taking them so long?"

Fernando walked quietly over to the bedroom and peeked in. "Little Juana sleeps peacefully. Why do you not join her for a nap?"

Shona shook her head violently. "I'll not sleep another wink until I have Stephen back here where he belongs!"

She threw herself into a chair and tapped her long fingers on the table. "It's unbelievable! After all we have been through! Oh, that Stephen's insufferable!" she exclaimed. "I can't believe he would want me to sell the shop!" She picked up a clay cup and threw it to the floor, taking satisfaction in watching it smash into splinters.

Fernando threw up his hands. "You two will never change. I thought you had overcome your violent temper, but you have not. And Esteban is no better, but you must remember he has been through much!"

She stared at him. "And I have not? Why, I've been through hell!"

He shrugged and pulled a chair over to the window, where he could sit and fan his face. "I will forget what you just said." He sniffed. "All I can say is that you are a survivor."

She lurched to her feet and began to pace again. "Yes, and I'll get that man back if it's the last thing I do! I'm going out. Maybe I can find them and talk some sense into that stubborn Spanish . . ."

The opening door stopped her. Stephen stood in the

doorway, his eyes boring into hers, and Shona walked stiffly toward him.

"Well, has Jephtha talked some sense into that stubborn, pigheaded mind of yours?"

"I have come home," he said simply.

She stopped before him, her hands planted on her hips. "And just exactly what does that mean?" she demanded.

He raised his head, his eyes flashing dangerously. "It means that I was mistaken in issuing you an order. I wish to discuss our problem quietly!" he exclaimed hotly. "Stop shouting like a tramp!"

"Mistaken! Is that what you call it?" She threw herself at him, her hands beating a tattoo on his chest. "You're damned right you were mistaken! Thinking I would sell my shop!"

Fernando slumped lower in his chair. Now the fat was in the fire! With those two angry at the same time, there was no telling what might happen!

Shona and Stephen glared at each other, their chests rising and falling rapidly. "I met with Don Cabrillo!" Stephen shouted. "He wants to employ me!"

"So what?" Shona screamed.

"I talked with Father Jerome!" Stephen bellowed.

"Why should I care?" Shona raised her fists.

"He'll marry us as soon as you are confirmed."

Shona's fists dropped to her sides. "And then?"

"Then we leave for the Tejas Territory. Don Cabrillo has offered me a position there."

"The Tejas Territory! I knew it! You're too ashamed of me to take me back to Spain!"

He grabbed her and held her tightly, ignoring her protests. "Listen to me!" he exclaimed. "Neither of us would ever be happy in Spain. I would never settle down enough to run a ranchero. We need adventure, both of us, and we will find more than enough where we are going."

He pressed his lips to hers, and gradually, she stopped struggling. As her tongue twined with his, she moaned. Then, her pulses beating wildly, she pulled away and looked up into his face.

"But I'm a tramp!" she said softly.

"You are the woman of fire I love," he answered in a whisper. "I am sorry, but you will have to sell your shop before we leave."

Shona's eyes began to sparkle. "But you are mistaken!" she laughed exultantly. "We'll buy a wagon and take the supplies with us! I'll set up a store in this . . . this Tejas Territory, wherever it is!"

"Never!" Stephen roared. "No wife of mine is going to run a shop!"

Fernando sat shaking his grizzly head as the argument continued. There were only two things he could depend upon as absolutes: death and the surety that, living with those two, life would never be dull. He shook his head and chuckled as he got to his feet. If they were leaving for the Tejas Territory, he would have to repair the broken shop window for the new renters.

SIZZLING ROMANCE
from Zebra Books